CREEPY COURT
A MONSTER MALL ANTHOLOGY

DARKLIGHT PRESS

Darklight Press

COPYRIGHT

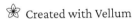 Created with Vellum

CONTENTS

LOST AND FOUND
VERA VALENTINE

FED AFTER MIDNIGHT
LATREXA NOVA

PLAY
SABRINA DAY

THE MONSTER OF DARKSPELL COMICS
SJ SANDERS

CREEPY PASTA
EVANGELINE PRIEST

PUBLISHER'S NOTE

Dear Monster Lover,

Due to page count restrictions, the print version of this anthology needed two volumes.

The first half of seven stories are in *Creepy Court: A Monster Anthology vol. 1:* https://www.amazon.com/dp/B0CKXZ7VFC

"Playing Mantis" by Clio Evans

"Frankie's Funhouse" by Beatrix Hollow

"Lost and Found" by Vera Valentine

"Fed After Midnight" by Latrexa Nova

"Play" by Sabrina Day

"The Monster of Darkspell Comics" by SJ Sanders

"CREEPY PASTA" BY EVANGELINE PRIEST

The second half of seven stories are in *Creepy Court: A Monster Anthology vol. 2.* https://www.amazon.com/dp/B0CKXZ3D88

"DREADFUL THINGS" BY MAEVE BLACK
"VAMPIRES TOTALLY SUCK" BY C. ROCHELLE
"THE BEST BOY" BY WREN K MORRIS
"THE PHANTOM OF THE THEATER" BY ELLE M DREW
"THE GOOD CHAR" BY YD LA MAR
"MALL RAT" BY ASHLEY BENNETT
"DON'T EAT YOUR HUMAN BOYFRIEND" BY LILY MAYNE

You are currently reading *Creepy Court: A Monster Anthology vol. 1.*

Creepy Court: A Monster Mall Anthology is a limited edition monster romance collection. It will be available to purchase exclusively on Amazon in both digital and print format. The eBook will also be enrolled in Kindle Unlimited.

It will be unpublished in early January 2024.

Much love,

EVA PRIEST
CREATIVE DIRECTOR, DARKLIGHT PRESS

CONTENT WARNING

Please note that this anthology features a diverse range of stories that span from sweet to spicy, and all the delicious flavors in between. Please consult each story's content warnings for further details.

They may contain the following themes, tropes, and triggers:

Abduction, Assault, BDSM, Criminal Acts, Dark Themes, Fighting, Forced Marriage, Graphic Sex, Heat, Hunting, Kinks, Menage, Nightmares, Power Exchange, Size Difference, Trafficking, Why Choose.

Please proceed with caution.

PLAYING MANTIS

CLIO EVANS

In this short story, you will find: instalust, pheromones, oviposition, breeding kink, cervix penetration, heats, and more.

CHAPTER 1

JAMIE

If I were a wizard, life would be so much more rad.

Instead, I was stuck like everyone else in this office for another two minutes. I stared at the clock, waiting for 5 P.M. to hit. I impatiently drummed my fingers on the desk, twirling the phone cord with the other hand, hoping time would move faster.

The phone rang, and I let out a hiss between my teeth. Another angry person hoping to catch an insurance agent so they could vent about whatever had happened.

"Are ya gonna get that, Jamie?" Lucy asked from her cubicle next to mine.

Hell no.

9 to 5, Monday through Friday, I was a driven business woman. I'd worked my way up through the insurance company I worked for, and was on the verge of getting another promotion despite the assholes I worked with. I did everything I could to be the best. Do the best work, get the most clients, make the most sales.

But the moment the weekend hit, my secret addiction called like a siren from the sea.

The clock hit 5pm, and I stood up, ignoring the petulant ring. "It's five o'clock, babe," I said, looking at Lucy.

Lucy paused, caught in the middle of putting on lipstick. Her teased platinum blonde hair radiated hairspray like a cloud of smoke, even from where I stood. She wagged a lace gloved finger at me, rolling her eyes.

The nice thing about Lucy was that she knew I always left like this on Fridays and was used to it. It meant I did her other favors here and there when she covered for me. "Fine, I'll answer it for you, sugar, but you owe me one."

"I'll bring you a chocolate suisse mocha on Monday," I promised.

Lucy gasped. "I can't wait!"

The phones in the office kept ringing in a loud chorus, some employees choosing to answer while others left. Like me.

On the clock, I was the best of the best—but it was the weekend, baby. I could already feel the tingle of victory in my fingertips.

"I would. I'm out of here," I said, grinning at her.

"You always rush out of here on Fridays," she sighed, picking up the phone. She winked at me as she put on her best customer service voice. "Hello, thank you for calling Haunt Insurance, where we help you make decisions that won't haunt you for the rest of your life. How can I help you?"

Good luck, I mouthed, already grabbing my bag. I rushed out of the office, squeezing into the elevator and riding down to the parking garage. I slung my purse over my padded shoulder, adjusting my plaid blazer as I almost ran to my cherry red BMW M3.

I slid into the back seat and slammed the door, looking around to make sure no one was peeping. I always parked away from everyone else because my backseat was my changing room on Fridays.

All clear.

I ripped off my blazer and turtleneck, leaning down and snatching my gym bag. I unzipped it quickly and pulled out a lime green crop top and high-waisted fade jeans. Within a few minutes, I was a changed woman. I had morphed from Career-Jamie to Arcade-Queen-Jamie.

The mall's parking lot was already crowded when I arrived. My radio blasted rock, a shot of adrenaline straight into my bloodstream. The neon sign above the doors burned bright pink, *Creepy Court* drawing all of us in like moths to a flame. I pulled into a parking spot, excitement making my stomach flip.

Home sweet home.

I grabbed my bag and got out of the car. The cool breeze

ruffled my dark curls as I crossed the parking lot, joining the masses that went through the front doors. A chill went up my spine, which I'd found to be my normal reaction when stepping foot onto the carpet lobby of Creepy Court. There was something strange about this place, but that only made it more exciting.

It was a wonderland.

Laughter and shouts surrounded me, the scent of burning corn dogs and popcorn wafting through the air. Teenagers moved in packs, adults stood in front of shop windows fishing out their wallets, and the elderly sat by the fountain at the center of the food court. Creepypasta had a line outside of it, the noodle sign blinking like a carb calling card.

Pasta sounded delicious, but my reward for making it to the weekend was waiting.

I strolled down one section of the mall, passing other shops. None of them mattered to me the way my destination did.

I passed Frankie's Funhouse, the only other arcade in the mall. That one served pizza, but I couldn't get over how it made me feel. I'd gone in there once before, but had felt like I was being watched.

The vibe of that place was really unsettling.

I let out a sigh of relief as I bounced to the front of GalaxyGames. The outside was painted dark blue with specks of white. The name was displayed on a glowing, planet-shaped sign. Two massive windows showed the inside. As per usual on Friday nights, it was jam-packed.

"Damn it," I breathed out.

Other people were waiting outside. I went towards the front doors, but a girl hissed at me. "Hey, lady, get in line."

My fingers itched. I had to be at my game, to make sure I'd maintained my high score.

"I work here," I lied.

She scoffed at me, popping a bubblegum bubble as an exclamation point of disgust. I ignored her and went through the front doors, sweat dripping down the back of my neck.

The clerk at the counter recognized me. Jimmy. He raised a brow but said nothing as I slinked through those that waited and eventually disappeared into the chaos of the arcade.

I was pretty sure he had a thing for me and I was chaotic enough to accept the favors.

I went down a row of pinball machines, squeezing past the shouting kids. I felt a little out of place here, sometimes, but all of those feelings drifted away as I rounded the corner and met my machine.

Playing Mantis.

No one was playing at the moment, so I stepped forward, claiming it as mine. I reached into my purse and pulled out the stash of coins I had.

I let out a soft breath as the screen flashed brilliant colors. I braced my hands on either side of the green and white machine, smiling as three digital hearts charged up.

I waited patiently to see my name at the top of the leaderboard as always. I grinned as it popped up.

But then my stomach dropped.

"No," I whispered.

My name was not number one. *JamieandtheJets* had been knocked down to number two by a simple name.

Mantis.

Fuck.

"No, no, no," I groaned.

Who the fuck was *that*?

I'd been playing this game for years, and no one—NO ONE—had ever beaten me. Never. I had held the golden spot for so long.

I was going to destroy them.

My heart hammered in my chest, moisture exuding from my palms. I swallowed hard as I slid two coins into the slot and slapped the red start button.

I felt autopilot kick in, fueled by adrenaline and the need to beat them. I knew this game like the back of my hand. I'd been playing it for years. Coming to this arcade for so long that I could tell when there was a new stain on the zigzag patterned carpet. I played the game, smirking as I hit a level I'd never hit before. Surely, this would be enough to defeat my enemy.

"Fuck," I whispered.

"Damn, you're totally rad!" A teen called.

I ignored them, and the weird feeling of being observed. They could watch all they wanted.

Hell, part of me hoped that the mysterious *Mantis* was

watching me right now, too. I wanted them to see me absolutely destroy them.

My heart raced faster as I played through the level. I slammed my hands down as I lost my last life; the screen turning black with the neon green Praying Mantis emblem.

The high score bloomed on the screen.

+++

1. Mantis

2. JamieandtheJets

+++

My name remained in second place.

My chest heaved with breaths. I stared at their name, stared at the game I felt had betrayed me.

I was superb. But I wasn't superb enough.

I blew a stray curl out of my face and reached for the coins. I slid one into the slot and started it over.

Whoever *Mantis* was, I *would* crush them.

CHAPTER 2

Mantis

My gaze drifted up and down her body, my cocks hardening as she spent the last of her coins trying to beat my high score. I watched from the darkness as the woman shouted at the machine, her frustration clear.

For years, she had come here. I had watched since the first day she'd stepped foot into GalaxyGames. Watching her from the shadows, wanting her but never daring to pursue her.

My mandibles clicked in satisfaction as she continued to play, even as the other humans left the arcade. The mall would close soon, going from a hub for humans to a place of monsters.

We didn't bother each other. I was aware there were other creatures that roamed Creepy Court, but they had their own domains. I heard them in the night, their growls and roars and the scratch of their claws over the linoleum.

GalaxyGames was mine.

And this woman who fought so hard to beat my high score?

She was mine too.

The attendant approached her. He tapped her shoulder, and I listened as he informed her the arcade was closing. She argued with him, insisting she had to beat me.

Where she was competitive and fierce, I was slow and methodical. It had taken me some time to decide that she was the one, but her scent called to me. Her body made me lust, and she was smart. Smart, cunning, competitive.

Everything I looked for in a mate. I knew she was mine.

I would give her my life and give her my eggs.

She gave the man a curt nod and then headed towards the front. I watched as she went—but then she did something she had never done before.

She ducked out of sight and then slid behind one machine.

She was *hiding*.

Both of my cocks hardened. I let out a low growl, looking down at them. Cum dripped from the tapered heads and I felt the eggs inside of me buzzing with anticipation.

I had to restrain myself.

I pushed both of my cocks back into their pocket, grunting as I adjusted myself. I was large—larger than any of the humans that roamed around. My skin was bright green. I had four legs that were long and angled. My upper half was humanoid, but my arms stretched long and ended in points, spikes running along the underside.

The lights in the arcade dimmed, the silence settling as the attendant locked the doors.

The woman was now locked inside.

With *me.*

At last.

I waited for a few minutes. She eventually emerged again, muttering curses as she went to the machine. It illuminated her, casting a soft iridescent green glow over her body. Her dark hair fell down her back in a tumble of curls, her faded jeans tight against her skin. She wore a green shirt too, one that was similar to the color of my skin.

I ached to pull her clothes off and admire her. To taste her.

"I can't believe I'm doing this." Her voice was full of surprise and determination.

My mandibles chittered together with happiness. I had been waiting for this moment for so long—the chance to be alone with her. To have her standing here in front of me, trapped in this arcade with me.

My yearning for her was obsessive. Ever since I first saw her, it was her face that came to mind any time I touched myself. My cocks seemed to have a mind of their own when she was around.

She bent over, slipping a coin into the machine. It whirled to life as the game began, her shoulders stiffening as she focused on it.

She would need more coins if she were going to keep playing.

I emerged from the shadows. I crept along the rows of machines, quiet as a mouse, as I went to the counter at the front. I found the bag of coins that they kept and picked it up.

My offering.

I hoped it would please her.

I went back into the maze of whirring machines, the bright sounds pinging here and there. The arcade was never truly silent. I slowed as I came around the corner, peaking my head around to study her.

She was standing in front of the machine, her hands on her hips. My gaze fixated on her ass, the shape of her hips. I wanted to grip them as I pumped my eggs inside her dripping cunt.

"Fuck," she growled. "I'm out of coins."

My mandibles clicked together, and I couldn't help it. A cloud of pheromones burst from me, invisible to the eye but pungent in the air.

She stood still for a moment, but then let out a soft breath. Her arousal became stronger, and she let out a confused moan.

"What the fuck?"

My pheromones would send her into a heat if she was truly my mate.

I left my hiding spot, creeping towards her. She gripped the sides of the machines, letting out a low moan as she fought the waves of need pumping through her right now.

My little gamer girl had no idea that she belonged to a monster.

CHAPTER 3

JAMIE

"What is happening to me?" I rasped.

Suddenly, every part of my body buzzed with need. I clenched my thighs harder, groaning in surprise as my pussy pulsed. I'd never had this happen before. I needed a cock inside me. My thoughts felt erratic, my heart beating faster in my chest.

My nipples strained against my clothes, my skin sensitive. I stared at the gaming screen, at the praying mantis emblem that gleamed there. My eyes widened as I focused on the reflection on the smooth glass.

The outline of my face...

And then *something* behind me...

I turned right as a giant creature leaned in.

I didn't scream. I should have. They were a monster, a creature, a massive *being* unlike anything I'd ever seen before. Their skin was bright green, their eyes reflecting the flashing lights of the arcade. They had a humanoid upper half with hard abs, spikes on their long angled arms, and four legs.

I stared into their strange eyes, shivering.

"You don't fear me." His voice was deep and raspy, a strange edge to it.

"I must be dreaming," I whispered.

I had to be. I let out a low moan as my pussy throbbed harder, begging for something to fill it. I'd never been this turned on before. My cheeks flared with hot embarrassment.

Not to mention there was a creature standing in front of me.

I leaned back against the machine as his oddly angled arm lifted, pinchers at the end dropping a bag of coins at my feet. They jingled, some spilling free and clinking against each other. They gleamed on the purple carpet, the GalaxyGames logo shining.

"A gift for my mate," he huffed. "Does it please you?"

"Coins," I whispered, staring at the bag. It *did* please me. Pleasure bloomed through my whole body, a tug in my lower stomach.

He let out a low, chortling noise. It sounded like a chuckle, but I couldn't be sure.

"My pheromones are impacting you..."

"Pheromones?"

"You're wet. Needy. In need of my cocks to fill your hot little cunt. Right, *JamieandtheJets?*"

I gasped. "How do you..."

"Who do you think has the high score?"

"*You?*"

He nodded, dipping his head lower until I was truly face to face with him.

It made sense, of course. Mantis was...a giant praying mantis monster. One that looked at me like he wanted to devour me. His eyes shone, gleaming. "I have been waiting for you, little gamer. I'm going to breed you over and over again. I'm going to make you mine."

"Breed..." A low gasp left me as his arm lifted, his pincher running up my body. The hardness of his skin, smooth against mine.

"I need to fuck you," he clarified, as if I didn't know what he meant by *breed*.

Just hearing him say that sent a thrill through me.

This was crazy. Crazier than anything else I'd ever done, and yet, all I could think about was taking him. I wanted to touch him.

I'd already broken the rules tonight. I'd snuck into the mall and stayed like some wild teenager, unable to accept the defeat. And now, here I was, pinned against the game machine by a monster that looked like he came from it.

Desire was like a heavy drug, pumping through me.

"Do you want me to relieve you? You are under my influence... I will only take you with your consent. And then I will not stop until you end me."

End him? I frowned, but reached up. I ran my fingertips over his mandibles, gasping. He opened his mouth, a long tongue unfurling.

Every muscle in my body tensed. I was staring up into the face of a monster, and yet all I could think about was what that tongue could do to me. What *he* could do to me.

"Like what you see?" he teased.

Apparently. My body certainly did.

"I want you," I said. "And then I want to beat your stupid high score."

"Why not both at the same time?"

My eyes widened as he leaned in closer. His long arms caged me against the machine, his torso pressing against mine. I let out a soft groan, feeling everything that I knew crumble around me.

I was about to fuck a monster. Hell, I *wanted* to fuck a monster.

I parted my lips as the tip of his tongue explored. He let out a gentle growl as it met mine, the taste of him turning me on even more.

His tongue drove deeper, pushing down my throat. I took him, my eyes fluttering as he devoured me. His mandibles tapped against my cheeks, our moans blending together as he pulled back.

"You will be the death of me," he rasped.

The two claws at the end of one arm reached for the hem of my shirt. I sucked in a breath as he pulled it up, drawing it free. I reached around and pulled off my bra, never taking my eyes off him even as his fell to my breasts.

"You are beautiful," he huffed. "A beautiful little creature. Undress further, little gamer."

I did as he asked, unbuttoning my jeans and pushing them down. A squeak escaped me as I was lifted and perched on the ledge. He pressed against the machine. My legs parted for him. The sounds and vibrations of our game surrounded me as he lowered himself.

"Oh," I gasped.

His tongue dipped between my thighs.

"Please don't kill me yet," he huffed.

Kill him?

I didn't ask him why he thought I would murder him. His tongue pressed against my clit, pushing against the lace panties I wore. I cried out, my head falling back as he spread my legs further.

The tip of his tongue worked around the patch of fabric, running along my slit. I was so fucking wet, my body responding to him. I'd never felt this way before.

I *needed* him. I needed more.

"Mantis," I gasped. "Oh god."

His tongue pushed inside of me and an orgasm immediately ripped through my entire body. My voice echoed through the entire arcade, every muscle tensing as the shock zapped through me.

His tongue kept working me until I completely melted. He pulled it out gently, looking up at me. His eyes shone in the flashing lights.

"More," I groaned. "I need more."

"I'll give you everything I can."

CHAPTER 4

MANTIS

I pulled her off the machine and turned her around, her ass facing me. Both of my cocks were fully hard, pre-cum dripping from them. She leaned against the game, her back arching as I reached around and pinched her breasts with my claws.

"Play the game," I breathed.

She let out a helpless whimper and reached down, sliding a golden coin into the slot. The scent of her cunt was driving me wild, my instincts feeding off of her own pheromones now.

Playing Mantis whirred to life. She gripped the joystick as I pushed her legs apart, stepping closer so that I could press the head of one of my cocks against her tight pussy.

Taking my eggs would be difficult for her, but I knew she was strong. I'd work her up to it. I'd make her cum over and over until her body accepted them completely.

"Keep focused," I commanded. "Can you do that?"

"I can try," she moaned. "I can feel the head of your cock..."

I looked down as I rubbed it against her. Did she know I had two yet?

My mandibles clicked, need rushing through me. My mate had accepted me, giving me everything that I could dream of. For years I had wanted her, never thinking she would let me touch her.

The taste of her was still on my tongue as I eased forward. She stiffened, her breaths becoming harsher as she took my cock, all while playing the game. I let out a low chuckle as she lost a life, the screen blinking for a moment before restarting the level.

"Be a good girl," I whispered. "Focus on the game while you take every inch. I can feel your body milking me."

Her muscles were squeezing me as I pushed further. She gasped as I went as deep as I could, feeling that she could take no more. I squeezed her breasts harder as I pulled back, only to slam forth again.

She yelled, her game ending as I took her. Her back muscles tensed as she gripped the machine, bracing herself as she took me repeatedly. Her scent was driving me wild, my pre-cum dripping from her cunt, the sounds turning me on even more. She fit me like a glove, tight and hot.

My long tongue ran up her spine, only to slowly wrap around her neck. She huffed as I tightened it, her body now completely in my grasp.

I fucked her harder, falling into a primal frenzy. She relaxed completely, taking a bit more of my cock with each harsh thrust. It wouldn't be long before I released for the first time inside her, and then...

Then we could do more.

My seed would make us even more desperate.

"Do you want me to fill you?" I asked.

"Please," she whined. "Please. I need it all. I need it all and more. Everything feels so good."

My hips jerked faster. I let go of her breasts and used my pinchers to grip her hips, holding her in place as I fucked her.

She cried out, her pussy squeezing me as another orgasm rolled through her precious body. I let out a low growl as I gave one last thrust, wanting to join her in our pleasure. I started to cum, using every ounce of my willpower to keep my eggs from joining as my cum shot out in hot ropes.

"Oh," she moaned. "*Oh...*"

Normally, I might relax from coming. Normally, she might too. But not now.

"I feel like I have a fever," she rasped, squirming against me. My cock was still buried deep inside her and I could feel her gripping me, squeezing out every drop. "What is happening to me?"

I let out a groan, fighting the urge to fuck her again. I was still hard. How could I not be now that I was with her? Everything about her was perfect.

She squeezed me harder, letting out the softest whimper. All of her noises turned me on even more. "Now that you've had my cum, your body will want more," I explained. "How do you feel, little gamer?"

"Good," she huffed. "I've never felt this good in my entire life."

"Good," I chuckled. "Stay still."

She stilled beneath me as I slowly pulled back. A shudder worked through her body as the last of my cock was freed. I released her, turning her to face me. Her eyes widened as they fell to both of my cocks, her lips parting with shock.

"Two? You have two cocks?"

"And you have two perfect little fuck holes," I growled. "I want them both."

Her eyes widened. She leaned back against the gaming machine, her legs slightly parted as my cum dripped down her soft thighs. Her eyes fell back to my cocks, taking in my form.

I loved the way she looked at me.

She hungered for me the same way that I hungered for her.

"I've watched you for years," I admitted. "I've watched you come to play the game. Always this game. Why?"

"It's my favorite," she whispered. "It always has been. I've been playing it since I was sixteen, and I've always had the high score. And even though I'm an adult now, I still like to play. It still makes me happy. Helps me escape…"

My hearts pounded a little harder. For the first time in… my entire existence in this place, I wondered what life was like on the outside. All I knew was the gaming store. All I knew was the scent of the different cafes that lined the food court or the remnants of butter outside the theater. The dark undercurrent that haunted this place, the monsters that were trapped within.

She was my window to the outside world. My ray of sunlight amongst the neon darkness of Creepy Court.

"Are you…from the game?" she asked tentatively.

I chuckled and reached for her. Part of me expected her to flinch or wince, but she did neither. Instead, she stepped closer, her hand touching my chest.

"No," I rasped. "I don't think I'm from the game. I don't know how long I've been here, or where I came from. I only know this place."

Her fingertips were light over the hard green shell that was my skin. She moved them up further until she pressed her palm over my hearts.

"This is crazy," she whispered. "But I want more. And I don't care if you came from the very depths of hell. I want you."

A low growl rumbled, and I tugged her closer, holding her to me. She looked up at me, a smile tugging at her full lips.

"I'll take you to my nest," I said. "If you're willing."

The nest that I had been prepping for years.

She nodded. "Take me there."

Delight rushed through me. I picked her up carefully, holding her naked body to mine as I turned. I moved to the room in the back, stepping past the dusty shelves filled with supplies and games. There was a door there, one the humans never opened. It was as if they knew a monster lived there.

I held her to me with my long arm as I opened the door, carrying her into the small room. She sucked in a breath as I closed us in, her eyes widening as she saw the nest I'd made.

This was where I would give her my eggs and my life. Everything I had was hers.

Soft blankets padded the floor. I'd stolen them from one of the stores, along with pillows.

"This is amazing," she said. "It really is like a nest."

"It is," I said proudly.

She wrapped her arms around my shoulders and then moved, her legs wrapping around my waist. My cocks were still hard, the tips brushing against her pussy as she held onto me.

A low groan left me. I lowered her onto the blankets, pinning her beneath me. Her dark hair splayed out, her hands running down my torso.

She was everything that I'd ever dreamed of and more.

"Can I explore your body?" she asked. "I just want to touch you."

"Yes," I said. "Please. I want you to touch me everywhere you want to."

She smiled and leaned up, pushing my shoulders until I rolled over onto my back. My body was large and angular, my many legs spreading as she rose and sat on my lower half, my cocks right in front of her.

Her hands wrapped around each one, her eyes widening. She studied them the way I studied her, running her fingertips over the ridges. My cocks were dark pink, the veins bulging as pleasure rolled through me. I let out a helpless moan as she seemed to take all of my control, my body submitting to her.

Whatever she wanted, I would give her. My body felt like it was on fire, the ends of my pinchers digging into the blankets as she stroked me.

Jamie leaned forward, her eyes meeting mine as she parted her sweet lips. I gasped as her tongue ran over my cock's head, slow and sensuous. She kept stroking as she sucked, soft moans leaving her.

"You feel so swollen here," she said, squeezing the base of my cocks.

"Eggs," I rasped. "My eggs. The ones I will soon fill you with, little gamer."

CHAPTER 5

JAMIE

I squeezed the base of his cocks, sucking in a breath as pre-cum dripped from the heads. Both of them throbbed in my grip as I licked them, the taste of his cum making my mouth buzz. I sucked the tip of one, groaning as I moved to the other, back and forth.

Tonight had turned into a dream. Perhaps a nightmare to some, but I'd only come to realize that I had a *thing* for monsters.

Especially ones that fucked me while I played my game.

I sucked harder, listening to the sounds he made. The

grunts and groans, the way his mandibles clacked. His hips bucked as I took him deeper, my eyes fluttering closed as he hit the back of my throat.

My pussy throbbed with need. I slid my hand between my thighs as I took his cock, my fingers rubbing my clit. Bolts of ecstasy went through me, my muscles tensing as I pushed the two of us to the edge.

"*Jamie,*" he hissed. "I must fill you."

In one swift motion, he rolled me onto my back, his body hovering over mine. I gasped as he pinned me beneath him, his eyes gleaming like disco balls as the head of one of his cocks pressed against me. I was already so wet, ready for him.

"Take me," I whispered.

He let out a low growl as he thrust forward, his cock filling me. I cried out as my cunt gripped him, taking as much as physically possible before he paused, allowing me to adjust to his length and girth. I gasped at the ridge that pressed right against my G-spot, an involuntary shiver working through me.

My nipples hardened, my fingers gripping the soft fabrics of the nest as he slowly pulled back. He thrust again, the two of us groaning in sync as he pumped into me.

He gripped my knees between his pinchers and pushed them back, holding me in place as he fucked me. I gasped as the head of his other cock pressed against my ass, almost pushing inside with each movement.

"Mantis," I moaned. "Fuck. I want your other cock inside me but we need *something*."

"Hold still," he growled.

I did as he asked, stilling as he pulled his cock out. I gasped as cum shot from the head onto me and then he leaned down, using his tongue to push it inside of me. First my pussy, and then slowly my ass. I groaned as he worked me, using his monstrous seed as lube until I was ready to take his cock there too.

I arched against him, close to the edge. He drew back, letting out a dark chuckle as he moved over me again, both cocks ready to push inside me again.

"I'll take it slow," he whispered. "Your little human body is not made for a monster like me. But the pheromones have put you in heat, and it's working its magic. You'll take them both."

I shuddered, heat pouring through me as he pushed forward. This time I took each cock, a long moan drawn from me at the sensation of being completely filled. Filled in a way that I never had been before.

"You're doing so good for me, little gamer," he rasped. "I'm going to fill you with my eggs after you cum for me."

The sound of his cocks taking me filled the small room, coupled with our gasps and moans. He fucked me harder, my body gripping him as I got closer and closer to coming.

A cry tore from me as an orgasm came, pleasure rushing through me. He stilled as I gripped him, shivering around both of his monstrous cocks. I moaned, relaxing as I felt the endorphins from coming so hard.

His hips gave a small thrust, reawakening the fervor. He let out a low growl as he moved again.

"You feel so good," he moaned. "My perfect mate."

"I want you to fill me," I whimpered.

"I will," he promised, thrusting harder.

My eyes fluttered as he pumped into me, sliding in and out until finally he let out a guttural snarl—hot cum shooting inside of me. My eyes suddenly widened as I felt my entire body tingle, his cum making me feel like a live wire.

"Oh god," I cried.

Another orgasm rolled through me, followed by another. And then another. It was like his cum was sending my body into a frenzy, his cocks pushing deeper with each mind shattering orgasm.

I felt pressure against my cervix, but instead of the pain I expected, I felt pleasure.

"What is happening?" I rasped.

"Your body is getting ready for me," he huffed. "Relax, little gamer."

I gasped as I suddenly felt something bulge at the base of his cocks, slowly working its way up both shafts.

"Oh god," I rasped.

It was a slow push, two round objects lodging themselves inside me. I gasped, an orgasm suddenly rushing through me at the invasion. I'd never come like this before, didn't even realize it was possible. I felt one egg be shoved in further, ready to be pushed deeper. I groaned, arching against him right as I felt another bulge at the base of his cock.

His cum dripped out of me as another egg pushed out, bumping against the one already inside of me. I gasped, writhing under him as it happened again. With each egg, I felt myself relaxing further, helpless moans leaving me. I felt like I was high, a mix of euphoria and pleasure.

He shuddered as he gave me the last of his eggs. I looked down, seeing the bulge of my lower stomach. He slowly pulled out. I could feel his admiration, his appreciation, his desire.

"Beautiful," he whispered softly. "If you wish to kill me now, I will die knowing I gave you everything I have."

"Kill you?" I whispered, confused. "What do you mean?"

"It is custom for you to behead your mate," he said sadly.

"I'm not going to behead you!" I exclaimed.

I started to sit up, but gasped as I felt an egg slip free. Fuck. I laid back down, letting out a short laugh. I couldn't believe this beautiful monster thought I was going to kill him now that we'd had sex.

This was not the kind of pillow talk I was used to.

"I will not *kill* you, Mantis. I was going to ask for a second date…"

"Really?" he whispered. "You want…you want me to live?"

"Yes! That's a crazy custom!"

"Where I'm from, it is always that way. Of course, there are rare exceptions. You honor me, little gamer. I never believed I would be…"

"Wanted? That I would want you?" I let out a helpless giggle. "What do I do now?"

He leaned down, pressing one of his pinchers to my stomach. I gasped at the pressure, moaning as all of the eggs slipped out, covered in our cum.

"Fuck," I groaned.

He chuckled. "I guess we...plan another date?"

"Yes," I groaned. "Another date."

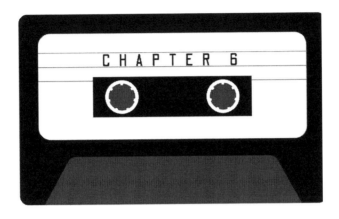

CHAPTER 6

JAMIE

I felt a sense of sadness as the mall came back to life. Mantis held onto me for a while longer, the two of us curled up in his nest. I didn't know how I was going to sneak out yet, but I would manage it.

After all the eggs, we'd cleaned up, and I'd shown him what snuggling meant. He discovered that was his favorite thing. I lost track of time when I was with him, it seemed.

I should have run and screamed, but how could I when he was so damn sweet? Monsters were real, monsters were hot, and monsters were better in bed than any human I'd ever met.

Now I just had to figure out how to sneak into the mall all the time...

He caressed the top of my head, his sweetness making me smile.

"I will be back," I promised him, letting out a sigh as I sat up. Every muscle in my body felt like jelly, as if I'd run a marathon. "I'll come back tonight and we can have another date."

"I will count every moment until then," he said. "I will prepare a new nest while you are away. I will do everything I can to please you. Your happiness means everything to me, little gamer."

I nodded, trying to fight the tears that suddenly sprang up. Why did he have to live here all alone? How hard would it be to bring him home? Could he even fit in my apartment?

"We'll find a way," I promised.

I reached for my clothes and got up, putting them on slowly. My thoughts were running like a freight train, trying to work out a solution.

I pulled my hair back and tied it up, and then turned to look at him. He stood up, pulling me close. I wrapped my arms around him as I accepted his monstrous kiss, one that had my pussy aching to be filled by him again.

"We will be together again soon," he promised.

"We will," I said.

I turned and went to the door, slowly opening it and

poking my head out. I could hear a voice out in the arcade. One that belonged to the owner, Buddy Bardot...

Shit. How in the hell was I going to sneak past him?

I slipped into the storage room and then went to the doorway, listening.

"I can't keep running an arcade. I'm getting too old. And I want someone that loves this place that can handle its... creepiness. Where would I even find someone that would want to buy?"

Oh my god, they were selling the arcade.

I peeked around the corner, spotting Buddy. He was dressed like an old wizard from a movie about a hobbit, his Motorola DynaTAC 8000S held to his silver sideburns.

I had enough in savings and could get a loan...And my family would be happy to help me out....

Excitement burst through me.

That would mean I could see Mantis anytime I wanted. And that he wouldn't have to be trapped here.

I had to buy GalaxyGames.

Before I could stop myself, I rushed out into the open, not caring if he wondered where the hell I came from or that my hair was a frizzy mess.

"Buddy," I said, startling him. "I can buy the arcade. I want to buy the arcade."

"Jamie!" he yelped, staring at me like I was an alien. "Where did you come from?"

"No worries about that," I blurted. "I love GalaxyGames

and have been coming here for years. I want to buy it from you."

Please, please, please let me buy it from you.

I loved my job but this would mean I was my own boss. I knew I could run an arcade.

"Hold on Phil, I might have the answer to all my problems," Buddy said, ending the call. He put the antenna down and frowned, sizing me up. He stroked his long beard with a deep *hmm*. "Jamie, you've been coming here for years. And I know you love that one game, but do you really love the whole place?"

"Yes," I blurted. "And I'm a smart businesswoman. This would give me the chance to flourish."

I'd never have to go back to the office again.

That thought made me feel giddy.

"Well...this place can be...different..."

"I know about the monster, Buddy," I breathed out.

His eyes damn near bugged out of his head. "Keep your voice down, Jamie," he said. "I mean. I don't know what you're talking about."

I raised a brow and smirked. "Sure. You don't think there's a...creature here?"

He hissed between his teeth. "No one can know."

"But I know and I'm cool with it, Buddy. I'm the perfect candidate."

He shook his head and crossed his arms. "Are you sure you want this place?"

"I am."

"Then it's yours. Including that...monster..."

I grinned. I didn't have the heart to tell him that the monster was already mine.

And that I was already his.

Want more Clio Evans?

If you like mafia romance, start with...

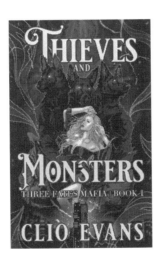

If you like alien romance, start with...

If you like short and hot reads, start with...

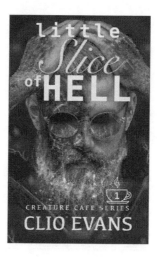

If you like dark romance, start with...

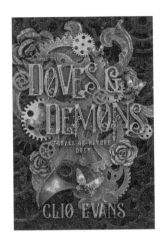

ABOUT THE AUTHOR

Hello Creatures!

My name is Clio Evans and I am so excited to introduce myself to you! I'm a lover of all things that go bump in the night, fancy peens, coffee, and chocolate.
IF you had the chance to be matched with a monster or alien — what kind would you choose?!
Let me know by joining me on FB and Instagram. I'm a sucker for werewolves (and swoony tentacle aliens) to this day.

facebook.com/Clio-Evans-Author-107243805025580
x.com/clioevansauthor
instagram.com/clioevansauthor

ALSO BY CLIO EVANS

Doves & Demons

Demons & Doves

THREE FATES MAFIA SERIES

Thieves & Monsters

Killers & Monsters

Queens & Monsters

GALACTIC GEMS SERIES

Cosmic Kiss

Cosmic Crush

FRANKIE'S FUNHOUSE

BEATRIX HOLLOW

AUTHOR'S NOTE

Desperation for cash has led me down a rainbow painted hallway to Frankie's Funhouse—a children's gambling casino. Or as my boss likes to call it, a pizza arcade.

The coworkers are strange, the patrons are disturbing, and the animatronics are possessed. Which I was willing to put up with until my boss died.

Well, he was murdered, actually.

Now I have to serve pizza and birthday cake while thinking about burning down the mall to hide a body for an animatronic that keeps hitting on me.

Drug dealings in the backrooms, puddles of blood seeping out from the storage closet, and parents threatening to talk to my (dead) boss if I don't get their screaming kids' pizza was all manageable...

Until I realized I didn't mind Frankie's possessed tongue in my mouth.

Content Warning:

MF human x animatronic; Explicit violence, gore, and death; Explicit sexual content; Dubious electric play; Sudden submission; Degradation; Side character drug dealing and drug use; A beheading and other loss of limbs; Unrecommended use of a chainsaw; Satanism; Violent use of a spork; Bad pizza; (NO harm comes to any children).

CHAPTER 1

All I wanted was to dive into a deep-fried piece of bread and questionable meat on a stick before my interview, which was in...I looked around for a clock but couldn't see any around. Elevator music was playing from the mall speakers as I maneuvered around throngs of shoppers to get to The Good Char.

"Shit," I huffed. My interview was likely five minutes ago but I was going to throw up on their lap if I didn't get carbs in me. My mom and I had cleaned out the wine coolers when no other family members felt inclined to imbibe last night. They stuck to their soda while we hackled like hyenas over sweetened peach-flavored alcohol.

Which brought me back to my purse, or should I say my mom's purse. I'd accidentally grabbed it since we had matching lavender pleather purses. How I didn't immediately realize something was wrong I was chalking up to early morning delirium. This thing weighed ten pounds and was digging into my shoulder.

It was bursting with Avon cosmetics that my mom was attempting to sell everywhere she went. I heard a lipstick liberate itself from the purse and drop to the floor. I kept walking, unconcerned where it rolled and happy to be free of one of the contents.

The scent of yesterday's fresh perm wafted in my face—a biting chemical scent I found oddly nice. My fingers pressed into the tight, dark curls, enjoying the texture and bounce.

Man, I was hungry and hungover. Enough that the line at the corndog place didn't even bother me even though it should, considering I was running late. My eyes slid around the packed mall hallway. A thriving mall was a dangerous yet exciting thing—more shoppers than ever, bright smiles, and multiple full bags in everyone's hands.

Ten minutes later I rushed through the mall while forcing corn dog down my throat. I ran past a store mascot and shivered in displeasure at the sight of it. I didn't trust people in costumes. Ironically, clowns were my least concern. It was the ones in those cartoon character suits that disturbed me the most. I didn't like knowing there was someone inside its body. Some unknown person I couldn't see and couldn't get a read on. For all I knew they were jerking off in there while holding a knife. Bunch of sick fucks.

I sent the mascot that looked like some peculiar fuzzy monster a mean look he didn't see and hurried down a less crowded hallway. The people petered out as I continued toward the back of the hall. The less popular shops were down here. The mall swords, the antique shop that gave a frightening aura, and my destination: Frankie's Funhouse.

I pushed the last piece of the deep-fried cornmeal and hot dog into my mouth and chomped aggressively. The thing about eating bread fast was that it gave me hiccups. So as I swallowed a too-large mouthful of only partially chewed breading, I began to hiccup at an alarming rate.

Frankie's was empty, hopefully because of the time of day. It was like an arcade with a few fun games like Pac-Man and Asteroids, but it was mostly carnival games. Bowl a cue ball into the hole. Shoot a basket. Win points and get tickets, trade in the tickets for prizes.

Essentially this was a kid's gambling casino.

I'd never been here myself but I knew places like it. Cheap pizza, screaming kids, bowling alley carpet. This one was special though...This one had Frankie. He was a has-been now but at one point Frankie had been the biggest thing on kid's television. And this wasn't some copycat Frankie, it was the real deal. The very same animatronic featured on the tv show that was also called Frankie's Funhouse.

Welcome to Frankie's Funhouse, kids! I could hear the intro in my head. The chipper music, his eyelids blinking one at a time over big round plastic eyes.

I saddled up to the prize counter where a girl about my age was blowing a bubble with her bubblegum. The uniform looked like a cross between a clown and a street walker and it was one hundred percent weird as a uniform for a kid's place.

"Hey, *hiccup*." Fuck. She looked up at me. " I'm, *hiccup*, here for the interview." I hiccuped again but just stared her down as if this was perfectly normal. My glare could make grown men redecide their actions. It was a bonafide superpower. She decided to ignore the hiccuping.

"Back there," she said, waving towards an opening to a large room with a stage at the back. Thick red curtains blocked off the stage. I thanked her, hiccuping more, and then made my way over. When I pulled back the curtain and stepped through I grimaced. A collection of horrifying animatronics littered the stage. Their lidless, huge eyes were all aimed at me. It was a strange ragtag of various human-like animals wearing black leather and chains as if they were a metal band.

Maybe I didn't need money for an apartment. I could just keep living at home for the rest of my life...

"Hey there, you must be Ramona." The voice came from the animatronics. I stared at them in a cold sweat. Then a man stepped from behind them, dropping a screwdriver into a toolbox.

"Gus?" I asked, eyeing him.

"That's me," he said, flashing a smile. He had rolled-up

faded jeans, white socks, new balance sneakers, perfectly cut blonde hair, light blue eyes, and a college shirt that showed off lean muscles. Which was really weird given Gus was the store owner and this guy looked the same age as me.

"Your dad—" he started.

"Not my dad," I hissed with vitriol. Ray was my mom's ex-husband and the scum of the Earth. It was almost comical how unlikable he was. Then he had to do something stupid like help me get a job. Which made me hate him even more because now I felt like I owed him.

"Okay," Gus said, giving a long blink. "Did Ray explain what the job is?" He flashed another white smile. I eyed him suspiciously. Why was the owner of a rundown pizza arcade a preppy college jock?

"How old are you?" I blurted out, my face heating suddenly because that was weird. He probably thought I was interested in him. I saw movement from the corner of my eye and slowly looked to the left but there was nothing there except an empty spot where an animatronic might stand between two others.

"Older than I look," he said with a chuckle, smiling even wider. God, he *did* think I was hitting on him.

"Ray didn't say much." I shifted the purse strap around on my shoulder to try and get a little relief from its weight.

"We're low staff at the moment so there will be a lot of hours."

"Perfect." The idea of a large paycheck sat well with me. Plus, I was tired of my house, cram-packed with my three younger siblings always running around yelling and being annoying. Their puberty stank like sweat, hormones, and unwashed ass.

"Maureen will show you the ropes the first half of the day but then you'll be on your own tonight. She has some concert she insists is necessary to go to or she'll die." I stood there a moment, slightly dumbfounded. Did that conclude my interview? It sounded like I got the job. He hadn't even asked me anything about my work experience.

"So if you don't know, this is a pizza parlor and arcade for kids all rolled in one." There was pride in his voice. The dark carpet with neon geometric shapes practically glowed.

"Aren't all arcades for kids?" I asked, looking back at the animatronics. There was a drawn-out moment of silence. I looked over at Gus and he was giving me the most scathing look I'd ever seen. My eyes bugged a little and I wondered what major offense I could have accomplished in my statement.

"No," he finally said with a very long sigh, mumbling under his breath about respect and gaming.

"Right, okay, got it. *Kids* arcade plus a Pizza Hut." Then I mumbled, "*Plus whatever nightmare fuel those are.*" I looked at the empty spot. It wasn't empty anymore. How had I...the dim lights and the neon carpet were playing tricks on me because there was no empty spot now, there was Frankie himself—a tall, humanoid coyote wearing a trim-fitted business suit of all things like some wall street banker who was rolling in cash. Broad shoulders, a thin waist. A smirk was on his face and his tie was rainbow striped. Christ, who designed him? Why'd they make him so...so...

Don't fucking say attractive, I growled at myself. He was *not* attractive. He was a fucking robot coyote and his eyes were oversized and practically lidless. I shivered, some archaic part of my lizard brain really disliked his almost but not quite human-like features.

Whoever thought that design screamed kid-friendly probably had the Night Stalker news reports recorded to video tapes to watch on repeat.

CHAPTER 2

I was wearing the slutty clown outfit and it was even worse than I anticipated. Worse than anyone probably could anticipate. It was as if they intentionally thought of all the ways an outfit could make a job harder.

Some parts were sort of cute, maybe. The white collar that hung over my shoulders was okay until I realized it ended in points that had jingling bells attached to the ends. The rainbow thigh-high socks would be cool if they didn't keep rolling down my thighs.

"Shouldn't work outfits, I don't know, be convenient for working?" I asked Maureen the bubble gum chewer as I held up my arm and saw the six inches of extra sleeve hanging from the tips of my fingers. It was a loose-knitted turquoise sweater that went over a pink tank top that covered little more than my chest. "Won't this drag through the pizza?"

"And cake, yeah," she said, popping a bubble.

"How do I grab things?" I asked in exasperation. My arm flapped around and I watched the extra half-foot of fabric sway back and forth.

"You have to roll them up every time. It's a pain in the ass but you get used to it."

"*How* do I get used to this?" I asked then my feet slid and I nearly fell on my butt because, of course, we wore roller skates. Of course. As I twisted around, trying to not fall, my rainbow-striped shorts crawled further up my ass.

"These are underwear, not shorts," I hissed, trying to grasp the locker door through the sleeves. I eyed my own clothes inside the locker with longing. My mom's purse was bursting with Avon products that wished for freedom. Dealing with that seemed like a piece of pie compared to my work outfit.

Maureen stood up and slammed the locker shut, making her point that complain-time was over. My arms spun around like windmills as I watched her glide towards the locker room door. Her blonde hair was blown out with a dreamy feathered look, her layers and bangs fluffy and with bounce. Practically a Farrah Fawcett stunt double, especially with how she skated with ease backwards, watching my arms spin around with both fascination and apathy. An expression I'd never seen anyone able to pull off before.

"You'll get used to the skates too," she offered.

"And what about the shorts?" I asked. Her ass was half out too but unlike mine, her butt was petite. Mine had underbutt cleavage and a jiggle. "This place is for kids, isn't it?" I asked.

"Kids love the outfit," she said. "Disturbingly so," she mumbled as she flipped around and glided down the hallway. I groaned and stumbled after her, half falling, half rolling the entire way.

"Ramona!" My mom's ex barked out. He was seated at one of the long tables in front of the stage wearing a thick golden chain, a sweater, and chunky sunglasses. None of these things were appropriate for the location. It was hot, dim, and kids were not impressed by gold chains. A half-smoked cigarette clung to life on his bottom lip as he talked.

"Ray," I growled, falling after Maureen. She turned and eyed me up and down, looking at me with a more critical eye now that she knew I knew Ray. He was ruining my reputation before my job really even started.

He scanned my outfit, glass blue eyes squinting, and barked out a laugh that was far too loud, spittle flinging from his lips and his face turning red in delight. His cigarette leapt from his mouth and landed on the table, sparks and ash flying out and dying quickly on the table.

"What are you doing here?" I grumbled. He had to wipe

tears of laughter from his eyes before he could talk. The cigarette continued to burn unperturbed on the table and I watched as a small blackened mark appeared before he finally plucked it back up.

"This is my haunt, me and my buddies like the *aesthetic*," he said with a weasely little smile. Aesthetic? I looked around at the kid arcade and aged animatronics in horror. Then I looked back at Ray and finally gave the two guys with him a brief glance. They wore matching windbreakers and also sported the sunglasses and gold chain Ray wore. Whereas Ray had black hair, these two had hair so golden it had to have been bleached.

"You all look like criminals," I commented. Ray spit out the soda he had been drinking from the yellow Frankie Funhouse cup. "Oh god, you are criminals," I groaned. In theory, I had already known that. Ray was a drug dealer but I had not expected him to run his ring out of a kid's funhouse in the mall.

"You need to learn to keep that pretty little mouth shut, Ramona."

"Okay that was gross," I practically threw up the words on the floor. "Is this why Mom finally dropped you? Because you sell coke at Frankie's *Fucking* Funhouse?"

"Your mom couldn't handle the fact that she didn't put out enough." He slapped one of his buddies' backs with a bark of laughter. "Hansel and Lars get it!" The two blonde men didn't give any indication they were part of the conversation. I'd learned not to be surprised by any crass or stupid remark from Ray's mouth. The man was a walking joke of a human, an infuriating one that I thought about strangling regularly.

"You'll learn this one day sweetheart—"

"Don't ever call me that again," I grumbled.

"When you get yourself a man, you need to be able to please his needs. Now I'll admit I've got more needs than most guys. It's all the extra testosterone," he commented, petting the little line of hair above his lip that he called a mustache.

"Ray, stop talking," I pleaded, my eyes shooting to Maureen.

"You listen here. I've got some fatherly advice." I felt nausea roil up in my stomach. "Your momma didn't spread her legs enough and when that happens I gotta find some extra snatch. It's natural for a man to spread his seed. For some reason, your bitch of a mom had an issue with that." I closed my eyes and took a deep breath so I wouldn't fling myself across the tables and punch him in the face repeatedly.

"This is neither advice nor fatherly. Thank you for the traumatic conversation I'm sure to relive at the most inconvenient times." I suddenly found the will to skate better and glided towards Maureen who had witnessed the entire shitshow.

"Skate, please," I hissed through my teeth. She snorted a

laugh and then did as I asked, taking us back to the front counter. As we rolled around the back of it I noticed there was a television set on top of a VHS player.

"You need to watch the tapes. I'll handle the floor as you work through those. You'll be on ticket duty while you do that." I let out a breath, thankful she wasn't going to bring up what just happened.

"Ticket duty?" I asked. She leaned against the counter and flicked her eyes out at the arcade machines.

"Kids win tickets for playing games then they come up here to trade in the tickets for prizes." She flicked her eyes at the wall behind us and I looked at it. There were a bunch of cheap-looking toys with numbers next to them.

She leaned over and pressed play on the tape player. Some static started, along with some warped music. Suddenly a woman dressed like us popped on the screen with a smile that looked stretched to discomfort. It never left her face, even as she began talking. It was a muffled noise under Maureen.

"Don't let them get toys they don't have the tickets for. It becomes chaos because they don't keep their mouths shut. They tell every other kid in here that you gave them free tickets and five minutes later we'll have to call the cops again."

"*Again?*" I asked, eyeing the welcome tape. The woman was talking about how she was so happy I was part of the funhouse family. *Sooo happy.* Her smile stretched wider even though it seemed impossible.

"The cops usually have to come down every weekend," Maureen said. My eyes snapped back to her.

"You're kidding. This is a kid's...funhouse," I spouted, not finding a better word. She snorted and rolled her eyes. Just then a group of kids ran into the restaurant at full speed. One slammed into the side of a pinball machine and fell to the ground wailing. Two moms came strolling in a minute later with cigarettes dangling from their mouths.

"Get up, you're fine," one mom grumbled at the kid. Immediately the crocodile tears stopped and he popped up and ran to her, sticking out his hands. The other kids ran up doing the same and the moms dug in their purses before dropping money in their waiting hands. They ran over to the counter, smearing around snot from runny noses on their cheeks. They shoved the money directly in my face, so close I could see a booger clinging to a dollar bill.

Maureen plucked the money from their hands and slid it into the cash drawer before retrieving the golden tokens she dropped in their hands. She accomplished this all without touching them or the booger. Maureen was a seasoned pro. The kids ran off, yelling at ear-splitting levels and I groaned, picking up the golden coin one had left on the counter by accident.

A drawing of Frankie was etched into the metal. At the bottom the logo curved around the edge: "*Where everyone is always smiling*".

"This is going to be a long day," I sighed. Maureen paused the tape and then pointed out the rates for coins on the wall behind me before she skated off toward the kitchen. I groaned and clicked play, starting the tape from where it was left off. The lady was showing a "new employee" how to cook Frankie's famous pizza. It involved a mechanical device that shat sauce onto a frozen dough circle before we were supposed to—with finesse and *significant* speed—drizzle shredded cheese on the top before shoving them in the oven to bake just enough for the center to be lukewarm at best.

My attention slowly drifted around the place as the video continued. The front was littered with arcade and carnival games. There was a ball pit in a mesh prison across from me. Behind the arcade, it opened up into a large eating room where people could sit at various sized tables. Off of that were the kitchen and a special "timeout" room for parents who wanted to pretend their kids didn't exist for a couple hours.

The stage was in the very back, the animatronics tucked away as if they feared putting them any closer to the entrance would frighten people off.

Right now the red curtain was closed but after a few moments of mindless gazing, I realized there was a small crack. A large mechanical eye stared out, appearing to be aimed directly at me. The hair on my arms lifted and I swallowed thickly. It was Frankie. I could tell by his purple eye and gray fur. Plus, there was a flash of his rainbow tie.

For a moment, I felt hypnotized—incapable of looking away. Perhaps too afraid that if I did, Frankie would move when he shouldn't be moving. The animatronics were turned off until dinner time, according to the tapes. My breathing quickened as I stared into the eye, an odd sensation of being watched pressing on me. His gaze felt like something alive was observing me—watching my every move, learning my actions.

Fists slammed the counter in front of me, violent and loud.

"Tokens!" A kid wailed demandingly. A scream blasted out of me, my entire body leaping up from the stool I'd been sitting on. The kid began laughing raucously, his eyes bugging behind his thick-framed glasses. I sneered at him before looking back at the stage. The curtain was closed.

I spent the next few hours trying to convince myself that Gus was back there and had fixed the curtain. That it most definitely couldn't be Frankie. That animatronics were not alive and had no soul or sentience. I began repeating to myself in a forced laugh that I wasn't being watched by a robot coyote like a serial killer learning about his next victim.

Frankie's oversized purple eyes wouldn't get out of my head though. Whether my own eyes were opened or closed it didn't matter. I kept imagining purple orbs behind the ball pit, beside the Pong video game machine, and peeking through the curtain.

By the time Maureen was bouncing from the back, wearing her normal clothes, I felt like an insane person. I was jumpy, my eyes darting around everywhere. Maureen snorted at me and leaned on the counter.

"Listen, it's the animatronics, right? Bad news vibes," she sighed.

"You feel it too?" I asked. She shrugged.

"It's the uncanny valley," she remarked.

"The what?" My eyes darted around the dim arcade.

"Uncanny valley. It's when a robot looks almost human but not quite. It makes us uneasy and like...gag me with a spoon, revulsed."

"Huh," I commented looking her over. Robot nerd was not something I'd have guessed for her. She raised an eyebrow at me and smirked, reading my face.

"Anyway, sorry to run on your first day. A Friday night too! Hah! You'll want to kill everyone by closing but if you can manage to handle it, you'll get as many shifts as you want and the pay is bitchin'."

"Is that because Ray's henchmen take tired moms into the parent's timeout room and they come out looking like they are ready to run a marathon?" I asked. Maureen giggled while fiddling with the pastel bangles on her wrist.

"Probably but this job needs to pay well because dealing with this crowd is bogus. Plus people don't like the overall vibes of the Funhouse, you know? Not just the uncanny valley. Most only last a day at the job." She cleared her throat uncomfortably, her eyes darting towards the exit.

"The vibes..." I let it trail off, wanting her to confirm the unsettling feeling that thickened the air with the cigarette smoke. Her eyes held mine and I squirmed a little from the direct eye contact.

"You *know* what I mean," she said before pushing off the counter and walking away. "I need to book it. I got Oingo Boingo tickets!" Then she was gone, leaving the dark cave that was Frankie's Funhouse for the bright yellow lights of the mall hallway.

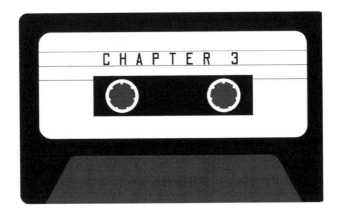

CHAPTER 3

A floppy disk was flapping around in my face. I was in the back with Gus, an office behind the stage that was filled with a massive computer. Or maybe it was multiple computers stacked one on top of each other. I wasn't sure but each black box had a label on it with an animatronics name.

Razzle Rizdog, Marabell Mozzarella, Dizzy Duck...

Gus was going over the finer details of the animatronic show that was about to get started and run until closing.

"Where's Frankie's floppy drive?" I asked. My eyes slid to Frankie, who was in the room with us. Not creepy at all. No, I definitely didn't have chills on my arms. He stood in the corner, his purple eyes aimed forward at nothing. My attention stayed laser focused on his eyes, half-expecting them to slowly shift my way.

"Frankie's a different model. He's special." Gus waved his hand around, the very one with a floppy disk.

"So how do I make sure the show for the night is installed for him?" Frankie hadn't moved, had he? He wasn't swaying slightly on his feet to keep balance, right? That wouldn't make sense for a robot. His legs were made of thick beams of metal with a coyote suit stretched over top. Plus, I was pretty sure robots didn't understand the finer mechanisms of balancing.

Gus sighed in annoyance.

"Look, I know Frankie is somewhat of a celebrity," he started. "You probably watched him on the tv as a kid."

"I was too old. My uh, siblings did though," I said, hyperfocused on the robot. I hadn't realized before but his dark suit was pinstripe—thin, deep red stripes so dark they looked black unless you were close. I swallowed thickly and took a step towards him. Perhaps if I conquered my fear I could get over this paranoia that he was alive.

Gus was rattling on about how he would handle Frankie because his system was more complex. Frankie really was different. He wasn't as bulky as the other machine. He was big for sure, probably seven feet tall. But he was almost slim in the middle, compared to his broad chest and shoulders that were accentuated by the suit.

"What happened to his overalls?" I asked. On the show he wore orange overalls and a rainbow shirt. I'd interrupted Gus again. I couldn't seem to stop because, for one, I wasn't really listening to him; and two, questions about Frankie felt important. Like I needed to know so I could soothe that uncanny valley sensation inside me.

"He wanted an updated look," Gus grumbled.

"He?" I asked, twisting around with wide eyes to look at Gus.

"I didn't say that."

"Yes, you literally just did."

"I meant I. *I* wanted an updated look." Gus's gaze bore into me, something like anger swimming in his expression. Suddenly I didn't like being in this room with him. I'd already been off put since Frankie was in here and not on stage where I expected him. However, I'd taken comfort that at least Gus was with me and I wasn't alone. Now, I realized I was in a small room with a man I didn't really know.

The door was open though and I could see out into the hallway. Plus, Gus hadn't shown any signs that he was interested in anything like that. At that moment Gus started explaining again.

"It's almost showtime. So each floppy disc is color coded for the animatronic. Pick out the Friday Fun Night. However, there's a birthday party later and then you'll need to come back here and switch it out for the Birthday Jamboree disc."

Frankie's fingers were thick, furred digits that ended in something metallic looking. I leaned forward, squinting.

"He has metal claws?" I asked in shock. That seemed like a major oversight. Why weaponize a kid's robot mascot?

Hands snatched me and twisted me around. Gus gripped my shoulders roughly and leaned in my face.

"Stop concerning yourself with him. He's not even supposed to be in here," he seethed, looking at the robot as if Frankie had walked himself in here. God, Gus was crazy, wasn't he? He thought Frankie had asked for a suit and walked around all on his own. I backed up at step and my back pressed against Frankie. He was radiating warmth and vaguely I wondered if that was a fire hazard but the thought was fleeting as Gus continued to grip my arms, his fingers biting into my biceps as his furious eyes glared down at me.

My feet slipped a little from the rollerblades and I had to lean harder into Frankie.

"You're a legit crazy person," I said. "Let go of me." My voice came out fierce and cruel. Fuck this guy. Fuck this job. I was almost happy Ray's little favor was going so horribly, meant I could hate him more.

"Your generation has no work ethic," Gus hissed.

"You're the same age as me!" What the fuck was wrong with this guy? He smirked, his eyes still cruel, his hands still gripping my arms. He had about two seconds before I kneed his groin and took a cheap shot at his face while he grumbled about his precious balls I'd smashed. Actually, I hope he did keep holding me because I'd really like to do that. My nose twitched and I stretched my fingers in and out, gearing up for a fight. A smile stretched over my face.

Everyone called me a psycho when I got like this. Psycho or not, I loved the thrill of a fight and once I tasted a brawl in the air I got way too excited. The smiling was the part people didn't like. The laughing upset people too. If I could just grimace while I threw a punch people wouldn't call me a psycho but I couldn't stop my expression of joy.

"What the fuck is wrong with you?" He snapped. I hissed a little as his fingers dug into my arms. Go time, buddy. Time to knock out my boss's teeth.

"Uh oh," Frankie suddenly said and we both stilled. It was the first time I'd heard him talk in person. It sounded like a programmed phrase, the tone mechanical and barely human. The end of it messed up, dipping enough octaves lower that it sounded almost demonic. Gus slowly looked over my head at Frankie. All the color drained from his face and he pulled his hands from my arms like I was made of fire.

"Frankie." Gus's voice shook. He took a few steps back.

"What's going on?" I asked and tried to take a step away from the animatronic. Frankie's arm snapped up and then fell on my shoulder. My eyes bugged. "What's going on!" I eyed the little metal claws on the gray hand.

"Is he malfunctioning?" My voice was getting high-pitched with panic.

"Th-th-th That's not good," Frankie said. Once again, the last word dipped down into a low pitch that felt startlingly ominous. The stuttering was off-putting too. Damnit, they hadn't maintained the upkeep of the machines and now they were freaking me the fuck out.

"Frankie," Gus said with a forced smile. "You can't do this. I control you." Odd chipmunk like laughter came out of

Frankie—fast and chittering. Gus's words sent me into a panic because there were only two reasons for him to talk like that. One, he was certifiably insane. Two, Frankie could do what he wanted.

"Sorry," Frankie said, the entire word that deep growl instead of the normal pitched friendly tone. It was slowed down too, a low growl that stretched on. I felt chills race up my spine. The paw-like hand on my shoulder had me trembling in place.

Then Frankie moved. He lifted his legs and gently pulled me to the side so he could step one foot in front of the other.

"I've had about enough of your shit, Gus," Frankie said, his voice suddenly completely human. A little wheeze left my throat as I clung to the back wall. That was no prerecorded phrase from a song or show act.

"Frankie—" Gus stopped talking and started screaming as Frankie lifted a hand and swiped. I saw blood drops splatter the side wall—wet, red dots that sort of reminded me of sprinkles because sprinkles painted on the wall of the Funhouse made more sense than blood. Gus kept screaming.

"It's quiet time, kids!" Frankie said in the pre-programmed robot voice again. What the fuck was going on? He swiped again, this time with his other hand. The metal claws splashed wet, red sprinkles on the other wall. The screaming cut off into a gurgle. Gus stumbled to the side and I saw four deep gashes in his neck, gushing blood between his fingers. His hand was on his throat, attempting to hold himself together and keep his blood inside.

Frankie shook out his hand, trying to flick the excess of blood off. He groaned with a sound of exasperation.

"I hate getting blood out of my fur," he sighed. It was all too human. Nothing was making sense. I felt like the world was tilting. Oh wait it was. I was falling over. My skates flew from under me and I landed on my hip on the ground. Gus fell over too, choking on blood, gurgles and snotty blood bubbles coming from his mouth. His body jerked as he inhaled sharply, blood pooled out over the linoleum.

Frankie turned around when I fell to the floor.

"Ramona!" He gasped, sounding worried as he turned around and came towards me. My eyes bugged but there wasn't much I could do except sit there as he kneeled down next to me and pressed one huge hand to my hip.

"Does it hurt bad?" He asked, large, robotic purple eyes a foot from my face. Frankie was huge and powered by metal. He could crush me.

"What?" I asked with a raspy voice, my eyes sliding to Gus who was no longer moving or breathing. "Fuck!" I hissed, pushing Frankie out of the way as I scrambled towards my boss.

"No, no, no." I pressed my hands to his gored neck and pressed down, trying to stop the bleeding. I felt some of my fingers slide into the wound and gagged as I fingered someone's insides in a way I never anticipated.

"He's dead, Ramona."

"Stop saying my name," I snapped. It was weird. Robots

weren't supposed to just know your name and talk to you like a person.

"Ramona, Ramona, Ramona," Frankie sighed, his voice smooth and almost sing-songy as he said my name on repeat. His large paw-like hand dug into his own thighs, gripping them as he purred my name.

"Fuck me," I grumbled under my breath, sitting on my ass with blood coated hands. Gus was certainly dead and there was no fixing that now. I heard the mechanical movements of Frankie behind me, making it clear he was indeed a robot. I stilled, my shoulders crawling up as I sensed his head hover near me. He leaned forward and I felt fur brush my ear.

"I think I love you, Ramona," Frankie said.

"Fuck me," I hissed again.

"Well if you insist," Frankie rasped and I screamed, my fight or flight response finally kicking in again.

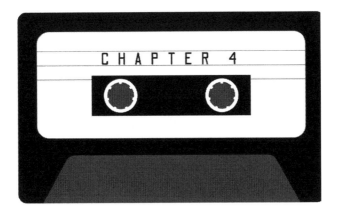

CHAPTER 4

A knock came at the door. A loud rattle and *BANG, BANG, BANG*. Frankie and I froze. I was certain the police were behind the door, ready to burst in. I could hear it in my head, an imaginary walkie talking giving a little beep and static.

"Uh, ma'am, we know what you've done and you're going away forever." Radio static, mumbled noise. *"Oops sorry, not forever. Just until the chair is juiced enough to end your pathetic, short excuse of a life, boss murderer."*

"Excuse me!" I heard an irate woman yell in the real world, outside my anxiety created fantasy. *BANG BANG BANG.*

"I think you better get that," Frankie said. Frankie, the animatronic who was...alive? I opened my mouth to ask him what he was but the banging continued and the woman was yelling some more, looking for an employee, a manager, a "goddamn district manager". I scrambled up, my rollerblades slipping in blood. Jesus, there was a lot of blood. It had just kept pooling and gushing from Gus like the mall's fountain— thick rivulets trickling out on the floor and spreading.

My legs were coated, my rollerblade wheels were dripping wet. My eyes briefly darted to the metal claw wounds and got stuck. They were just so...deep and violent. Frankie's claws had sliced through Gus' neck like butter.

When I tried to glide on my skates they slid backwards instead of letting me press off. My body lurched forward and I saw my own life flash before my eyes as the doorknob came hurtling towards my eye as I fell. Before I could brain myself, ginormous hands grabbed my waist and stopped my fall. Frankie's hands encompassed my waist. He squeezed a little, seeming to enjoy how his fingers could touch. It was very obvious that I was more the toy in this situation, he could pick me up and move me around like a doll.

"Mmm," he hummed, gripping me. I was as still as possible, a mannequin in a storefront, held in the air by an animatronic that claimed he loved me. The banging came again. Frankie took a deep, shaky breath and righted me, his furred, robot fingers slowly coming off me one at a time.

Immediately I reached for the door, turned the knob, and fell into the hallway into a blood-drenched heap.

"About fucking time," the woman said as I twisted around frantically to slam the door shut. *Don't see my dead boss. Don't see my dead boss.* That was this moment's calming mantra. Wasn't really all that calming.

It took several tries to get the lock twisted on the knob, on account of all the blood all over me. Finally, I flicked the lock it without my red fingers slipping off. Frankie and my dead boss were behind a locked door and I could take a breath. Except apparently I couldn't because the woman was talking a lot and her decibels were increasing rapidly.

"And if we don't get our pizzas in three minutes then I'm calling the cops because we both know what Ray is doing here."

"Nononononono," I said quickly, scrambling up onto my rollerblades. My earlier imagination was in the back of my mind. I could feel the steel cuffs biting into my wrists as they picked me up and shoved me in the back of a chevy caprice squad car, whispering to me about how I was never getting out while pretending they were telling me my rights.

"Don't call the police," I blurted quickly. "What's the issue...ma'am?" Ma'am rolled out of my mouth like English was my seventh language because I never used that word. I think she thought I was gagging instead of saying ma'am because she took a step back. She also sighed and pinched the bridge of her nose.

"I've paid for the birthday package. It's six-twenty and the kids were supposed to have pizza at six, Frankie at six-fifteen." Apparently, my boss dying and the animatronics coming to life weren't going to end my shift. If this was going to happen to anyone, of course it would be me. Of course. This was just my luck. My eyes shifted around while I thought. My bloody hand was gripping the doorknob to keep myself up. It started to jiggle a little and my eyes bugged. I was losing it.

"Yes!" I barked out to the woman. "I'll get on that right away. I'm so sorry. There was an issue with Frankie." *He murdered someone.* "And I had to uh..." I looked down at my blood-soaked body. The woman did too. I expected horror, what I got was judgment.

"Haven't you heard of a pad?" She scoffed. I looked at her in shock and horror. Were her periods capable of slicking her body from ankle to chest?

"Pizza sauce!" I said. "It's pizza sauce. Frankie was flinging it around," I said, making a confused face. No one would believe this. Apparently, that didn't matter though. This customer didn't give a shit what I was saying unless it was apologies and promises.

"Pizza in five minutes," she hissed, turning around and stomping off.

"It takes ten in the oven!" I belatedly yelled after her. She flipped me off and kept walking. The doorknob rattled again.

"Ramona," Frankie whined. "Let me out," he growled demonically. My eyes bugged.

"No," I hissed. "You killed my boss and it's going to look like I did it," I murmured to the door.

"Gus?" He asked, sounding shocked. "Gus is—"

"Shut up shut up shut up! You aren't supposed to talk."

"Would you like me to sing instead?" He purred in amusement.

"Oh my god, I have to go. If I don't make shitty pizza and defrost ice cream cake they are calling the cops and I'm going to prison." I skated off before Frankie could say anything else. I was pretending his banging and demands to be let out quickly were simply my mind breaking after what was already a too-long shift and only about to get way, way longer.

THIS WAS HELL. I SHOULD HAVE JUST QUIT ONCE MY BOSS WAS murdered but noooo, I had to pull up a clean pair of rainbow booty shorts and give kids partially cooked pizza and tasteless ice cream cake.

"Frankie! Frankie! Frankie! Frankie!" The kids had all joined in, the entire colossal, over-filled room of them, chanting like they were performing satanic rituals I wasn't sure wouldn't work to summon a possessed animatronic. Their fists were caked in pizza sauce and spit and banging into the table with each syllable.

The parents and Ray's crew had all left. That's how bad

this was. I was now the babysitter of the entire restaurant while all their guardians had slithered into the parent "break room" to make extremely questionable choices. They weren't here but a massive crowd of chanting, filthy children were and they had violence gleaming in their eyes.

I slid another partially cooked pizza on table three and they dove in, canines glistening. At least if I kept the pizzas coming they wouldn't eat me. That's all one could hope for at this point. They were furious that the animatronic band wasn't playing. Tonight was a full booked birthday bonanza and apparently, I was ruining everyone's year. A little girl had been inconsolably sobbing in the corner for thirty minutes because I wouldn't let a murderous coyote robot sing her children's songs and play guitar.

I bent down next to her. In the back of my mind, I recalled I'd left a pizza in the kitchen oven and it was likely burning. Maybe it would set the whole place on fire and hide the evidence of the murder and animatronics. That would likely mean burning the whole mall down. *Worth it.* This was my plan now. Burn the entire mall down.

"Sweetie," I said gently to the little girl wearing the pastel dress and hyperventilating. She shot daggers at me while tears rolled down her reddened cheeks.

"I want Frankie! I want to see him play guitar!"

"Oh, I see. You know, Frankie doesn't actually play the guitar right? He just holds it in his hands and the music is played from a tape."

"I want to see Frankie play guitar!" She was shrilling so loud I was certain she'd be hoarse for days.

"Well I want Frankie to go back to hell where he came from!" I snapped. Her mouth popped open and I sighed, skating off. There hadn't been an extra pair of skates so I'd been forced to keep wearing the bloody ones. They were still leaving blood trails wherever I skated. That was not going to work in my favor when someone realized Gus was dead.

When I looked over the room, I felt something had shifted in the air. Across the sea of kids, I noticed they were all glaring at me, faces coated in blue gel icing and chaos. My eyes bugged and I tried to skate backwards, out of the room. My extra long sleeve dragged across a slice of pizza some kid had peeled the cheese and pepperoni off of. Sauce coated the fabric and not for the first time. The sleeves were filthy which only added to my stress overload.

"Frankie, Frankie..." They started the chant. It started as a whisper but was gaining momentum and the kids were walking towards me as if they meant to claw me like their favorite *funtime* coyote had clawed Gus. "FRANKIE! FRANKIE!" I felt pressure in my throbbing head. This shift would already be a nightmare without the animatronic murder.

"FRANKIE! FRANKIE!" They were screaming now, their little voices breaking. And then it happened.

They began picking up handfuls of cake and flinging it at me. The ice cream cake came dangerously close to my new perm and I lost it.

"FINE!" I shouted, wiping off the cake from my neck. A slice of pizza slapped my thigh and slid down. "You want Frankie!" I yelled. The kids went quiet and nodded. "Okay!" I said breaking off in a deranged laugh. I'd lost it, they'd broken me.

"Buckle up kids, it's time for Frankie!" I growled out, chomping my teeth together. They went wild with cheers while I skated away, my entire body shaking.

"They want Frankie," I said, talking to myself. Probably not a good sign. "They can have Frankie." I got to the back hallway and stopped. There was about twenty feet between me and the door of death but it felt more like a hundred. I could see a puddle of blood had seeped into the hall. I grimaced. The lights back here were dim track lighting where the floor met the wall. Which created weird upwards shadows of everyone in it. It was also painted in rainbow colors—one wall red, one blue, the ceiling orange, yellow, and green. I swallowed thickly and skated down the hall, coming closer to the disturbingly quiet door.

I settled my hand on the knob and leaned close, listening for any noise. There was nothing. My hope was that I'd gone insane and imagined the animatronic killing my boss. I'm sure such delusions were an occupational hazard that everyone here had. Maureen had said the place was weird and most people didn't last a single shift. I was likely just one in many who skated myself into hallucinations involving murder and Frankie propositioning sex.

"Yeah," I whispered, nodding to myself. "I'm sure we all think about it." Well, the boss meeting an untimely end... maybe not the animatronic fucking. I wasn't going to linger on whatever subconscious trauma had made me hallucinate *that*.

"Okay," I said, standing tall and shaking out my shoulders. I licked my lips and twisted the lock. "Okay," I said again. Say it enough times and it's true. My mom always said that and right now, that saying was genius. I twisted the knob and pushed the door open a crack.

"Okay," I wheezed, looking down at the puddle of blood that was still there. A little whine left my throat. "Fr— Gus?" I asked. Better not to ask for the animatronic to respond because that had just been a hallucination. Just a hallucinat—

Frankie burst from the room, causing me to fall backwards. With one hand he grabbed my arm, stopping my fall. He held me dangling in the air as he slammed the door shut and twisted the lock again. A wheezing sort of whimper came out of me. Banging rattled the door and that's when my mind went from budding mental breakdown to confusion.

"Wait...who's banging on the door?" Frankie did some special move where he gave his arm a quick jerk. It caused me to fly back up and land against him. His arm wrapped around me and I looked up with wide eyes at him. He was smirking, his mechanical eyes half-lidded as he squeezed me a little tighter against him. His mouth opened up.

"It's Gus banging the door," he rasped the voice magically coming from the depths of his body. I peered inside his snout for a moment and only saw teeth, tongue, and blackness. Wait, why did he have a tongue? Another whimper came from me as I pressed my palms to his pinstripe suit and tried to push us apart. Too bad he was so strong he didn't even notice I was attempting to get away. I leaned back and he leaned forward.

"Ramona," he whispered.

"Frankie," I said high-pitched, my voice wavering. "What are you doing?" His tongue came out, licking his gray snout. "Oh my god, why do you have a tongue!" I slammed my eyes shut and shivered in his arms. I felt his warm tongue press against my jaw and slide up my cheek. It felt wet but when I slapped my hand to my face to try and wipe it off, my skin was dry.

Frankie pressed forward, his tongue pushing into my mouth. It was bigger than mine, maybe three times as large so when it went past my lips and filled my mouth it was huge. It was long too, sliding in deep. His tongue filled my whole mouth to my throat and he was licking into it over and over again. I shuddered, the action far too reminiscent of sex. My body felt lax and I was turning into a puddle as his huge tongue kept licking inside me. I squeezed my thighs together as the idea of his tongue in other places hit my mind because that size tongue could fully fuck a person. Oh my god, what was I thinking about?

He pulled back and I gasped for breath, my own drool on

my chin. He lifted a furred hand and wiped it up. Then he gave a little pleased laugh.

"Whoops, I just smeared blood on your chin." He was smiling like it was cute and it broke me from whatever evil magic spell he'd put me under.

"What the fuck!" I wailed. The banging on the door came again.

"Let me out of this FUCKING room, Frankie!" Gus yelled. I looked at Frankie and saw a demure blush creep up on his fur. The ears on top of his head flicked a little, giving a little mechanical noise as they did.

"I shouldn't have sliced open his throat," he whispered. "He's really moody now."

"*Moody*?" I barked. "He was dead!"

"Gus doesn't really die," he said, brushing my face and humming in pleasure as he looked me over. "Oh Ramona, I've never felt like this with anyone before."

"Like what?" I asked in a screech, eyeing his snout where that large tongue hid.

"Like..." He looked off smiling, he gave a little laugh of delight. "Like the very first episode of Frankie's Funhouse, the way the kids all looked at me with awe." He looked back at me with a wide smile. "I love you, Ramona and that's why I hurt Gus. He was grabbing you," he growled, his eyes flickered into a glowing red as he bared his teeth.

"Frankie!" Gus yelled and Frankie's eyes stopped glowing and he looked like a dog with its tail between his legs.

"We need to get everyone out before he breaks through the door," Frankie said.

"What?"

"Yeah, he's probably going to want to kill everyone. He's like that." Frankie explained it like saying someone didn't like pineapple on their pizza.

CHAPTER 5

"Run," Frankie whispered. My eyes bugged, my fingers tangling with the fabric of his suit as I clutched it harder, fear ramping up inside me. Pretty sure this was a very expensively tailored suit jacket. I did not run, I was glued in place because there was something terrifying about an actual monster telling me to run.

My arms were shaking a little as I looked up at him. Gus kept banging the door and then I heard it start to splinter but I couldn't stop looking at Frankie's purple eyes, the metal lids sinking lower and lower over his eyes until he was giving me a glare.

"Ramona," he said, pressing my face gently between his

clawed hands. He leaned forward, his snout peeling back from metal teeth painted white. They were sharp and excessive and my breathing was getting quicker.

"Don't kill me," I whispered.

"To be honest Ramona, I can't make that promise," he said and an undignified whimper came from my mouth. I was dead meat. "But if I do kill you, I hope you'll remember I didn't want to."

"Well," I croaked. "That makes it all better." Frankie chuckled.

"You are too cute." One of his hands slid down to my ass and I felt his claws graze under the shorts' fabric. "And these rainbow shorts are fucking killing me," he rasped, giving my ass a good grab. The thing was, he was so strong it lifted me clear off the ground and when my skates came back down to the floor I nearly fell over. My hands left his suit as I tried to balance.

"Shit," I snarled before I got my balance. I looked at Frankie and all the color drained from my face. The door cracked behind him and I saw an honest to god fire ax poke through the splintered wood. Gus's angry eyeball peered out.

"Frankie!" He yelled. Frankie only had eyes for me and he looked fucking terrifying because there was anger in his stance. With a creature as dangerous as that, even the smallest show of anger sent my fight or flight wild.

"Get the kids out," he growled at me as Gus tore through the door behind him.

"What?" I asked.

"Get the kids out and *run!*" He growled and that did it. I flipped around on my skates and attempted to get away. I couldn't run on skates though and to be honest, I couldn't even skate fast. The arch in my feet was burning in pain from using poorly fitting skates for multiple shifts and there was still a little blood in them. Which meant I flailed down the hallway barely going anywhere, screaming the entire time and shooting looks behind me at Frankie just standing there staring at me. He stood far too still for something alive. I didn't like it.

The rainbow hall seemed so much longer and almost as if it was twisted like a legitimate circus funhouse. But when my hands pressed against the green wall it was solid beneath my fingers and not moving. I was probably having a panic attack. And I could still feel the way Frankie's sharp, murderous claws had tickled the flesh just beneath my shorts. And oh my god, the way his tongue had literally fucked my mouth.

Now all types of weird visuals were in my head as I got to the end of the hall. Like Frankie running at me and tackling me to the ground, spreading my legs and ripping my clothes to tiny shreds until his massive tongue could plunge—

"God dammit," I hissed at myself. I needed therapy. To combat that alarmingly horny imagery I thought about what Frankie tasked me with and decided that yeah, the kids should probably not be inside Frankie's *Deathhouse*. Maybe I was a bit of a stickler but kids playing in a shitty pizza parlor arcade with murder robots and immortal bosses sounded sort of bad.

I flailed into the main room and the kids all turned to look at me as I panted and tried to speak without any breath.

"Where's Frankie?" They asked and I looked around at the crowd of kids, sitting and waiting for the animatronic band. Uh oh.

"You need to leave!" I blurted. The chanting started again, so loud they couldn't hear me trying to poorly explain Frankie was alive. The kids that did hear me looked at me like I was insane.

"Of course he's alive," they said. I screamed in frustration and nearly tugged on my perm before I remembered to not do that. I gently patted my hair with the sweater fabric and tried to calm down.

"We are playing a fun game of hide and seek in the entire mall!" I said, stretching what probably looked like a horrific smile across my face. I tried to give a charming chuckle like Frankie did but it came out too high-pitched and manic to sound anything but alarming. I felt grubby hands on my ass and jerked around to see a group of young kids running off giggling after harassing me.

"The job doesn't pay *that* good," I snarled. Fuck this, I was quitting. I could do it right now instead of trying to get the kids to safety. I let out another frustrated yell. Of course, I couldn't do that, even if they were a bunch of little shits. Even if the timing was perfect because Gus was no longer dead which meant I *couldn't* be charged with murder.

"Hide and seek in the whole mall?" A little boy asked with eyes as big as saucers.

"Yes!" I said, happy this was working. "The only rules are you can't hide in Frankie's Funhouse and can't leave the mall unless it's with your parents." I shot a look at the closed door to the parent's lounge. I'd uh, deal with that later, once the kids were safe. First things first.

"I want to see Frankie!" One troublesome kid wailed and enough joined in that it became clear to me these kids were not leaving until they saw the stupid fucking band play a happy birthday song.

Suddenly the curtains to the stage slid open on their own and the whole band was standing there motionless, including Frankie with his pinstripe suit and rainbow tie, guitar in hand. His empty eyes were aimed somewhere near the edge of the stage and it sent chills up my arms. He looked genuinely like a turned-off robot.

Then the whole band snapped up from their quasi limp positions and smiled at the sea of kids. I skated backwards as kids gasped in awe. Either this was going to be okay or a blood bath was about to start.

"Hi kids, welcome to Frankie's Funhouse. I'm Frankie!" My eyes bugged. His voice had a pre-recorded cadence about it, the exact phrase from the tv shows my younger siblings used to watch.

I wasn't insane. There was still blood on one of Frankie's paws. Which meant I hadn't imagined everything in the back. But this was fucking with my head.

"I heard it was someone's birthday!" Frankie went on.

Marabell Mozzarella, the opossum creature thing in a pink dress chimed in, "Oh I just love birthdays!"

This was insane. I couldn't handle this. The only thing I could do was straddle the back wall in terror as I eyed an entire group of animatronics, wondering if they were all alive and not opposed to homicide.

The birthday song started and Frankie's lifeless eyes stayed aimed at me. Maybe it was a trick, some type of optical illusion. I didn't think so though. I scrambled across the wall back and forth and I watched as his eyes followed me the entire way. That was until I bumped into my boss.

"Gus!" I barked out in shock, leaping away from him. His shirt was drenched in blood but the mess Frankie made of his throat was nowhere to be seen. His skin was a smooth, blemish free expanse and by the angry flush creeping up his face apparently he had blood again.

"Oh my god, I thought he'd killed you," I said in shock. This was a good thing, right? I mean of course Frankie was upset Gus was alive because he's the one who tried to kill him. I should side with the human, not the animatronic. Team Human for the win.

"You fucking bitch," Gus snarled, his short blond bangs falling in his eyes as he lunged at me. That's when I noticed one of his hands had an honest to god chainsaw in it.

"Holy fuck!" I snapped, ducking under his arm and then giving him a sharp jab between his legs. He wheezed, doubling over in pain. I tried to lift my leg to kick his face. That was always a great move—a broken nose, blood spraying out, their eyes tearing up. Except I was still in skates and fell over on my ass.

He loomed over me and I sent my skate directly into his gut. He barked out in pain and a smile stretched over my face. As he bent over clutching his stomach I sent my skate into his face and could actually hear the bone crunch. A little zip of excitement made me chuckle.

"Take that, fucker," I hissed. Guess I wasn't Team Human. Or hell, maybe *he* wasn't Team Human. I wasn't exactly sure what was going on here. However, the kids were still wide-eyed in awe as the birthday song continued. It wasn't the normal birthday song but some special thing about having fun at the fun house on your birthday and it was far too long at this point because I think I needed to re-kill my boss.

While the kids clapped and Frankie smiled and the band all swiveled on their robotic parts Gus stood up tall above me. He spat blood on the ground then reached up and pinched his nose, roughly jerking it back into place. I made a noise of disgust and shivered in displeasure to hear him crunch it back in.

"Frankie!" Gus wailed above the cheery music and giggling, happy kids. "Kill mode!" Frankie jerked to a stop, his eyes began to glow red, and Gus stomped through the kids and tossed the chainsaw to him. Frankie snatched it from the air with enthusiasm.

"Oh wow, this is gonna be messy, kids!" Frankie said, his voice a robotic, pre-recorded phrase from his show. It was... unsettling to say the least to see a childhood sweetheart mascot gleefully and with no hesitation talk about the mess one's body would make when he put a chainsaw through it. Particularly with the same enthusiasm and upbeat words used for when it was time to get pied in the tv show.

Slowly Frankie's entire body turned in my direction. His metal eyelids blinked one at a time, like some ancient reptilian beast. Then his large round eyes were on me, glowing red. I swallowed wondering if he was still in there or if this was something else entirely, just a killing machine operating on a floppy disc that told him *murder sure was fun, yipee!!*

Frankie laughed, still looking at me. Welp, I was dead. Hopefully, the chainsaw went for the throat first. I'd bleed out quickly and wouldn't have to labor myself with a bunch of screaming and cardio. Frankie lifted his hand and I heard his robotic parts humming under the suit as he waved at me.

"Bye-bye for now, kids!" Frankie said. The kids had gone quiet once the chainsaw came into play, awed by his ability to pluck it from the sky. One of his gray fingers played with the chainsaw's drawstring a moment before he gripped the thing steady in his hand and jerked his arm back. The machine came to life, buzzing loudly while the blade spun its teeth round and round.

Oh shit, someone was about to die.

"I'm going to make you regret what you did to me, Frankie. You were very bad," Gus reprimanded. His smile was cruel and I saw what he wanted. He wanted Frankie to murder the kids and it's something Frankie couldn't stop himself from doing.

"Hide and seek time!" I wailed. "I'm starting to count now! One, two, three..." Half the kids immediately scrambled for the exit, gleeful in the excitement of playing in the entire mall.

"Frankie's coming too, better hurry! Four, five..." The rest of the kids took off while Frankie robotically moved to the edge of the stage and tipped his head to the side, watching the kids flee with red glowing eyes. Gus growled, turning around to spew vengeance and hate from his eyes. He opened his mouth and Latin began tumbling out.

"What the fuck!" I yelled. Clearly, I was in over my head. Before I could turn and run, the parent lounge finally burst open and the adults came tumbling out like an overenthusiastic wave crashing to the shore. Some even fell over, their pupils blown. Ray had so much of one chick's ass in his palm that I was actually impressed he had managed to grab so much of it.

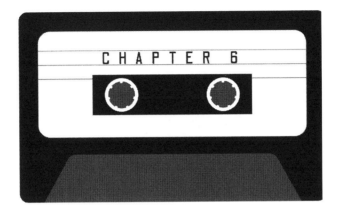

CHAPTER 6

The animatronic band was still playing which led me to believe they weren't monsters, just regular creepy animatronics that tickled the uncanny valley. They finished off the birthday song complete with a group moment where they congratulated each other on how good they played. All the while Frankie slowly turned towards a bunch of stumbling parents and their drug dealers who had yet to notice he was holding a chainsaw that had a sloshing full tank of gas.

"Funhouse Band," Frankie yelled with chipper glee, getting their attention. The animatronics all swiveled to look at Frankie.

"Time for some death metal," he growled, holding the chainsaw higher while his red eyes glowed violently. The animatronics looked at each other then Dizzy Duck, or whatever his name was, stepped up and started to riff his guitar.

That got the adults' attention.

"Hey, where the fuck is my kid?" Some dad yelled out, already belligerent before he knew what was going on. He was wearing a Frankie's Funhouse adult tee shirt that he'd cut the arms off of to make a muscle shirt. Admittedly, he had quite a bit of muscle. It was flexing right now—veins popping and his neck throbbing like an overfed eel.

I opened my mouth to suggest running and to tell them their kids were hiding in the mall. But I was in a very stressful situation and mangled the entire thing.

"I hid your fucking kids!" I screamed and they looked at me in a terrified expression that quickly morphed to rage. Luckily Dizzy Duck and the rest of the Funhouse Band really kicked off the song. Death metal blasted, Marabell Mozzarella was slamming her drumsticks on her set like she desired to obliterate them. Dizzy Duck's beak opened and Japanese lyrics came spilling out.

"What?" I said, not that anyone could hear me over the guitar, drums, and bass. Oh and Frankie's chainsaw. The belligerent dad stepped past the stage, coming at me like a silverback gorilla that intended to rip a threat in half. Frankie bent down while giving a squeaky, manic giggle that sounded wildly inappropriate as he dug the chainsaw into the throbbing eel neck of Belligerent Dad.

Frankie didn't bother trying to work his way through the thick neck. He ripped the chainsaw back out with a wet slurp and blood rained down from the chainsaw as the neck geysered red in an impressive, high-powered fountain half fueled by cocaine.

The parents started screaming, Frankie giggled, and Gus turned towards me and ran. I tried to work off my skates as fast as possible, shooting up looks at Gus barreling towards me. Frankie leapt off the stage to butcher an arm off one of the moms. She stood there watching in shock, screaming as good as any scream queen as he sent the weapon through the limb and it fell to the ground.

Dizzy Duck was now singing Welcome to the Jungle in Japanese. I must have accidentally loaded the wrong language floppy disc during the brief training Gus gave me. Man, I was shit at this job.

I battled the long, pizza and frosting coated sleeves of my work uniform sweater. I grabbed at the fabric, pulling and rolling to simply get use of my fingers so I could untie the skate laces.

It was too late though. I only got one knot untied by the time Gus got to me. I prepared for a fight, rolling onto my back and getting my skates ready for pulverizing his balls until his kids felt it. But then he just ran past me through the exit to the arcade area. Well, that was disappointing. I was all hyped for another round of fighting. The screams and music were really getting me pumped for it.

Then I heard the rattle of the metal door at the front of Frankie's and felt the floor drop out from underneath me. He was closing the place up with all of us inside.

"Fuuuuck," I wailed, scrambling back up to my skates, with no hope left to get them off. My shorts were riding up my ass fiercely, and the untied skate's lace kept getting dangerously close to the wheels. My arms windmilled with the extra fabric spinning around as I raced towards Gus at the entrance. He was most definitely pulling down the metal partition.

I slammed into it at the same time he pulled a deadbolt from his pocket and slid it into the lock.

"You fucker!" I snarled, slipping my fingers through the gaps and shaking the metal curtain hard enough to hopefully knock him in his preppy face. He stood up with a smile, pushing back his blonde hair and smiling at me.

"You'll all be dead by morning," he promised and I could see the complete surety on his face. I bared my teeth and thrashed the metal again.

"Why?" I hissed.

"Because I'm in a bad fucking mood," he said, glaring at me as he gripped his neck where Frankie had previously slashed it open.

"Who are you?" Because something was going on. Normal people didn't come back to life. Normal people didn't have their fatal wounds disappear without a trace. He just smirked so I screamed at the top of my lungs. He reached up frantically to grab the second metal partition, this one wasn't a meshwork but a solid steel wall. I watched the neon lights of mall signs blink out as he slid it all the way down with an ominous thud.

With the mall fully cut off, the screams and carnage behind me were louder. I felt cold as I realized there was a lot less screaming than before. A whole lot less. Then Ray rammed me and we went sprawling to the ground. My hip burned with pain from falling on it. Ray looked over his shoulder and two other people slammed into the metal partition that locked us in, hyperventilating and banging bloody hands against the metal while screaming for help.

Suddenly Ray had his hand wrapped around my arm so tight it hurt. I tried to jerk out of his grip, briefly wondering if it was the same hand just buried halfway in someone's ass.

"Get off me," I hissed.

"Where's a room we can go in? One we can lock," he asked, his bright blue eyes darting around. I heard the chainsaw revving like a streetcar getting ready to race and nodded, scrambling up and skating towards the back rooms. Ray and the two others followed me as I went past the kitchen. I could smell burning. Fuck, I really did leave a pizza in there.

"I got to get a pizza," I said.

"How are you this dumb?" Ray asked, not even angry, just shocked.

"It's burning, it could set the whole place on fire with us

in it," I hissed, pushing past the swivel double doors. The others followed as I raced towards the oven and pulled open the front. Black smoke came barrelling out making deep coughs rattle out of me. I noticed the others suddenly dart behind stainless steel counters and turned to look at the door.

The shadow of Frankie was there—two red glowing eyes and a purring chainsaw.

"I see you," he sang out before giving his little high-powered chipmunk laugh.

"Fuck, I hate that laugh," I said. He pushed the doors open as I flipped the oven off. The pizza wasn't on fire, just a blackened husk so I left it in there and booked it.

"Gather close kids!" Franky chipperly said, his sweet tone offset by the blood dripping from his dark suit and the deep growl of his weapon of mass murder.

"R-r-r Ra *mona*," the last part came out a garbled, deep mess. It sounded like he was malfunctioning. I stopped moving and looked at him standing in the middle of the kitchen. He was looking at me, his eyes flicking between his normal purple and glowing red. I felt for him all of a sudden. It suddenly hit me that he was trapped in his own body, a slave to whatever Gus programmed him to do. And he was fighting it hard, his eyes flicking while he called my name. Called *me* for help.

Then one of the other people in the room knocked over a stainless steel bowl sending shredded cheese everywhere and Frankie's eyes went full red as he turned towards the noise.

"I see you," he said chipperly, moving towards the person with intent to harm while waving his chainsaw around. He dove for the person and the rest of us weren't stupid enough to intervene. Frankie was huge and made of metal. His size and strength were far beyond what a normal human could accomplish, even what three humans could accomplish when working together...maybe. Honestly, I didn't think we were about to make a three person game plan to save the random person, especially since Ray was already running out of the room, even tossing a chuckle of relief and "sucks to be you" over his shoulder while a chainsaw dipped into the other guy's gut like he was gelatinous instead of muscle, sinew, and bone.

Blood splashed up on Frankie's smirking face as the rest of us made it out of the kitchen.

"This way," I said, skate-flailing down the hallway. I was scared, yeah. But I also still had the ultimate wedgie from hell, rainbow fabric tight in my crack and rubbing in a way that I didn't want to think about. I mean I could feel it in the front too, the tight fabric inching up both places and my legs stretching to skate, making me unable to ignore the sensation. People were being killed back in the kitchen. I saw something pink in the gore and was trying not to think of it and yet here I was squirming in rainbow booty shorts with a flushed face because my clothes were trying to get me off.

"I hate this fucking outfit," I said, trying unsuccessfully to pick the shorts out of my crack.

"Can you stop picking your ass a moment to tell us where to go?" Ray offered unhelpfully.

"Can you stop watching me pick my ass?" I snapped.

"You think I want to watch that? Your ass is so fat I can barely see the rest of the hallway behind it."

"Can you two shut up?" The other person hissed. I realized it was the mom from before who threatened to call the police if I didn't get her kids undercooked pizza.

I huffed and opened the stock room. It was filled with all the surplus cups, plates, unrefrigerated food, along with broken arcade games. Ray pushed his way inside quickly and the woman quickly slid in past him before I closed the door and turned the lock.

We all turned around and stared at each other, catching our breath. Then a box fell over in the corner and two eyes blinked out from the darkness. My breath caught as the light reflected off the eyes.

"Hey," a male voice whispered, then a normal guy came crawling out.

"Dillon?" Ray asked in surprise.

"Hey Ray," Dillon said. He looked like a douchebag and apparently worked for Ray. His eyes immediately flicked to my bare thighs and he readjusted his pants.

"Really?" I asked in exasperation.

"Shhhh," the woman hissed, spit flying everywhere, her eyes bugging in rage and panic. We heard footsteps. *Heavy* footsteps that were accompanied by the creaking and wheezing of a machine's moving parts. Oh God, where was the Frankie with his tongue in my mouth? I missed *that* Frankie. It was much better than murder Frankie.

"Ra-Ra-Ra moooooona," his voice called out. "Wh-wh-where are youuuu?"

"Fuck this," Ray said before lunging for the door.

"Don't go out there!" I whisper hissed.

"Me?" He scoffed before reaching back and grabbing my arm, he thrust me towards the door.

"What are you doing!"

"It ain't my name he's calling." Ray forced me out the door but I grabbed onto the frame, fighting for my life to stay inside. "Maybe," Ray huffed while pulling up his foot and kicking me in the gut. My hands slipped from the frame and I fell into the hall. "We give him what he's asking for and he stops killing." Ray smirked then slammed the door shut.

"Raaaaamoooooonaaaaa," Frankie's voice came. I could see his shadow coming around the hallway corner.

"Fuck you, Ray," I hissed, grabbing onto my untied skate and ripping it off. I ripped off my sweater, fully revealing the hot pink crop top underneath before trying to get the other skate. I forgot about the bells on the collar I was wearing. They jingled as the sweat went over my head. Frankie stopped moving. I swallowed.

Frantically I began working on my other skate. My fingers shook as I worked to open the knot I'd tied.

"I see you."

I ripped the skate from my foot, leapt up, and ran. The sound of heavy robotic thuds were fast behind me.

CHAPTER 7

"Ramona!" Frankie growled. Currently, I was diving between arcade games, working my way to the ball pit while plucking the bells off my collar and tossing them as far away as I could. Bad guys always fell for that. Not that I thought Frankie was a bad guy. Gus was certainly the bad guy. Frankie though, *was* trying to kill me.

Guess everyone had their faults. I tried to remember him telling me he didn't want to kill me but that minor detail was fairly unimportant while he chased after me. At least the chainsaw was gone.

I threw a bell and darted out from the Pong game towards the three skeeball games lined up together. Unfortunately, I didn't realize Frankie was in direct sight of them. He ran at me. I screamed and leapt on the skeeball ramp, clawing my way towards the top of the machine. My plan was to crawl up there and then...well I'd figure that out when I got there.

A furred hand grabbed my shorts at the waist and tugged me back down on the ramp. I landed belly down with an oomph.

"Stop running," Frankie growled.

"I'm not going to make it easy!" I raged back at him. *Don't run?* Oh yeah, sure, why don't I just stand there and wait for him to kill me! I clawed at the green, fuzzy fabric of the ramp and Frankie wrapped his enormous hands around my waist and held me down tightly, squeezing just enough that I had little hope of getting free. I donkey-kicked behind me and wailed as I made contact with metal.

"Stop that!" Frankie insisted and then he was on top of me, his body pressing against my legs to keep me from thrashing.

"Ramona," I heard him say over top of me, his hands moving from squeezing my waist to tracing down the curve of my hips. It was anyone's guess how he planned to murder me by feeling me up.

"You don't want to do this!" I blurted.

"I really do," he rasped. He lifted off me the barest amount. I took the opening, rolling out from him and onto the neighbor skeeball ramp. I kept rolling until I hit the floor and then ran through the maze of games.

I dove behind a Pac-Man game and listened. I heard Frankie stomping around and decided to take my chances.

I crawled on my hands and knees across the black and abstract neon carpet towards the ball pit with the last jingle bell in my mouth. Once I got to the ball pit I spit it out in my hand and gave it a big toss before slowly, and with as much delicateness as I could manage, submerged myself in the ball pit.

Rainbow plastic balls buried me. It was the only thing I could see minus the tiny cracks that showed the net ceiling above me. Then I waited, motionless and breathing as quietly as I could. Which was harder than I anticipated. My body wanted to adjust as the balls dug into my back, my lungs told me I needed to breathe heavier, burning inside my chest to get the oxygen they needed.

I heard him walk up to the ball pit and just stand there. I closed my eyes and held my breath, praying to Mary in case she wanted to listen. Frankie didn't move at all. No swaying, no blinking, nothing. Like a machine without power.

"I see you," that machine said, a moment before he tipped forward and fell into the pit with me. I screamed and thrashed, trying to find the bottom of the pit so I could kick off of it to get away.

There was no getting away though. I felt his hands grab my ankles and hold me. He didn't move an inch as I attempted to free my legs.

I kicked him with my one free leg but all I accomplished

was hurting myself. I wailed as my ankle rang with pain. He quickly grabbed my leg and held it back down.

"Stop hurting yourself. I'm not trying to kill you," he said. I heard the words but I'd been running for my life for who knew how long. One minute running for your life might as well be a whole day. I was exhausted, jittery, wild-eyed, throat hoarse.

"Prove it," I hissed.

"How about pleasure instead of pain?" He smiled, looking between my legs. I swallowed thickly and nodded, telling myself this was the only test possible when there were likely a million other ways. But I didn't care about those other ways. I cared about this one.

"God, these fucking rainbow shorts," he rasped and then one clawed hand tore into the clothing, shredding them down to the skin.

I felt his tongue dip between my thighs and I shivered, all the fight leaving me. Suddenly the exhaustion weighed me down, the adrenaline leaking out of my body as I felt Frankie's snout press against my body. His tongue pushed into me, making my back curve up, my soul trying to escape my body. I inhaled all the air in the room as his massive tongue breached my entrance, diving in as he hummed in pleasure. It was better than the brief imaginations before. My thighs shook and I wasn't even coming.

This was so wrong but I deserved a little treat after the shift from Hell.

He licked into me then pulled back a little.

"Don't you dare stop," I rasped, grabbing his coyote ears and thrusting myself up toward his mouth.

"Good girl, Ramona," he growled before his tongue pushed in again and again, licking into me, fucking me with his tongue. He lapped at the damn thing, long strokes over everything between my legs until I was squirming and panting, rubbing the little metal pieces hidden behind the soft fur covering his ears.

The large purple eyes, half-lidded with metallic lids were creepy, I had to admit. It had me half wanting to wriggle away but his tongue kept fucking me like nothing I'd ever felt. The pleasure and simmering fear that hadn't quite left made my toes curl in near ecstasy as an orgasm crept up.

"Frankie," I rasped, rainbow balls all around me, my face half buried in them as he hummed in pleasure, licking me in ways I'd never once been licked. His tongue thrust inside me hard then he pulled it back to roll it over my clit again and again.

Was he covered in blood? Yes. Although to be honest that was probably not the most important detail to me at the moment. That would be that he was an ex-children's show host. That was weird. Oh yeah, and that he was a possessed animatronic.

He licked like he knew how to fuck though and I nearly gave myself a Charlie horse straining as he gripped my legs and pushed his tongue in again. I could feel the press of sharp metallic teeth denting my body as he buried his face between my legs, moving his tongue faster, rubbing it over my clit back and forth before pushing it deep inside me.

I came and I came loudly. Frankie made me a screamer. My body tensed in a rainbow ball pit as pleasure exploded across my body all the way down to my very marrow. Melting was the perfect description, all that tense build-up turning into gooey, warm ecstasy as he concentrated on my clit before pressing his tongue inside me again. He was being selfish now that I'd come, exploring how deep he could get with his mouth, how hard he could lick, how wide he could spread me.

Once I was a full puddle, staring dazed at the netting above me Frankie finally pulled back.

"Can I fuck you, Ramona?" He asked.

"Pretty sure you just did," I sighed in a daze, loopy afterglow. Frankie maneuvered himself in the ball pit until I could see his hips and crotch. A hand went to his pants and unzipped. Then he pushed the fabric down and my eyes bugged.

"What is that!" I was almost afraid to look at the thing. Okay, I wasn't afraid at all but the damn ball pit was making it difficult. I think I saw flashing lights.

"It's my cock," Frankie said chipperly, a smile on his face. I blanched.

"Why the fuck do you have a cock!" I screamed.

"Of course, I have a cock," he yelled back in confusion, matching my decibels. "Gus is a bad guy but he's not a *monster*!" Frankie looked horrified.

"Gus gave you a cock?" I asked in equal parts fascination and horror. Frankie shrugged and began eyeing between my legs. "No," I said. "No way."

"What?" Frankie asked in dejection, his ears turning downward, his eyes almost looking capable of tears. It was odd with all the gore smeared over him. Oh my god, his eyes were actually watering. Which just made my trepidation about fucking a possessed animatronic even stronger.

"I'm not fucking you until I know what exactly I'm fucking," I said. Then I frowned. Wait, why am I a-okay fucking a mass murdering animatronic?

"Oh!" Frankie was back to being cheery as he rose up a little higher in the ball pit to begin showing off his cock. It was rainbow metallic with flashing light bumps on the side and it was big.

"It can even vibrate," he said in pride, flicking the tip with a metal claw. I heard it ding. My legs snapped shut as my mouth fell open.

CHAPTER 8

A loud noise distracted me from thoughts of having sex with Frankie. The metal partition was being lifted up. I heard the sigh of Gus and shifted to the edge of the net cage, peering above the rainbow balls I was swimming in.

Gus was bent over, fiddling with the lock for the metal grate.

He was already back? The clock in here still said it was the middle of the night. I guess he suspected Frankie to have easily killed us all by now. Body cleanup probably required this sort of witching hour, to avoid people getting suspicious of all the garbage bags shaped like humans being carted from Frankie's Funhouse.

Though what did I know? Maybe that was normal and he was just here to get an early start. It was going to take a lot of cleanup and I certainly wasn't going to help. Officially, I might still be a Funhouse employee but body cleanup was definitely janitorial and I had never agreed to that.

Gus pocketed the lock and pulled up the grate.

The very thing I was freaking out about at the start of this night, was what I now wanted badly.

"Frankie," I whispered. "I need you to kill Gus again. More permanently would be ideal."

"I can't," Frankie wheezed. I twisted around with an incredulous look.

"*Now* is when you get squeamish about murder?"

"What? No," he dismissed before sighing. "I can't kill Gus. It's not that I don't want to, I *can't*. I was lucky to have hurt him at all earlier. I think it was because he was caught off guard and wasn't sure what to do with you in the room."

"What would happen if you tried?" I asked.

"He can control me. Turn me off, make me kill. He's going to make me kill you," Frankie said in a panic, zipping himself back up his suit pants.

"Frankie?" Gus called out, trying to locate him. Frankie's eyes shifted back and forth, indicating he was nervous. He was also breathing heavily despite not needing to breathe.

"Frankie, where the fuck are you? Those damn kids." We could hear his voice drifting around the place as he walked through the maze of games. "Thirty kids running around the mall with no parents in sight. The police are probably already on the way because they all had very interesting things to say about being at the Funhouse, Frankie wielding a chainsaw, and one of the employees screaming at them to run." Frankie grabbed my hand, looking at me with big eyes. He was scared and this asshole Gus was to blame. Slowly I pulled us out of the ball pit and into the room.

The only things I had on were the rainbow sock thigh highs, the clown collar, and the hot pink crop top. My coochie being on full display wasn't an ideal way to enter potential combat.

"Frankie!" Gus yelled. I heard a door in the back open up and Gus went stomping back there. I off towards the entrance but Frankie halted, not moving an inch outside the store.

"Will you stop it!" I yanked on Frankie but he wouldn't budge.

"We got to go now, Frankie."

"He'll find me. He always finds me," Frankie whispered and my stomach dropped at the terrified tone. "You should go though. If I go kill mode again I'm not sure I'll be able to stop it. Like...yeah I think I might be in love with you but..."

"But what?" I asked, glaring. He grimaced.

"It's like a barely twenty-four hours type of instant love. I don't want to test that against Gus' magic."

"Well, that was enlightening," I grumbled. I jerked my hand from Frankie's and stomped back into the kid's arcade.

"Ramona! I didn't mean anything by that—"

"Stop," I sighed, twisting around to look at the

animatronic. "This isn't about the limits of your love for me against Gus' magic. Magic?" I asked.

"He's a much better satanist than I ever was," Frankie sighed. I took one long blink, then another.

"Let's revisit that later. This is about me killing Gus with a little thing I like to call Bloodlust," I said holding up my fist because I'd named my fist Bloodlust when I was in fights. I nodded, biting my lip and smiling at Frankie. He blinked at me.

"What?" He finally asked.

"I'm going to kill Gus," I said in exasperation. I turned around and started walking through the games again. I eyed the ball pit and a flush crept up my neck as I thought of getting eaten out by an animatronic not ten minutes ago in there. Now I was going to have to live with the memory of fucking around in a rainbow ball pit for the rest of my life. I was probably going to develop a fetish for the rainbow balls. I looked over at Frankie stepping up beside me, keeping pace. I wondered if he had balls and if they were rainbow.

No, stop. He wouldn't have balls. I snorted.

"What?" Frankie asked.

"Nothing. So like, how does one go about killing... whatever Gus is. A wizard?" Frankie snorted.

"Gus is human and in a demon deal...like me. I wanted to be famous so they made me famous," he huffed, shrugging. "Kind of thought it would be more Guns N' Roses instead of the Muppet Show but can't really ever trust a demon, Ramona."

"I'll remember that next time I see a demon," I joked. "Why isn't he an animatronic?"

"He wanted power, not fame. So they gave him power."

"He got magic powers and you got turned into an animatronic?" I gave him a look.

"No, he got put in charge of me. My manager. Power." Frankie began laughing and I joined in, it was contagious. Demons made some shit deals. This barely even made sense to me. The whole story felt vaguely unbelievable but I was chalking that up to the idea that actual demons existed.

"Well then why does he have magic and come back to life?"

"Gus is a committed Satanist, killing people all the time to stay powerful. He knows all those Latin spells." I looked around and then moved us off to the side. Gus was going to be back soon and I wanted to find a weapon.

"So you were a Satanist too, right? Because you also made a demon deal?"

"Not really, I just went to a crossroads like most musicians looking for a deal with a demon. All I wanted to do was play music for a crowd, see people happy because of what I created. Give them an experience." That was actually a really nice dream.

"How are you so sweet?" I asked.

"You're whose sweet," he said, smiling. I swallowed and tried to will a blush away.

"Right," I cleared my throat. "So how do I kill Gus?"

"You have to decapitate him," Frankie said.

"Why couldn't you do that when he was bleeding out earlier?"

"He's done his work protecting himself from me. If I killed him, I'd die too."

"You won't die if I kill him, right?"

"Is that concern I hear?" Frankie teased.

"No," I snapped out quickly, too quickly. Shit, I was being obvious. My face felt hot. How annoying.

"Mhm, sure," Frankie rasped, grabbing my arm and twisting me against a tall arcade game. My back pressed into it and he was just so big, blocking me in. "Look at your cute blush," he whispered to me.

"I'm not fucking cute, I'm cool," I grumbled.

"You are the very coolest, Ramona. I could tell that as soon as you stepped through that red curtain." Oh god, he was going to kiss me again. I was also still naked from the waist down and he was dragging metal claws up my thigh until I felt the pads of his fingers rubbing me just right. I gasped, gripping his arms to stay up.

"You like me," Frankie teased.

"I don't," I gasped, my hips moving back and forth for more delicious friction. Those claws could nick. I felt them skimming over my thighs as he rubbed me so excellently. I didn't care, I just didn't want him to stop because I was going to come and it was going to be glorious.

"Are you fucking the animatronics now?" I heard Ray ask. I screamed, pleasure scurrying away like a frightened woodland animal in the presence of something god awful.

And that god awful thing was my mom's ex-husband, the person I hated most in the world, walking in on Frankie the fucking animatronic fingering me.

"You are fucking dead!" I screamed at him. Mostly because of me wanting to die of embarrassment but also because he'd pushed me out of the safe room I'd shown him in the hope my death would keep him alive.

"Hey!" Ray yelled out over his shoulder. "Frankie's right here, Gus!"

"Where's the other two?" I asked.

"Well Gus said I can live but the other two had to go," he shrugged.

"Ramona, I don't think I like your dad," Frankie said.

"He's not my fucking dad!" God, how many people were going to make that god awful assumption?

"Wait...he's not?" Frankie asked. Ray jabbed his finger in Frankie's direction.

"Is that thing fucking talking?" He asked, eyes bulging.

"He's my mom's ex and I'm disappointed he's one of the survivors—" I didn't even finish the sentence before Frankie lunged forward, sinking his claws right into Ray's gut. Ray began to croak.

"My girl doesn't like you," Frankie said with a chipper voice. Ray fell off Frankie's claws into a heap on the floor. Blood gushed from his belly and he clutched it and began trying to pull himself in a crawl away.

About that time Gus came from the back with a look of rage on his face as he spotted me.

"Frankie!" He yelled. Frankie shifted back, his eyes wide in terror as he shot a look at me. I felt what I had to do in my bones. Save Frankie. Release him from the control of this evil man. I spotted the chainsaw over Frankie's shoulder, sitting on the edge of the stage, covered in dried blood.

"Kill her!" Gus barked out. Frankie was still looking at me with a pleading expression when his eyes went from purple to glowing red.

"Fuck," I snapped, running right at him. I had to get past him and to that fucking chainsaw before he killed me. Then I had to behead someone. Obviously, I could also choose to turn and run the fuck out of here to never see these two again but Frankie needed me. The poor puppy dog musician who stumbled into a dark deal with a demon didn't deserve this life. He deserved to be free.

I ran past Frankie just as the chipmunk giggle burst from him like a pinata spewing candy. He lunged towards me, claws striking out and scraping my arm as I passed.

"Ow!" I hissed but kept running at my weapon. I'd never killed someone before. Sure, I thought about it. Probably got close a couple times even. This was going to be way different. This wasn't going to be a brawl that could accidentally turn south. This was going to be a liberation of the head from the body.

I heard heavy footsteps behind me. Frankie didn't move super fast but he was huge, with long legs that ate up the space between us. I ground my teeth and reached for the chainsaw, noticing chunky bits on the blade before I grabbed the string and tugged.

I flipped around and faced Frankie, the chainsaw growling to life in my hands. I held it at my hips as a vicious smile cut into my face. The lust of a fight settled into my limbs. Frankie stood there eyeing me, his metal eyelids blinking one at a time, his smile wide to show off his many sharp teeth.

I looked over his shoulder and saw Gus standing there like a mannequin, waiting for my death to come quickly so he could get on with all the cleaning and fleeing that he wanted. That fucking bastard. He was doing something terrible to a sweet guy. A sweet guy who ate me out.

"Time to behead my boss," I grit out under my breath, twisting to the side and darting around Frankie. I ran as fast as I could at my intended victim.

"Don't worry Frankie! I'll free you from this bastard soon!" I yelled over my shoulder as I leapt over Ray, still crawling on the floor bleeding and grumbling. Gus' eyes bugged like a cartoon at my words. His eyes darted to Frankie in something akin to horror. Which was a bit rude considering I was the one waving a chainsaw near his face.

"No!" He yelled, throwing up his hands as I swung towards his neck. The machine went through two of his fingers like they weren't even there. I kept my eyes on the prize—that pale stretch of neck my weapon needed to plunge into.

Gus screamed and leapt back, missing my swipe of the

chainsaw. I nearly fell headfirst into the carpet from my momentum before I whipped the chainsaw around, spinning in place like Leatherface in Texas Chainsaw Massacre. As I spun I saw Frankie stomping slowly towards me and grimaced. I didn't have a lot of time to kill Gus.

"You don't understand!" Gus wailed. I ignored him. Best not to listen to the cries of a dead man. "He's not what you think he is! He was a mistake! My burden!" This all sounded a bit concerning but also pretty vague and like bullshit.

"Come here you fuck!" I yelled as he took off through the long tables, leaping over all the dead parents I'd been ignoring. I grunted and ran after him. I laughed a little as I leapt over dead bodies and held the chainsaw aloft. I really needed to stop doing that laughing thing when fighting. Even I could appreciate how unhinged that was.

"Ramona! If you kill me you'll let him free!"

"That's the fucking point, preppy boy!" I yelled. Gus tripped and fell and I leapt at him, lifting the chainsaw high. I had to do this quickly because the hair on my arms was raised, hearing the quick stomps of Frankie coming up behind me.

Gus held up his bleeding hand with its two missing fingers. I began to bring down the loud, rumbling chainsaw as Gus tried to talk some more.

"He'll kill everyone. He's a—" The sentence was cut off as the weapon's metal teeth ripped into him. Blood splashed up on my face, stinging my eyes. I had to squish them shut and just keep bearing down as hard as I could until I was hitting the floor.

I turned off the machine and didn't hear Frankie's footsteps. I swiped at my eyes and looked behind me. Frankie was standing there, blinking at me with red glowing eyes, not moving.

"You did it," he said before he began to laugh...a lot. I laughed a little too, I mean we just defeated the bad guy! I smiled at Frankie and tossed a quick glance at Gus to make sure the job was complete. Uh, yep, the head was *definitely* detached.

Frankie was still laughing though. He took a big breath and laughed some more even. This was getting weird. It wasn't the chittering chipmunk thing, thank god. But the cadence was deep and almost evil villain sounding in its nature. I chuckled a little with him, I mean it was contagious even if off-putting.

"You sure are happy I saved you, huh?" I asked. Frankie came walking up to me, a smile stretched over his face that could only look evil as he flashed all those sharp metal shark teeth. His hands came up and held my face tenderly. I bit my lip, feeling a little self-conscious being the hero and all.

"You are..." he trailed off with a laugh.

"So cool? Perfect? Lovely?" I suggested. I could really get down with being someone's hero. Especially when they had such a big tongue.

"So gullible," he said before breaking off into more laughter. My face dropped. Well, fuck.

CHAPTER 9

I started to struggle out of Frankie's grip but he powered down. Red glowing eyes faded to nothing, he sagged forward slightly and became stiff. I backed away, looking around at the carnage.

What was it Gus had been saying before I beheaded him mid-sentence? His words felt a lot more important now. Like just maybe he was actually telling the truth and that killing him was a bad idea.

Oh yeah, he said Frankie would kill everyone. Cool, cool. I should probably run and pretend I wasn't the person who started whatever shit show was about to rain down in Creepy Court Mall, maybe even Southern California as a whole.

Frankie still wasn't moving as I slowly shifted backwards. As I inched my way around my beheaded boss, I realized belatedly I definitely wasn't getting a paycheck for my hours. This sucked.

All the television sets in the room suddenly turned on, loud static hissing out. The pizza parlor showroom had about eight TVs strapped to the walls. They were snuggled high up so kids could watch reruns of Frankie's Funhouse, the tv show, during the daytime when the animatronics weren't in service.

"That's unsettling," I whispered. The static grew louder and then the TVs cut off one by one until there was only one left. It blue-screened before fading to a gray glow. Two glowing red eyes and a big glowing smile filled with tv.

"Thank you so much for freeing me, Ramona." Frankie's voice came from the tv, the mouth moving in time with the words. The hair on my arms rose up.

"Mmm, yeah. No problem. I'm just going to..." I flipped a thumb over my shoulder towards the dim mall hallway in the distance.

"Trying to leave already, Ramona?" Frankie asked.

"It's been a long shift." It certainly had been. I was exhausted, half-naked, *and* a murderer. Not sure anyone had ever accomplished this much on their first day before.

"I don't want you to leave." An electrical cord slid up my leg, wrapping around it tightly.

"What the fuck!" Another cord grabbed the other leg. I

struggled against them but couldn't move. I dived to the ground and tried to crawl.

"You see, Ramona. I told a few lies," Frankie said. "And you ate them up so easily." He laughed and the cords pulled me across the floor, dragging my body closer to the tv he was talking out of.

"You don't say?" I grumbled, trying to scratch at the carpet.

"All I had to do was throw a few puppy dog eyes at you and act like a fool." Clearly, I wasn't getting away so I gave up trying and looked at the tv.

Admittedly, I was embarrassed I fell for his act. My face was hot as he shamed me about it. The cords on my legs tightened and shifted higher. Yet another cord slipped around my body and headed between my legs, dragging itself across my center.

"What are you doing!" I gasped.

"Well, I didn't lie about liking you. What do you say, Ramona?"

"Say about what?" I squeaked as the cord lifted up, holding itself up like a snake with a pronged head. It hovered there a moment before it darted in like it meant to bite. The prongs dove towards my thigh, the metal sliding across my skin before a small shock of electricity jolted me.

As I gasped, the pronged head dove between my legs in a snap, delivering an electric shock right to my center. The sensation made my whole body jerk, my walls to tighten, and a chaotic pleasure to unfurl deliciously in its wake. It was a revitalizing jolt of pleasure that made me suck in a sharp breath before I let out a throaty groan.

"You gullible girl," Frankie rasped. "The truth is I'm the demon. Gus was a Satanist who managed to trap me inside the animatronic body to do his bidding and give him power. The little shit." The cord snapped forward again, the prongs sinking into me and jolting me with a sharp electric bite. My eyes nearly rolled in the back of my head as a shudder rolled over me. The pleasure was energetic and explosive, a fast-paced jolt that brought me higher.

"Demon," I rasped. "Why are you in the TV?"

"I'm incorporeal in this realm. But I can possess any device with electricity." More cords came from who knew where to slither across my body, sending tiny pronged bites of electricity to my skin over and over. My head fell back with a thud on the floor as I writhed in a frenzy of pleasure.

"Oh Ramona, look at you. I like the way you twitch on the floor from a few little stings. Pathetic, *gullible* Ramona." His words burned inside me, I felt like I was on fire, ready to rage like I normally do. I could feel the need to jump up and fight tight inside me like a knot.

Then it just snapped, melting away. My entire ego cracked open and left me feeling warm and guileless. My muscles went lax and my brain went numb. It felt like all my stress and anxiety had been taken out. The need to defend myself was completely absent.

I *wanted* him to keep calling me names and I wanted to nod my head as he did it.

"Gullible, Ramona," *Yes.* "So naive." I was and it felt good to admit it, to agree. All the tension leaked away until I felt malleable and soft, warm and gooey. All the while he kept teasing my body, getting me off, complementing the way I squirmed, and laughing at the way I agreed. I wanted him to laugh, I deserved it. I'd *earned* his teasing and disappointment.

I couldn't recognize myself, writhing submissively on the floor. It felt good to step outside all my roles—let them slither away until there was nothing left to care about. I cried out as the jolt of electricity hit me, my body shaking in charged revelry.

No one had ever talked to me this way. Or if they had, I didn't like it. But I totally loved this. Frankie, the tv star. Frankie the massive robot. Frankie the demon.

"More," I begged.

"Oh Ramona," he chuckled, a condescending edge to his words. The tv's light bathed the dark room, lighting my skin and leaving harsh shadows. I watched black cords tense on my thighs as a heavy one slid across my belly. It gave an electric kiss that made my muscles tense.

My back arched as I squirmed and moaned. Then a large coyote animatronic blocked out the tv's light. I looked up to see red eyes glowing down at me. The tv clicked off and the cords fell away. I kept laying there, waiting for him to do as he pleased, and hoping desperately it was fuck me.

Frankie reached down and grabbed me, pulling me from the ground and carrying me through the arcade all the way up to the ticket booth. His arm swept over the top and a handful of golden coins with his cartoon likeness fell to the ground. Then he set me on the counter, leaning over with a growl as I waited for what came next. Massive clawed hands settled beside my head.

The cold kiss of smooth metal pressed between my legs. The soft fabric of his suit and short fur brushed my thighs. Huge glowing red eyes looked down at me with curved eyebrows of judgment.

"You want to fuck an animatronic, don't you?" He asked.

"Yes," I rasped, reaching out and gripping his arms. He shook his head in disappointment even as I felt the tip of his metal cock brush my entrance. I gasped, twisting his jacket's sleeves, my body melting instead of tensing. All the fight was gone for *him*. I was loose and lax and needy.

His tip started to spread me open.

"You're such a disappointment," he rasped, causing a shudder to roll over me. Right next to my ears, I heard his metal claws digging into the counter as he pressed deeper inside me.

"I am," I mumbled in agreement. It felt so good just to agree, to not fight it, just be who I was even if it was the shittiest version of myself. He accepted those parts and even wanted to indulge them for me. I inhaled sharply as I felt the bumps up the side of his cock rub against my walls. I whined his name and he groaned, looking down to see how deep we were connected. Not deep enough.

"I'll give you what you need," he promised, pushing in

further. "How couldn't I give someone so pathetic what they want?" He murmured tenderly to me. He sounded almost breathless. His claws punctured the counter and a growl worked its way from his mouth as he thrust into me.

Despite his evident pleasure, he acted like this was all for me—because of how much I needed it. It did things for me.

"This is what you want, right?" He hissed with entertainment, buried to the hilt, my body clenching around him.

"Yes," I moaned. He pulled out and thrust back in, giving me what I needed. A gasp left my mouth. His cock was unforgiving, no give to it at all, barrelling its way inside me, the bumps rubbing.

"Tell me *how* you want it, Ramona. Maybe I'll torture you slowly," he said drawing himself back out before slowly pressing back in.

"No," I rasped. "I need it faster."

"That's good, Ramona, telling me exactly how you need your perversions fulfilled." He thrust into me fast, over and over, growling, claws scratching the counter. "Let's see how you handle what I can really do though," he whispered into my ear. He reached between us and pressed something on the bottom of his cock. The bumps on the side of his shaft lit up in blue, yellow, and red and the entire thing began to vibrate and twist.

He looked down at me with a shark's smile—manic, wide, unhinged. Then he pressed my thighs flat against the counter and pushed himself inside me again.

"Oh God," I whined, eyes rolling in the back of my head as vibrations and movement lit up inside me. I couldn't do anything but come while crying out and whining. And when it was over all he did was chuckle and keep fucking me. My legs tried to curl up and close but he held them down as I felt another orgasm burst through the surface and take over.

I clawed at his arms—whimpering as my legs shook with enthusiasm. The pleasure just wouldn't stop. I wanted the ecstasy but I felt like I was losing control. Tears pooled in my eyes and fell down my face. Frankie clicked his tongue.

"This ride only stops for emergencies. Crying is not an emergency," he said with a deep laugh, fucking me senseless until a third orgasm started to claw its way from the depths of me. I whined and my body tensed in preparation.

"I'm giving you just what you want," he groaned, fucking me faster, the vibrations a relentless attack on my sanity as the orgasm fully burst from me. I cried out, shaking and tensing as pleasure rolled over me.

A guttural growl ripped from him. I felt something hot gush inside me as my hips bucked on his cock, my body mastered by its pleasure. Not that I cared. I was still in that special headspace where it didn't matter how fucked up or embarrassing I was. I could just be everything I was, acknowledge it and enjoy it. I didn't even have to do any work to enjoy it, Frankie was there to give it to me. My reward for melting and losing all my fight.

Finally, his hips were still as he moved his mouth to my ear.

"The moment I saw you walk behind the red curtain I *wanted* you more than anything I've wanted before. I was determined to make you mine, even if I had to lie along the way." I laid there catching my breath and relearning how to be me. Frankie pressed his mouth to mine, his tongue owning my mouth. I moaned lazily, kissing him back.

"My pet," he rasped around the time I started to get post-orgasm clarity.

"I'm no one's pet," I hissed.

"How cute that you think you have a choice," he said with a laugh. Frankie pulled out and I felt something wet between my thighs. My fingers brushed through the liquid. It was white and plentiful.

"What is this?" I asked.

"Ectogasm," Frankie said with a wide smile, eyeing my pussy like he was considering ending my life via sex. He shifted closer, a gleam in his glowing eyes, and I scrambled away, behind the counter. I snatched up a pair of Frankie Funhouse basketball shorts and slipped them on before running through the arcade and back into the showroom. I would literally die if he fucked me again right now. I'd left exhaustion behind two hours ago. I was running on pure will to live at this point and it felt like shit.

"What's wrong, Ramona?" He teased while hot on my heels. I darted to the other side of a long pizza table and eyed him across it. He curved an eyebrow, a shark's smile with zealous eyes.

My legs felt like they could barely hold me. I was

clutching the plastic chairs to keep myself from falling into a heap. I could just imagine him descending on me if I did, killing me slowly with one orgasm after the other while telling me death also wasn't a good reason to stop enjoying the ride.

"What do you want, Frankie?" I asked. His eyes tipped down to my body.

"To fulfill all your sick perversions," he purred. I swallowed thickly.

"I meant other than that," I rasped before clearing my throat. "Why did you have me kill Gus?"

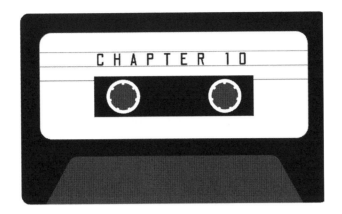

CHAPTER 10

"What I want is freedom to live my demonly ways without restraint," Frankie said. Then he began to go off in an excited rant about murdering the entire state and bringing an end to the world. Several times I tried to get a word in but he wouldn't let me.

"Frankie!" I snapped and he finally seemed to realize I was trying to talk. "So Gus killed someone and used Satanist death magic to trap you in the animatronic?"

"It's more complicated than that," he said, brushing the blood-stained arms of his suit. "He had to perform a massacre. Gus wasn't a good guy. I hope you don't feel bad about killing him."

"Not really," I said, looking over at the headless body. Though I wished I'd waited until he explained in full about Frankie. I looked around at the...massacre around me. Okay, I was forming an idea. One that might just save the lives of a lot of people.

I saw something glimmer near the edge of the room and realized it was Ray's glassy eyes staring at me. That bastard was still alive! I ignored him for now. Ray might be useful in some way.

I walked slowly around the table and then went over to my beheaded boss. Frankie watched me, standing his ground and observing me with oversized eyes.

"Uh actually maybe I do feel bad," I said, bending down and trying to discreetly pat Gus' body for a book of satanist spells or something.

"What are you doing over there, Ramona? You don't have a...*thing* for dead bodies, do you? I'm not sure I'm up for that." Interesting line in the sand to draw for him but okay. There was no book of spells. I lifted his shirt's sleeve and there on his arm was a tattoo, something scribbled in Latin. This had to be it. A fail-safe if he died and someone had to contain the demon again. I read over the words a few times, trying to memorize them before Frankie decided to get closer and see what I was looking at.

Discreetly, I eyed Ray again. He was leaning against the wall, holding his gut where Frankie had gored him.

Okay first, I was going to murder Ray and count that as a bonus. I wasn't sure if I had to kill him to make the spell work since there was already a massacre but no point risking it. Then, if that worked, I was going to be forever tying myself to Frankie and his really big tongue. Uh, I meant his demonic soul.

He was ranting again about his plans of pain, torture, and death.

To be honest, I didn't dislike the demon but he was far too cocky without someone controlling him. Rivers of blood wasn't really my aesthetic and I could never trust he wouldn't kill me or those I cared about when given the freedom to do whatever he wanted.

"Okay," I blurted, interrupting Frankie as he talked about ripping flesh from bones across the golden state. He was really attached to this idea. I pushed myself up from the floor and looked at the demonic robot.

"Okay?" He asked, the lids of his eyes sinking lower.

"Okay I'll be your sex pet," I said, my face burning as I glared at the wall, pissed I had to say this.

"Really?" He sounded unconvinced. "Why?" I swallowed my pride.

"Because then you won't kill me," I hissed. He kept staring down at me in anticipation of more. I groaned loudly and threw my hands up. "Because I'm into you, okay? You're a lying, mass-murdering demon and I kinda think it's bitchin'. I'm not totally normal, you know? I just beheaded my boss because of one thinly veiled lie an animatronic gave me."

The sad part was, I was telling the truth. Man, I was fucked up.

"Aren't you just the cutest, Ramona." Frankie sounded absolutely enamored and I tried not to swell with his compliment but my heart felt light and fluttery. I knew I was already addicted to whatever he had given me before, the moment with zero ego and pure sloppy pleasure.

"I'm not fucking cute," I said, shifting closer to Ray who glared at me, not trusting me one bit. He shouldn't. Bastard tried to get me killed, he deserved what was coming.

"Let's see how cool you remain when I test out just how many volts you can handle," Frankie rasped. My eyes bugged and I pressed my thighs together. I was hot over a possessed animatronic threatening to electrocute me. That was honestly a more surprising revelation learned at work, than realizing I'm capable of wielding a chainsaw against my boss.

I cleared my throat and focused.

"Tell me about your apocalypse plan again. I missed some of the big parts." I shuffled closer to Ray. He was in no shape to flee, thank god. Frankie had essentially already killed him, even if it was a slow death. I was practically doing him a service by ending it quicker. Plus the asshole might actually go to heaven considering he was being used to stop a demonic apocalypse.

"Oh you are going to love this," Frankie hissed in glee before he began to rant and rave again. He paced across geometric neon shapes on the carpet as he talked. There was a far-off look in his eyes and a smile stretched over his face, no doubt visualizing mayhem. Frankie had clearly been waiting a long time to talk about this with someone. The fact

I asked him for more info seemed to spur him into a greater hyper-focused deluge of details.

Perfect, it was now or never. I launched at Ray, grabbing a plastic spork from the table as I descended on him.

"You bitch," he hissed, grabbing my arm and ripping the spork from me. "I'll do it myself," he spat. He wasn't even going to allow me the joy of ending him—annoying until the end. Ray dug the plastic utensil into his belly. A final gush of blood left his body and he sagged to the side, limp.

That's when I whipped back around to Frankie and started to speak Latin. He twisted around with red glowing eyes and a furious look on his face.

"Ramona!" He yelled. He stood there looking furious with me as I spoke the spell. "Why do I have to like someone so difficult," he grumbled as I said the final line. Nothing happened and Frankie massaged his temples.

"You pronounced something wrong," he sighed before saying the word correctly for me.

"Uh, thanks," I said awkwardly before launching back into Latin. Frankie shook his head. I felt something snap inside me, a tight elastic band that was anchored to my heart and reached out, attaching to Frankie.

We stood there a moment in silence, staring at one another, and letting what just happened to sink in.

"Guess this means we are sort of forever now, huh?" I asked. Frankie gave a deep sigh. I expected him to be angrier —to have attempted to kill me actually. However, he just stood there like we were having a couples fight and he was being the bigger person about it. As the adrenaline settled and I realized nothing else was going to happen, I smiled.

"I've got a good feeling about us," I said, standing taller and putting my hands on my hips.

"I was this close to killing thousands of people," Frankie said, holding up his hand to show a tiny pinched space between his fingers.

"Yeah," I laughed. "That was a close one."

"Very close," he said, his eyes dragging down my body.

"I need some OJ before we do that again. Maybe something from the food court." I'd yet to try out Broth with a Bite but the smells it omitted were fantastically meaty. Frankie huffed in disappointment but looked resigned to my words.

"Hey, so do I have powers now?" I asked.

"Not unless you perform satanic rituals," he commented. I frowned.

"Well, do I at least become immortal?"

"Again, satanic rituals."

"Damnit, Frankie. You're supposed to be, like, a demon! What do I get out of this deal?" I asked. Frankie took a moment to think and then a smile spread over his face.

"Let me kill the rat," he said with excitement.

"The...rat?"

"Yes, the conniving bastard who stole my fame! A rat selling pizza, come on," he scoffed. Ohhh *that* rat.

"Is he a demon too?"

"Of course he's a demon. I'm trapped in a mall and he

gets made for tv movies!" He growled in rage. "Gus never wanted me to kill him or the execs that canceled my show. He was punishing me for trying to kill him one too many times." Frankie rolled his eyes like Gus was being dramatic.

"Oh," I commented. I wasn't sure what to say to all these revelations. "Well, I mean I'm cool with killing Chuck. You want a show again?"

"We can have so much more than a show, Ramona." Frankie strode towards me, his hands brushing down my arms before he held my hands in his. "We could have movies, theme parks even! Frozen pizzas in every supermarket. Gas station if we wanted to. We could be filthy rich."

"Gas station sounds random but the filthy rich part I like a lot," I said with a wide smile.

"We are going to have a good life, Ramona," Frankie promised, pulling me into his chest. His arms wrapped around me, giving me a tight hug. "I think I knew things were going to end up this way," he admitted.

"Can't say the same," I said, giving in and hugging him back. I pressed my face against his chest and inhaled. He smelled like blood and pizza.

"I really do like you, Ramona," he whispered. I bit my bottom lip to stop myself from smiling.

"I really do like you too, Frankie," I admitted softly. "Let's kill the fucking animatronic rat."

ABOUT THE AUTHOR

Beatrix Hollow survives in a puddle of mud sometimes called East Texas. She writes morally questionable paranormal romance that frequently has horror themes. Sometimes there's even a strange kink and interesting appendage. She finds dark, steamy, and humorous themes fun.
Beatrix studied creative writing and psychology at Virginia Tech, used to be a professional ice cream maker, and enjoys looking at artwork of raccoons.
https://linktr.ee/beatrixhollow

ALSO BY BEATRIX HOLLOW

Cute but Psycho

Run & Hide

Hookah Smoking Caterpillar

Flawed Creatures

Monster Island

LOST AND FOUND

VERA VALENTINE

BE KIND AND REWIND

A U T H O R ' S   N O T E

Ethan is a displaced Nix - a water spirit bound to a mall water fountain thanks to the tender mercies of unethical mosaic stone sourcing. When a plumber's son presents an interesting diversion to Ethan's days working the Lost and Found at the Creepy Court Mall, the handsome hunk may just be the one thing he's been searching for.

Content Warning:

This short story contains mature themes, including explicit

oral, anal, and manual sex, dirty talk, discussion of breeding, egg production (by MC, during climax), talk of breeding (non-pregnancy-causing), unprotected sex, and a magical coercion-into-mating situation. While MM pairings never need a warning, consider this your heads up that this is a love story between two men.

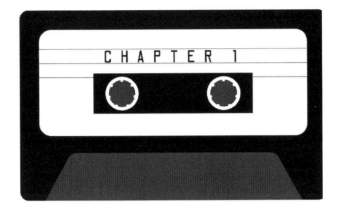

CHAPTER 1

I closed my eyes, grinding my jaw at a loud splash followed by raucous, idiotic male laughter and the echoing slap of retreating sneakers on linoleum. The sharp points of my teeth pricked at the inside of my lower lip before I got them under control again, soothing myself with a deadly glare at the source of the noise. The worst plague to ever descend on humanity, monsters far more destructive than anything I could call kin.

Teenagers.

Before I could indulge in any mental fantasies of drowning the little shits in the makeshift grotto I'd built beneath the mall, the phone rang.

"Mall Facilities, Ethan speaking." I bit back a sigh as I fruitlessly attempted to untwist the perpetually-tangled phone cord. Everything felt in disarray today. There were pizza grease smears on the curved edge of the information desk, whatever foulness the rowdy boys had left on the surface of my fountain-water, and now this knot of ugly beige coils, too.

A wailing, shrieking child in the background nearly drowned out the female caller's voice. "My Brittany's teddy bear is missing, has anyone turned anything in? We were in the food court and-"

"Nope, sorry." I cut off her pleas as I dropped the handset into the phone cradle, taking solace in the satisfying clunk and faint bell noise. Maybe one day I'd "accidentally" break the infernal thing and have an afternoon of peace for a change. The phone was my least favorite part of the job, one I'd begrudgingly had to take to stay close to my water source.

The phone immediately rang again, testing what little patience I had left. I was overdue to submerge myself—there had been an unusual amount of nocturnal activity around the mall the last few nights, which meant I couldn't safely slip into my grotto. The despair of feeling disconnected from my water had soured my mood and dried my skin. Yes, I could dip a hand into the coin-studded turquoise water without getting strange looks, but it wasn't as if I could ease my body into the fountain the way I longed to.

I lifted the receiver again, willing my voice to stay calm. "Ma'am, as I just explained, we don't have any toys here."

"No toys? Damn. What the hell am I going to play with, then?" The unexpected answer was delivered in a baritone smoother than the soft jazz muzak that murmured through the speakers overhead.

"I—oh. Um. Right, sorry, I mean—" I grasped at words, at sentences, with all the grace of that new gluttonous hippo game the toy store across the mall could barely keep in stock. Mercifully, the rumbling laughter of the voice cut in instead.

"Don't worry about it, man, I'm just messing with you. This is Ryan Gold, with Flo-Rite Plumbing. I'm calling about some kind of fountain leak, it says here. I know my dad scheduled your appointment for the beginning of next month, but we had a cancellation and we could come today, if that works?"

"Oh! Yes. Yes, we're leaking, definitely. The fountain is leaking, I mean. I'd love it if you came today, yes." Why did my face feel so hot? My nails shimmered blue-green, sharpening against the rubbery beige phone cord as I twirled it aimlessly. A strange current of anticipation rushed through me at the thought of seeing the man behind the voice, stomach tightening.

"Mhm. Good, that's perfect. We'll be there right around 2, then. Hey, listen, if you could shut off the water to the fountain beforehand, that would be super helpful." There were faint scratching sounds of a pen or pencil on paper as he wrote something down.

"Okay. See you at 2 then, Ryan." As I hastily hung up the phone to prevent further embarrassment, my face heated in an uncharacteristic blush. I dabbed curious fingertips at my warm cheeks, skin that normally ran water-cool and threatened to reveal my inhuman nature if I ever allowed contact. Why in the depths had I called him *Ryan*? That was stupid. Too familiar. I was at work, I should have called him Mr. Gold.

My stomach tightened with anticipation again as a jolt of recognition hit me.

I wanted to *collect him.*

That impulse was the only time I felt this way, when I shimmied after a particularly bright coin or lost bit of jewelry in the water, or when I spirited away something set with sparkling rhinestones from the dented cardboard box under the counter.

These little things I found? Those treasures tossed in the water or abandoned elsewhere in the mall? Those were *mine.*

This Ryan would also be *mine.*

CHAPTER 2

The giant neon-ringed clock that hung over one of the escalators read 12:30, an annoying distance from the 2 pm appointment I now eagerly awaited. Well, more time to get ready, I supposed. I grabbed the creased "We'll be right back!" sign and plunked it down, the peeling lamination scraping along the counter as I lifted the gate and squeezed out of the tiny kiosk. I swallowed with a wince at my pinched throat as I made my way through the mall—I was *very* dry, and I'd need to get into my grotto and relax my form tonight, no matter what.

I subtly leaned and trailed my hand through the highest part of the fountain as I passed it, a small relief against the dryness. My submerged pinky brushed the slick, cool surface of the tiles as the water swirled in eddies against my finger-webs with every step. I had to pull the thin membranes back in as I approached the far edge of the fountain and removed my hand, but it was worth that quick effort for the relaxation of touching my water.

I was a Nix, an ancient aquatic monster far from my ancestral home, forced to adopt a human persona for periods far longer than we were intended to. Countless years ago, a meddling adventurer making a name for himself stole a ring from my grotto, one forged from my own scales, and gained power over me. He'd been, unsurprisingly, an absolutely insufferable asshole about it, and once he'd commanded me to kill his enemies, fetch him wealth, and the usual array of boring mortal bullshit, he'd thankfully died without an heir. The ring settled into the silt of some forgotten river, and so did I, until an enterprising countryman unknowingly sold it in a load of decorative river stones slated for a mosaic. I was abruptly woken and forced to stow away on a ship to an unknown country, following the pull of my ring against my will.

The annoying checks and balances of that cursed jewelry kept me from finding it, reclaiming it, and eating everyone involved out of sheer irritation. I didn't have much of a taste for human flesh anyway, though I'd heard some of my local brethren weren't quite as discerning. No, I had to subsist on overly-processed fish, practically dehydrate myself to avoid detection, and wait for the impossible: another human to find my ring and willingly give it back. Until that happened, this job kept me close enough to water infused with my ring's magic to survive.

Oh, I'd still looked for my ring, believe me. Night after night that first year or two after my awakening, squinting at every inch of the hideous mosaic edges and walls and floors that shimmered under the foot or two of chlorinated water. But no glint of gold called to me, leading me to reluctantly admit it must be buried somewhere deep under the ugly tile shards and sloppy grout. I'd have to smash the entire fountain to even hope to find it, and the "monster" movies I'd rented from Red Light Video told me that sort of thing would get me the wrong kind of attention. The kind that landed you splayed out on a dissection table like a biology test.

No thanks.

Besides, the teenagers here were annoying, and loud, but overall life at the mall was far better than the one I'd had as chattel under the so-called "hero." I ran a lost-and-found that never really returned anything, because anything that remotely interested me ended up down in my grotto, neatly arranged on makeshift shelves. No one was ever really sure where their lost items ended up, so I escaped suspicion with a bored shrug now and then. Humans were simple, forgetful creatures and I liked pretty things—I wouldn't apologize for being what I was meant to be.

After spending a long minute drinking deep pulls of cold water from a nearby water fountain, I entered the "under renovation" bathroom that mall staff had effectively claimed as theirs with a fake sign. I locked the door behind me, wrinkling my nose at the persistent stench of perfume, hairspray, Marlboros, and weed that was practically tangible. Flicking a dirty hair scrunchie off the sink, I gave myself a once-over in the mirror, squinting through the crude layer of marker-scrawled curses and spurting cocks.

I looked like most of the 20-somethings behind counters at the mall, if a bit lanky and long-fingered. I'd modeled my look on mannequins in one of the nicer menswear stores when I first broke into the mall, following the mosaic artisans to this suburban oasis in the making. I'd recreated the outfits with clothes swiped after closing, furtively sneaking around before it occurred to me to try for a job here. My first pay envelope of off-the-books cash went to getting a simple haircut: a short tousled top and trimmed sides that made the most of my dirty blond hair, a look I hadn't deviated from since.

Light denim jeans, white sneakers, a button-up dark plaid shirt, and a black denim jacket made me just another face in the crowd. My features were soft and empathetic, a species trait that made it easier to tempt humans into drowning. Grey-blue eyes and a white smile that would give a Crest ad a run for its money put me on the right side of handsome, even surrounded by image-obsessed teens and college students on the weekends. My teeth were flat now, but if I didn't get these strange nerves under control they'd start showing points again, and I couldn't risk that.

I wet my hands under the faucet, letting the water wash over my palms for a few blissful minutes before finger combing my hair. My reflection's features took on the ethereal, dewy look that told me I'd chased away the worst of the dryness, and I was as attractive as I could manage in my strange pseudo-captivity. I didn't know why I cared that this *Ryan* saw me as beautiful, but I did. I knew it was likely futile anyway; unlike the ways of my own kind, some of these humans seemed to discourage intimacy between certain pairs for baffling reasons.

With a sigh, I eventually realized I was lingering too long and took one last look at myself before reentering the busy stream of bodies in the mall. Scores of parents were dragging squalling children after them, insisting they needed a new coat, boots, or a scarf for the fast-approaching winter. Even as obstinate as some of the little ones could be, I still found them charming. Lost children were the one thing I *did* return from my kiosk, mostly because reuniting them made the tiny humans so joyful. When you were designed for violent aquatic murder by magical creation and primal instincts, you enjoyed pleasant moments wherever you could find them.

Once back at my kiosk, I perched on the battered stool in the center and sullenly watched the neon clock, willing time to pass more quickly.

I'D BEEN FIDGETING, FROWNING AT THE 8-MINUTES-AFTER-2 ON THE clock, when an older man in grungy overalls cleared his throat directly in front of me. He smiled and thrust a callused hand in my direction, giving me a curt nod as I reluctantly took it and shook.

"Afternoon. Bob Gold, my son called you this morning. We're here to take a look at your fountain? I'm pretty confident we can get it patched up today, based on what your folks told us last month." He tilted his head back, indicating the large fountain directly across from my kiosk.

"Ah. Yes. Did Ryan come out with you?" I may have come across more blunt than I intended, but bitter disappointment *the voice* hadn't come with his apparent father colored my tone.

"That he did!" Bob laughed loudly, clapping a hand on the counter. "I'll tell you, that boy has more work ethic than I ever did. I told him this probably wasn't a two-man job, but he insisted. You two friends?"

I gave a faint nod, suddenly wanting nothing more than to find Ryan and resenting this small talk. "Yes. I'd been hoping to say hi."

Bob jerked a thumb over his shoulder. "Well, he mentioned something about getting a corn dog at the food court, our morning job took longer than we thought it would. Where's the leak in the lines? I'll get started while you track him down."

A cold dread pooled in my stomach; I'd *heard things* about

those corn dogs, I needed to steer Ryan to another food booth. I slapped the sign back on the counter and hastily exited while waving for Bob to follow me, the shorter man jangling behind me with a toolbox in his hand. I dropped to a knee by the far edge of the fountain, swinging open a small panel on rusted hinges and pulling down a switch that brought the rush of the central water jet to a gradual halt.

Ignoring the man's audible disappointment that I hadn't turned the water off beforehand - I'd been busy with more important things, like making myself irresistible—I hurried to the food court without a second thought. Halfway there, I realized that I had no idea what this *Ryan* even looked like. The sight of an equally-grungy pair of overalls over a blue work shirt blessedly solved the mystery for me. I gently tapped the man's arm as he stood in line to order, making him turn towards me.

"Ryan, right? Trust me, you want to eat elsewhere. This place—uh—failed...health inspection last month." I wrinkled my nose in a quiet, exaggerated show of distaste.

His appearance hit me like a flood-swollen river, all golden blonde perfection and chiseled features, marred by the slightest smear of dirt along his jawline that I longed to brush away. His smile was devastating, as was the equally-golden brow that arched above his bright blue eyes. "Toy boy?"

My legs went weak at that voice murmuring what sounded an awful lot like a pet name. It took a beat to realize he was joking with me, mind flickering like the stubborn fluorescent lights in the back storerooms. "Oh, um yeah. Heh. That's me. I'm Ethan, by the way. Do you like fish?"

"Love it." He craned his head over his shoulder. "Why, is there a place in the food court? I'd definitely prefer that over mystery meat hot dogs." He laughed, and it was clear to see that Bob was his father, his eyes crinkling the same way. My stomach writhed in equal parts anxiety and happiness, like I'd swallowed a mouthful of minnows that were fighting digestion.

I nodded and moved back to allow him to step out of the ordering line, and his hand spanned my lower back for a long moment as he guided me to lead the way. It was a gesture easily ignored at any other time, from any other person, but it felt electric coming from Ryan. I moved on autopilot to my go-to booth, ordering two of my usual fish and fries baskets and carrying them to a nearby table before I even consciously thought about it.

I shyly pushed one of the red plastic baskets towards Ryan as I dropped into a seat across from him, trying my damndest to act normal and promptly forgetting what the hell *normal* even looked like. He probably thought I was a nutcase, and I was certain I was blushing again. What the hell was it about this perfect stranger that made me feel so out of sorts?

"So. *Ethan.* I guess my dad's already working on the fountain? And look at me, over here slacking off, practically on a date." He folded down the checkered wax paper and popped a fry in his mouth, studying me with an intensity that belied his casual tone.

I elegantly choked on a piece of breaded fish at the word *date*.

Ryan seemed to deflate at my shock, his confidence rushing out as his brow creased with concern. "I mean, you know, just fucking with you. Not saying you're one of those— you know. Heh."

He quickly broke off a piece of his fish filet and chewed at it, a sadness creeping into his eyes for only a moment before he plastered on a smile. Desperate to put him at ease, my gaze fixed on a metal band button pinned to his overalls. Opportunity was knocking, and I flung the door open as wide as I could.

"So you like Nøkken too? I love them, especially the lead singer. He's...really awesome." It was a careful gambit to show my hand, the lead singer in question recently making headlines for kissing the band's drummer—the band's *male* drummer—on stage at an international show.

Ryan's fingertips brushed his pin as his smile softened again, voice quieting. "Oh yeah? Even with all the, uh, *stuff* recently?"

I swallowed thickly, and this time it had nothing to do with dryness. I was anxious to either pursue this strange, insistent attraction to someone I barely knew or to write it off and get on with my life.

"*Because* of the stuff." My nerves surged and I was worried for a moment my few bites of fish would be reappearing.

Ryan looked over his shoulder nervously before leaning over the table, tantalizingly close. His voice, just as sexy in a whisper, told me everything I needed to know. "Me too."

He jumped nearly a foot when a callused hand landed on his shoulder before I could answer. "*There* you are. I thought you were just getting a corndog? We're going to need some tools out of the truck, there's a half-busted junction in there, it's not the simple swap I thought it was. Oh! Good, your friend found you."

I smiled as broadly as I could, nerves sparking at Ryan's sheer look of panic. *Ah.* So his father didn't know. I wasn't surprised, what little experience I'd had with our current conversational subject told me that most humans kept it as private as possible. "Yes! Thank you, I insisted on buying Ryan lunch. He got mine last time we hung out. We were just discussing...football?"

It was another calculated gambit, if Ryan wasn't into the oddly popular human sport, I could always feign a one-sided enthusiasm. The way his shoulders relaxed told me I'd hit the nail on the head, though, and Bob launched into a spirited defense of a local team's latest game and ensuing fumble as Ryan quickly finished his meal and rose, dusting off the front of his overalls. Our hands brushed as he handed me his empty basket. We locked eyes for a long moment while his father was facing the other direction, rambling on about valve caps.

Ryan *winked* at me.

I was grateful my hands were obscured by the baskets and my coat was long-sleeved; the scales that rippled over my skin with delight would have outed me for sure.

CHAPTER 3

I'd trailed them back to the broken fountain and settled onto my stool, doing my best not to drool at the way Ryan moved. He was the kind of muscular that hid behind clothes, making him unexpected eye candy as he toiled alongside his father. The way his bicep bulged when he turned a wrench made him look like a work of art. The flex of his thigh when he stretched out alongside the utility door made my mouth water. The phone rang and I simply picked it up and dropped it right back on the phone cradle, cutting off the call that was attempting to cut into my precious sightseeing time.

Whoops. Technical difficulties.

I slipped away to the bathroom to check my hair again when I got restless, but most of the afternoon was spent staring at my new crush. As it looked like the project was making some headway, an unexpected splash of water sounded against the linoleum. I stood up to peer over the counter when a strangled curse and a *very wet* Bob struggled up from the floor, swiping water ineffectually at his overalls.

"Ry, what do you mean you don't see the part? It was *right there*. I don't understand how it could have gone missing, I damn well know I brought it in. If you can't find it, I'm going to have to stay here after closing to reroute that pipe manually, it's the only one we had on the truck!" Bob grumbled, cradling his head in his hands and glaring at the trickle of water that died off as Ryan pulled the shutoff lever.

"I'm sorry dad, I was just under there with the flashlight and everything it's just *gone*. Maybe it went into the pipes or something, it's a small valve. Listen, it was my goof, let me stay and do the repiping. I need the practice anyway, right?" Ryan gave his father a sad, wide-eyed look. I almost believed he was genuinely apologetic until he threw another wink my way.

Sneaky boy.

Bob sighed, nodding and clapping a hand on Ryan's shoulder. "You're a good son, Ry. Always working hard. Normally I wouldn't abandon you to all that work, but the game's on tonight and I'm already pushing missing kickoff. You really sure?"

Ryan gestured towards the exit, pulling keys out of his pocket and handing them over. "Absolutely. Enjoy the game, dad. Cheer them on for me! My friend Ethan will give me a lift home." He grinned as Bob grabbed the keys and gave him another pat on the back before hustling out.

Wait, what? I didn't have a car! My teeth pricked at my lower lip as I talked myself out of panic: plenty of humans didn't have cars, right? That wasn't suspicious. I'd just call him a cab when he was done; it would be easy enough to say it was part of the plumbing charge.

We both watched his father vanish through the mall exit before he pivoted on a heel and walked over to me like he had all the time in the world. Sliding a hand in his pocket, he produced a small white plastic piece, threaded on one side and sturdy-looking, setting it on my counter with a smirk.

"Damn. Would ya look at that, must have put that in my pocket and forgotten all about it. Makes this after-hours job more of a quick fix. Whatever will I do with the rest of my evening, Ethan?"

"You could, uhm, spend it with me. If you wanted, I mean." I nervously plucked at a loose denim thread near my knee, rocking my heels against the bar on the stool.

Ryan spun the plastic part like a top, playing with it on the counter and sparing me the intensity of his blue-eyed stare. "And do you want to talk about...football?"

He'd used the same long pause I had earlier, and delicious tension teased through my body. My voice took on a slight rasp, unable to believe that this pretty golden fish had swum directly into my lair. "Not particularly. I think I want to talk about...not football."

"Well that's a particularly fun conversation, I promise. Do

you have a place we could talk about...not football, Ethan?" Now his eyes met mine, and my teeth sharpened with excitement, forcing me to speak more carefully.

"I do, but it's different. Like, *really* different. Promise you won't laugh or think I'm weird?" I winced, certain he'd turn tail and run the moment he saw my shelves of trinkets, and oversized bed dressed with everything from stolen curtains to clearance accent pillows.

"The only thing I'm planning to be focused on is you." He said it casually, like we were talking about the weather, and something about that tone filled me with devastating lust. I was used to pursuing potential partners, albeit awkwardly and usually unsuccessfully, and I'd *never* taken anyone to my grotto. I don't know what was different about Ryan, but I wanted him in my sanctuary almost as much as I wanted him in me.

At this point I was reasonably certain I'd cursed the clock over the escalators with all the glaring I was doing today. An hour until closing? An *entire hour*? My body felt like I was swimming through a thermal vent, need cresting impatiently against unforgiving denim walls. Watching Ryan get back on the ground to finish installing the part he'd hidden didn't help anything, knowing I'd get to trace those muscles with my hands after an *eternally long hour* had passed.

Even though time stretched like taffy, I eventually got the call to read the evening announcements, politely telling everyone to get the hell out of the mall in corporate-speak. The lights started shutting down, section by section, the dimmer evening illumination taking over as I read the increasingly-insistent script: 10 minutes to close, 5 minutes to close, the mall is now closed. Ryan was seated on the fountain's edge across from me now, watching, the overhead lights reflecting off of the water to shimmer against his beautiful blond hair.

It was now or never. Taking a deep breath, I opened the gate on the kiosk, smiling at Ryan as I walked over. "Ready to go?"

He took a long look at me, gaze snaking up from my sneakers to my collarbone, hot and hungry as he grasped his toolbox against his thigh. "Been ready, toy boy."

The distance to my grotto had never felt so long.

CHAPTER 4

If Ryan had questions about the strange path we were taking down a forgotten hallway, he didn't voice them. As things got darker and less accessible, I held panels out of the way for him, mentally chiding myself for not picking up a flashlight. As we got to the darkest part of the secret shortcut to my grotto, I heard a few clicks behind me and light pooled suddenly at my feet—I'd forgotten that Ryan had a flashlight in his toolbox.

"So, feel free to tell me to mind my business, but do you... live down here, Ethan?" His voice held no judgment, but concern was plain to hear. I'd been so nervous about his reaction to the appearance of my grotto, I hadn't even considered how he'd feel about the situation surrounding it.

"I'm - well, I guess the best way to put it is that I'm an

immigrant. The kind without papers, you know?" My voice echoed faintly off the walls: we were deep in the access tunnels now, sections of the foundation management didn't even know about. "It's just easier for me to stay here, no one bothers me and I have what I need. Plus the commute is pretty low-hassle." I chuckled humorlessly.

His hand closed on my arm, warm and firm, and he turned me to face him, letting the flashlight beam play at our feet. "I hope you know I'll never tell anyone. Lord knows I'm good at keeping secrets." He hesitated, about to drop his hand, but changed his mind, pulling me closer to him and slanting his mouth over mine.

I groaned aloud at the relief of it, the contact with him at last, backing him into the clammy surface of the tunnel wall as our kiss deepened. It was everything I'd hoped for and more, particularly when he roughly flipped our positions, putting the wall at my back instead.

Oh yes.

The light danced around us as the hand holding the flashlight dropped to cup and squeeze at my confined cock. Ryan broke our kiss, panting softly against my mouth as he rubbed and squeezed at me. "Fuck am I glad I wore that pin. Please tell me you're a bottom, because every fantasy I've had since our phone call has gone in that direction."

I nodded mutely as I crashed my lips into his again with a soft whine. The flashlight clattered to the ground as he reached behind me, grabbing my ass with both hands and kneading it in strong fingers. I thrust up against him, hardness meeting hardness, the friction of fabric making me even more hungry for him. "Oh Ryan, please. *Please.*"

He trailed kisses down my neck, mouthing and nipping at it roughly with a low chuckle. "Damn toy boy, you beg so pretty. Come on, let's get to a bed so we can do this proper or I'm going to end up banging you against this wall."

That'd be just fine by me.

Still, we untwisted ourselves from one another, and I waited just long enough for Ryan to retrieve his flashlight before I grabbed his free hand, hauling him faster down the hall and eventually our destination. My grotto was a large circular concrete block room, the mall's main water line standing as a column in the center. It was the closest I could get to the water steeped in my ring's magic and the place I felt most at ease.

Along a curved wall, a huge pile of stolen cushions and padding created a harem-bed situation, walled off with mismatched sheer curtains hanging suspended from overhead pipes. Strings of colorful Christmas lights filled the space with a warm, festive glow, powered by loops of extension cords that probably wouldn't pass fire code. Shelves made out of discarded display racks and slats held a staggering variety of "lost" items, including the latest addition, a threadbare teddy bear I'd found in the food court. Stacks of rare coins, jewelry, and tokens from the arcade-pizza place upstairs spilled every which way, glinting in the low light.

"Oh. Uh. Wow." Ryan turned all the way around twice,

taking in the mismatched belongings, decor, and makeshift lighting before finally looking back to me. "It's not what I expected. But it's nice! It's got kind of a grown up treehouse thing going on." He clicked off his flashlight and shoved it back in his toolbox, setting it down on the floor and moving to me. "You still want to...you know?"

This time, I reached down between *his* legs, boldly palming the substantial bulge I found there. "I do, if you do?" He grunted happily in reply, thrusting against my curious hand.

"I'll admit, I brought rubbers because I was kind of hoping for this. Do you have grease, though? I don't have any with me and I'm...kind of big. I don't want to hurt you." He reached up to unstrap one side of his work overalls as he posed the question and my pulse quickened with pleasure. This was *really happening*.

"I can take you, I promise. It'll feel good. And you don't need rubbers if you don't want to use them, I don't have anything. I've been tested." It was a white lie, but monsters like me didn't need to worry about those sorts of things hopping the species barrier. It was effectively the truth, he was safe, and I *really liked* to feel my lovers bare. I shrugged off my coat, feeling self-conscious about my slender-bordering-on-scrawny body.

Ryan finished prying off his work boots and left his overalls in a puddle on the concrete floor. The front of his boxers tented obscenely forward, the fabric soaked and translucent with precome as he grinned, tugging me up against him and nipping my earlobe. "Why toy boy, are you asking me to *breed* your tight little ass?"

My momentary self-consciousness vanished in a puff of mental smoke and I shuddered in his arms. He'd said the magic words that went straight to the heart of my deepest kink. My fingernails shifted to scales against his forearms and I couldn't even find it in me to care, my need a throbbing, living thing inside me now. "More than *anything*. Please, Ryan. I'll do *anything*."

He shoved me roughly towards my floor-bed, sending me sprawling, giving me a quick, reassuring wink when I looked back up at him in shock. "Get on all fours where you belong then. I've got a lot to give you tonight and you're going to take all of it."

I squirmed and left a trail of clothing in my wake as I obediently crawled to the bed, snapping off one of my shirt buttons in my haste to undress. Once I was naked, I settled heavily on my knees, lowering my chest to the puddle of blankets and presenting my ass to him wantonly.

He left his work shirt on and unbuttoned, the edges of the fabric whispering on my hips as he kneeled behind me, his cock hot and throbbing against my ass cheek. "No underwear, even. Tsh, hit the jackpot with you, toy boy, you're the perfect breeding slut, aren't you?" His lips curved in a smile against my skin as he pressed a kiss between my shoulder blades, his hand reaching beneath me to grasp my cock in a firm, possessive grip.

I fucked his hand slowly, unable to resist the contact, and

whimpered, babbling without a single coherent thought, pleading. "Yes, I am. All for you, just for you, fill me up, breed me."

"Ah, wait just a sec." He slapped my ass playfully, leaving me with the perfect sting as he dropped my cock and got up again. He returned quickly, and the snapping sound of something opening made me look over my shoulder to find a blue-topped jar in his hands. "Lucky for you, plumbers occasionally need vaseline to waterproof valves. Not the fanciest stuff, but it'll do. I meant what I said about not hurting you. Now get that head down and show me what's mine, toy boy."

His fingertips nudged between my ass cheeks, sliding the makeshift lubricant against my entrance. His wonderful tactile swirls paused as he dropped to his knees in front of me, tapping my jaw with his unlubricated hand. "Open up. You're going to get me ready to take you, aren't you baby?"

My cock bobbed at yet another pet name, in heaven and ready to be penetrated any way he wanted. I opened my mouth happily, tongue extended for extra credit, because Ryan clearly had more experience than I did at all this and I was *definitely* hot for teacher. He slid his surprisingly thick cock into my mouth, little by little, a preview of what I was sure he intended to repeat elsewhere. My eyes rolled back in ecstasy at the taste of him, sucking so eagerly his hips kicked. "Mmph, careful now, toy boy. Ease it back. I got plans for that load and it's not going down your throat."

I went slowly, licking along his underside as he wrapped

his clean hand around the back of my head, using my mouth the way I desperately wanted him to. "Fuck, okay, okay. Damn. You're too good, baby, we gotta stop for now. We're gonna do this later though. Give me a kiss."

He let go of a handful of my hair to tilt my chin up, stooping to kiss me thoroughly, licking his own taste off my lips. He maneuvered me onto my side as we kissed, grasping my thighs to yank me down flat on my back under him. "With head like that, I need to watch you get bred, pretty thing. Do me a favor and hug your knees for me, now."

I did, pointed teeth nibbling at my lip as he busied himself between my legs, stroking his fat shaft with a glistening layer of vaseline. He planted his clean hand beside my head, biting his own lower lip as he lined himself up against my ass and leaned forward. "Let out a breath and push, baby. It's going to help you take me."

I did exactly that, but I was too eager to wait any longer, and I shimmied further down to impale myself until he gave a deep groan of satisfaction. He was a *lot*, but the burn was worth the pleasure once my body adjusted, and the first full stroke was pure heaven. I cried out, bracing my knees against his rolling thrusts so I could reach up and hold onto his shoulders. I whispered his name over and over in encouragement, my nails digging into his skin as our bodies crashed together in a perfect, primal rhythm.

He leaned forward, rocking as much as thrusting, resting his forehead on mine as our eyes met, chests heaving together. "You ready to be mine, Ethan? I'm going to breed you so deep you'll taste it." He grinned fiercely, grinding against me on the downstroke, angling against that sweet spot inside me that made me see stars. "Fuck...oh fuck, here it comes..."

He tossed his head back, golden waves sparkling in the multicolor lights as his cock swelled and shot his climax into me, holding tight to my hips to keep us locked together as he shouted in ecstasy, thrusting instinctually into me in hard, short jerks.

I watched him in rapture, wholly unprepared for him to divert his attention to me. Before I could stop him, Ryan wrapped a slick callused hand around my rock-hard cock and stroked me with purpose, turning his grin on me again. He was going to make me come with him, whether I liked it or not, and *oh* did I like it. That's why I forgot entirely. I was so lust-drunk that any thoughts of self-preservation were busy milking the cock in my ass and tightening my balls instead of keeping my secrets.

"Oh...oh god...don't stop...OH!" My hips thrust into the air, my ass tightening on him again as I shot an arc of luminescent white between us, splashing brightly on my chest and his stomach. I might have been able to explain the glow away as a trick of the light, had my egg not bulged up my shaft and spilled out the tip of my cock. It opened like a flower, ejecting the slick, glowing oval that settled into the curve of my stomach between us.

CHAPTER 5

After the big, unexpected reveal, Ryan had immediately eased out of my body and sat cross-legged on my bedding. He didn't say a word, but continued staring at the egg on my stomach, which rolled lightly with each of my panting breaths. His shocked expression told me I was in a precarious situation, one that would probably end with his death or mine if I couldn't calm him down.

"So. Uhm. This is probably pretty weird for you, but I'm going to start out by saying it's not going to hurt you and it doesn't hurt me, okay? Can we be cool about this?" I carefully palmed the egg, wrapping my fingers around it to obscure some of the glow. I winced as the luminescence shone through my webbed fingers. Fuck, I was losing my form, too. Too much emotion carried the risk of some features slipping out, and I was feeling a *lot* right now. Good, with a side of dread.

"What. The fuck. Is that." Ryan's voice was tight, just this side of hysterical, but I noted with a begrudging admiration that he was still half-hard. Now that was a libido I could get behind. Or under, for that matter. Maybe I'd found one of the rare monsterfuckers that was actually into creatures like me.

"It's my...well, I mean, I'm not going to bullshit you. It's my egg. Don't worry, it's not fertile, we can't have kids unless we, you know, we both want to. We'd both have to come on it again to kickstart...whatever makes little nixes, I guess." I uncurled my hand to look at the egg, which seemed bigger and brighter than previous eggs had.

"I'm a Nix, a monster, I guess. Kind of like that Monster from the Black Lagoon, you know, the one from the movies?" I gestured around me at my grotto. "It's probably not a huge surprise, given how I live. I have to, though. Very long story short, I'm bound to a ring that's buried somewhere in the fountain upstairs so I kinda make the best of it. No you're not high, no, this isn't a dream." I sighed the last bit, having had to give this speech twice before. One man, I'd had to kill, and the other had just taken off screaming. I'd never seen him again.

"Are you going to...eat me? Or something?" Ryan just looked so damn *worried* that I couldn't help but bust out laughing.

"No. *No*. I'm definitely not going to do that, though I'm happy to make you my own personal lollipop, if you want." I flicked my tongue teasingly along my lips. "You did say you wanted more of that."

Ryan got to his feet, clutching his temples as he paced, naked, across my bedding. "This is *insane*. Oh my god, is this like, punishment for being gay? Was dad right about this shit?"

I frowned, gently placing my egg on a pillow: fertile or not, it was still something precious and I always treated my eggs that way. I got to my feet and stopped Ryan's circuit of my bed by pressing a palm to his chest. "Absolutely not. You can be scared of monsters, of me, if you want to, but I'd like to think that what we did is never a *punishment*. Don't cheapen it like that, please. I'm not some penalty for loving a different way."

He had the decency to blush with embarrassment, wrinkling his brow as he looked at me. "No, not you, Ethan. No, I'm...I'm sorry, I just don't know what the hell to make of this. Of you. You look like you're going to kill me, man. Those *teeth*." He backed up a step, tugging at my heart.

"I can't help it, certain features come out when I'm experiencing heightened emotions. You affect me like no one ever has, Ryan. Even your voice...there's something about you that's turned everything upside down." I offered him my palm, webbed fingers and all, hoping with everything in me that he'd take it. He did, albeit cautiously, and I wrapped my fingers around his with a smile.

I squirmed, squeezing his hand as I rubbed my thighs together reflexively. His eyes dropped to my inner thigh, where a slow, sluggish trail of his cum flowed out of my body. "I couldn't stop thinking about you either. I - I needed to do that. Needed to be with you. God, I need to be with you again, to be honest, I don't think I've ever been this turned on. I'm terrified and turned on at the same time, and I think I like it."

He abruptly pulled me against him again, kissing the side of my neck and running his tongue along the fin-like membranes that had unfurled at the edges of my ear. My Nix form was really coming through now, and judging by the state of Ryan's cock tapping against my stomach, he was into it.

"Fuck. God you're hot. I have to have you again." He dropped his head onto my shoulder, kissing my skin with surprising tenderness. "Your ring, Ethan. Does it...is it magic or something?" His fingers had already crept down my body to tease at my entrance, two thick tips wedging inside of my well-lubricated, well-filled ass to thrust lazily.

"It grants a heart's desire to the wielder, but why do you... ask?" My voice notched up on the last word as he buried his fingers to the first knuckle inside of me, fucking me with them.

"Because I found it while I was fixing the junction, put it in your lost and found box while you were in the bathroom, and this was literally all I've wanted since that moment. Get down on all fours." He purred the order against my ear, pushing me down gently but insistently. He dropped behind me and immediately notched his cock into my hole, pushing forward with a sigh of deep satisfaction and riding my ass with hard, demanding strokes.

He grasped my hair again, tilting my head forward to kiss the back of my neck. "My second O always takes longer, so get comfortable, baby. I'm going to fill you up again and you're going to make another egg for me. Sound good?"

"Sounds like the best fucking thing I've ever heard, Ryan." I smiled at the wall in front of me as my new lover made the most delicious sounds of enjoyment, rocking my body back and forth against his.

A human had found my ring and returned it to me willingly, and my heart's desire was barreling the both of us towards a second orgasm with enviable, singular focus. As his hand wrapped around my cock and stroked, a second egg tunneled up my shaft to fly up and out, landing with a soft clink against the first on my pillow.

Ryan tensed at the sight, his cock jerking deep inside me, frantically whispering my name like a desperate prayer against my cheek as he came. Each hot jet in me came with babbling words of affection and loyalty, and in the afterglow he pulled me to him, stroking my hair with a softness more suited to magical mates than nearly strangers.

Dating was for mortals, after all, and Ryan had been *mine* from the start.

As we curled up to sleep wearing nothing more than matching smiles with a lifetime together in front of us, I knew the ring had done its *true* work. This was the happily ever after a monster like me—and a man like Ryan—truly deserved.

The end...for now!

Thank you so much for reading *Lost and Found!* If you'd like to read more sexy monster goodness, try my MMMF paranormal romance novels Carnal Cryptids: East Coast and Carnal Cryptids 2: Southeast. For more unique / unexpected characters, including balloon animal shifters and a door shifter, stop by my website, ValentineVerse.com for a freebie story, titles, content notes, and more!

ABOUT THE AUTHOR

An unapologetic book-huffer and devourer-of-stories, Vera Valentine has carried on a torrid love affair with the written word for nearly all of her 41 years. Grown in the diner-laden wilds of the New Jersey Pine Barrens and transplanted to North Carolina, she lives with her husband, eight cats, and two dogs, most of whom are house trained. An avid fan of the Paranormal Why Choose genre, she tossed her author hat into the ring in September of 2021 and never looked back.

A self-professed chaotic capybara, Vera can usually be found spending too much time on social media, chilling with fellow authors, or scribbling down ever-expanding plot bunny ideas in her trusty paper sidekick, the Bad Idea Book™.

If you'd like to stay up-to-date on Vera's latest projects and preorders, stop by her website - ValentineVerse.com for information, links, newsletter signups, ARC opportunities, and more!

ALSO BY VERA VALENTINE

The Carnal Cryptids Series

Unhinged: An Erotic Door Romance

The Holiday Hedonism Series

The Moriverse Series

FED AFTER MIDNIGHT

LATREXA NOVA

Billie Beringer has teased me relentlessly for the past five years. As a friend. But ever since she kissed my cheek, I've harbored a raging crush on her. Only problem is, if I give in, the monster in me might just get out. And once he's out, who knows if he'll ever stop.

Content Warning:

This is an unusual MF turned MFM friends-to-lovers story. Intrusive sexual thoughts, edging, denial, self-repression (and some familial), a sexually free FMC, an MMC that becomes two, 3 special rules get broken, unreliable narrators, public play, sweet kisses, nearly screwing each other in public, fucking in the center of the after-hours mall, absolutely drenching oneself in pussy worship, interrupted sex scenes, mild body horror, ethically ambiguous doppelgangers, body transformation, size difference, grinding on a giant cock, some stupid cute shit, love bombs, getting fucked by two giant oversized cocks, and magic precum that makes that possible.

PROLOGUE

WILLIAM

SUMMER 1980

B illie Beringer was the gnarliest girl I'd ever met. She wasn't supposed to be. Her parents were bankers.

But her? She was a rockstar.

I knew I shouldn't have gone near the stage the first time I saw her perform, but I couldn't resist. She was deadly up there with her neon pink leggings and gold spandex. She might have belonged in one of Jane Fonda's workout videos if it weren't for the spiked belt and gartered fishnets. Or the beaten up pink leather jacket.

Billie could have been singing anything and I would have looked on in awe.

But I messed that all up the second I got close. The speaker system went on the fritz. Electronics and the Liu's do not mix—thanks to our family trait. The feedback was killer —everyone covered their ears when moments before they too looked on in awe of her. Even I had to clutch my hands over my ears, as much as I tried to stay my ground. At least I knew why it was happening, unlike everyone else.

"What is doing that?" one of the mallrats shrieked from her posse of pink.

"So this is the future of music," an elderly man whined, pulling his wife away.

The band started pulling out cords, trying to stop the feedback from whichever instrument was the cause.

Me—I was the instrument of discord. So much was happening all at once. I couldn't move to stop any of it. I watched in horror as the crowd dispersed. Chaos overtook the stage, the sound only worsening as the band ran out of cords to unplug. People rushed to the exits, desperate to free their ears. The pups over at the Twisted Whisker howled in pain. Poor things. They couldn't escape like everyone else.

Billie looked on, glaring at the crowd from behind her smokey eyes—how dare they run from her. Even her bandmates bailed. She didn't budge, simply tried to find the source of the problem, ready to take whatever it was head on. The aggravated noises and screams of the stampede nearly overwhelmed the ever-growing whine of feedback.

And then it was just me and her.

A quirk of her lip, drawn up at the corner...

And then she smiled at me.

My heart flipped, did somersaults, and scored a perfect ten.

But the beast within me? He wanted out.

Did she know it was me? Was it that obvious? There was something showing, there had to be. Why else would she be looking at me?

I looked around frantically, worried that someone would see. It didn't matter that monsters lurked around every corner of this mall. No, the Liu family was perfectly normal. We weren't like the rest of them.

At least that's what mom and dad wanted everyone to think.

The feedback needed to be stopped. My thoughts were already jumbled enough in Billie's presence. I ran over to the sound system and ripped out the last plug, like I wish I could rip out that monster from within me. It was the one that keyed everything into the main power, not one that led back to a specific instrument.

Silence. Except for my parents' warnings cycling through my mind.

'Stay out of the light, William.'

They didn't just mean daylight. No, attention was a much worse sin.

"God, that is so much better, isn't it?" Billie called from the stage, rubbing at her ears. "You just don't notice what a relief it is until it's over. Felt like I was going to hear that noise forever."

I dropped the cord and started shuffling away.

"Happy to help," I mumbled, wishing she'd ignore me like everyone else.

Doing anything but admiring her from afar was too much. Too dangerous. But my body still slowed, hoping for kernels of her attention.

She hopped off the stage and pressed closer to me, until she was so close her perfume drowned my senses. It was a heady concoction of sin, bad decisions, and nights spent driving through town, dancing drunkenly in the open sunroof of a stranger's car. They should ban the scent from the cosmetics counter in Frillard's.

"You didn't run," she observed. *Like everyone else.*

"No," I said, noting the irony that at current I *was* trying to run away.

"Thanks," she said, reaching a hand out to take mine in hers.

Callouses lined her fingers from playing guitar. I don't think I'd ever held a woman's hands before. Too afraid of what I might become. But there we were, holding hands, and the monster stayed within. My fingers traced the outline of her fingerless gloves before I realized what I was doing.

"No problem," I said quickly, pulling my hand away and turning to leave.

"You got a name, Gizmo?" she asked.

I stopped in my tracks. "Gizmo?"

She shrugged. "You're at least useful enough not to run away until everything's fixed."

My eyes narrowed. "Are you calling me a tool?"

She grinned widely before leaning forward and planting a *wet* kiss against my cheek.

An innocent move. Or maybe less than innocent.

But one that would cost me.

"William," I got out before I felt my cheek pulse.

Not here, not in the middle of the mall. My hand covered the spot where she kissed me as my legs bolted out of there, running back to the shadows. Who knows if she laughed behind me, or what. I was a ticking time bomb, and the only person who could help was on the other side of the mall.

I bolted down the restroom corridor, pushing open the Employees Only entrance to the backrooms. Pushed past a few other disgruntled mall employees on break and didn't stop running until I got to the Past Present, our antique shop. My lungs burned from the effort as I shoved the door to the storage area open. Climbing over the older and broken pieces of furniture we couldn't sell, I made it to the front-facing door and paused. After taking a breath, I pushed it open slowly.

"A fine selection—oh! This one is four hundred years old.

You must be careful with it," Dad urged, carefully wrapping an old vase in paper.

"Wicked," his young customer exclaimed, some teenage skater punk. "Mom will be psyched."

Dad chuckled as he finished bagging the centuries old artifact.

I tapped on the door as unobtrusively as I could, trying to get Dad's attention. Mom was at home, prepping the house for a visit from my grandparents, so he was all I had for help. When that didn't work, I cleared my throat. When his eyes caught mine, I turned my cheek slightly towards him so he would see the issue.

"All done," he said quickly as his eyes flared wide, shoving the wrapped vase in a bag and into the guy's hands.

"Don't I need to pay?" the teen said with astonishment.

"It called to you," he made up, pinching his nose. "It's yours."

"Legit? Righteous, dude!"

"Treat it well," Dad spat out, coming around the counter to chase the teen out. "Thank you, enjoy!"

As soon as the teen was gone, Dad spun around and stared me down. The growth on my face felt heavier with every passing second. So did his disappointment.

"Three rules," he grumbled, rushing over to the storefront to pull down the grate. "Xiǎo guǐ."

Little demon, roughly. The words didn't come out in anger. But they were incredibly patronizing, especially because I was not a child anymore. They took me back to when I would sneak food after bedtime and he'd wake up to me fully transformed, or when I ran outside to play in the rain. The words were drenched with as much disappointment as love.

"I'm sorry, father," I said through gritted teeth as the curse swelled against my cheek. "I know better."

"Reckless."

He pulled me into the back room, lit the torch we kept there for emergencies, and placed the flame against my cheek. I held back the scream as much as I could, but I have always been weak.

It's not enough to be nice when you're fighting the monster that lives inside you.

CHAPTER 1

BILLIE

SEPTEMBER 27, 1985

"When was the last time you left this place? The start of the decade?" I asked, joking.

William got this faraway look in his eyes that made me think for a minute it's true. Except I knew he'd left the shop. I had it on good authority the little gremlin found ways to help every single person in the mall, should they need a hand.

Except for me. Maybe he's a one wish genie. I already got my good deed five years ago.

Which meant five years of watching everyone sing his praises. Five years of hearing how helpful he was from everyone I encountered in the mall. Five years of trying to lure him into my grasp by way of having him help set up for Nonspecific Symptom—my band.

Serves me right, I guess, for smooching that smooth cheek of his. But he just looked so cute back then, I couldn't help myself. Not that he wasn't still choice, just that he made it pretty clear he was off limits by booking it away from me at light speed after I made the most innocent of moves. That cheek of his was still smooth, though. Except for a light scar that I didn't remember seeing when I first met him.

Everyone else abandoned me that day, but not him. And that goes a long way in my book. That's why I hunted him down and forced him to be friends with me. It was hard for him to say no. Actually, I think he had trouble saying no in general. Though he did seem to practice on me an awful lot. I wished he would find someone else to practice saying that word to.

With my gig all done for the day, I threw my guitar in its case, said goodbye to my bandmates, and made my way to the quaint little antique store in my favorite semi-abandoned corner of the mall.

He jumped as soon as he saw me. Tried to pretend like he hadn't even noticed. But the funniest thing about this guy was the mild look of fear I seemed to instill in him every time he saw me.

And god, I couldn't help myself. It was fun to dig into that.

"Afternoon, Miss Beringer," is all he gave me.

So polite. There's something inside me that wanted to break him wide open. Figure out all his secrets and find out if he's ever more than just a perfectly nice guy.

"Miss Beringer?" I cooed. "William, if you wanna call me that, you'll have to put on a collar."

His face bloomed red instantly, and he turned away.

"Okay, *Billie*, Jesus," he whined, finally turning back at me.

"What're you drawing this time?" I asked, peeking over the counter.

He leaned over the drawing, trying to hide it with his body until he realized it brought him closer to me. Instead, he slid it off the counter and shoved it under, out of sight.

"It's not good," he grumbled.

"I just wanted to see."

William didn't answer, just set his jaw, staring at me. He was still blushing. Being that he was so much paler than me, it was fun to bring the color into his skin. He had a narrow face and high cheekbones. His puppy dog brown eyes made him look like he was still in high school, even though he was only a few years younger than me. The pout on his face, the attempt to seem stern and unaffected, really did me in. He was too easy. Maybe so was I.

Stop crushing on William Liu. It's pathetic to be this hard up for a guy who doesn't even want you to touch him.

I let out a sigh.

"What I do to put a stick up your ass this time?"

He shook his head.

"My parents went back to China to visit my grandma. Someone has to hold down the fort."

He stepped out from behind the counter, made his way over to the back wall that housed various cabinets full of porcelain—plates, bowls, dolls, you name it.

"Didn't you say last week that you were reconsidering working here another holiday season?" I asked, trailing behind him at a respectable distance.

He readjusted the porcelain cabinet, trying to occupy himself so he wouldn't have to show any emotion. William never showed emotion if he could help it. At least nothing that would expose him as anything short of the poster boy for customer service. Teasing him was essential. He'd never get better if he stayed cooped up inside his own head all the time.

He wasn't answering because we've already talked at length about how he feels trapped here. Telling him that maybe going outside the mall might help always ends in him shutting down completely. *'You just wouldn't get it.'*

"How long are they gone for?" I asked, leaning back against the cabinet instead of pushing us into an argument.

He pulled away, like I had some sort of disease. *Too close,* apparently. Went behind the counter and pulled out a rag. He lifted up all the items on display and wiped underneath, dusting the shelves and tables as he spoke.

"They don't really like Halloween, so they're using a couple of festivals and my grandma's fake ailing health as an excuse not to come home 'til November."

I sucked in a breath. "Look at you, Mr. Responsibility for an entire month."

He shot me a look over his shoulder, his hand gripping on a rather naked brass torso that served as the base for a lamp.

"Don't you usually make fun of me for being Mr. Responsible every month?"

I moved away from the cabinet to hop up on the counter. His jaw twitched. I could see him fighting the urge to tell me to get down. He still had his hand on the lamp base, his thumb pressed between the feminine figure's breasts.

"I think you should use this time as an excuse to live a little," I said, kicking my legs.

"That sounds like the exact opposite of what I should do."

His eyes followed the movement of my feet. Today was a Doc Martens and fishnets kind of day. I wonder if that did anything for him. If he's a fan of the short shorts. No, of course he isn't. But a girl can dream.

Sometimes I liked to think the reason he didn't go after me is out of some sort of sick familial dedication. Like he had to give up his whole life for them. Not that I would know what that was like. My mom wanted me to have kids, my dad just wanted me to stay out of trouble. Neither of their dreams were coming true since I chose the life of a punk rock musician, but they were coming around to seeing how my idea was much better than what they ever had in store for me.

Even if I was still struggling to get cheap mall gigs. Last week I worked a kid's birthday party but at least we were so good those babies started a mosh pit. Proudest moment of my life.

"No, hear me out," I said, jumping down and advancing on him like a predator. "They're all the way in China. You've been helping them run this store ever since you were a kid, and now you'll be thirty any day—"

"I'm younger than you—"

"And you've never had a selfish moment in your life."

His eyes fell to the floor. "I don't think that's true."

I crossed my arms over and glared him down. "Prove me wrong."

"I'm not telling you."

I scoffed.

"Sure. That sounds more like you can't even be bothered to make something up."

"No. I'm just not telling you."

I laughed, gloating that I was right, and followed close behind him.

"Liar."

"No."

"Pants on fire."

"Are you twelve?"

"No, but I'll call you king of the jungle, cause you're li-onnnn."

He spun around quickly, so fast that I didn't have time to process what was happening. Next thing I knew, he had me pushed up against one of the sturdy, ancient cabinets, his hands on either side.

"Don't you ever stop?" he growled.

Growled.

William Liu. Growled. At me.

"How much do you want me to?" I said, not backing down even when he did have me practically underneath him. We weren't too dissimilar in height, but it was the presence he had in this position.

It was the most dominant I'd ever seen him. The closest he'd been to me in *years*. And I fucking loved it.

"I'm not telling you," he repeated one more time.

His eyes dropped, a move that should have been submissive, but in the moment felt like he was laying me bare. Like he could see right through my clothes and savored every inch.

His eyes flicked up, meeting mine finally. I swear I saw the strangest flash of red. Maybe the reflection from one of the glass lampshades. But the look that was in his eyes was one I couldn't believe was real.

When we were younger, I showed him I liked him. And he always had his life so together. So if he was attracted to me, he should say it. We were both almost thirty. That meant we acted like adults now.

Or it should. Except that I haven't spoken of it since that day. But in my defense, he practically ran screaming after I kissed his cheek.

My breathing had grown noticeably fast, and I realized we had been in this position just breathing at each other for a whole minute. That's some fucking tension.

Every fiber of my being begged for me to lean forward, for me to force the kiss that lingered in the air. But I already sent out the first move half a decade ago. If William Liu wanted me as much as I wanted him, he'd have to prove it. Cause I refused to beg.

...Anymore than I kind of already did.

I mean, I'm hot shit. I'm in a rock band. Maybe I was a weirdo in high school, but getting older only proved how much high school just couldn't handle me. If he didn't want me back then, then he didn't deserve me now. *Not that he knew me in high school*—I don't think.

These are all the things I told myself as we stared at each other. As despite my head saying *'don't beg,'* my eyes didn't get the memo.

"God, you really know how to mess with a girl," I grumbled, shoving him away.

I hated it when guys played with my emotions. Too many of them have taken advantage of the fact that it doesn't take much to get me in the sack, and then change as soon as they get what they want. I'm not asking for their sweet words or their offers of love. If a guy just straight up told me he wanted to fuck, that's all I'm asking for. Just a little honesty.

But not even the best of them, William Liu, could be honest with me. Or maybe he was. Maybe I was the problem, because I wanted too much and he'd laid it out for years that he didn't.

CHAPTER 2

WILLIAM

OCTOBER 1, 1985

"What are you doing?" I asked Billie.

She had barged her way into the Past Present every day, 'to check up on me.' She insisted if she didn't, 'who knows, maybe you'd get lost in all the piles of antiques and never make it out alive.' That without my parents to look after me, there was no one who cared about me.

Really knew how to make a guy feel special, that girl.

Today, she had a whole box of ridiculous knickknacks.

"You heard what Chesa said, you need to decorate for Halloween."

The hella peppy mall admin came in yesterday to tell me about her plans to bring in more traffic. My instinct was to turn her down—the thought of keeping all those kids off the furniture and their grubby little hands out of all the delicate, ancient artifacts was headache-inducing even as a thought experiment. But Billie jumped in, talking a mile a minute about what a great addition to the trick-or-treat map the Past Present would be. She even offered to fill out the paperwork for me, which meant I really had no idea what was going on there.

"None of the kids are going to come back this far for Trick or Treat Street," I sighed.

"You really underestimate the draw of candy. Plus, I bet you could totally get people buying some of your old looking shit to zhuzh up their houses for the holiday."

"What?"

"You have old shit. People need to decorate."

"No, what is that word?"

"Zhuzh? Make fancy. Get with it. There's all sorts of like vampires and witches and ghosts that are going to be running around."

Billie didn't know about the monsters that ran the mall, so what was she talking about?

"C'mon, dude, this isn't your first rodeo. I just assumed

you guys never decorated because your parents are set in their ways or something. But I bet you could show them how good you are at managing the business if you pull in a bunch of extra customers with all your fancy decorations."

I stared at her—because I loved watching her talk. But also because she was right. Except that I didn't want to impress my parents. This shop was not something I wanted, only something I was stuck with because who could hire a guy who can't even go out in the daylight? The Creepy Court Mall was a sanctuary for people like me. Where we wouldn't have to face the world or be ridiculed or hunted for what we were.

"What, is it that insane of an idea for someone to try and help *you* for once?"

That shook me out of my reverie. *Of course, Billie had no idea. She was just trying to help. Maybe I should just let her.*

"No, it's fine. Go ahead."

She paused over the box, pursing her lips in a variety of directions as she thought. It made her look ridiculous, but I liked it when she looked a little ridiculous. A little less cool rock star and more like the girl who kissed me on the cheek half a decade ago.

When she didn't move, I sighed and looked through her box. There were a bunch of pumpkins in there, some stuff that looked like it had been painted as well. Black cats, bats, skulls and paper skeletons.

"Hey, wait, I'm supposed to be doing all that," she

asserted when I pulled out a string of paper ghosts to hang across the sign outside.

"You said you were here to help, right? So that means I can do things too," I said. "Never heard anything about you doing it for me."

"Why do I still feel like you're helping me when this was my idea?" she grumbled.

We got the decorations all over the store before lunch. To be honest, it surprised me she was even here so early. I wondered what she was trying to get at.

"Man, I'm hungry after all that," she said, taking a big breath and patting her stomach before she looked at me.

My eyes flicked up towards the food court.

"I won't keep you. Thank you... for making the store more, uh... festive."

She smiled at me and leaned forward.

"C'mon, my treat!"

She pulled at my hands, but I didn't budge.

"No one's here to watch the store. We just did all this work to bring in customers and you want to leave?"

"They'll try to pop their head in and see what's going on in there. It'll add to the mystery. Trust me, not being able to go inside is just going to make people want what's in there more."

She smiled back at me with so much moxie I had trouble separating if she meant the store or me. I mean, obviously the store. Not me. I think she got over whatever kind of crush she had on me five years ago while mine only deepened.

"I really can't, Billie. If anything happens to the shop while I'm gone..."

She let go of my hands and dove behind the register, looking through the counter.

"Stop, what is this, a stick-up?" I asked, laughing to hide how incredibly anxious it made me she was back there.

Not like any of the pictures I drew of her were back there. Other doodles, yes, but none of the stuff that would be find-the-nearest-coffin-and-die embarrassing to find. No, what I was worried about was all the stuff that looked like a bunch of odds and ends to regular humans. Some of the stuff behind the counter had serious magic.

"Hey, please don't touch anything back there, okay? The uh... oils on your hands can really mess them up. Some of that stuff is like thousands of years old."

Her head popped back up over the counter.

"What the hell is a cheesy antique shop in the Creepy Court Mall doing with ancient artifacts? Shouldn't you guys be a museum at that point?"

I just shrugged at her. Explaining to any sort of proper authority how valuable the stuff we sold here was would bring the government on us. So we just sold them all as "tchotchkes" as Billie liked to put it. Most of the things we had, we had to undervalue. The monster in us meant we lived a lot longer than most humans. What we sold was a mishmash of things my parents, their parents, their parents' parents, etc, had all collected over at least a thousand years. I was a kid still, compared to all those years of history, which didn't help me feel like I'd ever get out from the store.

"You'd be surprised at how worthless some of this stuff is," I explained. "Like it has value cause it's old, but people don't have a genuine connection to it. If you tell them a story, they'll spend a lot more, though."

Billie gasped, looking at me with a slight smile tugging her lips.

"William Liu, are you telling me you lie to sell your stuff?"

I blushed.

"Well, I mean. We're just uh... 'zhuzhing' things up."

"You never cease to surprise me," she murmured.

Her eyes caught on something under the desk.

"Aha!" she cried out, holding the keyring above her head.

"No, c'mon. I thought you were just getting distracted with all the stuff under the counter. I didn't think you were still serious about leaving."

"Yes, I'm serious. You're always out and about in the mall when I'm here, doing errands for everyone else. Well, here's an errand for *me*. I don't know how I'll find the food court without you."

Her stubbornness made me smile. She always had such an easy time twisting me to her will, though she didn't know it. Sometimes I'd have to imagine saying yes to her just to let go of the desire to follow her every whim. But ever since that day she kissed my cheek, I had to learn to say no to her.

So here I was, imagining now what it would be like to follow her out of the shop. For us to pull down the gate and leave a 'back in 30' sign. To have our bodies brush against each other, and that familiar speed of my heart rate grow just from touching her. To us sharing soup and smiling over our meals at each other. Watching her lips as they suck up the noodles and wondering what it would be like to kiss them. To giving up on the fantasy of it and throwing everything on the table to the side.

To prowl over the table and press my face to hers. The whole restaurant freaking out. Screaming. But our kissing turns more and more primal, our teeth biting into each other. Pulling her up on the table and feeling her all over. Sliding my hand against her sex and feeling that she wants me as much as I want her. Ripping her clothes off and growing into the monster I know is inside me. Fucking her in front of the whole food court and feeling completely satiated for it.

But that can't happen.

"Knew I'd be able to talk you into it," she grinned at me, having just pulled down the grate.

CHAPTER 3

BILLIE

Somehow I had succeeded in swindling some genuine personal time out of William.

"Make it quick," he grumbled. "Or I can drop you off and go back, you know, *so you don't get lost*. I really shouldn't have left."

"That's too bad, because we're about to pass Frankie's Funhouse. You want some pizza?"

"Absolutely not," he groaned.

Maybe an arcade is exactly what he needed. Though...

maybe not Frankie's Funhouse. The screaming of all the kids hopped up on pizza and candy was grating, even from the opposite side of the walkway. Peering in, it was clear there wasn't a parent in sight. Maybe there's a room in the back or something for them. My parents were always too busy to take me there, but they did drop me off at the mall with five dollars on their date night. So whatever happened to the parents in that place was a mystery to me.

Frankie always made me smile, though. The animatronic did *not* keep well—in that it looked pretty close to terrifying nowadays, and the fancy pants Wall Street suit they put him in recently did not make him more approachable. But I grew with the show. Sometimes it would be nice to be a kid again, not have responsibilities or anything.

"Did you ever watch the show?" I asked William.

He shook his head. Sometimes I thought that guy never had a childhood.

"Tragic," I mused, and pulled him away from the house of screams.

We passed by Broth with a Bite, and the smell made my stomach growl.

"Soup?" I asked.

Being fall, it was finally soup weather. But William stayed stoic, just kept walking. Like he had something against the place. Someone would think they served people or something.

"I thought you liked soup," I muttered.

He looked around the food court and folded his arms, looking at me. "Soup takes too long."

"Ah, so you're just trying to get rid of me," I mused.

"As I've said," he pouted.

I saw him tilt his head towards the Good Char, just slightly, as the smell of it wafted through the food court. His throat worked.

"Hot dogs?" I asked, tilting my head much more obviously towards the stall.

Not that they served anything I could eat, but I'd sit there and pretend to eat one just for him.

He narrowed his eyes. "You don't eat meat."

Shit. Did William *actually* pay attention to me?

I shrugged. "I could start."

"For *me?*" he balked. "For *the Good Char*? They're great, don't get me wrong, but I expect a vegetarian to have issue with the fact that they could grind up just about anything and put it in the hot dogs."

"You're impossible! I thought you wanted me to choose something fast!" I laughed, throwing my hands up in the air. "If you're so picky, you choose."

"You're the one that's hungry."

His stomach growled.

"Okay, kettle," I teased. "If you don't choose in three seconds, I'm picking and you can't argue."

William sputtered all through my countdown as he tried to make his choice.

"Great! Creepypasta it is!" I exclaimed, linking my hand

through his arm and dragging him over to the *slow food, sit-down restaurant* at the edge of the food court.

The restaurant was bustling with customers. We were lucky to get a seat squished into a booth in the corner. I was so elated to be eating with William that I didn't really pay attention to what was going on around us. He seemed to have his focus completely on the plate in front of him.

"Imagine you could do anything. What would you?" I asked.

That got his attention. His deep brown eyes met with mine as a flurry of hidden emotion passed over his face. Out of the corner of my eye, I saw his knuckles turning white, his fists balled. When I shifted my gaze, he pulled his hands under the table and out of sight.

"What're you doing down there, William?" I asked with a lurid tilt to my question.

His hands were back on the table, spread flat in a second.

"So jumpy," I laughed.

To be fair, I was feeling jumpy, too. Not just because there was some strange buzzing in the back of my head, almost like feedback or static. But also because our knees kept brushing against each other under the table. Because our hands were close enough to touch, to hold each other. Because the lighting was dim in our section, and there were other couples sat near us on actual dates, doing things I wanted to do to William.

I think the server came to take our orders, but I couldn't remember. Minutes later, two steaming plates of pasta set down in front of us. I went for a simple Linguine al Pesto—green food always made me feel better.

William, on the other hand, opted for *pizza* carbonara.

"I see, you wanted pizza, just something more extravagant than what they had at the kiddie arcade," I laughed.

He shoved a bite in his mouth, glaring at me. "I said fast."

"And I," I said, spinning the linguini around my fork, matching the challenge in his gaze, "really know how to milk a fast date."

I cringed at my phrasing as I sucked a noodle into my mouth. I was a slurp-the-whole noodle kind of gal, I didn't like cutting it off. The taste of cheesy basil spread across my tongue, and I closed my eyes, indulging in the taste of it. When I opened them, William was staring at my lips, pizza held just before his mouth. A jolt of excitement went through me.

I think I've gotten it wrong all these years. William Liu might actually be into me!

I licked my lips slowly to lap up all the drippy pesto and oils. His breathing slowed. My heart sped up to a million beats a minute. I ran a finger across my lips before sliding it into my mouth. When I moaned in appreciation (of the food) —*really pushing it*—that might have been going too far. He dropped his pizza in his lap, hit his knee on the table. He also managed to knock his drink over, sending the liquid splashing across the table and onto me.

He was blushing now, hardcore, and I savored every second even as the cool liquid froze my tits and lap.

"Ah, shit, Gizmo!" I laughed. "Watch yourself."

Instead of grabbing napkins or a waiter, as you would expect of a perpetual helper like him, he jumped up and out of the booth like it was lava moving across the table and not water. The other pastafarians in the room all gawped at us, one woman coming up behind me to help pat me down.

William was breathing heavily. I liked to believe it was because he was so turned on by my impromptu wet t-shirt contest entry, but there was something fearful about his behavior.

"I need to go," he said, his voice strained like he didn't want to say the words.

"Okay, fine," I grumbled, looking around for the waiter.

When he came by with the check, William paid. I offered to pay my portion, but he insisted he'd pay since he 'ruined lunch.' He tried to leave, but I scooped all our food up into boxes and chased after him.

"What was that about? A glass of water kill your parents or something?"

He didn't answer, just kept speed walking back to the Past Present.

I grabbed his arm, stopped him. The bag of leftovers swung wildly from the inertia and I winced, thinking about all that sauce I'll find at the bottom of the bag.

"Seriously, dude, what gives? You treat me different than *everybody* else, like you're always on edge. I was starting to think that maybe you liked me back, finally, but... I should just give up."

His eyes softened, a flurry of anxieties flashing across his forehead as he stared down at the place where I'd grabbed him. I thought I'd grabbed him too hard, but I was finding that William was a lot stronger than I'd realized. He hadn't moved my hand away, which meant I could feel the muscle under his sweater. I sucked in a breath, even though I was trying to have a serious adult conversation with him for once.

His other hand brushed against the top of mine, sending tingles up my skin and down my spine.

"There's a lot you don't know about me, Billie," he breathed. "A lot that would probably send you running. Whatever you think I am... I don't know why you're attracted to me. But you don't deserve to have to deal with my crap. There's a lot I want, if I didn't have to be me. *A lot.*"

My heart twisted at his words. He was letting me down.

Wait. Wait, wait. He was also...

Admitting he liked me enough to look out for me. To try and protect me from whatever it is he thinks is too big for me to deal with. That 'a lot' was dripping with innuendo and promises I wanted him to follow up on.

Well, if that isn't the sweetest thing anyone has ever done for me. Nobody looks out for me first.

Before I could overthink it, I leaned in, parted my lips.

His breath was shaky, but I waited for him to complete the connection. He was like a deer in the forest; I didn't want to spook him by moving too quickly this time. I almost wanted to make myself small and docile so he wouldn't think I was attacking.

The next three breaths we took were the longest moments of my life. Our lips moved towards each other, drawn by some irresistible magnetism between us.

Then, at the last moment, he turned away from my lips. I started to grumble, until his mouth found my neck and left the sweetest, most arousing kiss just under my chin.

"I want you too much," he whispered against my ear.

His hot breath sent a fire across my nerves. My eyelashes fluttered. I felt wobbly for a second.

Holy fucking fuck.

We didn't even *kiss*.

My vision blurred except for him. Nothing else in the mall mattered.

He bent down low, grabbed the bags from my hand and peeked into them before handing back my linguini, his eyes barely straying from mine.

"But I can't do just anything. So... give me a break. Please."

I stood there, flabbergasted at how honest he was being. That I didn't imagine all the signs he gave through the years. That my feelings were actually reciprocated.

He walked away, and when I tried to follow, he turned, gripping my shoulder like he wanted me to stay still.

"Please?" he asked again.

My whole head was a mess. But I let him go.

This time.

The thing is... I really liked it when William begged. And I liked it when he told me he liked me *too much*. I needed to hear it again and again.

Giving him space didn't get me that result. No. It was berating him until he had to finally admit everything to me.

So no fucking way I was going to back off now.

CHAPTER 4

WILLIAM

I knew I'd regret telling her how I felt. If she was a nice person, she would have respected when I told her to back off.

But instead, she dragged me off to a new destination every day during lunch. Lunchtime before was spent standing over the counter at the Past Present while the occasional customer wandered in, filled their eyes with our trinkets, and left.

Today, we shoved pastries in our mouths as she pulled me to GalaxyGames. I groaned, knowing how this would go.

Neon flickered as I passed under the sign. The owner, Buddy, was busy tormenting some kids in his Gandalf costume, and didn't notice when I walked in. The stoners on the games near the entrance sure did, though.

"Aw, come on!" one of them growled, shaking his machine.

"The fuck, I HAD THAT!" another shouted, kicking the machine before looking around for Buddy.

I bit my lip, hoping Billie would grow tired of the games malfunctioning quickly so I wouldn't get in trouble. Maybe Buddy didn't know exactly what I was, but he could connect the dots.

I pulled Billie towards the games that weren't so technologically advanced. Like the coin pusher that was essentially gambling. It was largely mechanical except for the display. And the sensors.

There wasn't much I could do. She pulled out a few quarters and put them in, squealing with joy as the coins fell off.

"You're like a lucky charm!" she beamed, grabbing my arm and pulling me close to her.

I could feel her soft breast press against me. The heat of her. The way her hips wiggled with delight.

"Look at them go!"

I wanted her, wet and wild for me. Screaming my name as I pound into her. I wanted to rip off her clothes and fuck her right here in the middle of the arcade.

"I am a servant of the Secret Fire, wielder of the flame of

Anor. You cannot pass!" barked a withered voice from behind me.

Then I felt him tugging against my neckline from behind.

We twisted around to see Buddy Bardot in his stupid Gandalf costume towering over us. The shtick was so much.

"Come off it, Buddy," Billie chided, shocked he was talking to us like this.

No surprise to me.

"He that breaks a thing to find out what it is has left the path of wisdom," the overdramatic wizard spouted off.

I got the hint.

"C'mon, let's go," I mumbled, pulling Billie towards the exit.

"What the?" she asked, still looking back and forth between me and the owner.

Buddy slammed his staff against the floor. "I said beat it."

I felt Billie stir to fight back and pulled her a little too hard to get out of there.

"The fuck did you do in there?" she asked, her face full of awe.

Another emotion ran across her face before she turned it towards the store.

"Your stupid games are on the fritz anyway, loser!"

I reached my hand towards her mouth before realizing my error and slipped it to the back of her head, pulling her focus forward.

She let out the sweetest noise. It went straight to my cock.

"William," she purred. "How'd you know I liked it rough?"

I pulled my hand away. Thoughts of twisting her hair in my grasp, shoving her to the floor, mounting her from behind, using her hair like reins as I rode her ass. Nobody wanted to see some guy hard outside an arcade. This wasn't fair.

"Lunchtime's over, Billie."

She pouted.

I felt shaky all over. We couldn't keep doing this. Fighting the monster was too much, and the sexual impulses were the least of my problem. It was the desire to destroy, to hurt, to maim. It was the lack of all control that she inspired that was scariest to imagine letting loose.

I should have told her the whole thing was off. Whatever *this* was, this tentative 'oh they're not dates, we're just having fun' thing that I know meant more to both of us than we were admitting. She was too good at working around my boundaries and wedging herself deeper into my heart.

Truthfully, I didn't want any boundaries with her.

"When are your parents back?" she asked out of the blue, easily switching away from the heavy flirtation. She knew she went too far. We walked back to the Past Present.

"In a few days."

"Just in time for Día de Muertos," she grinned.

I didn't know much about the holiday, but Billie told me about the sugar skulls and the ofretas. She always joked about being a mutt—some mishmash of Mexican, Jewish,

German, Russian, Irish, and Italian that could only happen in America. Not that China wasn't full of a bunch of disparate identities within itself. But to Americans, we were just Chinese.

And to humans, *mo guai* like me were just monsters.

I was half-terrified to see my parents again. I was worried they'd be able to smell the way I'd grown lax over our rules. That they'd stop me from leaving the Past Present at all, keeping me there and home only.

"Can we go on a real date?" she asked, turning to me as we stood outside the antique shop. "Like... out of the mall?"

CHAPTER 5

BILLIE

Operation William Liu's Day Out was a go.

He seemed terrified to leave the mall at first, but once we got to the mini golf course, he actually started having fun. A couple of times, our balls went into the fountain and he yelled at me as I stepped over the barrier, ignoring the "stay out of the fountain" sign to get them. When I dropped his red golf ball back in his hands, he dropped it, wiping his hand quickly.

His behavior was a little strange after that. It occurred to me that maybe William was a germaphobe. He kept looking at his hand strangely, like he expected it to grow fangs.

"Lighten up, Gizmo, it's your ball," I said, nudging him playfully.

I still couldn't believe he agreed to an actual date. We must have looked a bit ridiculous, him in his sweater vest and t-shirt, me rocking a lazy punk outfit, complete with a ridiculous tutu to really give people a shock. The prep and the loser. I gloated at the juxtaposition, at how people gave us strange looks for even being together. It fed that hurt kid inside me that used to get made fun of, even if I was mostly past that.

Finally, when a chestburster did not rip out of his hand, he shook it off and took his putt. When it bounced off the side and landed four feet from the hole, he just chuckled.

"I really thought more stuff would go wrong today," he said, watching me putt.

My hips wiggled extra for him. I checked to see if it worked, and was pleased to see the way his eyes followed my ass.

"'Cause I'm such a troublemaker?" I asked.

He snorted. "I wasn't worried about you."

I stood straight and looked at him. Stepped closer, dragging my putter behind me.

"You, Mr. Responsibility?"

He shrugged from where he sat on a rock. I leaned down, putting my hands on either side of him. Our breath slowed, hitched. I gulped, knowing that I was about to push him again.

"You don't know what I'm capable of," he whispered.

This time, I wouldn't wait for him. I pressed closer until our mouths hovered just next to each other.

"I'd like to see it," I whispered back before closing the gap.

His hand fisted against my button up, pulling me closer. I fell into his lap, slid my arms around his neck. He growled, pulling me right on top of his erection.

His erection.

I'd fucked tons of guys, but William got me excited to dry hump him on a rock. That's how desperate he made me after all this time. I bit his bottom lip, dragged it between my teeth as he thrust up. I moaned at the feel of him. He was the perfect size. My pussy ached for him. His hands slid up my shirt, squeezing at the soft flesh beneath until he forced his fingers under my bra. I broke from the kiss and buried my face in his neck.

"Yes," I hissed, dragging my teeth across the soft skin there.

In the next moment, I was on the floor, my legs up in the air.

"Excuse me, this is a family establishment!" came a man's voice. "Security!"

We stopped, stared at each other for a moment. Giggling, William pulled away from me and helped me up. He turned to the man, blushing scarlet.

"Sorry, sir. We'll show ourselves out. We're so sorry for what you had to witness."

William *bowed*, as subservient as he could, and then grabbed my hand and started running back to my car. He didn't have one, so it was mine or bust.

"I'm so sorry," he eked out as we bolted from the mini golf course. "I totally ruined your outside-the-mall date."

"No you didn't," I huffed out once we got to the car.

I leaned back against the car, trying to catch my breath. He was huffing and puffing too, but that didn't stop him from pouncing on me like a lion, attacking my neck, my chest, my lips.

You unleash the monster, and he really goes at it.

"Stop," I laughed, even though I was afraid I'd break the spell. "We have to go somewhere way less public or we're gonna get arrested for indecency."

"I want to be very indecent with you," he growled, his hands teasing along my waistband.

"Oh my god, yes. Fuck. Agh!" I squealed. "Stupid other people. Fuck. We can't go to my house. My roommates are..."

He shook his head. "I can't take you home. There's stuff at my house that..."

My eyebrows furrowed. "What does that even mean?"

"I'll explain one day. But... we could always go back to the mall. There's like no one there and we do have the shop to ourselves."

I quirked a brow at him. "God, you're a lot kinkier than I could have ever expected."

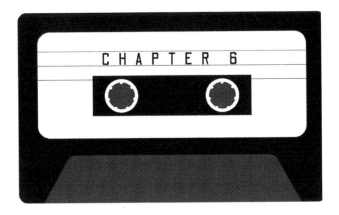

CHAPTER 6

WILLIAM

Billie was singing something that sounded vaguely familiar until I heard the words "at Frankie's Funhouse." It must have been the jingle for the TV show. The Funhouse in question was right in front of us. As soon as she sang the words, a strange mechanical sound emanated from the kids' arcade.

Billie grabbed my arm and started laughing. "God, that place is so creepy at night."

I tugged her in the direction of the employee corridor. Being here at night terrified me, and if I wasn't so horny when I suggested coming here, I would have thought of literally anywhere else to make love to her.

Oh god, I was going to have sex with Billie Beringer.

I'd never had sex with anyone. I didn't have a clue what I was doing.

Okay, that wasn't true. I'd slipped into the back of Red Light Video enough times to have a *very* good idea of what I was doing. The guy who ran it had to be a sex demon or something. He had all the best shit and knew exactly what you wanted just by looking at you.

Billie had grabbed us each a can of beer from the trunk of her car, but we hadn't even started drinking yet and she was already being silly. Maybe she knew I'd be anxious. She didn't have any idea I'd never had sex before, though. 'Almost thirty' as Billie kept putting it, and still a virgin. Maybe I just wouldn't tell her.

Oh god, there was a lot I was *not telling her*. I'm such a tool. No wonder she calls me Gizmo.

When we got to the Past Present, she pushed me in and tried to kiss me, but I was freaking out in my head too much to kiss her back.

So she cooled it.

"We can just have a sleepover, no rush," she said, trying to play it cool.

I could tell she was just as *not cool* inside as I was. I just hoped she didn't think I wasn't into her, that I'd changed my mind. The real issue was I couldn't figure out how to tell her everything.

She grabbed a fairly sturdy looking bottle from a cabinet and pointed it at me. "Since it's a sleepover..."

"I am not playing spin the bottle with you," I grumbled. "What are you, twelve?"

"Truth or dare?"

I sighed.

"C'mon, William, we're having a sleepover in the mall. Where's your sense of nostalgia?"

"It ran off with my sanity. I don't know. I'm nervous we're going to get caught?"

"You like literally work here."

I groaned and lay back on the antique couch. It was shitty to continue anything without telling her. But also I was so worried I'd lose her after everything.

"Truth or dare?" she asked again, plopping next to me on the couch.

My body angled towards hers, pulled in by gravity.

I groaned. "Dare."

She grinned. "Still hiding your secrets. That's fine. I dare you to do something that scares you."

I turned, looked up at her from my position on the couch.

If you could do anything, what would you?

The thing I couldn't get over was how my hand didn't start growing that awful boil that used to when I got wet. Rain did it. *Billie's lips did it.* Except... now they didn't. And my hand didn't mutate after she dropped the wet golf ball in my hand. Maybe getting older had cured me. Or maybe I had some semblance of control after all these years of trying to fight back against what I was born to be.

Maybe all the things that used to hold me back weren't anymore. That clarity I felt when she started kissing me at the golf course flooded my mind again. There was nothing to fear.

I sat up and turned towards Billie, kissing *her* this time instead of being kissed. Slipping my tongue between her lips and exploring what it was like to French kiss. She giggled a couple of times and told me to loosen up (still so tense, I guess). Her hands smoothed across my chest.

"Fuck, William, you're so sexy like this," she whimpered. "I like it when you take what you want."

Her words sent a hunger into me, gluttony for more. For the taste of her all over. All the porn I'd seen from the video store gave me ideas on just how much of her I could taste. With a growl, I pushed her back, so she was the one lying on the couch. She squealed with surprise when I ripped her shorts away.

"God, you wear so many fucking layers," I huffed, threading my fingers through the laces of her Doc Martens, eyeing the fishnets and tights.

I couldn't stop myself, kissed the bared flesh that poked through the ripped sections of her tights as I worked those stupid boots off of her. It took everything in me not to rip the laces off.

"Believe me, I would have made things simpler if I had any inkling you were such a beast," she giggled, leaning forward to run her hands through my hair. She shoved her tits in my face, and my mind went blank for a moment. She was so soft underneath all that punk crap.

Her hand snuck to my waistline, under my belt, and then to my aching cock. I whimpered, realizing how screwed I was if she got to play around there. She felt amazing. Her hand was so small against that inflamed skin, it made me feel huge. I always felt I was average at best, especially compared to the guys in the porn.

I shoved her back against the couch, finally freeing her feet of the Docs so I could pull down her leggings. Except I didn't pull them down... I might have ripped through them. At least the fishnets. I realized what I was doing and tried to be gentler with the second pair, pulling it down fast, but without the strength that took over me.

"Fuck, William," she purred. "Are you for real?"

CHAPTER 7

BILLIE

*J*esus *Fucking H. Christ, this man ate pussy like he needed it.* Who would have thought underneath that sweet exterior that William Liu was a sex fiend?

And *the moans* coming out of him. I've been with a lot of men who thought they knew how to eat a girl out. Some of them *exceptionally* confident. But William? Even if I didn't enjoy every single thing he was doing right now, I could get off on the noises coming out of him alone. It really changes things when a guy lives to eat pussy, I swear.

I watched in rapt fascination, surges of even more heat rushing through me as his gaze trailed up to meet mine.

Whatever that lustful fire in him was, it burned so strongly it turned his eyes red.

But...

Wait, like, actually.

This totally can't be happening.

"Billie," he groaned, his voice almost coming out like a growl. "You taste so fucking good."

Those lips of his were coated with me. I couldn't help myself and dragged him away from the meal he was so enjoying. The glistening pink of his mouth did me in. He growled as we connected in a fury of lips and teeth and tongue. His body rolled against mine as I felt how much he was enjoying this, too. His fingers dug into my sides, gripping so tight his nails nearly cut into my skin.

He dragged his mouth down to my neck, licking and biting in feral possession.

"Fuck," he muttered, his voice almost whining. "You're so wet, I shouldn't be—"

I shut him up with a bite to his neck. He whimpered and when I pulled back to look at the gorgeous expression on his face, my breath caught. He looked something between terrified and deadly.

His eyes seared red now, almost glowing. And his face?

"Oh no," he groaned, pushing me away. "Fuck, I thought—"

Wow, William Liu swearing. This night was full of surprises.

I was almost so distracted by his eyes I didn't see the way his lips drew apart wider and wider. Something strange was growing from inside his mouth, like skin.

I think he was trying to swear again, but whatever was in his mouth made it so all that came out was choking sounds.

"William, are you okay?" I said stupidly.

It occurred to me that maybe I could help him after what felt like an eternity of gawping at him while he continued to choke. Running forward, I circled around to his backside and wrapped my arms around him. I wasn't sure if the Heimlich was the right move, since I had no idea what that weird skin thing in his mouth was, but I was sort of out of options. Especially since we were in the mall sort of illegally.

He wretched as I thrust my fists just under his ribcage and hoped for the best.

"Really thought I was going to make you ejaculate something else tonight," I bit out in between thrusts.

He pushed my arms off him and fell forward. I watched in horror as something slimy and flesh-colored spilled from his mouth. And didn't stop spilling out of him. When I ran forward to put a hand to his back, he pushed me back.

"William!" I cried out.

I might have started to tear up, feeling so hopeless and useless that someone who might be my boyfriend now was having a medical emergency.

I should have called the stupid cops.

William slumped forward, finally no longer wrenching. I crawled on my hands and knees to get close, but the dark light of the hallway made it difficult to see. He rolled onto his back, revealing the fleshy mass that had come out of him.

It was... for all intents and purposes... *him.*

Naked.

And slimy.

"William?" I let out, now afraid to get too close.

What *was* that? What was *he?*

The clothed William lay panting on his back. His eyes turned toward me, lashes fluttering.

"Shit, Billie, you shouldn't be here," he groaned.

The him that he... puked up? The naked him writhed slowly, as if it was testing out its limbs for the first time. Which, I guess it was?

I couldn't help it and backed up until I was pressed against the wall. My heart was hammering in my chest, my breathing erratic. The nakedness of the slimy William reminded me that I had nothing on my lower half except a stupid neon tutu. It made me feel excessively vulnerable considering the situation.

"What the fuck is that?" I spat.

I didn't know what to call it. William Two? Twolliam?

"You should run," William choked out, looking absolutely wrecked.

Twolliam's back muscles moved like a wave as it—he?—acclimated to his new body until he could rise onto his hands and knees. His head turned oddly to look at William, then circled around to look straight at me.

His face was something like William's, but like he had a permanent evil grin etched into his face. Lines warped his features, and his eyes were resiliently that odd red.

"Billie, you taste so good," he said, his voice a bastardization of the reverence to which William had said those words earlier.

"No!" William groaned, turning onto his side. He was still huffing from the exertion of coughing up this strange chimera.

I tried to hold my ground, unsure if it was a mistake to run or stay. At least if I stayed, I could help William if Twolliam tried to hurt him.

His body contorting like a snake, Twolliam rose onto his feet, rolling out his muscles along the way.

It was unfortunate that my first sight of naked William was by way of his creepy doppelgänger. Even worse, that I couldn't get over how hot he was. Twolliam's cock was quite a surprise, not just because of its size and girth, but for the strange markings around the base, and the odd shape to his shaft. Is that what I felt under his jeans at the mini golf course? In my hand just moments ago? He was surprisingly ripped for someone so lithe, and I wondered how much of this creature was just like William himself.

Because I wasn't entirely sure William Liu was human anymore.

"Come here, Billie, I wasn't finished," Twolliam purred.

William grunted behind him, still attempting to get up.

"What are you?" I repeated, this time to Twolliam directly.

His terrifying grin spread wider. "In love with you, don't you know?"

His eyes flicked to William for a split second. The original blushed fiercely, even as he struggled to stand. The words made my heart leap. And at the same time, a sinking feeling formed in the pit of my stomach. Was he making fun of me? Yes, I'd finally worn away at William enough to convince him to have sex with me. And he had said he liked me a lot, but *what did that actually mean?* That he found his head between my thighs only moments ago wasn't much to go off of—most guys would be pretty happy to get laid.

Except that William wasn't most guys. I think he would have jumped at the chance years ago if that's all he was in it for.

This is not the time to have a love life crisis.

"Don't touch her," William growled.

Twolliam just laughed, spiting William by stepping closer to me.

"I won't do anything you wouldn't do," he giggled.

William's eyes flared as he struggled forward. "Billie, run!"

I shook my head. "I'm not leaving you. He said he wouldn't do anything you wouldn't do, so I don't think I'm in danger."

No, I was not getting the sense that Twolliam would hurt me.

"What the fuck is going on, William?" I tried again.

"So used to keeping everything kept under lock and key," Twolliam murmured, now just a foot away from me.

It was becoming very difficult to not think about the fact that he was hard. If he stepped any closer, he'd poke me without lifting a finger. My body didn't know what to do. As far as it cared, that was William in front of me, even if my head knew differently.

Or did it?

"I am William," Twolliam cooed. "Just as in love with you, just as curious to know every bit of you…"

I shuddered, his sensuality dripping from him in a way the real William kept locked up.

His hands reached forward, one wrapping around my hips as the other wrapped around my neck. His thumb lingered behind, stroking up and down my neck like a sexy threat. Before I knew what was happening, his mouth pressed against mine. His cock against my stomach as well.

"Stop," William said weakly from behind his double.

I shook Twolliam off, but he just redoubled his efforts, kissing my neck instead when I turned my face away from him. His hands slid up my t-shirt, quickly seeking out my breasts.

"You should really stop that," I panted, caught between really loving this and feeling incredibly guilty for having the guy I like watch from only a few feet away.

Twolliam just chuckled, shifting so that his cock slid between my legs instead of pressing up against my stomach.

"C'mon, you've wanted me for years," he hissed against my neck.

Could William see it too? Or was that just his evil twin who could see right through me? I thought he always dismissed me as just trying to push his buttons until tonight, but everything was so new I didn't know where we stood.

"Stop it!" William grunted again, this time wrapping himself around Twolliam's naked shoulders as he attempted to pry him off.

"Ohh, a threesome?" Twolliam laughed, holding on to me even tighter so William couldn't pull him back.

"I'm not having a threesome with anyone until someone tells me what is going on!" I screeched, pushing back at Twolliam until he finally let go.

The fucker just laughed. But next to him, William looked on, his face full of worry. It all bottled up inside of him, his lips pursing as he tried to keep it inside.

For once, he couldn't. It came out in the form of him punching Twolliam. That just made the doppelgänger laugh harder.

"Tell her, I'm sure she can *take it*," the doppelgänger laughed, thrusting his hips forward for emphasis.

I'm not going to blush just because a very lewd copy of the guy I'm into makes dumb innuendos.

"Fuck!" William said, the word growing more and more comfortable on his lips with each use.

Wild to think he never swore in my presence before this night. There's a lot of things I never knew he was capable of. You think you know a guy.

Finally, he stopped hitting Twolliam and calmed himself, taking a wide stance and breathing in deeply. When he looked up, the red of his eyes seemed to be gone. The lines around his face softened again to almost nothing.

"I guess what's happened is crazy enough it won't sound completely insane for me to tell you the truth," he said with a sigh.

I nodded passively. "I'll take any explanation after what I'm seeing."

He reached a hand forward. I stared at it a moment before realizing he wanted me to take it. As soon as I did, he guided me over to an antique chair covered in plastic. He pushed on my shoulders, urging me to sit. I got caught up in the smell of him, the heat of his body bringing out the smell of his soap.

Both of them looked down at me as I sat there, Twolliam with an almost gleeful smirk on his twisted face and William himself wide-eyed with worry.

"I come from a long line of *mo guai*... ah... basically... monsters. Ogres? Sort of..."

This probably should be a bigger deal than it felt. But now I was just curious.

"Why have you never had problems before?" I asked. "You've been like the picture of sweetness the whole time I've known you, well, except for..."

The day I kissed his cheek was the last time I ever tried to get close to him. He made it pretty clear he didn't want me to touch him. Well, that's what I thought. Until today. He rubbed at the mark on his cheek. My eyes flared wide.

"That's not from me, is it?"

He shook his head and blushed all at the same time. "No... Not entirely. It was a very... um..."

"Wet kiss," Twolliam interrupted. "We love wet kisses."

Twolliam bent to sit next to me, wrapping his arm around my shoulders as he looked directly at William. "Don't we?"

William kicked the doppelgänger's shins. Twolliam leaned forward to rub the sore spot, removing his arm from behind me.

"When my great-great-great grandfather fell in love with a human woman, he desired to live with her among the humans. For him, it was hardest, because he was full yao guai. Much of the time, despite his best intents, he was chased out of the villages. It didn't matter how well-mannered he was. But my great-great-great grandmother loved him anyway. Their children came out human—at least they thought so at first, except for their dislike of the sun, which caused them to wail and scream. But then the eldest took his first bath—and suddenly they had far more than just him. Like you saw, wherever he got wet, more of him sprouted."

I was so engaged in William's story, I didn't notice Twolliam getting closer again—so close that his breath was hot on my neck.

"I love being wet," Twolliam whispered in my ear before licking my neck.

William let out a growl and pounced on Twolliam, caught between trying to pummel him and hold him down. Twolliam giggled all the way through.

"Stop it!" I called out, trying to wedge myself between them. "Fight later. I'm still trying to understand."

William stopped aggressing, but was still straddled across his double's lap. Twolliam reached out fingers to tickle him with, which sent William flying back off the couch.

"Dick," William hissed.

"Right here," Twolliam said with a smirk, rocking his hips to show off his *still very naked cock.*

I looked away, staring at William's feet instead.

"So your family, what, reproduces by budding? Like a sponge?"

"That's a good one," Twolliam guffawed, slapping his knee.

William shook his head. "No, that would imply he's my brother. Or worse, I guess, my child?"

His nose wrinkled.

"I already told you," Twolliam said, lowering his voice as he leaned in closer. "I *am* William."

I shrugged him off, feeling him trying to get close again.

"Well, I mean, that's weird, yeah, but not really monstrous," I concluded. "So I guess that explains why you're such a baby about sunlight... and I guess I just won't get you... wet."

Now I was blushing again. Hard. I wanted to go back to that moment in the hallway when I was riding his mouth and he was lapping up my enjoyment like he'd been parched for months. I guess, in a way, he has been. Wait... has he ever...

"Have you ever been with anyone else? Has this happened before? I mean, it did happen because... because of how..."

"How wet you were," Twolliam purred. "I wonder if you still are... just waiting for us."

Breathing got a little harder for a second as I turned away from Twolliam to focus on William instead. And William was also affected by his double's words. I could see it in the protrusion in his pants. The one that I wanted so desperately to grind on earlier.

Twolliam's fingers grazed along my arm, teasing up towards my neck.

"You are the only one," William bit out, stomping his foot as a sign to his double to quit it.

My heart flipped.

"Does that mean you're a virgin?" I asked before I could stop myself.

I guess it made sense, if he had this big terrifying change looming over his head, that he wouldn't have had sex like most of the guys I knew.

"It's embarrassing," he groaned.

I stood up, took his hands in mine.

"I don't think that at all," I said, waiting for him to look at me.

His eyes seemed transfixed by where our hands joined. To

be honest, my eyes fell too, wanting very much for more connection. A reminder of how just minutes ago we were worlds more intimate.

"Besides, if that was your first time eating pussy, I don't stand a chance," I laughed.

That got him to look at me.

"Stand a chance?"

"Dude, you're going to destroy me."

"I can't do it again, though... not if..." he looked over to Twolliam, who sat on the couch with a strange expression on his face.

"Does it only happen to the original, though? That's the question," his double murmured. It was the most serious he'd sounded since William spat him up like a bad hairball.

William pulled me close, putting himself between me and Twolliam, like he was trying to protect me.

"No experiments."

"No fun," Twolliam pouted. "Such a big stick up your ass."

"Don't I get a say in this?" I cut in.

They both turned to look at me.

"You can't possibly..." William mumbled.

"Oh, please tell me that's where this is going," Twolliam giggled.

"No! I'm just saying that obviously I was attracted to William, and he's who I was doing things with, right?"

William nodded fervently. His double did too.

"You're absolutely right. I still remember how you taste," his double said.

There I go blushing again.

"No, I mean... *That* William, obviously."

"Did that kiss on the cheek after your gig mean nothing?" Twolliam pouted. "Because you know, I had to run back to our store as fast as I could. It was such a wet kiss... Dad cauterized the bud before it could grow into another me."

"Shut up!" William grumbled, nudging his double with his elbow.

If they really are the same... I'm not sure I can figure out loyalties. I *really* like William. I always have. He's always been so sweet to me, but I wish he would have taken the initiative with me so much sooner. And Twolliam seems just like William, except that he's so much... looser. Like he never wants to be bottled up again.

And if I never get eaten out like that again, it will be a crime.

"I think maybe we do try some experiments," I said, my voice a bit uncertain.

My stomach twisted as I tried to pick an ethical stance on this. But my pussy seemed to be more in control.

CHAPTER 8

WILLIAM

This might have been my worst nightmare.

She's actually choosing my fēnshēn?

"Why?" I asked, my voice far weaker than I liked.

She shrugged and let out a huff.

"He's you. But... More..." she lets out a breath, trying to find the words. "Greedy, I guess."

My stomach dropped.

I could be greedy. I felt so greedy all the time. Like I want too much. Like I want the world. But all the years of being told to hide what I am meant that it was second nature to pretend. To always give up those dark desires in me for the sake of everyone else.

I guess that's not greedy at all.

"I can be greedy," I snarled. I wouldn't let the *fēnshēn* win.

"Prove it," she scoffed.

I grabbed her by the throat and pulled her close. Only hesitated for a moment as years of keeping everything inside warred with me to stop, to back off, to stay away. But then our mouths crushed together.

When she kissed me after I went down on her, it was a revelation. But this... This was dominance. It was staking my claim on what was mine. She was mine. She needed to know that.

She whimpered against my mouth, and it was the most beautiful thing I'd ever heard. My teeth pulled against her bottom lip, drawing out another delicious sound. My other hand dug into her hips, pulling her tight against me. I pressed my hips forward, making sure she could feel the desire between my legs. There was no way she could let that *fēnshēn* touch her if I gave her everything she needed.

Her hands clawed into my back as her head fell backwards, away from me. I felt him brush against my thumb before I realized what he was doing. He was kissing her fucking neck. And she wasn't stopping him. She was into it.

I grabbed her by the back of the throat and pulled her back to me. Moved my hand at her waist down, filling it with the plump flesh of her ass and ground into her.

"William," she gasped when I came up for air.

"Mine," I growled. "You're all mine."

Hands pushed against me, his hands, as he wrapped them around her and began to tease at her breasts. His mouth moved to her ear, nipping and biting. Licking at the space below.

"You're right, she's mine," he teased.

His hand snuck low underneath the elastic of her stupid tutu to play with her pussy. No. Mine. I grabbed him by the wrist with one hand while I sought out her pleasure with the other. If anyone was going to touch her there, it would be me. Not the fucking *fēnshēn*.

"So *wet*, isn't she?" he mused, his exploration of her neck slowing to watch my hand on her soaking cunt.

Fuck.

I pulled my hand away like it was on fire. It almost made me want to cry. How fucking stupid is this? All I wanted was to have sex with the girl of my dreams, but if she got too wet, then I'd have to deal with another fucking *fēnshēn*. Billie squealed with neither of us touching her, the *fēnshēn* only holding her.

"Don't you want to try our little experiment?" he cooed. Fucking cooed.

But she looked so hot, desperate and panting.

"Please, fuck, I don't care who touches me, I'm so fucking—"

The *fēnshēn* didn't even wait for my input. Not that I could have protested. Maybe he was right. He is me, right? And I don't want to deprive Billie of a lifetime of stimulation just because I could produce another *fēnshēn* if I do too good of a job.

That possessive monster in me wanted to keep fighting. To forget about the consequences and take our pleasure. But I was too good at holding back.

Be greedy.

I couldn't. Not truly. The *fēnshēn* could be greedy for her.

And she loved it. She writhed in his grasp, twisting her head back to match his lips as his fingers plunged into her wet core. It felt so weird. Like watching custom porn or something. That was me behind her, fucking her with his fingers. As erotic as she looked, as much as she was a treat that felt designed just for me...

It was so strangely arousing to watch someone who looked just like me, who treated her just as I would if I didn't feel so restrained all the time. Who acted on all the impulses I buried.

"Oh fuck, William, are you jerking off to this?" Billie moaned, her eyes heavy with desire.

There was so much I was already giving up. I refused to give this up. I kept stroking myself, in time with the movements of my *fēnshēn*'s hand. To imagine what it would be like to press myself between her legs with more than my fingers.

"You're so hot like this," she said, her face rapt with fascination.

At least I was more entertaining than kissing the *fēnshēn*. That was a nice boost to the ego. That she would rather watch me stroke my cock than make out with him while he fingered her. I grinned smugly.

"Where has that expression been my whole life? Oh fuck," she panted.

Her eyes couldn't decide where to land, my face or my cock. The *fēnshēn* was whispering something in her ear, something I couldn't hear. It made her bite her lip as her eyes raked me up and down. Like she had laser vision or something. Like she could see through the clothes I still had on. Clothes I very much regretted wearing at this juncture.

"Yes, please, I need it," Billie gasped out in answer to whatever the *fēnshēn* said.

A grin spread across his face as our eyes locked.

"Experiments," he said simply before dropping to his knees.

He looked up at her, pulled her towards him. I growled. The least he could do was let me watch. But I still felt guilty about interrupting, so I moved to the stupid couch they were sitting on earlier.

"Take this stupid thing off," the *fēnshēn* grumbled, tugging at the tutu.

"Yeah," Billie eked out, pulling the tutu up over her head. It dragged her shirt up, revealing her breasts.

"All of it," I added. "Holy shit, Billie, your tits. Fucking unreal."

When her clothes were off, she looked back at me almost... demurely. Like she was amazed I thought she looked so hot. As if I could think anything else. Imagining what Billie looked like under all her little rock outfits had been my pastime for over a decade.

Nobody knew self-repression like I did.

But here, with the real thing right in front of me... It was a mistake to sit on this stupid couch and watch. Maybe I couldn't go down on her, maybe I couldn't finger her...

Maybe I couldn't even fuck her with my cock...

But I sure as hell could touch her.

She slumped forward as the *fēnshēn* kissed between her legs. He was surprisingly gentle, tentative. It felt like the opposite of how I'd devoured her. Maybe with that experience behind us, he wanted to take his time. I know I would. Fuck. It was so unfair.

"So good," he murmured.

I still remembered what she tasted like. The memory of it sat on my lips as I bolted forward, wrapping myself behind her so I could kiss her neck and play with her breasts. All the immediacy of our battle over her affection had dulled into an effort to bring pleasure to the person we both loved.

"Shit, you feel so good. Both of you," Billie mumbled between her sweet whimpers.

My nose filled with the scent of her hair: apple-scented shampoo and the slightly burnt smell of her curler. I ground my hips against her ass, reveling in the feel of her cleft. Of the three of us, I was the only one still wearing clothes, and it both felt like a mistake and a necessity. My cock was going to break out of my pants. The fact that I wasn't wearing a shirt anymore meant feeling the soft skin of her back against my chest.

I bit into her shoulder, fighting not to bite too hard. The monster within me wanted to, but I didn't think she was ready for that. That kind of bite meant more than she could handle. Pinched at her nipples as I gyrated against her. Her hips matched mine as she ground herself into my *fēnshēn*'s mouth. He pulled her forward until she was fully sitting on him—

"No, I'll crush y—"

He lifted her legs, and we held her upright between the two of us. The *fēnshēn* groaned as she dug her hands into his hair and bucked into him.

"I don't want to break your neck," she whimpered.

"You'll have to try way harder than that," I hissed in her ear. "Violence is in our DNA."

"Oh," she said simply.

To prove it, I forced her hips to ground even harder against the *fēnshēn*'s mouth, until she slid forward on his shoulders, forcing his neck back far more than any human should be able to.

"Oh fuck," she groaned.

The impossibility of it seemed to do her in. She came loudly, a noise that rattled through my bones. I heard a noise that reminded me of the strange creatures that wandered the mall at night. Those that would love a tasty human treat like Billie. I covered her mouth with my hand as we guided her through her orgasm. My other hand roamed over her body, teasing out the shivers and quakes that fell over her.

"Shhh, you're okay," I murmured against her ear.

My eyes locked with the *fēnshēn*'s. The strangest little thrill ran through me from looking at him, still licking and sucking his way through her release. He seemed so carefree. So pleased. Happy. Like he could do this forever. Like he was made for this.

And it occurred to me that maybe he was.

Because he wasn't bent over, coughing up a *fēnshēn*. Maybe he was made to do all the things I couldn't. All the ways to please her that I wanted.

Life was real fucking unfair.

CHAPTER 9

BILLIE

I was dazed, and that was putting it lightly.

I thought William had ruined me the first time he went down on me, but the combined efforts of him and Twolliam *destroyed* me. And what's more, they were still kissing me, licking me, holding me. We were nestled against the couch, not that I knew how we got there. Twolliam stroked at my legs, running his fingers along the skin with featherlight caresses.

William, on the other hand, held my head in his lap. Unlike Twolliam, whose gaze caressed me as much as his fingers did, William was staring into space as his hands played with my hair. The look on his face...

"You okay, Gizmo?" I asked, reaching a hand up to stroke his cheek.

His eyes fell to meet mine. His smile turned up.

"Peachy."

"Penny for your thoughts?" I asked, a little worried. Something was off.

He leaned down and pressed a soft kiss to my lips in answer. "I'm just glad one of us can give you what you need."

He tried to pull away, but I held him to me. Kissed him just that much harder as my heart ached for him. I didn't know why his doppelgänger could pleasure me and be fine. Maybe because he was just a copy. But it made me ache for William.

"God, I'm starving," Twolliam interrupted the tender moment. "You guys could go for some food too, right?"

William lifted his head slightly, his eyes searching mine with an energy that made me almost think he was looking for a way out. And at the same time, that he was looking for any excuse to stay near me.

"Everything's closed, dude. It's after hours."

Twolliam clucked his tongue. "It's a *mall*, dude. C'mon, let's break into the Good Char."

He slid his hand up between my legs playfully. "I bet Billie could really go for some sausages."

I squirmed until he took his hand away. "You know I'm a vegetarian, but I'll allow the innuendo."

"Feisty," he laughed, lifting my foot up to place a kiss on the inside of my arch. "Let's get your energy back so you're fun again."

He jumped up and turned to us expectantly. "Well?"

"You're a fucking nuisance," William hissed.

"But a useful one, no?" Twolliam sniggered, holding out a hand.

I didn't want to get up. I could melt into this couch for all I cared.

"Leave me," I said with a great level of theatre. "Tell them that though I have died, it was a little death."

"What does that mean?" they both asked in unison.

My cheeks blushed. "You guys didn't take french in high school, huh?"

They shook their heads, William biting back his words when Twolliam spoke.

"My parents said Spanish would be more useful. This isn't Canada."

"How many languages do you speak?"

They shrugged.

"Four-ish." In unison.

"Hot." I smiled.

They both blushed. Cute.

"Maybe someone... friendly... is still up. We're not going near Broth With a Bite."

"Man, soup right now, though? No one there is friendly?" I pouted.

They both looked at me. "No."

"What, is the secret ingredient people or something?"

"Hot dogs are out too. I'm not eating that around her, it's... dangerous," William added, glaring down Twolliam.

"For sinners like us?" Twolliam joked. I think. Whatever the joke was, I wasn't in on it.

"Cookies, then?" Twolliam said with a sigh. "C'mon, I need *something*. Don't tell me you're not as hungry as I am."

"One of us has all the self-restraint," William grumbled.

"Thank god it's not me," Twolliam laughed.

He leaned forward, took my hands in his, and pulled me up. "C'mon, Water Wiggle, let's get on your feet."

Proving him right, I almost slid right out of his hands and onto the floor. He laughed and pulled me close.

"I'll take the excuse to hold you," he murmured, before placing a kiss on my lips.

Kissing was nice. Kissing didn't require thought. The heat radiating off his body was another problem. It made me want to nuzzle into him and cling on like a koala.

"I can carry you," William said quickly, shooting up from the couch and pulling me off of Twolliam.

"You're like almost the same size as me, no you can't," I scoffed.

He didn't listen, just wrapped my arms around his neck and pulled my legs up around his hips.

"I stand corrected."

That whole *mo guai* thing came with a lot of perks, I guess. Satisfied I didn't have to move a muscle, I tightened my hold around his neck.

"I'm not choking you, am I?" I asked against his neck.

His shoulders tightened. "I'm stronger than I look."

"He gets off on it," Twolliam chuckled.

William kicked towards his twin. The double stepped away, laughing before shoving his hands in his pockets and leading the way down the corridor.

"Cookies taste better the second day, anyway. Gives the sugar time to age a little or something. I don't know the science behind it. But one of the girls who works there always has some for us at the end of the day," Twolliam said.

"Yeah, she's really nice," William agreed idly.

She's really nice. Has he ever said I'm really nice? Who is this girl? I'm trying to remember if I recall what the stupid cookie girl looked like. If she was prettier than me. I mean, guys go for me because I'm unattainable in their heads. Because I come off like a bitch and they like a challenge. But sweet cookie girls are the kind that you settle down with. That bake for you and cook for you and raise sweet-faced kids. Nothing like me.

"I don't want your girlfriend's cookies," I grumble.

Twolliam just laughed. William cocked his head to the side, slowing his pace a little as he tried to look back as he carried me.

"They're just cookies."

I hardened my jaw. Of course, they were just cookies. I'm being ridiculous. But I feel like I was dealing with a lot tonight, what with finding out he's a secret monster or something and watching him split off into two people right in front of me and then getting pleasured so hard I felt drunk. It was like running on giggle juice, but if everything that wasn't coming at me wasn't just our little world, the whole universe felt like it was crashing in on me. Couldn't we just fuck and cuddle and kiss and do nothing else forever?

"Yeah, obviously," I said.

I wish it had sounded more natural. But it came out like an accusation instead.

Then William made a strange sound. A choked sort of laughter.

"Oh my god, you're jealous."

If I didn't feel the vibrations of his voice through my chest, I could have thought it was Twolliam talking. A shiver ran through me at the realization that they were one and the same, ultimately. I buried my face in his back.

"No," I pouted. "She obviously has a crush on you, is all I'm saying."

He readjusted his grip, his hands grabbing just under my ass before giving my cheeks a squeeze. It made me yelp.

"Shhh," he laughed. "Wow. Jealous, huh?"

The stupid man had a spring to his step the whole trek to the cookie stand. I refused to say anything else in case it only encouraged him. Twolliam, at least, seemed wholly preoccupied by his stomach, which felt like a blessing, so I didn't have to deal with two smug dicks. Maybe William felt like it was payback.

"Are you really okay with this?" I asked, keeping my voice low so it could stay just between us.

I felt sort of bad leaving Twolliam out of the conversation. I mean, he was a whole person. A whole William, too. But he seemed so much more carefree. Maybe being a copy of William meant he didn't have as much pressure holding him back. It certainly seemed that way.

He slowed a little, losing whatever spark had flitted through him from gloating about my jealousy. Not that I was trying to rain on his parade.

"He's me, right?" William sighed. "So if he can do what I can't... and it makes you happy... That's all I want."

I hummed against his back and squeezed him lightly. He coughed faintly, which made me giggle.

"Too strong for your big, tough muscles?" I purred.

"If you're gonna be a brat, missy, I can carry you like one," he grunted.

I giggled. "What does that mean?"

Maybe I shouldn't have. He crouched low and slid his hands away. When I didn't move, he chuckled.

"Off."

I grumbled. "No, you were carrying me."

"Look at you, you are a brat. I'm still going to carry you."

He wiggled under me until I slid off, despite my best intentions.

"Rude," I said.

He spun around to face me, his mouth spread in a grin that made my heart melt. It was the most devilish expression I'd ever seen on *him*.

Who are *you?*

Then he bent forward and threw me over his shoulder. I squealed.

"Put me down!"

"Act like a brat, get treated like one," he laughed.

"Aren't you a virgin?!" I huffed out indignantly as my ass raised to the air and my head dropped low.

Needing something to grab onto, I wrapped my arms around his waist.

"You wouldn't believe the sinful stuff they've got in the back of Red Light Video."

This mall was proving to be way beyond anything I could ever expect.

"I'm beginning to suspect this whole mall is made up of people like you."

He bit into the side of my ass playfully. "You have no idea."

The worst part about hanging upside down is I felt like I could fall at any moment. And my stupid arms didn't know where to go. Holding tight around his hips jostled my head way more than I liked, although I had to appreciate the proximity to his beautiful little butt. It occurred to me it might be slightly more comfortable if I just held him at his hips and pushed myself slightly away from him, and I'd get a better view.

The best part? Fuck, it made me feel all twisty inside. Exposed... and like a little plaything. Like *his* plaything.

"Why are you squirming?" he asked, his voice caught between amusement and something much more lurid.

"Maybe one day I'll carry you over my shoulder and you can tell me how comfortable it is."

He patted my butt condescendingly. "I'd like to see you try."

"We're practically the same size."

"Monster strength," he pointed out.

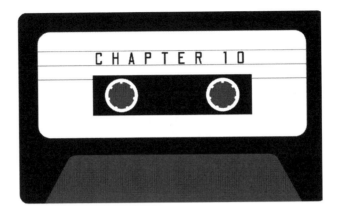

CHAPTER 10

WILLIAM

Maybe it wasn't the worst thing.

This whole sharing her with my *fēnshēn* thing.
He wasn't terrible. I mean, he was me. In a way.

"You want any?" he offered, extending the bag of stolen
cookies out to me.

They were warm and everything. The *fēnshēn* made a
point of warming them up in the microwave like Candy did. I
did not miss out on the way Billie's eyes lingered on his
fingers as he sucked the melted chocolate off them.

"I'm good," I said.

There was a little sneaking thought in the back of my head as soon as I heard my watch beep midnight.

Never eat after midnight, my parents had told me.

But the fēnshēn? He was free of all the stupid restrictions I had to endure, right? So it didn't matter for him. He was like an alternate universe version of me who didn't have centuries of repression to uphold. I wanted him to be free. Wanted to see one of us enjoy ourselves.

Getting to be with Billie at all was enough for me.

"God, these really hit the spot," the fēnshēn moaned. "So fucking good."

"I'll swing by and leave some money with Candy tomorrow," I said, knowing we didn't have a way to pay since the cash register was locked up tight.

"You're always so thoughtful," Billie grinned back at me.

I wasn't carrying her anymore. Instead, we walked hand in hand. It was everything I could have ever dreamed of. All the years of repression built up a million kinky ideas in my head, but fuck if I didn't want to just hold her at the end of it all. And that smile of hers? Those perfect lips, lipstick smeared after the way we pleasured her earlier, her eyes gleaming back at me, frizzy hair sticking out in all sorts of odd angles...

How could I not be in love with her? Every moment with her just reinforced that I would do anything for her. It only solidified how important it was that I be the responsible one.

"Can't get enough," I heard the *fēnshēn* groan.

Despite my pushing for moderation, he'd grabbed the

entire tray of semi-sweet chocolate chips and dumped it into a bag. That bag looked like it was almost empty. Billie only had a couple of cookies before patting her stomach and claiming she was more than full. I don't know if she was just being a girl or if she really wasn't hungry anymore.

I know I was.

But truthfully, I always felt hungry. It wasn't the kind I could satiate, though.

Billie gasped, like she just had a thought.

"What is it?" I asked.

"Can we swing by the fountain?"

"Aren't you tired yet?" I laughed.

We were coming up on our thirties.

"I want to make a wish," she said.

I narrowed my eyes at her. "Be careful making wishes in a place like this."

She cocked her head. "That sounded like a threat."

"More like a warning. We really shouldn't bother the guy who..."

She lifted a brow.

"Kind of lives... there..."

"There *is* something weird and magical about this mall. How else could it stay in business?"

We were walking back through the main part of the mall. As much as it worried me the security guards would catch us, I did know all the places you could slip away in a pinch. Billie's sloppy, wet kiss on my cheek wasn't my last foray into hiding what I am.

"I don't really like being near the fountain," I sighed.

Too much freaking water.

She halted. "Oh. That makes sense, actually."

"Yeah," I said.

"Oooh, let's take a picture. I just want to remember this night."

"Um—"

She ran ahead and put a quarter in the photo booth, then turned back towards me. I really didn't like bright lights. Under normal circumstances, I would avoid the photo booth like the plague. But she just looked so beautiful looking back at me. So earnest and hopeful. I couldn't resist.

She sat me down on the stool first and slid in after me.

"Hold on," she said, "Where's Twolliam?"

"Twolliam?"

"Your uh... doppelgänger."

That sinking feeling in the pit of my stomach was back.

The light flashed.

"Shit, it's just us then. We'll do another round with him."

She turned towards the camera and beamed. I did not.

Flash.

"C'mon, smile, you dork."

'Twolliam' wasn't like me. He could be bad, he could break the rules without the same consequences. Right? He didn't need to worry about getting wet or eating after midnight, because he was just a *fēnshēn*. *Fēnshēn* didn't work the same way.

"William, c'mon. Kiss me, then. I want at least one cute one."

She pulled my mouth towards hers and cleared my thoughts as her tongue dove between my lips.

Flash.

"That's better," she breathed, smiling back at me.

I returned the smile. Fuck, she was so pretty. Made me feel like I didn't have anything to worry about.

"I love you," I whispered, our lips still close enough we could feel each other's breath.

Hers hitched.

Then, a flash of green pushed through the curtain and tugged at her.

She screamed.

Flash.

CHAPTER 11

BILLIE

As I got dragged from the photobooth, all I could think about is how annoyed I was that William had just told me he loved me, and the moment was ruined. We almost had that shit on camera.

Being whipped around was enough to drag me out of sulking. I could hear William shouting, but with how much I was being thrown around, it was hard for me to get my bearings. All I could really think about was *green*.

Some sort of monster had hold of me. William and Twolliam kept insinuating there might be other monsters in the mall, but I guess I just didn't expect to find any. Not really. I mean, it was hard enough coming to terms with the whole doppelgänger thing.

"Smell so good," came a low, deep voice.

And then I felt something hot between my legs. I was no longer being whipped around.

Huge, piercing red eyes stared back at me from across a snarled nose and mouth. A long, thick tongue pushed out between those terrifying lips. This thing's head was huge, like three times the size of a normal person. I squeezed my legs together, realizing where its tongue was going.

The monster frowned.

"C'mon, Billie, you liked it so much earlier," it said.

"What the fuck—were you watching us?" I squealed.

The monster burrowed into my legs, attempting to spread them open again.

"I can fill you so much better now," it said with a gleeful little laugh.

One that kind of reminded me of Twolliam.

I looked away, desperate for help, and saw William below us.

Kind of far below us.

Like we were on the second story, except that we weren't. The monster was holding me up with a single hand across my back, laying me out like a pastry, ready to consume me. He pressed one thick, huge finger down between my breasts, down my stomach. It sent shivers across every part of me.

And deceitful waves of heat to my core. I did not know I got off on being terrified.

"Stop!" William yelled up at the monster. "You're going to scare her!"

He kicked at the monster and jumped back, holding his foot.

"Fuck, I should have stopped him from snacking," William muttered to himself, nursing his foot.

The monster huffed and looked down at William.

"Aren't you hungry, too?" the monster grumbled.

With one easy scratch of its claw, my leggings ripped apart, leaving me exposed. Cool air rushed across my pussy as I squirmed. The monster groaned and smiled. It moved its hand away from me and reached down for William, grabbing him before he could outrun the creature's huge limbs.

"Ahhh fuck, fuck, fuck," William yelped out, writhing in the monster's strong grasp for freedom.

"Have a little fun, William," it cooed. "Look how free I am. That could be you, too."

"Don't touch her!" William grunted out.

"She's not even afraid of me. You should smell her, you'd recognize the scent."

The monster flipped William over and mashed his face into my lap like we were Barbie dolls. Unlike a Barbie doll, though I had genitals, and I was pretty uncomfortable with this monster just assuming things about me just because he could smell my dirty little secret.

"Let go, *Mo Guai*. What's the worst that happens? You are free."

"I'm sorry," William mumbled against my pelvis. "Fuck, you smell so good."

That traitorous heat between my legs spread them apart. This whole situation was so fucked up, but I mean, I'd already been eaten out tonight by William's doppelgänger while he dry-humped me from behind. How much extra fucked up was it to get turned on by a monster shoving my maybe-boyfriend's face in my crotch?

"I can't," William whimpered, dragging his hands across my hips, sending sparks of need through me.

He kissed everywhere but my cunt. I ached for him. My legs spread wider. Both he and the monster groaned in unison.

"Please, William," I begged.

The monster's claw curled around my neck, pressing into it.

"You can't deny her. We never could."

The realization that this monster might be Twolliam settled in, making me feel a whole lot better about the insanity of this situation. His sharp claw grazed across my chest, leaving in its wake a ripple of biting pleasure.

"Shit. Fuck. Shit," William spat out, his hand moving between my legs.

Until finally, he grazed across my clit.

"Yes!" I gasped, bucking my hips as much as I could while held within Twolliam's grasp. "Please more, yes!"

"Fuck, Billie, when you beg like that," William groaned.

He circled my clit again and again until I wanted to scream.

"No more teasing, please," I begged.

Our eyes connected. In my peripherals, I saw how he bit his lip. Unfair. He slid his fingers down, spreading them all across the slickness he'd created.

"So wet," he groaned. "So fucking wet."

Two fingers pressed inside me. My legs flailed about, trying to hook onto his body and pull him close. I wanted so much more than his fingers, as good as they felt.

"Not enough," I moaned.

He let out a shuddered sigh as he slid in another finger. When I whimpered and twisted, trying to drive him deeper, he slid in a fourth.

"Fuck me, please," I begged. "This is torture."

"My fingers aren't even enough for you," William sighed.

He stared down at his hand, flexing it like he was expecting his hand to break or something. He looked at me and then back at his hand and licked up the wetness. Moaning over his fingers, he stared at me as he sucked up my arousal.

"If you don't, I will," Twolliam mused.

The monster drew me away from his original. When I tried to latch tighter, the monster just lifted me over William's head. He laughed when William grabbed at my hips, trying to keep me close.

"Stop!" William cried out. "I will!"

The monster shook his head. "Still too afraid."

And then I was straddling the monster. Being so high up meant I never got a good look at the rest of him. Obviously, he had busted out of the clothes we'd found for him earlier when he grew three times the size of a normal William. What also should have been obvious is that the size of his cock would grow as well.

William was the perfect size. Perfectly shaped, and I still wanted to know what he felt like inside me. But this monster? The strange decorations I saw on Twolliam's cock looked terrifying.

The monster pulled me along his cock, stroking himself with my whole body. I let out stuttered moans as the ridges stroked along my pussy.

"Oh my fucking god," I whimpered. "Oh, William..."

Before I knew it, William was behind me too, straddling the monstrous cock with me. He wrapped his arms around me, rubbed my clit. Kissed my neck.

"If you can't beat em," he grumbled into my neck. "Fuck."

I chuckled. "One hell of a fuck."

His fingers teased my clit as he ground his cock against the cleft of my ass. His free hand pulled my mouth back to slide our tongues against one another.

Twolliam rubbed the precum from his cockhead and brought his giant finger in front of me.

"Taste," he urged.

William held my chin as his doppelgänger stroked his

huge fingertip against my lips. The precum got all over my face, tingling like mint.

"Oh," I groaned, opening my mouth wider and licking at his fingertip with my tongue. "Why does that taste so good?"

"You think humans fuck monsters without incentives?" Twolliam chortled before sliding his still-wet finger down my breasts, down my stomach, and pressing against my clit. William moved his hands to hold my legs wider.

It tingled there too. A rush of pleasure burst through me, just shy of a climax.

"Did you know?" I gasped out, writhing against William behind me.

"He's me," William huffed. "I just didn't realize you'd be such a slut for me even before."

"Oh, Jesus," I groaned.

He had a fucking mouth when he wanted.

The monster pulled his finger away, readjusting his grip on us smaller beings as he continued to slide us up and down. It was agony. Torture. I just wanted to get fucked—I *ached* to be filled.

"Please fuck me," I whimpered. "Please."

William squeezed at my tits before sliding his hand back down between my legs. "She's so wet. Let me fuck her."

CHAPTER 12

WILLIAM

My legs were shaky as the *fēnshēn* set us down. But Billie looked like a goddamn treat, bent over and whining for me. She held her hips up in the air, her face sweaty, blushing, and desperate.

"Bratty little Billie, desperate for my monster cock," I mused.

Not that I was going to let the *fēnshēn* fuck her first. Though I knew our precum had magic in it to aid our girth, I didn't want her broken. Or unable to even feel me. I was grateful he at least let me go first.

"Fuck me already," she whimpered.

My cock twitched. It was nice to hear her beg outright after all the years of her trying to manipulate something like this into being. Well, something she probably didn't expect to be quite so... complicated.

I leaned down, palmed her ass, marveling at the way she pushed back into my grasp. That cunt of hers was absolutely dripping. Surely whatever magic had spawned my *fēnshēn* wouldn't torture me twice. It seemed I could palm her wetness without breeding more *fēnshēn*s, so maybe I was confused as to why he spawned in the first place.

Yes, I was just looked for excuses to eat her out again. Her taste was unbelievably addicting. I pressed my mouth to her cunt, sighing at the taste of her. Even if this spawned another *fēnshēn*, it had to be worth it. Plus, I could only think about how we might be more fulfilling with three of us.

"Oh, oh! William—ah—but—ffff—I'm so wet!"

She was. She was so wet. She drenched my face, washed me away in a tidal wave of arousal. I could swim in her cunt, learn to breathe in her.

Hungry. So hungry.

My tongue couldn't reach deep enough. I could not suck on her strongly enough. I needed more. So much more.

She let out a wailing cry as finally I felt like I could fill her enough. Her hips bucked against my mouth as she screamed, "Yes! Yes! Yes!"

After all these years of practicing "no" on her, those were my favorite words. I brought my hand up to scratch along her back and marveled at how small she felt beneath my palm. I licked through her orgasm, sucking and fucking her with my tongue until her cries turned to blubbering ecstasy, eating my fill of her.

When I lifted my head, I jumped at the strange green hand on her back where I thought mine was. Clearly I was so enraptured by eating her out that I didn't even feel the *fēnshēn*'s hand on mine. I tried to move mine out from underneath, but the *fēnshēn* moved his too.

I pulled my hand back against my chest. The *fēnshēn*'s hand—

No. No, that was my hand.

I was the *fēnshēn*. Or... No, I was the original. No copy.

Mo Guai.

The monster inside of me got out. This is what I was afraid of all those years.

But I felt powerful. Right. I was fucking the girl of my dreams right in the middle of the mall and I didn't care who saw. If there were security guards here, they knew better than to interrupt this. This was destiny. Primal need. Inevitability.

Looking over, I saw my *fēnshēn* staring back at me, a mirror image.

I spun Billie over until she could look up at me, see me for what I was. I stroked back her sweaty locks, the perm completely gone from her hair. She looked up at me, her face twitching with a swirl of emotions.

"You're so big," she slurred with a happy giggle. "C'mon, big boy, let's see what you've got."

"My tongue wasn't enough for you?"

She moaned, whimpered, tittered. Her hands covered her face, barely any strength left in them.

"Never greedy," she teased.

I wrapped my thumb around her throat as I licked up from her cunt to the lips of her mouth before choking her with my tongue. She moaned with approval.

"Careful what you ask for," I hissed, pulling apart.

My free hand spread her wide, the pad of my thumb rubbing against that tender little cunt. My cock was just as decorated as the *fēnshēn*'s now. I thought it a small tragedy I never got to feel what she was like in my human form, but something told me this would be even better. As I rubbed the head of my cock against her pussy, she giggled as the tingling sensation overtook her. I wasn't sure how much the precum would loosen her up. It seemed an impossible fit, but my father always said our bodies would adjust to each other. I shook off the thought, not wanting thoughts of him to taint this moment.

Impossibly, after everything, I was still a virgin. I couldn't help but laugh.

And then I pressed in. Softness. Heat. Tight. Good. Wow. Bliss. Absolute bliss. I would do anything to be inside her twenty-four-seven.

Billie whimpered, writhing against my grasp on her torso. Her head lolled, as a strangely blank expression took over her face.

"Billie, okay?" I asked, my whole body tensing with worry.

She nodded, but that wasn't enough for me. For all I knew, she was possessed. Gone from this world, though.

"Tell me," I urged, pressing my too-large lips against her shoulders, nuzzling as much as I could against her neck.

"Fuck me, Gizmo. Be greedy."

It didn't matter how many times she told me. I was still so afraid. But I let it go. Pressed harshly within her and she yelped in delight. Her breaths came out in shuddered moans to the rhythm of my pistoning. I pulled her close to me, to move her like a doll on my cock. Looking down between us, I watched in fascination the point of our joining. My eyelids fluttered when I could see the shape of my cock through her womb. That couldn't be comfortable, but I couldn't stop now. Well, unless she asked.

"Okay?" I asked again.

She yipped yes with each thrust. Her pitch went higher and higher until she was sobbing another orgasm. Her walls spasmed around my cock as her delicate arms came around to grip me tight.

"More," she slurred, drunk from the nirvana of orgasm.

I chuckled, ready to pull her off even though I hadn't even come yet, but the *fēnshēn* stepped up behind her.

"As you wish," he murmured, teasing his own cock against her ass.

"You'll break her," I protested.

"You haven't," he pointed out, his finger tracing the shape

of my cock along her torso. I hissed, feeling the pressure of his finger through her.

As it was, Billie seemed pretty beat. I felt bad that she had to hold herself up at all, so I lay back against the cool marble of the mall and lay her against my stomach, holding her still against my cock. She nuzzled her head into me, pawing her fingers into my stomach. The *fēnshēn* groaned as he drenched her backside with his precum, squeezing at her ass to keep her attention.

"Please," she begged, too frustrated by his teasing.

And then he slid into her, and I felt the pressure of him through her walls. It was too much. I slid out, letting him slide in fully. When he slid out again, I slid back in. She writhed against my stomach, her voice growing hoarse with every moan. She drew her head to look up at me, her face a canvas of blotchy red joy as she reached her hand towards mine.

My heart squeezed. I was far too big to hold her hand properly. But I held it anyway. Her entire hand closed up within my giant grasp.

"Love you," she whimpered, on the verge of another orgasm.

She turned her head back to the *fēnshēn*, too. Reached out for him. He took her hand too, as awkwardly as I did. Her tits bounced as we continued to pound into her.

"Love you," she repeated to him, her whimpering moans growing higher and higher pitched again.

As finally I felt the surge of orgasm rush through me, the

same happened to the *fēnshēn*. I wanted to tell her I loved her, but it was hard enough to keep holding her hand as release filled my every cell. We kept pounding into her until the *fēnshēn* collapsed forward onto her.

I was afraid he was going to crush her until I realized we had both come back down to human size. We wrapped ourselves around her, kissing her and telling her how wonderful she was. The *fēnshēn* started to doze off, but I woke him when I realized we were still in the center of the mall. I groaned, pulling at him until he woke up and we carried her back to the Past Present between the two of us before passing out on the centuries-old furniture there.

CHAPTER 13

BILLIE

Wow. So. Monster boyfriends.

If anyone had told me I'd be going into Halloween finally dating the guy I've been lusting after for half a decade, I might have laughed. But two of him?

William and Twolliam weren't the same person anymore. They both started to experience things differently—and especially because Twolliam was much more spontaneous, he wanted to do so much more than William had ever allowed himself.

The Lius were coming back tomorrow. We'd have to explain to them, or hide Twolliam.

"We can't both be William," William grumbled. "It'll be too confusing. The easiest thing to do will be to tell everyone you're my twin brother who grew up in China."

"So, what? I'm not changing my name."

I laughed. "You're both being stubborn. You could always split the name down the middle."

"What do you mean?" they asked in unison.

"Will," I said, nodding towards William, then towards Twolliam. "And Liam."

I'd never tell Twolliam that Liam was actually short for Twolliam in my head. I'd grown too attached to calling him that.

They looked at each other, testing it out in their minds.

William reached out his hand first. "Liam."

Twolliam—Liam—took it as they shook slowly. "Will."

Then they looked at me.

"Are we splitting you right down the middle, too?" Liam asked, a mischievous quirk to his smile as he stripped me with his eyes.

I bit my lip. "I mean, you can try. With your dicks. If you manage to split me in two, you can each take a part."

Will made a face, but still laughed. "You have such a weird sense of humor."

"I like that challenge," Liam grinned, stepping over to kiss me.

He reached his hand around to squeeze my ass and pull me against his already hardening cock.

I looked out towards the mall, afraid someone might see. Will growled, pushed Liam out of the way.

"I'll win."

Just then, I saw some people walking over and pushed them away.

"Boys, boys, there's enough of me to go around."

They each reached a hand behind me, stroked along my back and my ass where no one could see. Heat rushed to my face as the new customers entered.

"Welcome to the Past Present!" we all three said in unison.

Liam squeezed my ass, making me jump forward. My hand brushed against my water cup and I squeaked as it flew towards Will. He didn't seem bothered, though. Didn't even try to wipe it off this time.

"Are you sure?" I asked, my eyes wide.

He shrugged. "What's the worst that could happen?"

ABOUT THE AUTHOR

Latrexa Nova's mind is a Rube Goldberg machine of puns and monsterfucking.

A California native, Latrexa has always seen the weird in the world and seeks to share their outright lust for the strange and unusual. Their hobbies include sculpting unnatural horrors, running from their inner demons, and trying to celebrate Halloween all year round. They write for the weirdos, with a lust for darkness and off-beat humor.

Subscribe to their mailing list on
https://www.latrexanova.com
or follow them on instagram or tiktok for manic updates:
@latrexanova

ALSO BY LATREXA NOVA

More Halloween Monster Goodness

The Thirteen Kinks of Halloween

Spicy short tales of classic halloween monsters

Halloween Spirit

A pun-spewing clown somehow manages to seduce an on-the-job grim reaper

Willing Sacrifices

Tributes are needed to keep these monstrous gods from breaking out of their prison to eat the world. But Bee will only let them take the willing.

Check out their first full-length novel

Love the Sin, Hate the Sinner

Friends-to-enemies-to-lovers genderfluid, shapeshifting sex demons

Got a hankering for aliens?

Mated to the Xirashi

Four stories of spunky leading ladies falling for electrifying pink alien bounty hunters.

PLAY

SABRINA DAY

BE KIND
AND REWIND

"Welcome to Red Light Video: Purveyors of your deepest darkest desires. Yes, even that one."

The first rule in the Red Light Employee Handbook? Never go behind the curtain unless you're willing to sacrifice everything. But when punk video store clerk Seren finds herself suddenly broke, homeless, and staring down a 24-hour pawn shop deadline, her only solution is to break the first rule — and her gorgeous, mysterious boss is only too happy to accept her sacrifice.

Content Warning:

Due to mature themes, parental discretion is advised. This love letter to the VHS tape features: a nomadic art punk, dream invasion, extensive role-play, "I want to F a priest, a hot one" energy, irreverent and constant 80s movie references, an incubus with big Jareth vibes, a toxic friendship, misuse of a fax machine, HR violations of employee-boss fraternization, a "Please, Mr. Serial Killer, don't kill me, I want to be in the sequel" primal chase sequence, fang-play, knife-play, copious fluids, a confession booth that's seen some things, memory-removal with consent, dream pregnancy (no actual pregnancy), and graphic depictions of sex between sentient and consenting adults, sometimes with an audience.

CHAPTER 1

Hell is a barren pawn shop, manned by a roid-ed out, Magnum PI look-alike.

"Just give me my stuff," I hiss at him. I can see my whole life staring up at me from behind the glass display case, sitting on a piece of filthy, thread-bare velvet.

"No marker, no gear," the overly-muscled owner of Hock It to Me says again.

"But it's mine! I'm not the one who pawned it."

He snorts with a raised brow. "How do I know you're not just trying to steal it?"

"Do I look like a thief?" I snap the heels of my 10-holes together and straighten up to make my five-foot-nothing self as intimidating as possible, hoping the shit-kicking abilities of my favorite pair of oxblood Docs can get me through another round of this endless argument.

These leather boots have seen me through shittier situations. I fled NYC in these boots. These boots outran cops who took issue with my sprawling tribute to Basquiat tagged on the side of a railcar depot in Oakland, all while Janie did a performance striptease protesting the demonization of sex workers. We got away both times. These are my lucky boots, and I'll be damned if a two-bit pawn broker in this sleepy Southern California beach town's weird-ass mall breaks my lucky streak. Why else would the universe make sure I slipped these puppies on today? It's a sign that I'm not leaving this shop without getting my entire life back from this man-shaped mountain of muscle squeezed into a pair of acid wash Z Cavariccis.

Fueled with the righteousness of the perfect pair of shoes, I reach back in time and summon my best Mother Constance glare of divine outrage — the one she'd unleash during class whenever she'd find me drawing one of my "infernal" cartoons of the nuns engaging in their favorite vices after school hours.

The key to nailing the glare requires the upper lip to do a lot of heavy lifting to sell the "Obey me or I will crush you" undertone. Do it wrong, and you're looking at an immobilized jaw for at least a day, but it's well worth a lip cramp if it means I look like the last person McGruff the Crime Dog would haul in for questioning.

"Don't matter what you look like." His easy-going, Cali

drawl grates on my Brooklyn-born-and-bred ears as he shrugs a boulder of a shoulder. The action drags the obscenely deep vee of his Hawaiian shirt wider, exposing the thick gold chain wrapped around his neck. The chain glints under the fluorescent lights as he settles onto the stool behind the pawn shop's display case counter. Shrewd, deep-set amber eyes assess me, lingering at the base of my throat. He fixates on the small metal spike I punched through the stiff tab of white paper tucked under my button down's black collar. His gaze drifts lower, tracing the silver chain dangling from my neck.

He jerks his chin at my chest. "Might want to flip that guy right side up if you want to sell the man-of-God look, Sweet Cheeks. Better yet, you should get some padding down there." The owner's smirk is swallowed up by his mustache as he nods towards the crotch of my black pants. I'd hurriedly grabbed the cross I fished out from Red Light Videos' lost and found; now, I'm cursing under my breath—it's inverted.

"Told you there's no such thing as lady priests." The pip-squeak standing beside me chimes in. Jelly's esses come out in a lisp through the mouth slit of his Darth Vader mask.

I palm his tiny head and scoot him back. "Stuff it, Jelly. I'm negotiating here."

"No, she ain't." The jerk contradicts me with a chuckle that makes me want to hock it to him, preferably with the nearest sharp object.

"Yes, *she* is..." I glance down at the yellowing business card taped to the counter, "Drake Krabopolis. She, I mean me," I shake my head, "*I* am one second away from calling the police."

No, I'm not.

"No, you're not." Hazy, gray curlicues of smoke rise from the smoldering stogie clamped between Drake's meaty fingers, the ember a third glowing gem wedged between two serpentine signet rings. Unbothered by my threat, he moves his smoking fist with a grace at odds with his size and rests it on the sign propped up on the counter, tapping the glass front with calloused knuckles. A snowfall of ash floats down as I read the bold, block print.

NO MARKER, NO REDEMPTION.

Yeah, I read it.

"See, here's how this goes. You call the police. They send Kelsey from Creepy Court security down to scope out if it's worth the police's time. Kelsey gets here, gets the lay of the land, remembers that top shelf Scotch I gave him at Christmas last year, and then he boots your cute little ass out of my shop. You know why?"

"Because I don't have a marker."

He grins grossly. "Because you. don't. have. a. marker."

I swallow back a frustrated scream. I don't have a marker because the marker is with my best friend, the bane of my existence, the person who pawned all my belongings in the first place before stealing my car.

Freaking Janie.

A soft burr buzzes against my hip, the vibrations rattling the spikes dotting my belt. I snatch my pager from its clip and hope bubbles up in my chest. Maybe Janie has felt my imminent melt-down, wherever she is, and finally decided to make contact.

To my dismay, instead of a random pay-phone callback number, a series of digits scrolls across the display so familiar, I don't see the numbers, just what they stand for.

Red Light

The back of my neck tingles as I clip my beeper to my back pocket and ignore the persistent buzz. The pushy bastard can wait, and even if he can't, what's he going to do about it? Come and find me?

Actually, he might.

"Fine. Just sell it back to me." I fish out my wallet, the metal chain connecting it to my belt loop clinking against the counter. It's the one thing I took with me when I came to Creepy Court this morning. My plan was to shoot some eerie, mostly-empty-mall and parking garage footage. I wanted to fan the flames of the stories of a Rat Lady scurrying around the grounds by editing some suggestive footage together on a VHS tape. I had this idea that I would leave the videotape out for a group of teens to find, start my very own urban legend. I'm grateful for my own devotion to sowing chaos, because taking my wallet is all that saved my remaining cash from Janie.

Still, wallet half-out, I pause. Until I get paid next week, this is all I have. Sure, I'm flush with more cash than usual, thanks to Chessa insisting on paying me for helping her out, but if I spend all this on liberating my stuff, there will be nothing left for the butt-load of problems I still have. I'll still need money to make those issues go away, including a ride to hunt down Janie's ass.

I stare across at the glass case, finding six years of bootleg cassette tapes, Polaroids of strangers with their secrets scrawled across the back in red Sharpie marker, and videos from every place we touched since we fled Our Lady of Unsavory Memories. Those tapes, those ones right there, are the infant beginnings of the Creepy Court documentary — a film I just started shooting a month ago. All of it will be lost if I leave it behind to chase Janie.

Not this time. I'll chase her down just like she wants, but I'm doing it on my terms, not hers. I'm not going to play her game anymore. It's too much; I can't let it go.

I shove the sweaty wad of money at the pawn broker. "There. That's five hundred, double what everything back there is worth."

In a flash, the wilted twenties disappear from the counter and into Drake's hairy hand.

With agonizingly slow movements, Drake reaches down into the case. The scrape of his stool against the linoleum briefly drowns out the music tinkling up from Creepy Court's atrium. "Five hundred gets you this," he grunts as he tosses a bundle covered in pins and frayed, colorful fabric onto the counter.

"Are you kidding me? Five hundred dollars gets me my backpack?" My backpack—held together by a riot of band patches—is a sight for sore eyes. My "kind-hearted degenerate" button pinned to one strap winks at me under the fluorescent light. Even as I protest, I snatch it up and hug it to my chest, wrinkling my nose when a whiff of Drake's Drakkar Noir wafts up from it. I quickly unzip it and take stock, confirming he didn't take anything out.

Clutching the fabric close, I ask, "What about my camcorder, tapes, and clothes?"

My punk-ified priest outfit, complete with a huge, severe bun in the back and oversized crimson glasses swallowing my face, is probably the most respectable look I've worn in forever. Baby needs her shredded crop tops back.

The bastard shrugs. "Not for sale."

"Of course it's for sale. This is a pawn shop."

"So?"

"So, it's not like you have a stampede of people throwing cash at you. Why not take five hundred for it all? If you think there's a thriving market for beat-to-shit camcorders, I've got some tough news for you friend."

I do an exaggerated scan of the store, taking in aisle after aisle of no shoppers and empty beige shelving, save a knockoff Teddy Ruxpin bear and a demonic, oversized, Raggedy-Ann doll. Despite the treasure trove of high-end gear spilling out of the stockroom, attracting customers is clearly not Drake's strong suit.

"Everything back there is mine and stays mine until I decide otherwise." He smiles blandly.

It's over. There's nothing I can do. If he's going to keep it all, he'll keep it, and I'm stuck with the sticky end of the lollipop, like always. Utterly destroyed, I motion to Jelly, and we turn to leave.

Just as I reach the door, though, Drake calls out to me. "Hey."

I whip around, probably looking more hopeful than I have the right to.

Drake sighs as I hurry back to the counter, Jelly on my heels. "Lookit, I'll give you one chance to get your stuff back, free and clear."

"All of it?" My pager rumbles against my ass again, and I, once again, ignore it. Instead, I snap my gaze to Drake's, trying to read the impassive slabs, looking for the catch.

"All of it will be yours, Sweet Cheeks, if you can answer one question."

"I suck at Jeopardy," I blurt out. "Unless the category is how to jimmy the lock to a Ford Pinto in under two minutes, I'm useless."

"Noted," he says, his mouth twisting up. "I promise this is a question only *you* will know the answer to... because it's about something you own."

"Oh, okay." I frown, unsure where he could be going with this.

"Tell me, how did you get this?" Much to my astonishment, Drake whips out a trick too fast to track, and bands of delicate silver are suddenly twisting around his arm to form a familiar cuff, complete with my crimson opal soldered to its center. It's the most beautiful stone I've ever seen—the deepest shade of merlot—and it's around the wrist of a stranger when it should be around mine.

I'm momentarily shocked into silence by the whole situation. Jelly gasps beside me, clearly impressed by the magic trick, but Drake the Magician ignores the praise and grunts in annoyance.

"Tell me where you got it, and I'll give you the whole lot without a marker. I promise you, girlie, giving you something from my horde for free? That's an offer I've only made to one other person in all my years running this shop. So, answer honest and answer true, because this is your only shot."

I stare at my opal in chagrin. A bone-deep itch starts up around my wrist, calling to the stone that was pressed against my skin until late last night. I was really hoping this bastard hadn't rummaged through my backpack, but obviously, that was too much to expect.

Thinking carefully, I scratch the inside of my wrist through my sleeve. The stiff fabric doesn't dull the itch or the pain from where I had already rubbed that same spot raw last night.

I hadn't taken that cuff off in months — *couldn't* take it off, honestly — until right before I fell asleep last night. Yesterday, the urge to scratch the crap out of the skin beneath was off the charts, and I had to spring the release or go mad. Of course, I had to leave the one piece of jewelry I love behind this morning and let it get packaged off to Drake's emporium of whack-assery.

"Well, what's the answer, girlie? How'd a baby punk like you get a rare piece like this?"

Any happiness I was feeling about this shot at freeing my life from a cologne-scented prison evaporates into thin air.

"She got it cause she's a princess like L-L-Leia," Jelly announces.

"That so, princess?" He raises a brow.

"It's t-t-t-true," Jelly says, nodding emphatically. "She's a princess, and that's her..." he pauses for a moment, searching for the words before he says triumphantly, "her token of affection. From a prince."

"A prince, huh?"

"No, I got it at a...at a party," I answer quickly over the whoosh of blood in my ears. My skin goes hot then cold at the mention of that night.

"Mm-hmm, very convincing. Go on. Tell me more about this party. Who saw their princess there and had to make sure she left with a token of their affection?"

The thing is, I can't tell him. I can't because I don't know who. If it was a prince like Jelly said, then the charming lad must have slipped me a quaalude—or four—because that night is a blur streaked in neon. Trying to jostle the memory free only brings forth a cocktail of adrenaline and the feeling of a high so pure and intense, it beats the euphoria I get after finally nailing a tricky film edit.

Drake doesn't care about what I felt that night. He wants facts.

"There were people there," I start vaguely, but the harder

I strain to bring those people's faces into focus, the more a familiar ache builds behind my forehead. I've done this dance a million times, always with the same result: a splitting migraine and the thick taste of defeat.

The facts are these: Janie and I rolled up to an abandoned warehouse on the edge of this sleepy town, our party pitstop for the night. One of the club kids back in L.A, who loosely follows the same party circuit we do, said the next best DIY show was going to be there. He raved it would be a total body experience, an insane collision of performance art, drag, and hardcore bands breaking shit and releasing our collective rage into the night sky. It was a feast I couldn't wait to tape, and something Janie couldn't wait to debauch herself in. So, we did what we do: we set fire to our existence in L.A. We loaded up my hearse, Elvira, with our meager haul of permanent belongings and took off down the coast, following a shitty set of directions until — mostly by chance — we stumbled on the warehouse, just as the sun was setting.

That's it. That's the last memory I have until the next day, when I woke up in Elvira's driver's seat, an overexposed Polaroid crumpled in my palm with an address written on the back and the cuff cinched around my wrist. I was still struggling to understand what was going on when Janie banged on my window, startling me so much, I cracked my head against the steering wheel.

Janie ignored this, telling me in no uncertain terms that I needed to get my hungover ass up because her new boy toy

— as of last night — Eddie the drummer was going to show us where to get banging chilaquiles for breakfast.

Janie was no help when I cornered her later that day and asked what happened. My head was still fuzzy from the drinks and scent of cinnamon and lavender seeping from my pores. She said we got separated early on, that she caught sight of me doing my thing, asking strangers questions and snapping their picture while they answered. Then, she "bumped" into Eddie after his set was over, and her memory became almost as unreliable as mine.

"You know how horny drummers make me, Seren! They can multitask like a mother and can keep a beat doing *anything.*" So that was it for my safety buddy. She lost track of me after she went off to test Eddie's finger dexterity in his band's van.

Drake's dark brows are raised in expectation, still waiting for me to answer, and I know none of this is going to satisfy him.

"I just... went to a party, and someone gave it to me."

Drake frowns. "Right. 'Fraid that's not going to cut it. Get me the marker for lot 2306 and you can have this," he taps my cuff to the counter, "and the rest back."

"Come on, man, there has to be a price, please. What are you going to do with a bunch of pictures and VHS tapes?"

"For starters, Imma look to see if you took any other topless photos with poems by Rilke written across your tits." Drake smirks.

My stomach twists. "You shouldn't go through people's stuff."

"Course I did. 'Cause it was mine at the time. Weird little menagerie of items you got going there, but that pic was a nice surprise. You've got a banging rack, baby."

At that moment, Jelly's new stepsister and his current babysitter, Molly, appears behind us, returning from whatever errand she's been on. Her name is Molly to everyone else, but she's PB — as in Peanut Butter to Jelly's jelly — to me. Hearing Drake's description of my attributes, PB gasps, whispering my name.

I ignore her because, first of all, I have bigger problems, and, second of all, Drake may be a douche, but he's not wrong. I *do* have a banging rack, and the least Drake can do right now is give it the respect it deserves.

"I don't care what you say. You have to give me a price. Otherwise, I'm going to post flyers all over this town about your shady business practices. Give me a chance, a real chance, to get my stuff back." That's a thing suburban moms would threaten, right? I slam my fist on the counter to sell it. If there's one thing I've learned from hanging out with Janie, it's that when in doubt, cause a ruckus.

"Is that so? Well, I wouldn't want my good name dragged through the mud," Drake says dryly. "You're pushing it, Sweet Cheeks, but since I've got a soft spot for nice tits and early nineteenth-century expressive poets, I'll give you a price tag." He studies me with an enigmatic expression. "Let's say ten grand."

"You've got to be shitting me?"

"You kiss the big guy upstairs with that mouth? Yeah, you heard me. Marker or ten grand by this time tomorrow. I'm breaking all my rules for you, sweetheart, and I have no problem with yanking this offer back, so think long and hard before you pull the trigger on whatever you're about to say." Rocking back on his seat, Drake takes a pull from his eternally smoldering stogie and puffs out a perfect ring, as if he wants a frame to capture the rage stroke paralyzing my face.

"What's the matter? Ten grand is nothing. Ditch whatever this is." The cigar draws a line of smoke down my unholy priest outfit. "A pretty girl like you just needs to toss on a mini skirt and bat her lashes at any of the marks wandering around out there to get the moola in no time. Now, get out of my shop before I make it twenty."

"But that's not fair!" I yelp. Shame, hot and heavy, blankets me head to toe. The urge to strangle the childish retort and shove it deep back inside is instantaneous.

The discordant screech of Hock It to Me's fax machine cuts in, saving the day from whatever shit I was about to spew that would most assuredly get me kicked out. Drake shoots the machine a surprised look, like he's just now noticing its existence, before he snatches up the paper being spit out. He gives the message a cursory read, and his face splits into a grin so wide, even his ridiculous mustache can't cover it. Deep lines of amusement crinkle around amber eyes as he slides the fax across to me.

"Life ain't fair, kid. Now, get. You're late for work."

Red Light Video's trademark logo and star standout from the stark white of the sheet on the counter. Below the header, in slanted, looping script, two short sentences send a sweet-sick twinge to my lower belly:

"My star isn't where she's supposed to be. Send her back. Immediately."

I jerk my head up and scan the ceiling. There, in the corner, I find what I'm looking for: the spy that took over when my pager failed to bring me to heel. Through the dusty lace of cobwebs, Hock It to Me's security cam blinks a red light down from the darkness, sending the same message my beeper tried to.

Time to go to work.

CHAPTER 2

A group of nuns scatter like a flock of judgmental pigeons, clucking their tongues as I storm past them, Molly and Jack hurrying along in my wake.

"And a good-day to you too, Sisters." I toss a mocking nod to the bobbing black habits as I yank my collar open and release my hair from its cage. With a sniff, the scandalized lead nun gathers her group together and pointedly turns back to joining the winding line of corndog groupies at That Good Char's kiosk.

"It's weird that the Sisters come here so often for lunch." Molly examines the nuns with curiosity. "It must take them an hour to get to Creepy Court one the bus. The Lagerfeld Mall has a bigger food court, and it's just a few blocks away from their nunnery."

Bad mood temporarily forgotten, I grin at her. "Trying to drum up business for your new family?"

I went too far, and I know it as I watch PB's dusky cheeks turn rosy with anger. "You know that's not how it works. It's their family's money, not mine. Mom and I are just the low-class interlopers."

PB is PB to me and Jelly, but she's Molly Lagerfeld to everyone else. She used to be Molly Bhattacharya, but her mom decided she was done being the wife of a convenience store owner and ditched her dad last year. She traded slushies for ski-slopes and married the patriarch of the Lagerfeld family. Lagerfeld owns the "good" mall and pretty much anything else worth owning in Dorian Bay, the très chic enclave for Southern Cali's old money.

"That's not true, Molly. You're not a 'loper. You're the best sister I've ever had." Jelly, earning his nickname, glues himself to his stepsister's side with earnestness you only get from a seven-year-old as I make a sharp detour to the mall's payphones on the other side of the atrium.

"I'm your only sister, silly."

"Yeah, but I love you more than Ruthie, too. He never takes me to the video store and lets me hang out with Seren." Darth Vader's mask can't hide the pout adding a tremble to Jack's defense.

"Stop it. It's not a competition, and don't let him hear you say that."

I let their chatter fade to the background. I prop up

against one of the payphones and rummage through the front pocket of my bag.

"Need my phone card, Seren? Mr. Lagerfeld-"

"Just call him Dad!"

"*Mr. Lagerfeld* just got me a new one, so there's tons of time left on it."

"Naw, that's okay, PB. I got my own calling card right here." Triumphant, I produce a paperclip from the grody bottom of my backpack. Why pay the man when you can get your phone breaker on instead?

I bend the tip of the paperclip against the lip of the payphone booth, right under the "Rat Lady Iz Real" graffiti, working it until it's just one smooth, metallic line. I take the straightened bit of metal and poke one end into the receiver and the other end in the keyhole where the coins are collected, and viola, free phone call. Score one for Seren.

I dial the number to what *was* our apartment until this morning, when I found myself locked out. From what I could see from the window, Janie had packed everything up except for our answering machine. Listening to the phone ring, I twist the phone cord and hope that she at least left a message to explain this little bomb she set off.

"We aren't home right now because we're off being imperceivable amorphous concepts of grace and beauty." My husky voice greets me. "And objects of mass destruction!" Janie's soprano screeches from the background before descending into peals of laughter. "Please leave a message, and we'll make sure to haunt your dreams until you go mad as soon as we can."

Tears prick behind my eyelids. Stupid Janie. If it was time to blow out of this town, she could've just said so. Through blurred vision, I tap in the code to listen to any stored messages.

click *Hey, uh, Serena, I mean Seren. It's Glen. Gotta say, I'm disappointed. I rented to you girls even though you looked flighty as hell. To wake up to a note scribble on the back of a diner napkin that you were breaking your lease and not paying this month's rent is a shit way to start my day. It was a month-to-month lease! If you girls wanted out, we could've worked something out. Now, I hate to take action against you, since it's just you on the lease and not your roommate—and I get the impression this is more her doing than yours—but unless I get this month's rent by Monday and a visit from you apologizing for all this mess, I ... Well, I'm going to have to do things I don't want to do. You take care now.*

Dammit, I really am going to kill her. I squeeze the phone until the plastic creaks and whines in protest. Why did I think Janie would limit her exit to just disrupting my life? No, she made sure to go full scorched earth so I would have to follow her.

"What's the matter? Finally realized the gutter punk lifestyle isn't all it's cracked up to be?" Rutherford "Ford" Lagerfeld the Third's chiseled jaw widens into a smirk as he leans on the other side of my phone booth. His dark hair smoothed back, his cool arctic gaze scans the defeated slump of my shoulders, nostrils flaring, as if he can scent that I'm wounded.

Not one to get kicked without kicking back, I fire back, "What's it like wanting to bang your stepsister so bad, NASA can see your hard-on from space?" Ford's neck practically snaps as he tries to both check his fly and guiltily whip around to see if Molly heard me. Luckily for him, she's distracted with wringing out Jake's cape, which he somehow dunked in the atrium's fountain.

Because I stay ready, I grab my Polaroid camera and snap a pic of Ford sporting a rare look of disheveled, horny self-loathing.

People have to be poked before they drop their masks and show you their truths, but capturing that moment is worth pushing them to the edge.

Maybe now, he'll stop being a tool to Molly and just admit he has it bad for her, even though, in his eyes, she's just one step up from my gutter punk status.

"Jacob, bring Mole girl and meet me at the south parking garage entrance. Lagerfelds have better things to do than slum it with the Creeps." Ford sneers the last bit at me, shoving his lacrosse-fit body away from the phone booth with enough force to send the chained Yellow Book Pages careening out of its cubby and swinging wildly in the air. With one last look of disgust, he pops his collar and spins away in a smooth move they probably teach all the rich dicks in private school.

"But Ruthie, Seren was going to make me a character

sheet on her break. She said I could play D&D with the AV kids at Red Light tonight!" Jake whines over Molly's frantic shushing as she drags him behind Ford. She mouths an apologetic "sorry and good luck" over her shoulder at me.

click click

Thanks to Ford's interruption, I forgot the answering machine was still playing all our stored messages.

This is your last message.

A velvet-edged timbre flows out of the receiver. The command underlying the caller's soft vocal fry strokes a path from the shell of my ear down to an invisible hand around my throat.

Starlight, star bright, you are missing work tonight.

I wish I may, I wish I might, have the pleasure of punishing you tonight.

Seren, Seren.

I'm a generous benefactor, but standards must be maintained.

Be where I can see you soon, or a penance must be paid.

Hurry back to me, Star girl.

End of messages

The nice robotic lady severs my connection, leaving me alone with the persistent bleat of the dial tone.

Right. That just happened.

I need to scare up ten grand, get written up by my stalker boss with a fetish for hacking anything electronic to keep tabs on me, and sling some tapes.

Gotta love Friday nights.

C REEPY C OURT IS THE FUN, KITSCHY KIND OF CREEPY, LIKE A
roadside tarot card reader draped in dollar store scarves with
a pack-a-day cough, who you're sure is pickpocketing you,
but damn if their fortunes aren't dead-on creepy.

In a way, Ford isn't wrong. People go to Lagerfeld Mall to
shop and be seen; they come to Creepy Court's beautiful,
slightly gothic walkways to slum it and satisfy urges they
can't feed anywhere else. Tucked away on the east end of the
mall, Red Light Video is a perfect fit for this place. It's why
working here is the most enjoyable legit job I've ever had.
Where else would I be given carte blanche to run the store
like the anarchist film punk I am?

I hustle past two wide-eyed teens taking in the waterfall
of gauze streaming down the front window. It's lit with
spotlights of pink and blue, a soft frame to the glam rock
horror scene of crushed disco balls and a ripped and bloody
backdrop. Their attention is stuck on what looks like a nearly-
nude, waifish mannequin dressed up as a ballet dancer frozen
on pointed toes, her pink mouth a perfect O of terror as a
masked dance instructor looms behind her, gloved hands
wrapped around her throat. The tagline of the movie of the
month is spray-painted above the couple's head: *"The Only
Things More Terrifying Than the Last 12 Minutes of This Film...
are the First 80."*

Amid all the stress of today, a small curl of satisfaction blooms as a pair of permed high-schoolers decide my Suspira display is "bitchin". So, it's with a light step that I finally make it into work.

"You're late." The dry, vaguely Germanic-accented admonishment sounds out as soon as my Docs touch down on Red Light's galaxy print carpet.

"Whoa, Ronnie, careful with the emoting. Your face might crack." I try and fail to stifle my laughter when the only other employee at Red Light raises a perfectly-manicured eyebrow in confusion and not one muscle else.

One of the AV kids swears that Veronica, with her stone-cold looks and accent, must be the love child of an Eastern European model and an African oil tycoon undercover as an international assassin. She rocks a complexion so dark and perfect, it looks like she was carved out from the night sky, coupled with a bone structure and figure Annie Lennox and Grace Jones would die for. Ronnie's remote androgynous sex appeal has men and women tripping over themselves for a hint of attention.

I swear, she's why half of them come in.

"Look, you're lucky I'm here before the Friday night parade of perverts comes through." I skirt past the hollowed-out TV I converted into a fishbowl and scoop up Nyx from his perch above the goldfish as I slip behind the rental counter.

"Ronnie, would it kill you to keep Nyx from eating the goldfish?"

"It would not kill me, no."

I roll my eyes. "So, why is our devil kitty threatening death from above to our babies?"

Ronnie glides over to the front of the rental desk, looking like she just got in from Milan in her slim-fitting suit, manicured onyx nails clicking on the counter as she considers the purring bundle cradled to my chest. "It wouldn't kill me to keep the young master away from the fish, but it is also not within the scope of my responsibilities to prevent it." She makes a gesture with her fingers, as if to say her hands are tied. "It *is* within your position's responsibilities to not refer to our patrons as perverts."

"Yeah, yeah. I know, but the point stands: I still beat our patrons here. Besides, Friday nights are all VIPs who only have eyes for whatever you and the bossman do behind the curtain with your stable of pretty young things." I waggle my brows at her and set Nyx down. The cat grumbles his displeasure and leaps off the counter, disappearing behind the stacks.

That's the difference between Ronnie and me. Front of the house is my domain, in all its film nerdery glory. Her role is to serve as the stern-but-sexy guide to the backroom. Between the two of us and whatever our invisible boss does, there's no reason to go to a chain rental place when you could come to ours. Here at Red Light, the tapes are shelved according to actor or director or mood. The shelf of movies to watch when you need an ugly cry so you can feel something again? It's behind the beanbags. Want all of John Carpenter's movies sorted from best (The Thing) to worst (Starman)? Under the mounted TV that only plays David Bowie movies. Taking a break from movies but need to disassociate from reality? How about you take a load off in our Gary Gygax Grotto with the AV kids; they'll pair you up with just the right tabletop game.

"Movies my invisible boss thinks are good but are not and we should shun him for his bad taste", "Movies where Ronnie has made out with someone on the cast -You'll never guess who!", "Movies my invisible boss thinks are bad but are Perfect and this is proof that he has no soul." All of these shelves exist and bring me joy.

Yes, most members are here for the other half of the store, but since I joined the team six months ago and implemented this stocking system, I've found my ragtag collection of geeks, punks, and oddballs, along with a small group of stray normies. Janie thinks I'm a freak for what I've built here, and maybe she's right, but I kind of love the thought that this quirky corner of the world will persist once I leave.

I check the register and make sure I have enough singles and fives to break all the twenties that will come through tonight. Satisfied with what I find, I snap the cash drawer closed and turn to check the returns bin to see which dipshits didn't rewind, but before I can start checking cases, a glaring problem presents itself.

"Stop putting Die Hard as Movie of the Month, Ronnie! We voted on horror as the theme." I snatch Bruce's bloody mug down from its perch and place Suspira back where it belongs.

"Yes, we voted and nominated a horror movie, but our

employer and I thought that would mean something with oversexed-camp counselors and phallic knife shots. Not," Ronnie puckers her lips in a wan expression of distaste, "stressed-out, dancing Italian girls."

"Slashers are fine, but Argento's subtext-"

Bored with me already, Ronnie drifts away and returns to her post in front of the crimson velvet curtain hiding the entrance to the back room. Customers have started to trickle in, along with the impossibly beautiful VIP room employees who sashay past Ronnie, leaving a cloud of Clavin Klein's Obsession in their wake.

The customers circle the shop, gawk at the back-room staff, and dawdle like they don't want to be caught making a beeline for Ronnie to ask for the eight-page application to become a VIP member and gain access to whatever raunchy goodness happens back there.

I ignore the looky-loos and do a quick loop around the store to make sure everything is in order, acutely aware of the five different security cameras slowly tracking my progress.

When I was first hired, the cameras pissed me off. After my first day, I flipped them off and told Ronnie I quit, that I wouldn't work for a boss who was going to monitor the black girl as if I was going to make off with the cash register.

Ronnie smiled in response, and the sight of her stunning cheeks scrunched in laughter stunned me enough to stop me in my tracks. "He isn't watching you because he thinks you'll steal our money. He's watching you because he regrets hiring you for up here and not back there. His penance is seeing what he's missing."

At the time, I'd calmed down enough to remember I needed this job to fix up Elvira, who promptly shit the bed the day after Janie and I attended the warehouse party. I thought Ronnie was full of shit, but I decided not to care.

But now...

Now, after months of the quiet whirr of cameras following my every move, I'm starting to wonder—maybe having a stalker for a boss could solve all my problems. If only I can work up the courage to ask.

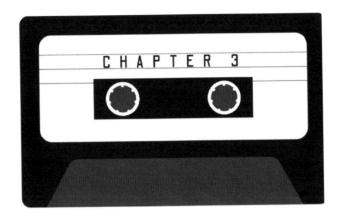

CHAPTER 3

FAX

To: Bossman

From: The Employee of the Month

You know, I thought your fetish for faxing was just a quirky, "while we're working" thing, not a "you control an intricate web of security cameras around the mall and will fax unsuspecting asshole pawn shop owners" thing.

FAX

To: Employee Number Two

From: The entity who controls your paycheck

The beauty of faxing is that I can reach you whenever I need to. That's the whole point.

Creepy Court's administration team appreciates my efforts to man their security cams, and if I should happen to spy a tardy employee exchanging explicit photos with a business rival during my efforts, then I think I'm well within my rights to use any means of communication to remind said employee that her shift has started, and she is needed where she belongs.

Unrelated, do I need to add a section to the HR handbook about outside of work conduct?

FAX
To: Sauron, the All-Seeing Eye of Capitalism
From: Does this mean Ronnie is Employee Number One because no

I am a model employee who has never done anything wrong in her entire life.

Currently, the employee handbook is a single page, and the only rule listed is "Front of house staff must adhere to the same rules as Red Light Video's patrons. They will never go behind the back-room curtain unless they are willing to sacrifice everything."

Cryptic, passive aggressive, and vaguely threatening. You conveyed so much with so little. It'd be a shame to add more and throw off the perfection of this one.

Now, speaking of you being the entity who controls my paycheck, I'm willing to overlook the managerial overreach of obtaining my real phone number (and pager number!) when I definitely gave you a fake ones if we can talk about renegotiating my salary.

FAX
To: The person who'll be tasked with telling Veronica she's now Employee of the Month
From: Your Video Overlord and Master

I cannot wait to see where this is headed.

FAX
To: My Master
From: Your humble but plucky servant

Given the uptick in walk-ins and memberships due to my window dressing and marketing efforts (did you even look at the Giallo Spread in the front window? The local PTA committee wrote a letter against it, and we got twenty new VIP members the day I put it up), I think I'm overdue for a raise, but I'll settle for a simple advance on my next ten paychecks, effective tonight. Sound good?

FAX
To: Call me that again, but slower and to my face

From: You may be my servant, but you are anything but humble

No.

No. That's it? *No?* I unbutton the rest of my shirt, baring an opaque, black lace bustier underneath and fanning away the flush that started creeping up my chest when I read the first line of his last fax. It had been a joke —*just* a joke—calling him master. His reaction was unexpected, and honestly, so was mine.

How could he end it, just like that? We were having fun abusing the store fax system, as usual, unexpectedly dipping our toe in flirty banter, and then just *no?* I fall back into my childhood self-soothing habit of running my fingers through my hair, teasing the wiry strands out until my head is hidden from that asshole's camera by a dark cloud of hair.

The store phone clatters to life. Annoyed, I answer it and plop back in the desk chair, throwing my feet up on the counter. "Hi, you've reached Red Light Video, Where You're the Star."

"Hey."

"Janie!" I snap upright. "Bitch, what the hell? Where are you?" I scan the store for Ronnie and find her huddled with a golden surfer dude and his reedy friend, walking them through the thick VIP application. Clutching the phone receiver, I duck under the counter and sit crossed-legged in musty semi-darkness. For all I know, our boss can read lips through those cameras, and I don't need anyone to hear this conversation.

"What the hell do you mean, what the hell? You had to know this was coming. I told you it was time." The sound of honky tonk and rough male laughter muffle her response.

"No, you didn't."

"Yes, I did, over and over again. You just didn't hear me because you lost sight of the mission, playing with all your new little friends."

"Janie, I wasn't playing. I was working. Remember that massive car bill?"

"The one you finally paid off last month? Sure, I remember it, because that's when I brought up ditching this place and heading somewhere new. You shot me down and said you wanted a little more cash before we headed out, but guess what? Week after week, it was always some new reason why we couldn't leave. Some made up urban legend you wanted to interview people about, or batty old lady you wanted to tape talking about which president she banged in 1920." Janie is crescendo-ing into another register as she lists all my crimes. "You brought home a butter dish from Southstrom's and *paid full price for it* because you thought it was cute! What was next, investing in a home security system? We are not home security people!"

I frown. I'm proud of that butter dish. I named her Mrs. Butter-Tits because the sloping top looks like a perky set of boobs. If that's really what set this shitshow of a day in motion, I don't know what to say. The staticky silence grows between us.

"You weren't going to leave unless I blew up our lives here, Seren." Back to soft and coaxing, Janie wills me to see it her way. "You were being lured into the capitalism of it all, working in that damn mall. Life isn't about how many toasters and butter dishes you can buy. It's about art-"

"And art is trash," I finish dully. *Life is art and art is trash* was the motto we coined when we were two seventeen-year-old, Catholic school dropout runaways. It was supposed to remind ourselves that our mission in life was to fuck up the status quo wherever we landed, but always be ready walk away in an instant before any of those places could turn us into the suburban walking dead.

"You've pulled me out when I've started getting too comfortable, and I owe it to you to do the same. When you figure out how to get out of there, you can meet up with me in Vegas. I'll be crashing with Dennis for the next few weeks. I got a line on a rager coming through out in the desert next month. A nomadic commune of hippies and freaks are throwing it. It'll be just what we need to forget that stupid beach town." Janie sounds tired but resolute. "I'm not sorry. You got in too deep, Seren. You aren't built for planting roots. Sooner or later, all your new friends are going to decide you're too loud, too weird, too angry, too into sex, and everything you stuck around for will fall apart."

"Right." Every sentence of hers is a splash of cold reality. She's right. I *am* in deep. I have wings; I don't plant roots.

As my invisible boss just proved, it's all fun and games until I ask for a little too much, and then I get shut down. I may have poured more of myself into this store than I have anywhere else, but it doesn't count for anything. It's all trash.

"So, you'll come to Vegas, yeah?" Little kid yearning breaks through Janie's tough exterior. She's always been the more insecure one, convinced I was going to ditch her once someone better came along. That's what started all of this; I can see it now. She thought Creepy Court was seducing me away from her. This was her latest test to see if I would finally make good on her prediction.

"Yeah, Vegas." Janie is Janie. I know her; she's my constant. Where she goes, I go.

But not quite yet.

"Tell Dennis I'll be out there in a week or two. You hocked things that you know I love and would've taken with me, and I need to figure out how to get them back before I join you."

Janie mumbles something about how she needed the money for a bus ticket to get to Nevada.

"Whatever. It's done. Try not to bang all the drummers before I get there."

"No promises, bitch. Get your ass out here before I burn this city down." Janie laughs and then hangs up.

I crawl out from under the counter and flop back into my

chair. My stomach is churning with a gross mix of guilt, anger, and melancholy. Until I got Janie on the phone, a tiny part of me was hoping I could talk her into coming back. I pull out my sketchpad from my backpack. As I press the pencil to paper, I let my worries run away as I start to storyboard a movie I will probably never make. Even I know it's pretty pornographic, but that's the point. Too much, too intense, too sexy.

I channel my mess of conflicting thoughts into an orgy of aristocratic vampires feeding on the plump cunts and cocks of writhing, rosy-cheeked servants as the Queen of the Damned watches with approval high up on her throne.

"Why the face?"

I loll my head up to find Ronnie inches away, staring down at me and my sketchpad.

"Personal space, Ronnie! We've gone over this." I wheel back a bit and snap my sketchpad closed.

Ronnie holds up her hands silently, but she doesn't apologize, and she doesn't back away. She just stands there, watching me, her hands at her sides and her face calm and even, like she knows that I'm about to tell her everything. And here's the kicker: I want to tell her.

I swallow hard before I open my mouth. "My face is because the real world sucks. I need cash, a lot of it, to...fix some problems before tomorrow, when I-" I frown and look behind Ronnie to the blinking red light tucked into the corner above her. The Big Boss is watching, which means it's definitely not the time to share that I plan on leaving as soon as I get my tapes and cuff back. "Before I lose some belongings that mean a lot to me."

"Bullshit," Ronnie says without heat, except it sounds more like "Bool-Sheet."

"What's bullshit? Money is a hard-to-come-by thing for most of us working stiffs."

"It is bullshit that you can't think of a way to acquire the money. You dress like this." Ronnie reaches over, and one slender nail scrapes gently against the swell of my breast to pull the edge of my lace bustier away. She holds it there for a single breath before letting it snap back. "You look like this. Where I am from, people would pay to be in your presence."

"Got a plane ticket there?" I cock an eyebrow at her.

Ronnie cocks her perfect head to the side. "In a way, yes. The VIP experience has been a success, much more so than our employer anticipated. We'll need to bring on more backroom staff." A sly smile ticks up the corner of her lips. "Just imagine getting paid more money than you've ever had just to exist. You should come back and ask for an interview."

I stare at her, utterly dumbfounded. I don't know what to say first—thank you for implying that I'm hot enough to get paid for it? No one has ever actually told me what happens back there. Preternaturally beautiful people go in, followed by VIP members, and the members come out with dopey smiles, clutching jet-black VHS cases, not the fire engine red cases I package all the front of the store tapes in. The black tapes never get returned.

"It's against the rules," is what I croak out instead.

Ronnie lets out a delicate snort. "I thought the spikes and the black make-up and all your costumes meant you didn't concern yourself with such things?"

I scowl at her and grab my camera, quickly snapping Ronnie's picture. Fanning it until her stupidly beautiful face appears, I write "Get Bent" under her portrait and tack up on our wall of renter shame.

Unbothered, Ronnie loosens her tie and leans over the counter, booping me on the nose. "Back there, I do the bending of people over, but for you, mein liebling, I might make an exception. It would be like getting mauled by a little kitten. Fun." She smiles, and for the first time, it actually reaches her eyes that glitter with mischief and humor. "Besides, Boss likes people with an eye for a good scene."

Unable to process an almost *playful* Ronnie, I can only sit as she taps a finger against my fantasy goth, vamp orgy sketches. The way she lingered over the word *scene* makes me shiver just a little bit. "How else do you think we live up to this?" She points to the "When you're here, you're the star" neon sign hanging over the velvet curtain to the back room.

"You know that if I go back there, I risk being fired."

Ronnie sniffs and saunters back to her post, but I hear a muffled "squawk" as she goes.

Jittering with the prospect that I could beat Drake's deadline if I just stormed back there and asked the jerk for a new job, I pace around the store. I shelve and reshelve the "Motivational sportsball movies that actually are good" section before popping in Die Hard, fully intending to borrow some of Bruce's walking-on-shattered-glass energy. I can do this. I can risk my job and do this.

There's nothing I'd be giving up of myself, my true self, if I worked one night behind the curtain. So what if giving a handie to some local I'll never see again after I beat it out of here next week? That's just the sacrifice I have to give Red Light. Joke's on the bossman, because I've done worse.

Before I can talk myself out of it, I task Georgie with watching the checkout counter. She's our D&D DM, and she practically lives here on Friday nights anyway. Then, I roll my shoulders, take a breath, and plow through the curtain as if I've done this a thousand times.

I'm greeted by a dark hallway lit with neon runners, which cast a technicolor glow that makes it difficult to see where the hall ends. In fact, a few steps in, and I can't even tell there's an exit behind me. The floor vibrates with a faint bass, but I can't hear any music. I can't hear anything.

As I creep further down the passage, neon red signs appear on the wall, illuminating dusky paintings of writhing bodies.

TRUST ME

LOVE ME

FUCK ME

The signs go on, but I can't see any doors or any hint of

where all the VIPs could be. Disconcerted, I almost run into the final sign mounted to a door that's cracked open an inch.

BAD DECISIONS MAKE GOOD STORIES

"Is that advice, or a warning?" I ask under my breath. Moving as silently as I can, I peer through the crack in the door and catch sight of a flash of Ronnie's tan suit jacket and dark skin. I'm triumphant, and not above shouting Ronnie's favorite movie line to rub it in her face that I didn't chicken out of her challenge. I kick the door the rest of the way open and jump inside.

"Yip-kay-yi—what the fuck?"

Blue-black wings spread wide in surprise, and pure crimson eyes, two sets of them, blink out of a face I know but don't. Ronnie, still dressed in her slim linen suit, cradles a stack of papers to her chest. The rounded ovals of her manicure have elongated into sharp onyx points that make her nails indistinguishable from her fingers, and her night sky complexion is polished to an iridescent sheen. It's like looking at a beautiful, black marble gargoyle come to life.

"Ronnie?"

Crystalline lips glitter as my co-worker smirks at me. "Seren. So happy you could join us. I was just talking about you."

A cough jerks my attention to the brutalist concrete desk to her right, its sleek surface barren, save for a TV perched on the left of the creature sitting behind the desk. Four merlot eyes stare out at me.

Pain cracks down the center of my forehead with an explosion of static, the feeling of the inside of my skull being roughly fine-tuned by an indifferent god too much to bear. My knees hit the floor as my vision clears, and a memory surfaces: endlessly deep merlot eyes, navy skin, delicate fangs pressing into a sinfully lush bottom lip, and taloned fingers tapping a tune I know but don't know.

The world boils down to a single word, a name, one I always knew but didn't know until now.

A name from my lost night.

"Poe."

CHAPTER 4

"I know you!"

His name is Poe—a soft, round name at odds with the sharp creature staring at me. I clutch the name to me in a tight fist; it's the first solid bit of evidence that a hazy night six months ago is just waiting to be unlocked somewhere inside me.

"Do you?" Poe steeples his talons under his chin and contemplates with an unreadable expression.

"You were there that night! The night I—" The ache starts to build again, pressing in on the back of my eyes. I rub my wrist in frustration, uncertain again about everything besides the name of the monster looking at me like he might casually tear me apart and study my insides.

Tired of being on the defense, I do what I do best and go

on the offensive. "If I don't know you, then how do I know your name?"

"I am your boss." Gucci-clad shoulders, the same shade as Poe's navy skin, shrug. His smooth baritone rolls out and hits my right in the chest, the sound ten times as potent as it was on my answering machine. "I'd expect you learned my name from the training manual, like any obedient employee. You know the one in the same drawer as the Employee Handbook? The handbook that contains the sole rule of this store? A rule that you have blatantly violated?"

"Who needs to be trained on how to rent tapes? I used that book to prop up the Kindergarten Cop cutout of Arnold my second day here." I plant my feet and call on the power of my Docs for the second time today. "Besides, I can't be in violation of any rules, because you're not human. Therefore... the Geneva convention." There had to be something about informing your employee that you were... whatever Ronnie and Poe are.

"How limiting. I expected you to have a more expansive mind, Star."

Ronnie beams at the both of us. It's the second smile she's given me today, and the sight is vaguely threatening. "I'll see myself out," she says gleefully. "You," she flicks one talon at Poe, "audition her. You," she turns to me, "don't be a little shit, but make him work for it."

Work for what? Bewildered, I don't get a chance to ask, because Ronnie just winks out of existence. Poof, and no more Ronnie. Just me and Poe.

Why does she even have wings if she can do *that*?

"She likes you," Poe muses, staring at the void where Ronnie once stood.

"I'm pretty fucking likable, unlike other entities in this room." His abrupt dismissal of my request still hurts, but if he's bothered by the simmering anger in my voice, I can't see it. In fact, he bares his fangs in a viscous grin at my prickly response.

"That you are, Star."

"Stop calling me that," I snap.

"I'll make you a deal," he continues, as if I haven't spoken. "Ronnie informs me you are in need of money. I presume it's for that meathead dragon. He won't give you your belongings back, will he?"

"Drake is a *dragon*?" I can almost feel my eyes bugging out of my head at the knowledge.

"Yes, and like all dragons, once he comes into possession of something, it will take a much stronger force than yourself to get it back. Hence the deal you'd be wise to take from me."

"I'm listening." I saunter forward and drop into the wingback chair opposite his desk, like I make deals with monsters every day. My heart is pounding, my stomach fluttering, but I throw my boots up on the edge like it's nothing. I don't miss the way he tracks the bounce of my breasts as my back hits the chair.

Eat up the view, monster boy.

"I am not going to hire you for what we do back here. You're not a good fit," he states.

It takes more willpower than I like not to curl in on myself at yet another rejection, especially now that I know the person rejecting me looks like a fallen angel.

"But I *will* get you the marker you need, in exchange for a night." Poe tilts his head, a fringe of silky white hair shielding his gaze from mine.

"A night of what?"

He shakes his head. "If you had read the handbook, you would know that the only people allowed back here are those willing to sacrifice everything. It's in the contract you signed as an employee, and these things are ironclad. So, for my help with your matter, I need a sacrifice from you."

I blink slowly. "What does that mean?"

"It means I want to play with you for a night." He snaps his fingers, and the darkness behind his desk clears. I watch in astonishment as row after row of lights flicker to life behind him. Floor to ceiling racks filled with jet-black VHS tapes line the walls as far as I can see.

"I have watched you, Star. I've watched as you make your little tapes, your fantastical bits of truth and fiction, watched as you gloried in collecting other people's secrets and leaving them all over town." Poe circles a finger behind him. "Some of them have made their way here. I was just watching this one before you came in." Plastic scrapes against concrete, sending a shiver down my spine as Poe nudges the TV screen to face me.

Bea's soft, wrinkled face grins back at me as Poe clicks the play button at the bottom of the screen.

"Woodrow loved to have his balls licked and then kicked. My god, I could come on the spot when that man went down on me. Didn't matter if we were in the presidential motorcade or on the desk in the oval office; the man ate my pussy like a five-course meal."

Bea's face dissolves and another old face appears, telling an equally raunchy story involving a cucumber and a drunken sailor. The film I spliced together from years of asking people to tell me a secret from their sex life rolls on as Poe turns the weight of his gaze back on me.

"I want to make a tape with you."

"Of me asking you about your sex life?" I mirror his self-serious pose and steeple my fingers under my chin.

"Of us acting out our secret fantasies."

I snort rather unattractively. "That seems a very intimate thing to do with someone I just met."

He quirks a marble brow. "Have we just met? I like to think I know you better than most after all our time together."

I think back to the reams and reams of faxes that have piled up between us over the past six months.

Arguments.

Debates.

Sketches.

Snippets of my past.

Goddammit, he's right. He knows me almost as well as Janie, maybe more so.

Sensing my self-doubt, Poe presses on.

"Let's play together. One of your deepest secret fantasies and one of mine."

"That's it? Then you'll get the dragon to give me my stuff?"

"That's it. I'll even throw in the ten grand."

I blink once before I answer. "Okay. Let's make a tape."

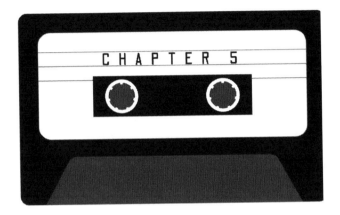

CHAPTER 5

"So...this is where you monsters make your bespoke porn, huh?" We've traded Poe's office for what looks like a miniature high-end movie theater. Loops and loops of brocade curtains in alternating maroon and black hang down the walls, and thick, maroon carpeting squishes between my toes. Against my protests, my Docs were confiscated at the doorway.

Can it be a theater if there's only one seat in front of the screen?

"Bespoke porn? Is that what you think I do?" Since he left his office, the hard-to-read corporate stooge mask has fallen away, and the edgy, kinetic Poe from our faxes is here. Bouncing on the soles of his feet, he stretches side to side, a taunting slice of navy abs peeking out from where his shirt has worked itself loose from his low-slung pants.

"Want to grab your camera?"

Caught, I cough and look away. "About the porn—it's not hard to put two and two together. This is obviously some kind of sex club, where you make videos of your time with the VIPs. Am I getting warm?" Our voices are muted to half their usual volume, the sound swallowed up by all the fabric. I could scream, and I doubt a whisper of sound would escape this space.

"Do you mind if I get comfortable while I answer you?" Poe prowls closer and circles behind me. My knees buckle as the art deco movie seat I thought was bolted to the floor is shoved at me. I fall backwards into the seat, and before I can spring up, tight bands of film tape cinch around my arms and torso, tying me to the chair.

"You're handling things surprisingly well, but just to be on the safe side, I'm adding some restraints to make sure you stay in place."

Poe emerges from behind the chair as a new man. A cropped corset cinched tight around his feline frame, he looks like a wet dream version of a marauder. Golden skin, kohled eyes, billowy canvas pantaloons set so low, a crispy trail of hair peeks out of the band—it draws my attention to the shadowy bulge swinging freely as he settles into a chair across from me, one he has conjured out of nowhere.

"Which of these is the real you?" I twist stealthily to test the bonds keeping me in place, but they only tighten more with each movement.

"I'm whatever feels right in the moment. Sometimes this, sometimes that, sometimes a little kitty-cat," he sings-songs, kicking his leg back and forth over the arm of his chair.

I blink as realization dawns. "You're Nyx!" The asshole has been prowling around, sleeping inside my shirt as the store cat.

He chuckles but doesn't deny it. "Moving on. Where were we? Right, what we do back here. You're a bright star, darling, and you aren't far off. You might have sensed this whole mall is a little off. Different from everywhere else, yes?"

I think of the fanatics who clamor for hot dogs from The Good Char and the sheer number of unusual sightings and happenings around the mall. Yeah, I would say it's a little off. It's part of what drew me here.

Accepting my silence as an answer, Poe continues. "There's a split in reality here. Runs the length of the mall, actually. It makes it easy for all sorts to slip through, including us."

"What are you?"

"I'm far more than you can comprehend. For now, let's make this easy and say I'm an Incubus. I—we—feed on desire and need. The more intense the better. Only strong passion can summon us to this plane, and even then, we still have the process of hunting amongst the dull and uninspired sheep to find a mind that contains the kind of true desire that calls to us."

"Poor babies."

"Indeed; that's what I thought. Poor babies, all of us." He nods approvingly, missing my sarcasm in his zeal for storytelling. "Sure, the break gives monsters like us opportunity and access, but what good is an escape if we have to hunt so hard for receptive minds to feed on?"

Poe rolls his chair closer. "To find open..." He wedges a knee between mine, and buttery leather kisses my ankle as his booted foot kicks my leg wide. "...hearts to accept us. Others hunted in the streets, but I figured, why work hard when we could work smart? So, I built a honeypot and baited it with the sweetest nectar." He strokes one talon up the inside of my thigh. "I embraced this modern place and found a way to have our meals come to us. It's a non-stop smorgasbord of the kinkiest, horniest, dirtiest fantasies served up to us every night, all night long. Partners who are desperate to come back again and again because it's only here their true desires can come true and be committed to celluloid to watch again and again whenever they want."

Poe's saturated image shimmers and distorts in time with the static of the screen behind him. His slutty pirate crop top and corset melt into gray, pinstripe pants, the knifepoint edge of his crisp white, popped collar embroidered with a tiny crocodile with blood-soaked fangs. Sexy bluebeard is gone, and in his place, a coke-eyed Gordon Gecko slouches forward and throws a wink at me. "It's all about the ABCs, sweetling: Always Be Coming."

He claps and leans back, looking entirely too pleased with himself, white hair practically crackling with excitement, the restless hunger of a predator about to strike dancing in his eyes. "But first, before we get to the coming, we mustn't let Veronica down. Time for your audition, Starling. I need to see what I'm working with before we can truly begin our dance."

I start to struggle in earnest again, rocking back and forth. The brass fasteners holding my seat to the floor groan as I throw my weight around, but it doesn't stop Poe from eating up the space between us.

"How can I audition like this? Want me to whistle Dixie? Do a seated tap dance for your viewing pleasure?" I bat my lashes at my captor; the second he cuts these film stripes, I'm introducing his balls to my foot.

"Whistling, hm? No." Sharp talons skate across the thin skin of my throat, one claw circling the jumping pulse at the base. My eyelids flutter as Poe's hand burns a collar around my neck, forcing my face to tilt up to where his mouth is just a hair's breadth away from mine. "But I do want you to pucker those pretty lips together," he adjusts his grip higher, catching my chin in his palm as sharp talons dig into my cheeks, "so I can blow."

Silky trails of pitch-black smoke billow out of Poe's mouth and into mine, sliding an icy-hot path down my throat before settling in my belly. Sweet, hazy disorientation immediately sets in.

"I knew you would take me so sweetly. Now, swallow

every last bit, Seren, and we can begin." What had been a thin stream of smoke becomes a fat column as Poe dissolves into the black fog. My jaw aches as he slithers inside me, tendrils of him twisting and writhing down my throat, invading every hidden part until I can't tell what is him and what is me.

The exertion of consuming Poe is overwhelming. My eyelids droop, and I struggle to keep them open as I slump back into the pillowy softness of the seat. I register that the lights are dimming, and the sound system lurches into action as a distorted jingle starts up. Through slitted eyes, I watch as a trio of stoned looking cartoon popcorn, fountain soda, and pack of Red Vines smile with vacant eyes, shuffling and jiving across the screen while singing a warning that our feature presentation is about to start. They dissolve into the glitching static, replaced by the words "Let's Play" growing larger and larger on the screen.

The theater spins, turning into a carousel of lights and sounds. Just when I think I'll be sick, it all stops, and I'm tipped forward into the vortex of static devouring the screen.

Then, I'm gone.

Caged wiring crisscrosses the yellowed, dirty window. Through the decades of grim coating the glass, I can make out the view I saw every day for most of my childhood. A slice of Brooklyn's overgrown, red brick jungle sprawls out and up, the muted roar of buses and taxis battling it out below soothing white noise. Taken aback at seeing the wrong coast staring back at me, it takes a second to realize that I'm standing up. I'm free.

I cautiously turn around, only to find that I'm alone and not unaware of where I am. The cracked webbing of linoleum, the ancient metal coffee service gathering dust in a cart by the door, the stack of chairs just waiting for a rowdy group of CCD teens to come in and set them up—that means the thing that haunts my dreams more than I care to think about, the anachronistic treasure our lead priest was so smug about landing from a condemned Cathedral in Queens, sits behind me. The ornate confessional booth.

It's almost laughable how out of place it looks now that I'm older, but back when I spent most of my afternoons on my knees inside it, the last thing I wanted to do was laugh.

"Seren, Seren." I scream and whip around to find Poe, now dressed in a blue-jay colored habit and neat nun's dress, curiously examining the old rectory room. "I have to say, I didn't expect a basic priest and parishioner scene to be what your mind conjured up. The bones of a good fantasy are here, but you're holding back." Blinking his bottom set of eyes open, he examines me. "You took all of me, Starling, and you're still able to resist my poking around in your mind." He nods to himself. "You know what you need? A costume change to get in the mood."

I look down and find I'm back in my faux-priest get up from earlier.

"No more of that outfit. Strike it, reverse it. You can't submit to me if you're wearing that, or if we're out here. Now, how does it go? Forgive me, Daddy, for I have sinned." With a wicked grin, he snaps two claws together, and I'm plunged into the velvet darkness of my teens. There's no light, but I don't need it to feel the barely-there nightgown.

He truly *is* inside my mind. Deeper than anyone else has ever been, apparently, because I've never shared this place with anyone, not even Janie. This was my secret place, where I was broken and then born again.

It's funny how absolute darkness isn't actually pitch black. Used to being surrounded by it, I widen my eyes and wait. This is the kind of absolute dark that's so encompassing, you start to imagine acid trip-worthy strobes color if you're patient enough. I've been chasing this type of dark since I left Saint Mary's School for Wayward Girls years ago, but I've never been able to find it anywhere else.

Slowly but surely, pulses of purples and blue emerge from the darkness. The absence of a floor or ceiling makes me feel weightless, like I'm Alice, endlessly falling down the rabbit hole.

"Now, tell me, child: why do all the paths in your dreams lead back here? What is it about this place that makes it so special? Confess, and you will be rewarded." Poe's sonorous voice wraps around me from all sides, and I swear I catch a glimpse of crimson pupils among the shifting blacks and blue shadows.

So used to being stripped bare and being brutally honest in this space, the words flow out of me without hesitation.

"I was a difficult teen. Too loud, too much, too womanly when I was too young." *An upstart tart*, Mother Constance's voice echoes off the sides of my invisible cage. "There was a sister who was determined to break me. She knew the only thing I feared was the dark, so that's how my confessions started." The pulsing swirls of purple start to solidify into gloved hands, the thick fingers steepling together to form eyes and mouths until I'm surrounded by makeshift faces. Other hands reach out from the darkness and grasp my arms and ankles in a firm grip, anchoring me in place. A stray hand ghosts up the curve of my ass and settles there.

"What did she do?" the finger-mouths ask in unison.

"She knew the reason why this confessional booth was stored here instead of on display in the main nave. The door to the parishioner side jammed, locking whoever was inside in until someone could let them out. So, she boarded up the partition and would drag me in here every day after classes to reflect on how I was not the center of the universe. I was small and inconsequential, and I should think on how I could better shrink myself to be what the world expected of me, which was nothing."

"But that's not what you did, is it?" The finger-faces frown down at me, and more stray hands appear to tug off my nightgown, the cool air my only cover.

"Nope. I spent the first few times having panic attacks, but eventually, I distracted myself with a little game. I spent hours coming up with the wildest, most sacrilegious fantasies to get off to, and I'd see how many times I could come before Connie dragged me back out. A particular favorite was Father Andrew, the hot young priest, deflowering me during midnight mass while she watched."

Huh, maybe *that's* where my vampire orgy scene came from.

Pleased with my answer, the hands lift me higher and tilt me forward, throwing me off balance. Strong, invisible arms pull my legs apart as nimble fingers spread the lips of my cunt wide, a thick finger pressing in, stroking in and out, making a mess out of me. The sensations of so many hands, exploring, teasing, slipping into my mouth, my ass, plucking my nipples to the point of pain, drives me out of my mind with need. This is better than anything I imagined back then. Being used by an invisible, godlike force that I couldn't stop even if I wanted to is everything I didn't know I could ask for, but it's something I know I'll crave from now on.

Poe's face emerges in front of my own. A hand—his hand —collars my throat, trapping a groan and forcing me to swallow it back down.

"I knew we would be a match made in hell." Poe emerges from the darkness, back to his creature self now, but dressed in my priest's outfit. As he places an affectionate hand on my head, the even whiteness of his sharp smile is alive with delight.

"Let's drop deeper."

All my anchors disappear, and my stomach swoops up as I freefall down.

Poe's ivory grin is the last thing I see as I tumble into the darkness.

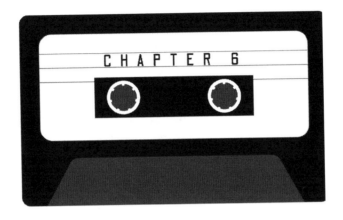

CHAPTER 6

I'm in the woods.

From a nearby cabin, Duran Duran's *Girls on Film* sounds, mixed with whoops of a party reaching its peak. The chorus of bullfrogs and crickets hiding in the forest circling the lake try to compete, but they're drowned out by the rhythmic chants of "kegger, kegger."

The full moon hangs in the night sky, and I'm.... on a wooden porch with a bunch of hot camp counselors? Tiny, tight orange shorts with white piping cover everyone's impossibly tight asses, and mulleted dudes and feathered-haired girls alike rock crop tops with the words "Camp Titicaca 1979" across the chest, with socks that stretch to their knees.

What in the teen-coming-of-age-movie nonsense is this?

Everywhere I look, it's a mess of beer bottles and groping, half-naked bodies. A breeze brushes against my stomach and the bottom of my butt cheeks.

Oh, jokes on me, I'm wearing this ridiculous outfit too. I twist and try to catch my reflection in the glass window. These shorts are doing things for my ass.

"Oh cool, you made it." A lean arm circles my waist and spins me around, gluing me to a hard body. The golden surfer boy I saw with Ronnie earlier tonight grins down at me.

"I was worried your kids wouldn't go down easy and you'd miss this rager."

"My kids?"

"Your cabin? The cabin 44 girls? They drank the punch at dinner, right? Cody laced it with enough NyQuil to put down an elephant."

I stare at all the other counselors in horror. A bonfire rages out of control down in the front yard as a group of guys streak past to go skinny dipping. Who is in charge of licensing this place?

"Uh, yeah. My kids are asleep, but I should probably get back to make sure none of them wake up and come looking for me." I shuffle back and try to break Surfer Dude's hold.

"Nah, you're good." Cocky and confident may do it for me when it comes from Poe, but on this jerk, it's just obnoxious. "I was thinking, after all that eye-fucking we've been doing all summer across the arts and crafts table, I could take you down to the Stabbin' Cabin tonight." The douche thrusts his hips against mine, grinding himself into me, leaving no doubt as to what kind of *stabbin'* goes down there.

"Who signed off on that name for that place? Because I want a word."

"See, this is why I like you, Serena. You're so funny."

"Seren," I automatically correct.

He frowns and then shakes off the correction like the golden retriever he is. "Babe, c'mon. Loosen up." Wine cooler and weak beer-laced breath hits me as Surfer Dude leans in open mouthed. I duck to the side and stomp on his foot, but unfortunately, I'm wearing tennis shoes and not my Docs. Still, his squeal of pain is satisfying as he releases me.

"Serena, what the fuck? Why are you being such a bitch?" Surfer Dude stalks away from me and snaps his fingers at the reedy guy manning the keg. "Cody, brah, beer me. I'm going to see what Brittney is doing. She's someone who knows how to have a good time."

"Whatever, dude. Enjoy peaking at nineteen," I mumble as I escape off the porch to put distance between myself and the party.

I follow the lip of the lake, my path illuminated by tiki torches. The burning kerosene mixes with the funk of the algae coating the surface. Whose fantasy is this? It sure isn't mine.

I kick a rock and mutter about stupid hot demons under my breath. I passed the audition, and he drops me into a lame-ass party?

Rude.

The farther I walk, the more my tiny shorts ride up until, with every step, the crotch grinds against my clit, still swollen and needy from all the teasing Poe did in the confessional booth. The ache grows and grows until I can't take it anymore.

I step off the path and lean against one of the towering oaks at the edge of the forest. Not wasting any time, I look out at the rippling surface of the lake and trace a path along the ruched band of my shorts before dipping my fingers inside the slick mess between my thighs. Bracing one foot on the ground, I bend my knee and plant the other against the rough trunk behind me, widening my legs so I can dip two fingers inside my pussy. I coat them with my dripping arousal and then swirl a path around my clit.

I close my eyes and conjure up Poe in the movie theater, blocking out everything, forcing his essences inside of me, stuffing me full of him. I imagine that instead of smoke, it's his cock I'm choking on. Saliva pools in my mouth, as if he's already pressing against the back of my throat.

Snap.

I scramble away from the tree and peer into the evening gloom.

"Hello?" There's a flash of white out of the corner of my eye deeper into the forest, followed by some childish giggles. Surfer Dude's comment about the sleepy punch comes back to me. Maybe some of these kids decided they weren't thirsty.

I walk a few feet deeper into the forest, and the undergrowth soaks my socks with dew in seconds. Did the kids wake up and decide to have fun while the counselors got wasted?

Wait, why do I care? None of this is real.

None of this is real!

"Oh, you asshole. This. *This* is your fantasy?" I call out into the night air.

I double over laughing until my ribs ache. Poe is a lot of things, but being this square with his fantasies is not what I expected. "Is all of this because you're still mad I chose Suspira instead of Sleepaway Camp as movie of the month? So now you have me playing the role of the slutty camp counselor wandering around in the dark, fingers in my pants, flicking my clit, when I should be finding the nearest cabin and locking the door?"

"That's exactly what you'd do if you knew what I'm about to do to you." Warm breath skates down the side of my neck, accompanied by a slicing, fiery line of pain down my forearm.

I gasp and stumble backwards, tripping over a root and landing on my ass. Now covered in mud and leaves, I scuttle backwards in an ungainly crabwalk, away from my attacker, but there's no one there. The leaves on the top of the trees rustle in the wind, but I'm all alone.

My new injury is here, though. Blood flows from newly-opened skin, the moonlight rendering the red river black as it drips from the tips of my fingers. I slap a hand over the wound to slow the bleeding. The cut doesn't feel deep, but in the low light, I'm flying blind. Swaying, I get up and run. Light-headed, from blood loss or adrenaline, I'm not sure, I miss the turn that would lead me back to the well-lit trail. I'm on a less maintained path, kicking up rocks that slice my shins with each stride.

This isn't real, but it is.

It's a game, but is it?

How far does this slasher fantasy go with Poe? I thought I knew the game being played. Even now, huffs of nervous laughter puff out of me. Exhilaration like I've only felt once before hums through my veins. I half want to get caught to see what he gives me. Pain? Pleasure? Both? Still, my throbbing arm says I'm a fool to think I'll escape the fate of every other black girl in a horror movie. Maybe there's no safety net here. I'm playing tag, but Poe could be setting the stage for a snuff film, and I'm just the dumb bunny whose neck will be snapped before the first act is over.

I run faster. I don't even know if Poe is following me. The tip of his knife whispers down my spine, but whenever I twist back, no one is there. Caught between horny and scared, I don't see the fallen branch until it's too late. I trip over it and skin my knees, landing hard on my shoulder.

My top is caked in mud, soaked through with puddle water, one side of my shorts ripped almost to the band on my hip. Something rustles in the leaves nearby, and I spring up before I freeze. Twenty feet ahead, a dark cabin sits in the middle of a clearing.

The Stabbin' Cabin!

I don't wait to see if the Poe who jumps out of the bushes is friend or foe. I sprint for the cabin, or at least, I try. My knees scream for me to slow down, but this time, I know Poe is closing in. I can see the shadow of his form rising up behind me, a foot-long knife raised over my head.

I hobble up the stairs and throw myself against the door. I grope and find the doorknob, but I'm slammed up against the wood before I can open it.

"Never caught a shooting star before. I wonder what my prize will be." Poe spins me around to face him, fangs bared.

On instinct, the animal in me rises up to meet the predator. I slam my forehead against the bridge of his nose, and the sick crunch of crumbling bone giving way makes me gag.

"What a gorgeous, murderous little beastie you are." Poe looks downright proud at my attack as he flicks his tongue out and tastes the bloody mess I've made of his face.

Poe's split second of distraction is all I need. I push the door open and duck inside. The echo of Poe's surprised laughter slips the crack of the door as I slam it shut. I turn around to find a weapon or a hiding place, but —

I'm back at Creepy Court.

It's a muted version of Creepy Court, where all its warm colors have been leached away, leaving behind an eerie ghost town.

The cabin door rattles.

"Seren, Seren," Poe sings. "The longer you fight, the harder I get. So please, darling, make me work for it. I can't wait to catch you and tear you apart."

I take off down the mall corridor. I don't have a plan. I'm

not sure how to get off this ride or if I even want to, but I know I'm not ready to be caught yet. A flash of blonde hair and fur scurries past, a bony shoulder knocking into me.

Rat lady?

I limp as quickly as I can, searching for a hiding place. The mall isn't as empty as it first seemed, but it's definitely stranger than I left it. Good Char still has a line twenty deep, but instead of the usual high school meatheads, it's populated by werewolves, vampires, and men with impossibly long arms and legs. At its head, behind the grill, a demon is turning hot dogs. He looks up at me with a face so monstrous, I'll be seeing it every time I close my eyes for years to come.

I duck my head to evade detection, but the monster falls silent and tracks my path as I hurry by. Horniness long gone, I speed into Frillard's. The box store appears to be truly abandoned: half the lights are blown out, and the remaining ones flicker on and off, the circular racks graveyards of droopy dress and wire hangers.

Starlight, star bright, your master is missing you tonight.

I wish I may, I wish I might, have the pleasure of punishing you tonight.

Poe's off-key tune whistles out, making my heart skip a beat.

Out of time, I dive under one of the clothing racks by the door and climb up on the center platform so he can't see my feet. I'll be able to see him enter from this hiding spot, and once he's deep enough into the store, I can make a break for it.

I hold my breath until my lungs ache, scared that any disturbance in the air will give me away. Poe's combat boots stomp past a few minutes later, and I force myself not to move for what feels like an eternity but is probably closer to fifteen minutes. The last sounds I hear are the slap of his soles down by the escalator.

That's good enough. Back to an almost childish state of glee, I burst out of the rack, choosing speed over stealth... and immediately find myself clotheslined by a trench-coated arm.

With a low "oof," I fall flat on my back, watching as a trio of gas masks float above me. Slowly, they come into focus as one. Poe tugs up the mask just high enough to expose a filthy smirk, flecks of dried blood still crusting his upper lip.

"Hiya, honey. Time to go home."

Battered, bruised, and wondering if I can get a concussion in an alternate reality, I don't protest as he swings me up over his shoulder.

"Time for the big show, Star."

I hiss when he lands a sharp smack to my ass and chases the sting by biting the fleshy meat of my cheek, where I can still feel the brand of his hand.

We don't go far. He probably takes only a hundred steps before he places me back on the ground like I'm precious and not someone he spent the last hour terrorizing. I blink up to a tangle of pink and blue gauze I'd recognize anywhere: we're in Red Light's display window. The Suspiria scene is gone, and in its place is a makeshift graveyard.

I flop my head to the side and see we've collected a silent audience of ghouls and beasties. The eyes gleam with anticipation. The scene is set, and the curtain is about to rise.

"Eyes on me, Star." Poe's deep command hijacks my nervous system, and I automatically look up into the blackened goggles that make up the top of his mask.

It makes my face ache, but I smile up at him. "'Fraid I'm going to scratch your eyes out?"

"Nothing would give me more pleasure than if you did. Pain from you is a sweet kiss to a monster like me." He tugs the mask all the way off, and the rough motion sets his nose to bleeding again.

"See, this?" Droplets of blood drip from the tip of his nose into my parted mouth as he kisses his sweaty forehead to mine. "This is how I knew we would be a match made in hell. You get it."

"I get what?" I ask softly, the question a puff of air from my mouth into his.

He taps my head and then his. "In here, you understand love is violence. You revel in its destruction and the primal fear it inspires as much as I do."

He does a push-up and stares down at me. "You laugh, but those camp counselors are what your life will be like if you leave me for Vegas."

I stiffen beneath him; he's dragging in reality where it doesn't belong.

"You've spent forever running, running, running, and for what? The secrets you crave aren't going to come from the Codys of the world." He rises to his knees and whips off his belt. With a single, swift motion, he manages to loop the leather strap in a figure eight around my wrists before hooking them above my head.

I'm the sacrificial lamb, and he, my butcher.

"You need someone to push you so you can see yourself as I see you." Knife in hand again, Poe straddles my hips, trapping my thighs between his. In two, quick swipes, he slices open my tattered shorts and tosses them away.

"You need the focus of a killer." He trails the knife up and up and up, a thin red line blossoming from the split of my pussy through the valley of my breasts. The soft pad of his tongue follows, licking up his handiwork. The shallow cut stings, but my nipples go hard at the bite of pain combined with the most tender of care.

Crouching back down, he spreads my legs wide and makes a pillow on my thigh. Two ghouls are pressed against the window, torn nails clawing at the partition, trying to break through the glass. From this angle, the audience of monsters can see all of me, but only Poe can touch.

"You run. I chase." Silky hair tickles my pussy as Poe presses a kiss against the artery that's hiding just below.

"You bleed. I feed." His fangs sink into my thigh. Sealing his lips around the wound, Poe sucks until blood flows, pooling with my arousal.

Poe drinks deep of the cocktail he made, making sure that

with each lap, his tongue drags and swirls around my clit. I moan, desperate for release after being brought to the edge so many times just to be yanked back.

As if sensing my thoughts, Poe pulls back, licking his lips clean, and I cry out in frustration.

"The only chalice I want to drink from, from now until eternity." His chin glistens in the soft light of the window.

I whimper, and feel sorry for myself and my poor, needy body as he pulls me up, arranging me like his personal mannequin until I'm pressed face first against the glass, smearing our combined arousal all over the window. Poe presses in behind me, covering me from head to toe. He leans in and bites two talons off his fingers as his other calloused hand covers my mouth.

He works his newly declawed fingers between my legs, plunging them roughly into my pussy, fingerfucking me hard and rough, the sound of how wet I am a testament to the constant strokes against my g-spot.

The fingers disappear, and his cock slides in, splitting my lips apart, teasing my poor, battered clit until I'm clawing at the window, hips bucking backwards with no shame, tears and sweat and salvia painting a picture of my desperation to just be fucking filled, much to the amusement of the shifters and demons watching.

Then, in one, vicious stroke, Poe slams up and in. <y pussy, done with his shit, clamps down around the thick cock in a stranglehold, afraid the asshole is going to try to stop before we're done with him.

"Naughty star. You're not the master here."

Breaking my hold on him, Poe's cock swells larger, and it feels like it splits in two. He's officially everywhere all at once, and I short circuit.

Cunt full, head empty.

Legs shaking and supported only by Poe's weight pinning me to the glass like a butterfly, my eyes roll back in my head, and I'm gone.

CHAPTER 7

"Wakey-wakey, sleepyhead." Eyes closed, I wrinkle my nose as droplets of water hit my face. I slip down and sputter when bubbles and water go up my nose. I sit up, and water sloshes over the lip of the tub. "This is what I get for leaving you unattended for ten minutes."

I blink up at Poe. He wipes a fluffy hand towel down the front of the cashmere sweater I bought him for Christmas. "Oh no! I'm so sorry, baby. Here, let me." Slick with bubbles, I slip and slide as I try to gain some traction and stand-up.

"Nope. You know the drill. In here, you move when-"

"You move me." I sit back and hug my knees to my chest, propping my chin on top with a grin. "It's a hard life, having you as a master."

Strong arms slip under my armpits and help me stand. I

glow under Poe's indulgent gaze, watching him watch me as he thoroughly dries every inch of exposed skin before lifting me out of the tub and settling me on the vanity counter.

"Did I set the heat high enough?"

"You know you did. Otherwise, I would be wrapped up in all the bathrobes," I tease.

"Can't have that happen. I love this view." I gasp as he tweaks a pearled nipple. The surprise pinch fades from memory as he lotions up his hands and palms my breasts, kneading them until I lock my legs around him.

"How'd I get so lucky to get a guy like you?"

"A guy like me?"

"Not every man is secure enough in himself to let me decorate our bathroom to look like a pink mermaid's grotto."

"You love pink," he says, as if that explains everything.

"I do love pink." I smile and rub my nose against his.

"And I love your pink. In fact, I want a taste of it right now." Then there's the firm pressure of his mouth against mine, his tongue slipping between my lips, and I get lost in his kiss.

"You keep falling asleep on me, sweetheart, I'm going to start to develop a complex."

"Wha-?" I jerk up and frown at the Persian carpet beneath me. "Where am I?"

"Uh, your studio, you weirdo." Shirtless, Poe leans against the door jam. The strong planes of his muscles are glowing a soft gold under the lamplight as he steps into the room. "Are you ready for me?"

"Ready for you?" I echo. Bookcases of black VHS tapes line the wall beside Poe on one side, and a projector dominates the opposite corner.

"I know they said to expect you to be tired and forgetful, but I didn't think it would start this early." He holds his hand out to mine. I automatically take it, and he hauls me up.

"Here, I'll help you get set up, and then you can put me where you want me." He moves over to the projector and starts fiddling with it, leaving me dazed and confused. This room feels like me. It has my wall of Polaroids of all our friends and the secrets they shared with me scrawled on the back, but I don't feel quite right in this space.

I wander over to the wall of tapes and run my finger down their sides, reading their names.

"Bea bangs a president and other old people sex stories."

"Rat Lady is real, and I served her coffee."

The tapes go on like this until I see a pair of names that make me stop. This next batch of tapes stand out from the rest.

Poe and Star Slasher Scene.

Poe and Star Confessional Booth Scene.

Poe and Star Doctor's Office Scene.

Each title strikes a chord, but I don't know why.

Poe comes up behind me. "Oh, is it going to be that type of night?" I find myself wrapped up in a hug from behind. "I thought I was here for art purposes, Mrs. Star, not one of your smutty films."

"Oh, is your hard-on your way of protesting?"

"You know it." Poe presses a kiss to the top of my head. "Come on, I got the tape rolling."

The Persian carpet is now awash in undulating blue light. Poe stretches out across the rug, his golden body now submerged under translucent waves. "Last time, you had me this way; want me here again?"

"Uh, yeah." On autopilot, I grab a marker from the table. The sense of having done this before is strong. I straddle Poe, settling on top of his semi-hard bulge, rocking back and forth for a bit, enjoying his groans of pleasurable frustration.

"Enough! I'll walk!"

"Okay, okay." I uncap the pen.

"Wait. What about the tape? Here." Poe reaches to the side and hits play on two portable stereos. From one set of speakers, Rilke's poem *I Go To The Sea* starts to play. From the other, Galaxie 500's *Tugboat* drifts out.

The feeling of being on autopilot comes back, and I settle back on top of Poe, covering him in Rilke lines and Tugboat lyrics.

Then, I stand up and grab my camera.

Drowsy, content, and drowned in blue, Poe is the most beautiful creature I've ever seen.

"I like you in navy." I smile softly at him and snap his picture.

"I like *you* in navy." He rolls up and pulls me down beneath the imaginary sea. Smoothing my hair away from my face, he looks at me with intense concentration.

"What is it?"

"I could spend a millennium filling up tapes of you, and it wouldn't be enough." Merlot eyes bore into me.

A headache starts to build behind my eyes, and I wiggle out from under him. "What do you mean?" The feeling of wrongness comes back tenfold. The TV besides us crackles to life, snowy black and gray pixels dancing across the screen.

Poe shakes his head. "Don't worry about it. I'm not feeling myself tonight." He blinks, and chestnut eyes stare back at me, merlot gone. Was it ever there to begin with?

"Right, I get that feeling."

"Come on, time for bed. Let's get you comfortable. You're sleeping for two now."

Wait, what? I look down at my stomach, which I could swear was flat just moments ago. Now, it swells out, filling the bottom of my dress with a small bump.

"No."

"What's that dear?"

"No, this is wrong. This isn't right. I'm not pregnant. We aren't... We aren't this." I pace around the room, the static from the TV rising to a dull roar.

I whirl around, bits and pieces of the night coming back to me. "This is another of your fantasies, but I don't want to play anymore. Let me out, let me out, let me out." I slam my palms against his chest over and over again. "Take off that face and let me go." My lungs tighten, and I can't suck in enough air.

"Seren, breathe!" Navy talons out placatingly, Monstrous Poe's two sets of eyes are resigned. "We can leave here, but you need to know something before I let you go."

I shake my head. I don't want to hear it. I won't believe it, whatever he says.

His hands grip me tightly as he says, "This is your deepest desire, not mine."

CHAPTER 8

Magic *does* make things less awkward.

Like when you're confronted with the knowledge that your deepest, sexiest desire is a bougie apartment on the Upper East Side where you're an art professor at NYU and make smutty films with your super-hot husband on the weekends. Oh, and you're having a baby with him.

Sister Constance is laughing her ass off somewhere.

Right. Magic.

Magic means there are no awkward morning afters. Just poof, you wake up in front of Hock It to Me with a silver marker in one hand and ten grand in unmarked bills in a plastic A&P grocery bag.

Wham, bam, thank you, monster boss?

Unable to process what last night was or what it meant, I decide not to try. Instead, I stride into Drake's and slap his marker on the counter.

"Pony up, lizard breath."

"The little peacock outed me, huh?" Drake lets out a wheezing chuckle. Seemingly unbothered by the revelation of his secret, the dragon unlocks the case behind him and piles my stuff on the counter.

"Guess you know who gave you this now?" With no small amount of reluctance, Drake removes the delicate bracelet and surrenders it back to my care. I stare down at it, trying not to choke on the pang of longing in my heart. Staring at one merlot opal leaves me longing for the merlot eyes of another.

"I have my theories," I respond.

"I bet you do."

Ignoring the dragon's scrutiny, I start to scoop my life off the counter and into my backpack.

"Oh, hey. Don't forget this." Drakes drops a black VHS case onto the counter.

"That's not mine," I say slowly.

"No, it's the lady's who brought the rest of the lot in. She said she needed the money more than she needed the tape. Said she already knew what was on it, and it told her what she needed to do." Drake shrugs. "It's part of the lot. You gave me the marker, so it's yours now."

Something is wrong here. Why did Janie have a VIP video from Red Light? What was on it that sparked her desire to leave? A rush of anger at my friend boils over. All that shit about Mrs. Butter-Tits was a lie.

leave? A rush of anger at my friend boils over. All that shit about Mrs. Butter-Tits was a lie.

She didn't blow up my life for me; she blew it up as part of a cash grab to go follow whatever Poe put on this tape.

"Oh, I know that look. If I could close the store down, I would love to watch you tear him a new one, Sweet Cheeks. I'll have to get Ronnie to give me the play-by-play at the next gin rummy game." He chortles to himself as I storm out of the shop, fingers pointing a V between my eyes and the security camera.

Watch out, boss. I'm coming for you.

I storm straight through the front room and into the back, straight up to Poe. "You caused all of this!"

"This is progressing nicely!" Ronnie looks delighted. "I'll leave you to it."

"Hello, Seren. I was not expecting you back here." Poe drums out an agitated beat against the concrete surface of his desk.

"Oh, I bet you weren't." I circle around the desk and crowd up right next to him, ignoring that even sitting down, Incubus Poe dwarfs me.

Docs, do your thing.

"If this is going to work, you need to start sharing and stop manipulating."

I snag my camera from behind me and snap Poe's picture. Without even looking at it, I know I'm going to carry it with me everywhere. I doubt I'll ever catch this mix of weariness giving away to startled hope on his impeccable face ever again.

"My missing memories of the night we met, this cuff, Janie's tape, her taking off, and I'm sure a million other little machinations, they all lead back to you. I can't stick around and play with someone long term if they can't be honest with me."

"Say it again, but slower." The rumbled command sends a fun shiver down my back.

"Which part? That I'm going to stick around and keep the lights on in this place, or that I want to play with you some more?"

"Why would you do that? You just said that I've been manipulating you this entire time to keep you with me." He scowls down at me like I've failed a remedial puzzle.

"Bad decisions make good stories." I climb into his lap, kicking my boots against his rock-hard calves. "A wise neon pornshop sign once told me that. Besides, If I run-"

"I'll chase." He growls into the side of my neck, biting the tendon there for emphasis.

"So, I suss out all your secrets from here. I'm like the sea, Bossman. I'll wear you down eventually."

"I'm sure you will, Star."

THE BEGINNING

When I heard her tell the opening band her name as she asked them overly familiar questions and snapped their photo, I had to laugh.

Seren.

Meaning star.

Of course, with a name like that, she would be the one to guide me through the inky abyss separating her world from mine.

Only a star with an aura that bright, that insatiable, could sing a siren song to my own hunger and draw me to this loud, garish plane.

"She's a tasty little powerhouse, isn't she?" Draconis watches my star spin and twirl on her chunky-heeled boots around the bonfire in time with the driving beat of the band.

"Avert your eyes, Dragon. She is not for your horde."

"Oh, it's like that is it?"

Yes, it is like that, but not for the reason my ancient friend thinks. He sees my star and sees an anchor to this plane, a crown jewel for his horde.

She is so much more than that.

I apparate near her and snap the neck of a Nightmare creeping too close to her bright light. I toss their limp body into the fire. I will play every role for her. Her protector, her nightmare, her jailer, her assassin, her thief. I'll take her screams, swallow her joy. I want every filthy fucked up inch of her beautiful mind under my care.

No one else will ever have her.

Seren.

My Star.

ABOUT THE AUTHOR

Sabrina loves writing characters who find strength in softness, prefers monsters to men, and has never said no to more world-building. When she's not yelling at her laptop, Sabrina can be found wandering around New England, pushing book recommendations onto people who didn't ask for them.

She loves connecting with readers!
Stay in touch with her in any of these places:
https://sabrinadayauthor.carrd.co

ALSO BY SABRINA DAY

The Hidden Omegas

A Hallow Bargain: A Hidden Omegas standalone prequel

Fleeing Fate: Hidden Omegas Book 1

Fate Found: Hidden Omegas Book 2

THE MONSTER OF DARKSPELL COMICS

SJ SANDERS

BE KIND
AND READ

Welcome to Dark Spell Comics where worlds come alive. Or at least Pashar does his best. As a night-terror demon on sabbatical, he's enjoying his vacation in the human world tending to his little corner of Creepy Court Mall, stuffing his face with hotdogs from The Good Char and listening to the newest rock release while he sees to enjoying his work.

Everyone finds the nightmare they are secretly searching for... even if they are a human who breaks into hops afterhours. But this human is a special treat who intrigues him like no other, and one he especially wants to savor. Perhaps even for the rest of time.

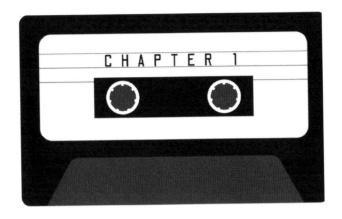

CHAPTER 1

PASHAR

I lean against the counter as I watch the demon industriously working on the order ahead of mine. The humans are all smiles and waiting eagerly, practically slobbering all over themselves, as they make appreciative sounds at the smell of the meat cooking. My lips quirk with amusement as their order is turned over to them. They immediately dig in, looking for all the world as if they are having the best meal of their life. I shake my head as I watch them go and glance over at the lumbering male behind me.

No Cassanova in his true form, he's an ugly bastard as a human as far as I'm concerned.

"You do realize that's sick, don't you?"

He smirks as he wipes down the counter with a swipe of his rag before starting my order. "It's not like they know where it's coming from. And why waste good meat?"

I snicker and he gives me an impatient look when I don't move away from his counter. He may get a kick out of feeding humans bits and pieces of those being tortured in the pit, but he sure does get a pike up his ass when it comes to serving a fellow demon.

"What will it be?" he grumbles, slapping his rag on the counter to glare at me.

My smile stretches wide, and I know he can see behind the illusion to my oily dark purple scales, the hint of my corethi slithering over me, and the monstrously large sharp teeth grinning at him. Nightmare demons are just built special that way. Even other demons prefer not to look too close at what goes bump in the darkest parts of various demonic realms.

"Three to go. Extra crispy and extra mustard. Hold the red crap," I instruct, delighting in watching the other demon curdle resentfully beneath the yoke of his punishment.

Unlike Dzik, I'm not on Earth for punishment. I'm on vacation—a lengthy one in reward for my exceptional services. Or to remove competition, but when it comes right down to it, I don't really care. I'm able to come and go as I please through the portal connecting my shop to my dwelling in the nightmare realm of the infernal abodes, and running the comic book store gives me an outlet for my creativity while allowing me to enjoy the chaos that is humanity.

As far as vacations go, I'm having a great time. I also have to congratulate myself on my timely vacation. The eighties has it all. Beyond the nicotine soaking into everything and the drugs that seemed soaked into the skin of many adult humans that pass through, there is a blatantly energizing glamor to everything that sparkles like hellfire. And there is rock and roll.

It is a hell of a lot more entertaining than my last vacation in 1348. What was supposed to be a leisurely vacation with an idea to torment some of the rank clergy and local populace in Florence, Italy while enjoying fine meals and a good Tuscan wine ended up being dead in the water—quite literally. The Black Death probably was a good time for some demons, but everyone was a little too dead or dying to be much fun. I did spend most of it drunk on said wine so I suppose there was a kind of fun in that.

I consider the casks I still had from all of those I smuggled back to my den and smirk. The landholders had not lasted too long after they let their servants die and rot in the fields but first, I was quite happy to liberate them of their stock while they ineffectually cursed me in a nightmare-fueled state, their decaying bodies covered in lesions. Normally I don't send nightmares to those suffering or dying but I made a special exception for them, leaving just enough lucidity for them to watch as I stripped them of their wealth.

I scratch my jaw thoughtfully. Come to think of it, I have some nice jewels as a take-home gift for myself from that vacation as well. The wine, however, was the gift that keeps giving. I found so much of it stored at the winery due to ports closing down that I had to construct an entire basement level beneath the lower levels of my home just to fit them all. At my current rate of drinking, I suspect it will take a few more centuries before I get through them all. Unless I find someone to share my life and wine with.

I snort in amusement as my gaze follows Dzik as he puts my order together. There is little chance of mating. It is rare for my kind to mate at all since we are terribly territorial. The only thing a nightmare demon enjoys sharing is...well... nightmares.

Dzik squints at me as he slaps my order on the counter in front me. My grin simply widens as I toss the required paper bills on the counter beside my to-go bag and pick up my order. His upper lip curls in a sneer as he snatched the money up and puts it in the till before shutting the drawer a little too forcefully. I hear it clang loudly as I walk away. Snickering to myself I remove a corndog and take a healthy bite, my eyes landing on a couple of pimply faced boys loitering around the food court.

A maniacal cackle escapes me before I think better of it and two pairs of eyes snap to me warily.

"Relax boys," I soothe as I take another huge bite of my corndog. "How would you like to make a couple bucks?"

As it turns out, even the wariest youngling will react

greedily when coin—or in this case, cash—is offered. I relay my instructions and grin with wicked glee as they scamper toward The Good Char, their eyes alight with mischief.

Let's see how that pain in the ass demon likes that. He would have to hope for a cold day in hell to provide them their icy treats with hellfire fueling his grill. Another cackle leaves me as I head toward my shop. Because I'm something of a hobbyist even when on vacation, owning my own little comic store appeals to the youngling in me. That each comic book drags its unsuspecting own into the nightmares woven into it while they sleep at night is part of the charm of my own little slice of eternity. That... and chewy, who is far less "charming."

For all of my shop's considerable charm, it's unfortunately hard to keep servants... ah... staff. I can tell immediately I am about to lose another employee the moment I step inside. It probably has to do with the fact that he's not breaking speed at all as he barrels toward me, his face white as a sheet. I bite back a sigh as he shoots out the door and slowly turn to look over at the menace occupying a shelf in a roped off corner of the store. I narrow my eyes at the innocent looking fern.

"Chewy," I growl, stalking toward it.

Its enormous fronds slowly curl inward at my approach, her numerous pod-like heads and stinging vines tucked out of sight, but I'm having none of that. Chewy is the one inconvenience of this whole vacation. A sentient, carnivorous plant from the nightmare realm, she can be a real bitch to deal with at times. It's bad enough that she will try to eat a customer who gets too close if someone isn't keeping an eye on her—something that putting the ropes in have mostly solved the problem of—but the fact that she gets her kicks out of frightening my employees is what makes her company unpleasant at times. She thinks this mournful routine will work on me? Ha!

Pointing a heavily glamoured claw at her, I snarl deeply. "No more of this. No more trying to attack or eat customers or employees if you don't want to end up mulched and thrown into the flaming pit."

This time I mean business.

CHAPTER 2

FANNY

"Fanny Yang?" The barista calls me name, her nose scrunching slightly.

I force a polite smile to my lips, trying not to wince at the way she butchered my name as I push through the crowd to retrieve my coffee, dropping a couple of quarters into the tip jar. It's the last of my cash but the lure of coffee is too hard to resist. The liquid nearly scalds my tongue in a satisfying away as I take a sip and I hum with pleasure as I scope out the mall.

Creepy Court. Weirdest name for a mall that I've ever heard of. It doesn't look any kind of creepy to me. Bright, fluorescent colors of the lit-up signs distract from the yellowish paint used on the walls so that the nicotine stains from their numerous smoking customers isn't so noticeable. Frankly, it looks much like any other mall I've been to.

The food court itself is a riot of eye-bleeding colors slapped disharmoniously together, and smells that make my stomach grumble in complaint even as I try to silence it with another, larger, sip of coffee. The coffee will have to do for now, at least until the mall closes and I can break into some of the kitchens to find something to satisfy my belly. A girl has to do what a girl has to do. It's better than the alternative. I have nothing against the girls peddling their wares on the curbs, but I'd much rather just steal what I need rather than resort to that method of feeding myself. There is a lot my parents believe about me since I decided to eschew family traditions and start living my own life, some of them ended up being true, but I'll be damned if I make that one a reality.

I try to make the coffee last as I wander around but, all too soon, I'm down to the last little bit in the paper cup. I down the rest and give the cup an unhappy sigh before tossing it in the trash can. Popping a piece of Bubble Yum into my mouth, the overwhelming grape flavor accompanies the shock of sugar flooding my system. Pulling my scrunchy out, I sweep my hair back into a tight, high ponytail at the top of my head and secure it once more with the shiny pink scrunchy. The feathery ends of my old perm tease my neck as my head tips, and I peer at the sign with a maniacally grinning coyote. Frankie's Funhouse. The smell of cheap pizza, cigs, and booze, and the scream of what I assume is children's laughter amid all the strange clamor coming from within, emanates from the place like a thick haze that sends a little shiver up my spine.

Okay. Perhaps it wasn't quite like other malls. I dig the dark atmosphere. Very rock and roll. As busy as it appears to be, it looks like a good spot to hole up for the day. It's unlikely that anyone will notice me loitering there with all of that madness going on inside. Nor is anyone likely to notice when I slip into the restroom to wait it out while the mall closes. That's my regular method, and it seldom fails me.

Taking a deep breath of the riot of smells, I step inside as if I belong there. Just another paying customer. My eyes drag over the animatronic band moving stiffly through a routine, the music pleasantly creepy in tone despite its somewhat jovial lyrics. A game lets out a death scream that makes me jump and I clench a hand to my chest and laugh. Wow, this place is great!

Noting a family vacating their spot, I slide in and lick my lips as I examine the untouched slices remaining on the pan. They are stone cold and there isn't much left over. Even the soda remaining in the pitcher looks flat as hell but I'm not going to scorn my good fortune. Grabbing up a slice, I take a healthy bite, my eyes following the movements of the grinning coyote on the stage in front of me. There is something about him that makes me think he is looking right back at me and leering, but I mentally push it away with another quiet chuckle as I focus on my food. As expected, no one even looks my way much less approaches me. I find a few coins and play some of the games that have a surprising monstrous theme. It's enough to keep me entertained anyway until I see my cue to tuck into my hiding place. Families are packing it in and the older children who were dropped off are slowly detaching from the place and melting back into the mall.

It won't be much longer now.

The bathroom smells disgusting like someone puked in here recently, it's entirely bogus but I ignore it as I sit on a toilet and prop by feet on the closed stall-door in front of me. Sliding my backpack off, I put it in my lap and unzip the top to pull my headphones out. It only takes me a minute to rifle through my coveted mixtapes before I select my favorite and slide it into my Walkman's tape-deck. I smile and lean my head back on the wall behind me as the world is muffled out by my music. I spent tireless hours making each tape, perched next to my boombox just waiting for the right songs to come on the radio so that I could record them. My music had resulted in the first major blow out—the first of many—between me and my parents. Demon music, they called it, their eyes rounding worriedly as they turned it off at every opportunity as if that would somehow miraculously make my love for it vanish.

My nose wrinkles disdainfully at the memory. Demon music. Ha! Joke's on my parents because if demons like rock and roll, as far as I'm concerned, they can't be that bad.

My foot bounces a little in time with the music, my head

bobbing. I pause and frown, moving one of the headphones off my ear when I think I hear a strange sound. I shrug when it doesn't repeat and plop it back into place. Whatever, man.

I stay in that putrid stall for an hour or two, waiting until long after the last of the lights have gone out before I make my move. Zipping my backpack mostly closed, leaving just enough room for my headphone cords to have some give to it, I shoulder my backpack and bound out of the bathroom with a relieved sharp inhale of fresh-ish air.

As fresh as a pizza-arcade joint in the mall can be, anyway.

Humming along to the music, I make my way from the restrooms in the back through the labyrinth of games. I am briefly debating whether or not I want to dip into the kitchen here to look for more filling sustenance or hunt something out a little quicker and easier someplace else when I feel a strange tickle at the back of my neck. Stopping in my tracks, my eyes sweep around the arcade warily. It feels like I'm being watched. Creepy I can handle. Creepy I love. Being watched in a darkened arcade, abandoned for the night, goes straight from creepy to hell no.

"Yeah... no, I'm out," I whisper, my gaze making for the entrance. Surprisingly the grate is still wide open to the dark interior of the mall and I feel a prickle of unease.

The soles of my funky ankle boots scuff just a little too loudly and I race for the entrance and my heart slams a staccato rhythm in my chest. A terrible, unnatural sound that I can't quite identify rises up behind me as if something is rising out of the gloom to hunt me. I desperately want to scream but I swallow it back as I slide gracelessly out of the entrance door. Just as quickly as it started, the sound cuts off, leaving the entire mall silent except for the sound of my pulse thrumming loudly in my ears and the faint music from my headphones banging out the rhythm of one of my favorite songs from where they now hang loose around my neck.

Biting back a nervous laugh, I give Frankie's Funhouse one last fleeting look before striking back into the mall again. My stomach rumbles loudly, reminding me that I haven't eaten since the meager slices of cold pizza this afternoon. Food it is, and then I will explore a bit before finding a suitable place to bed down. That's one thing about malls. If you are sharp enough to evade security, it is a hell of a safer spot to sleep than out there on the street.

I slink at a more unhurried pace down the dark hall, picking up my pace momentarily when I come nearer to The Mall Swords. The antique store which only gave me a pleasant buzz of something vaguely horror-esque in the light of days feels even more threatening in the gloom as if something is rattling dangerously inside. Not one to commit dumb horror movie cliches, I run past it and don't stop until I turn out from the hall in the main part of the mall again. The aura of the place is a bit more settled here even if the carousel looms like something from an abandoned carnival, casting long, monstrous shadows. It overshadows the food court just beyond it. I give a carousel horse with oddly sharp looking teeth a wide berth as I make my way back into the midst of the food court.

Taking my place at the center, I survey my options. The Good Char is the closest to my right. I peer at it speculatively, the smell of hotdogs and grease clinging to the air. It looks promising. Pulling a small hatchet from my backpack that doubles as a deterrent for those with less than innocent intentions for me, I smash the lock with the back end of blade and lift the security grate just high enough to squeeze through before lowering it again. The scent of food is deliciously thicker inside but I can't seem to figure out how to work the grill, which has a menacing aura to it anyway. Stepping close to it feels like walking to the edge of an abyss and it has an unnatural heat as if the fires are lit and burning though it seems to be off. Haunted stove is out. I consider the deep fryer for all of a minute before I realize that it's fruitless without the batter to fry a dog. Batter I obviously have no clue how to make. Cue the sad violin. I give it a disappointed look but raid the bakery across the way instead, giving its lock the same treatment and coming up with a few forgotten stale donuts for my trouble. Shoving one in my mouth, I head out into the mall, both nervous and curious to see what it has in store for me.

Either way, I locked in here until sun-up. I'll just have to find a relatively safe place to sleep.

Heading down another hall, I pause in front of a comic book store. Although the outward facing shelves are lined with horror comics, there is an orderly sort of quiet to it that seems almost inviting. It could be the fact that an entire corner is left empty for an enormous fern that's obviously been babied to grow to such proportions in the mall where space is always a premium. Smiling, I "let myself in." This looks like the perfect place to bunk down for the night. A thousand apologies for the lock but at least I anticipate sleeping well tonight.

CHAPTER 3

PASHAR

I pride myself in knowing everything that goes on in my shop even when I'm resting within my den. It highly benefits me that nightmare demons are armed with a variety of skills when it comes to spell-work and manipulating energies. Not only is that what allows me to create my comic books, but it's what gives me a very effective alarm system with the network of energies I leave in place every night when I return home. The tremble of energy announcing the presence of an intruder brings a scowl to my face as I heave myself off my very comfortable reclining chair and storm toward the portal.

I'm half naked, I don't have my glamour in place, and I don't give a flying fuck. It is a welcome opportunity to scare the piss out of whatever idiot decided to invade my territory. Besides, it's the middle of the night. Who would believe them?

I smile nastily to myself, my corethi trembling at the bottom of folded wings, and step out into my stockroom. With an impatient growl, I enter my shop, my eyes falling on the sleeping form curled up suicidally close to Chewy's barrier. My eyes snap up to the plant. Several of its pod like heads are visible on their long stalks, their sharp clearly visible as their mouths gape open as a long, uncoiled vine inches closer to the sleeping human huddled under a thin blanket. I'm a bit shocked that it's not one of the heavily barbed vines utilized to flay and weaken Chewy's victims but I still don't hesitate to snarl threateningly, stopping her in her tracks. I want a terrified human, not a dead one. Unsanctioned deaths from nightmare demons is more paperwork than I want to deal with on my vacation.

Head's tipping toward me, the vine rapidly retreats back into her pod with a snap. I squint at her suspiciously for a moment as her mouths move slightly as if whimpering in protest. I should have destroyed her the moment she hitched a ride with me to this world. The infernal lords damn that soft spot in my black heart.

Grumbling, I give the human a brisk nudge with my foot. Not at all pleased that they inconvenienced me and then had the nerve to fall asleep before I can get up here and terrify them good and proper.

I purr with satisfaction as the human let's out a shrill squeak in response, their eyes flying open as they roll to face me, their blanket falling away. My snarl slips slightly in surprise as I meet the honey brown gaze of a petite female staring up in complete shock at me. Her golden complexion pales as she stares at me in abject horror. It's only then that I consider the sight I must be, snarl fixed in place, corethi looming threatening around from where they've emerged, my exceptionally long tail twitching in the air around me. I'm not at all surprised when she manages to stop choking on her scream to let it out in an ear-piercing shriek. I'm also acutely aware that it will draw attention from the night security guard, and I can't have that.

Her slender fingers scrabble against the floor as she tries to scurry away from me, but she isn't fast enough to evade my tail. I snag her effortlessly before she is able to get more than a foot away and haul her up from the floor with ease as my tail winds more firmly around her body, holding her aloft in the air in front of it. My mouth waters at the scent of her skin. It strikes a considerable hunger within me but not for tearing flesh from her dainty bones. Her mouth is still wide open, but her scream seems to have lodged within her again now that I have a hold on her and I'm starting to worry that she's stopped breathing. I poke her with one finger in the belly and a terrible sound erupts from her that is a strangled shriek and giggle all at once. Wincing a little and fighting to hold back a chuckle of my own at the terrible sound despite my best effort to remain unmoved, I shrug. I'll just carry her out and throw her on her little rear end personally and be done. There are strict rules regarding holding unsanctioned humans, and more paperwork than there is for killing them. Which is sad because she seems like a tasty little thing.

With a regretful grunt, I hoist her a little higher with my tail as I bend down to retrieve her bag and upon picking it up, it tips, dumping several of my precious comic books out in the process. I stare at the mess in dumbfounded silence. She was going to steal from me? Steal my comics?

Comic books I've spent many hours and days crafting horrendous nightmares with my woven spells.

I bristle, feeling numerous sharp spines pushing up from my skin along my back and arms as fury coils deep in the pit of my belly to mingle with the blaze of lust swirling there. I ignore the strangled scream she issues in response and my eyes narrow on her. Now, punishing a thief and getting compensated for it—that is minor paperwork. I grin at her and she shrinks within the clutch of my tail. Poor little thief. Chuckling wickedly, I turn back to my portal carting my prize. Having my last employee serving me was nice enough —what was his name Chuck? Larry? No, Tyler!—but this little morsel won't escape me during neither hours of the day nor night. There will be no clock-in and out times by which she can make her timely escape.

With one last weak cry, her eyes roll back, and she goes limp. Drawing her toward me, I give her a sniff. Ah, still alive. She just fainted. Good.

She is all mine.

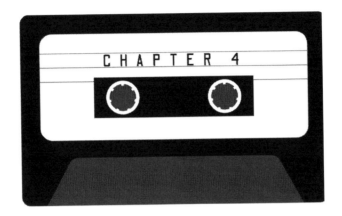

CHAPTER 4

FANNY

W hy does my head hurt? I moan softly, my hand going up to my temple. It feels like I hit my head on something. There is a piercing ache and a throbbing behind my eyes.

"Good, you're awake," a deep voice growls in a way that is frighteningly animalistic.

Startled, my eyes pop open to meet the yellow glow of a predatory gaze staring directly back at me. My pulse jumps and I suck in a breath, overwhelmed by the monster looming over me. And that I'm sprawled on the floor. My mouth downturns, puzzled as my eyes somehow manage to drop from the terrifying face above to take a covert look at my surroundings. Why am I on the floor?

I start to sit up just so I can inch away from the demonic monster looming over me, dread coiling within me that perhaps in this too my parents were right that I would end up caught in something demonic. Well... someone demonic, anyway. My head swims for a moment and a hiss of pain escapes me as I quickly shoot up and clench the side of my head again. What the hell?

The demon grunts, his eyes narrowing on me before shifting away to a point beyond me. "Come on, get up," he grumbles. "Washroom is the door on the right over there. Then we need to get going."

"Going?" I echo, caught by surprise.

Apparently, it's the wrong response because his gaze snaps back to me and he glowers like he's entertaining the idea of eating me. A clammy sweat breaks out over my brow. When I was a kid, we had a neighbor with a pit bull. The dog was as mean as its owner and I remember staring fearfully at the dog's heavy, square, crushing jaws. The day it got loose from its chain still gives me nightmares. Looking up at this demon with his heavy, wide jaw roped heavily with muscles in proportion to his wide, powerful neck reminds me of that dog and yet infinitely more dangerous. When he speaks his large, sharp teeth are something from a horror story, barely cover by his lips, his tongue sinuous, long and thick lashing along them. Now that I think of it, with his oily dark purple scales and incredible long tail, he almost looks like he belongs on set for Aliens if only his head was shaped more elongated and barer rather than boasting long black hair and several large horns along with a multitude of bony protrusions studding his face.

Not to mention he has wings, I note. And whatever the barbed peacock things whipping around him. Their lethal points nestled among their feathery ends catch the light in such a way as they move that its hard to miss. Yeah, somehow, I think this is far worse.

"Yes," he snaps impatiently. "I need to show you the ropes before the mall opens at nine. It isn't going to wait on a lazy thief."

Wait... what?

I rub at what feels like a knot on my head. I don't know what I hit it on, but it must be making me delusional. Did I somehow get offered employment without realizing it?

"Are you saying that I have a job?" I ask, just to clarify.

He chuffs a deep laugh, his terrible teeth flashing in a horrifying grin. "That would infer you are getting paid, wouldn't it? No, little thief, you don't have a job, you have duties... endless duties in all waking hours, assigned as I see fit. Now move!" he barks.

I reflexively bolt to my feet and hurry to the washroom, groaning inwardly. Ok, so I'm being punished for breaking into the shops and stealing... that much I get. It sucks but if it means that he doesn't intend to eat me, I'm not going to complain too hard and make him change his mind. I just need to report to work every day until he considers my debt repaid.

I ponder this as I step into an obsidian washroom lit by what looks like several small, glowing mirrors. I look at the large basin tub with longing. It's not in any style that I recognize having an appearance more like a large, elongated bowl, but I would give anything to be thoroughly cleaned. Any impatient growl at the other side of the door makes me jump and I turn toward the sink and press on the tap above the mounted bowl. Freshwater flows for a measured count before gradually slowing and turning off.

Pressing it again, I take one of the small, folded cloths stacked neatly in a bit and quickly wash my hands and face before giving myself a brief sponge bath. I feel a little better with the freshening up and considerably more optimistic. This whole situation makes a strange sort of sense. My grandparents were full of stories regarding transactions with the world of spirits.

Assuming that I'm remembering correctly, I recall from stories that I grew up with that the relationship with the spirit world is often transactional between debts and balances. By that logic, I just need to pay off my debt.

This puts me in a much better frame of mind as I walk out of the washroom. The demon is still terrifying, but I feel like I have a better grasp on what's expected now.

"I'm ready," I tell him, and I feel a prickle of warning when he smirks in response.

"Not quite," he says succinctly. "You need your uniform."

"Okay," I agree, expecting a shirt or something to be thrust at me.

I jump when he suddenly leans forward but he moves too quickly for me to properly react. I jerk back but before I know what's happened, a band clicks around my neck and I'm released so suddenly that I stumble backward a few steps, my hand slapping up to my throat where a flexible metal band curls around my throat.

"What...What's this?" I squeak as I try unsuccessfully to get my fingernail up between the metal and my skin.

Whatever it is, there is something unnatural to it as it seems to twist in a way that evades my grip and hugs close to my skin without choking me.

"My stamp of ownership that magically binds you to me," he replies with a deep rumbling purr of satisfaction. "When I said that you have duties for all waking hours, I was very literal. You are now mine."

This...is a lot worse than simply working off my debt in the mall. I have a sinking feeling that I will be returning here at the end of the day. My face falls, and he chortles gleefully.

"Come along, little pet," he hisses. "There's much to be done."

His fingers snap and I feel an overwhelming compulsion flow through me to follow after him as his tail coils around him and a shimmer of inky darkness appears around him and slowly reforms around him. If I didn't know any better, with his faded jeans, long ponytail, and band shirt, I would have mistaken him for any other human fan of rock and roll. I open my mouth to question him about it but the mirror in front of us takes on a slick appearance of shifting black oil. It looks way too menacing but there is no avoiding it as I follow after him right through the mirror and into the comic book shop that I fell asleep in. Comic books litter the floor still from where they fell from my bag but the demon walks by them, motioning for me to follow him as we head to the enormous fern taking up the corner of the room. Pick up a spray bottle from the storage cupboard beneath a nearby display, he stops and turns to me as he motions toward the plant with the bottle.

"This plant that you idiotically fell asleep next to is Chewy." Another grin briefly splits his face before sobering once more as it sets into a scowl. "If you value your quality of life at all, you will stay away from her. You will not die, since you are bound to me, but you will be surprised what suffering that you will survive through," he casually remarks.

I give him a look of disbelief because seriously—this is a freaking fern. His eyes narrow at my expression, and he chuckles a cruel cackle. Lifting the bottle, he sprays the fern liberally and I feel something cold slide through my veins that the fronds tremble before suddenly numerous pod-like, teeth-filled head poke up from among it and thick vines uncoil as if enjoying the mist. It's very Little Pet Shop of Horrors and I can't help but to stare in a mixture of fascination and horror. The movie trailer is strange as hell but I kind of wish that it was already out so that I have some small idea of what to expect. I have a feeling this is no mere carnivorous plant. There is a mind of some sort behind its movements as its mouths open to catch more direct spritzes.

"She requires misting several times a day. Keep an eye on her at all times that you or anyone else in the store is near her and remain a safe distance behind the marked off area. She is a lethal predator and can move faster than you will expect. I'll feed her for now, so you don't have to worry about that yet, just keep her hydrated throughout the day," he instructs blandly as he puts the spray away. Tipping his head toward the comics scattered and the floor, he resumes glowering. "Once you've cleaned up your mess come to the register. And be quick," he snaps as he turns away to leave me to my work.

I give Chewy a nervous look and have a feeling that she is looking curiously back at me, her vines curling like little question marks around her as if she is curious. I swallow and give her a tight smile as I shuffle back a little further. Bending I pick up the first comic book, and then another, my eyes trailing around the shop to note that the shelves have nothing but more horror comics filling them.

Perhaps that would have been pertinent to notice *before* I fell asleep in the shop.

CHAPTER 5

PASHAR

Having a human pet is actually quite nice, I decide. Sadly, I can't keep calling her pet or human without rousing suspicions among those running the mall. I've caught the administrator of the mall, that Rizal woman, glancing curiously our way throughout the day as she makes her rounds preparing for something called Trick or Treat Street.

I squint at the flyer she gave me to pin on the board behind my counter while my pet straightens up after the last slew of customers. I do not understand. Instructions to don a costume and I am supposed to give unhealthy quantities of sugar to human offspring?

"Human, come here and take a look at this," I snap, drawing my pet's attention to me.

Her dark brows lower as she puts the last comic book on the shelf and heads toward me. Somewhere around hour three she lost most of her fear of me, much to my dismay, and has been showing an increasing amount of irreverence and attitude that I plan on curtailing.

"Since there appears to be no end in sight of you ordering me around, you could just use my name," she grumbles. "Like I told you four hours ago when 'pet' got old."

I frown, promptly losing my train of thought. She did?

"Remind me."

She makes an exaggerated roll of her eyes in her disgusted exasperation that is as annoying as it is ridiculously amusing. "Fanny," she huffs and leans forward to peer at the flyer behind me, her ass tipping in the air.

I stare at its delectable curve, my tongue snaking over my lips as I imagine sinking my teeth right into it. And then blink.

"Fanny?" What a peculiar name.

She shoots me a sharp look, the long tail of gathered curls grazing me with the turn of her head. Her lithe, little body suspended over the counter so near me that it would take little to no effort to pull her toward me—or push her over onto her ass, however the impulse at the moment drives me.

"Yes," she bites out. "As in a fanny, and if you think you

have any lame butt jokes, I've heard them all. It's short for Francine, but I can't stand that name either," she grumbles, her attention returning to the flyer.

The annoyance on her face shifts to one of curiosity and I eye her, trying to not to enjoy the natural perfume of her body mixed with whatever annoyingly sweet substance she seems to be constantly chewing.

"Oh." I hadn't been aware but now I'm intrigued with the way her face has turned red. I can feel the smile pulling my lips and my tail twitching with maniacal amusement despite being restrained around my waist.

Her slender finger shoots up in warning and she drops to her feet. "Don't even think of it. If you can't be nice then I will get you back."

Bah! I would like to see that. I regard her silently, weighing the matter and then snort. "There is nothing you can do to ridicule Pashar."

Her brow furrows. "What the hell is a pashar?"

"Not a what," I bark, incensed. Hasn't she ever heard of any good, respectable demon names? I'm the fourth in my line to be rewarded with such a distinguished name for my incredible skill at terrifying mortals and all other beings susceptible to nightmares. "It's my name, diminutive female."

"You're name, huh?" She crosses her arms over her chest and regards me for a long moment before making a derisive sound of amusement. "Okay, I give. I've got nothing."

"Give what?" I eye her suspiciously.

Her lips twitch. "Give up. As in, you win."

I scoff as I give her my back and peer at the confounded paper once again. "Of course, I do. I'm a demon." A scowl pulls at my face as the strange cheerful smile on the gourde in the picture mocks me. "But this," I growl, waving a hand at the flyer, "I don't understand."

Fanny's smile rivals that of an imp. "I thought you were a know-it-all demon. Don't tell me that you don't know what trick or treating is? Does Halloween ring a bell?"

I sniff disdainfully, my wings folding together against me beneath the illusion spell. "Some ridiculous human tradition, no doubt. I have some vague memory of humans celebrating a holy All Hallows Day." I don't recall that being much in the way of fun or having anything to do with the projected merriment suggested on the flyer.

Her eyes widen. "You really don't know what Halloween is? Oh, you're in for a treat!"

Somehow, I doubt that. My doubts are largely confirmed when Fanny gives me a quick run down on the festivities. As if moving on their own accord, my arms cross over my chest as I pin her with a glare. I'm privately amused by the way she throws her hands up in up in the air and huffs at me in response, but I wrestle it down so that my expression doesn't crack.

"How can you, a demon who peddles horror comic books, not like Halloween?" she finally asks with an air of complete disbelief.

I give a taciturn grunt in response. Truthfully, the

administrator's idea doesn't sound half bad. Especially if the large plastic skeletons that I can see the administrator struggling to haul down to hall just over Fanny's shoulder is any indication of how the mall is going to be decorated. More skeletons, monsters, and horrors are always better. I can see the night being very lucrative if the swarm of small children doesn't scare away my usual sort of clientele. What use do I have for extra children roaming around the mall? Unlike some of my brethren I hold myself to higher standards when it comes to my victims.

"First, they're not horror comic books, they are woven nightmare enchantments. Second... I don't have much experience when it comes to children," I admit on a grumble.

The idea of having to interact with a large number of them makes me feel on the brink of breaking out in hives, complete with festering colonies of stinging wasp-like parasites.

Fanny's mouth down turns, her head tipping to the side. "I would think that a nightmare demon would be someone pretty familiar with children. Don't they make you most of your business?"

"For some," I agree, my tone turning sour as I move away, determined to find something for my pet to do.

Unfortunately, she doesn't give up so easily. She scampers after me, her dark eyes lit up with delighted curiosity. "You don't scare children, do you? Holy cow! This is totally rad. A demon with a soft spot for children."

"I didn't say that either," I sharply rebuke. I have no idea what rad is, but I'm quite certain that's an insult. "Don't go putting words in my mouth."

"You realize we are going to have to wear costumes," she sing-songs behind me, obviously taking far too much joy in my predicament. "We will have to do something really gnarly but not super scary. We can do a matchy thing. It will be the perfect way to introduce you to the Halloween spirit... and kids!" She lets out a gleeful giggle that is just on the verge of a demon worthy cackle.

I have the sneaking suspicion she knows how much the prospect of being surrounded by children terrifies me. It's kind of cute that she honors with me a good scare. Cute but not going to happen.

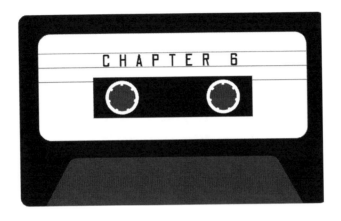

CHAPTER 6

FANNY

A WEEK LATER

Having a grumpy demon around is kind of adorable once you get used to all the grumpy growling and fussing. I spend the night curled under a thick blanket on a pretty nice-looking couch—something that looks a little familiar from the Sears and Roebuck catalog actually, which makes me suspect his furnishing come smuggled straight from Earth—and upon waking, accompany him back to toil all day in the comic book store. If you can call what we do toiling. If Pashar's human disguise is to resemble a rock and roll grifter, he certainly runs his store with similar laid-back vibes. He spends the majority of the day muttering to himself over his sketches while I care for Chewy, organize the comics, and watch for customers. Every now and then he has a new issue that practically sends sparks shooting up my arms the moment I touch it, with orders of what shelf to put it in.

Apparently, there is some sort of system to the madness within the shop that I've yet to work out. To my eye, there isn't any organization to the shelves at all but all of my offers to reorganize them are met with steely refusal.

Most hours there is little for me to do other than watch the people milling through the mall and the gradual arrival of Halloween to the mall. A trick or treat street *inside* a mall. What a clever idea. I just need to find a way to convince Pashar that it can be fun. I know that his human appearance is just an illusion but there still must be some joy that a demon can find it the admittedly silly customs of the season. Maybe I need to suggest a few good costumes and get him into the spirit of things, but what?

I start rolling various ideas through my head. The obvious answer would be for him to go as himself but there are two problems with that. One, his real appearance can be terrifying for someone not prepared for it. Even spending day in and day out with him and never once being offered any kind of harm, I only recently have stopped recoiling in response when he releases his illusion of humanity. It's not that I find him distasteful to look at. Quite the opposite, actually. I always enjoyed some aspects of fear a little too much and that trickle of remaining fear has resulted in flipping a switch that I didn't even know I have—to which he thankfully hasn't caught on yet so that I'm spared from dying from embarrassment. Two, there is no way any sort of human-made costume can come close to looking like him.

I tap a finger on my bottom lip as the administrator walks by with her arms laden with two large boxes that appear to be filled with little goody bags, a black witch's hat flopping on her head. Despite her burden, she tries to shift it anyway so that she can give me a cheerful wave. Smiling, I return the gesture. Miss Rizal is super nice. Looks like she needs a hand. The store is dead at the moment anyway.

"Hey, Pashar, are you going to flip if I go on break?" I shout over to the male brooding over his drawings at the counter.

His eyes lift and it strikes me how yellow they are even beneath his human illusion. A very bright golden brown that toes the line of being natural. His brow furrows slightly and he grunts, flicking his fingers at me.

"Take your lunch break," he growls, his gaze returning to his work.

"Sweet. Want anything?" I already know his order, it's the same thing he always gets. "I'll be heading to The Good Char."

Strange how learning what exactly that demon's special ingredients are hasn't dissuaded me from eating there. I don't know what that says about me. If it makes me a monster, I guess I just fit in better with the Creepy Court this way. In the days I've been working here I've slowly seen the normal world peel away as I become increasingly more aware of the monsters living peacefully among humanity here.

"Yeah. Don't forget to tip the brats," he says, a satisfied smile curling his lips.

I shake my head and pinch my lips together to contain my own smile. I'm so not encouraging him with this. "Still on that? I figured the feud was over when Dzik picked up the fleas from you. I'm still trying to figure out where you pulled those out from, by the way."

His smile widens showing teeth with a definite sharpness to them, his yellow eyes gleaming brightly enough that I can see a hint of their true color bleeding through. He looks evil as all get out but strangely, he's just my kind of evil. "Secrets of the trade," is all he says, and he makes another shooing motion at me. "As for Dzik, he would get bored if I didn't torment him. Now get out of here before I change my mind."

I can't quite keep a giggle from slipping out as I book it out of the shop. Whatever magical leash he has me on is relaxed so I don't feel the sharp tug that I normally would. That I automatically miss the proprietary tug of it is some heavy shit. Therefore, I choose not to think about it. Instead, I immediately pick up my steps to catch up with the administrator lugging her box, the charms on my cute, little chain belt looped through my jeans tinkling cheerfully as I walk.

"Hey, Miss Rizal, wait up!" I shout.

She wobbles a little with her burden, the double stacked

boxes teetering precariously as she turns to me, but her smile is wide and friendly. Swooping in, I rescue the top box and beam at her.

"Let me help you with this."

"Oh! Thank you, Fanny. I think I misjudged my carry capacity," she jokes. "There's just so much to do! But I think the mall is really starting to come together."

My gaze skims over the decorated displays set up in the hall and the smaller decorations in the corner of the shop windows and smile. "It is looking super bodacious, Miss Rizal."

She brightens with pleasure. "Thank you, again, Fanny! Are you and Pashar getting ready?" She glances back toward Dark Spell Comics meaningfully.

I grimace a little as I follow her gaze back to the shop. Pashar is visible through the window as is the fact that there has been zero decorating done.

"It's a work in progress," I admit slowly, my mind working frantically to explain as we make our way down to the Guest Service desk. "They don't celebrate Halloween where Pashar is from so I'm trying to warm him up to the idea."

Her mouth rounds briefly in surprise. "Oh, I didn't realize. Well, if you need any help, flag me down. I really want this Trick or Treat Street to kick off with a bang."

"I'll be sure to let Pashar know how important it is," I assure her.

My eyes catch on a large, black German Shepherd walking

his owner down the hall and my smile returns. Awwww. JJ found himself a friend. I was a little concerned when I learned that there was a for-real werewolf masquerading as a pet at the Twisted Whisker—because, for real, no one around here can keep a secret worth damn if you are in the know— but the two of them look so damn happy that I can't help but to be thrilled for them. The woman holding his leash certainly doesn't seem to be the one in charge, but she looks ecstatic as hell as she cheerfully waves to me.

We finally reach the desk and the monster stationed behind it gives me a polite smile as she returns to work while Miss Rizal and I set our loads behind it with all the other boxes rapidly accumulating there. I have to hand it to her, she's going in full tilt. A tingle of excitement sweeps over me. I can't wait, even if it means dragging Pashar in, kicking and screaming the entire way. There has to be a way to convince him that it will be fun, preferably with as minimal fuss as possible.

Giving a cheerful wave, I head toward the food court, my stomach growling. I spot Elliot handing one of his special orders out over the counter to a customer. His eyes meet mine when his customer leaves with a pleased gurgle and I give him a friendly wave in passing. His face creases with laughter as I wiggle a little to Cyndi Lauper's hit blasting through speakers overhead before continuing on my way. I'm still bopping with the lyrics when I reach The Good Char's counter and Kimmy giggles behind her hand at my antics while Dzik the Dick glares over at me from where he's perched over the grill. I know that's Dzik being his usual friendly self, so I give him a wave. If he was actually annoyed, he would be looming over the counter, attached to Kimmy like a tick.

"Hi Fanny," she chirps. "The usual?"

"Yes, thanks!" I reply, leaning one hip on the counter as she hurries to pour my lemonade while Dzik grumbles and grabs several wieners and coat them in his special batter.

"How's it going?" she inquires as she sets my cup and straw in front of me.

"The usual. I do what Pashar says while he growls and snarls at me like he's contemplating eating me. That, of course, is when he's not complaining about 'the Halloween nonsense.' The fun is never ending."

Kimmy giggles again and gives me a sympathetic look. "Still trying to convince him to get in the groove for Halloween? How's it going?"

I grimace. "Let's just say that you are fortunate that Miss Rizal's staff takes care of the food court. He's about as willing to contribute toward festivities as Dzik would be."

"Waste of time and money is what it is," Dzik grumbles, looming behind Kimmy as he plops my order on the counter in front of me. My eyebrows raise when he sets a large hand on her shoulder and Kimmy blushes. What's this? New developments? "Just begging for extra lunacy around this place."

He shakes his head grimly as he stomps back toward his

grill and drops unceremoniously into his chair tucked back there.

Kimmy makes a face and sighs as she grabs a soda from the cooler and cracks it open. "Point taken. Does that mean you're throwing in the towel?"

I snort in amusement. "As if." My gaze trails over to the clothing store kiddy corner to the food court where an employee is busily hanging up costumes on wracks at the front of the shop. My eyes land on a bright red, horned mask wearing the biggest evil grin and I brighten at the sight of it. "Actually, hold that thought. I have a great idea."

Kimmy leans over the counter and giggles. "Good luck!"

I may need it. But does that deter me? No, it does not! Digging out cash from my pocket, I hand it to Kimmy, and with another wave goodbye, I hurry away from the food court with my order in hand. My lips curling with a wicked grin that would do Pashar proud, I make my way over to the shop, my idea blooming vividly within in my mind. This is totally going to be righteous!

CHAPTER 7

PASHAR

I look up from my work as the smell of corndogs fill the shop, my long tongue snaking over my lips. My weaving pin, with which I stitch the nightmare to form the images into the paper, lifts from my current work and I set it down as I turn toward the door. Fanny gives me a sly smile and I notice that she has a second bag in her other hand. I give it a curious glance as she sets the takeout bag from The Good Char on the table beside me. I dismiss the bag she continues to hold as my attention rivets fully on the paper bag filled with mouth-watering food. Besides, it's not the first time she has decided to shop while on her break.

The name of the clothing store is not one I've seen her with before since she usually visits, usually either Sizzling Discourse or Xolotl's Gifts whose signature brands are easy to spot, but I'm just glad she didn't make me wait too long this time for my meal.

Fishing out my corndogs, I shove the bag in her direction as I promptly open the to-go cup of mustard and set it beside my meal. I'm salivating as I dip a corndog into it and take a satisfying chomp. I purr happily and close my eyes contently as I chew. Dzik must have got a fresh batch rich with suffering. It is delicious. My eyes cracking open so that I can take another bite and note that Fanny is watching me with a worryingly thoughtful look on her face as she nibbles on her own corndog. As much as I usually take considerable pleasure out of watching her eat the flesh of the damned—who knew it would be so erotic as well as incredibly satisfying?—I am put on alert by her expression.

And she's still clutching that bag. In fact, she is hugging it strangely close to her chest. Noticing the direction of my gaze, she promptly drops the bag to the floor and kicks it under the table. Like that's not suspicious. I pin her with a scowl, but she doesn't cough up an explanation. Instead, she takes a large bite of her corndog as if she hadn't just acted peculiar.

"What was that?" I growl, suspicious.

Her round, hooded eyes widen perceptively at me, and I'm distracted by the fine hair teasing the soft curve of her jawline as she glances down in the direction of the hidden bag in surprise. "Nothing. Just picked a few things up that I need."

Giving me a particularly sweet smile, she dips her corn dog in her own little cup of mustard and takes another crunching bite followed by a delectable moan that makes my cock harden aggressively in my pants.

My eyes narrow at her, a soft growl starting in my throat. I promptly quash the sound and blank my expression when I notice the corner of her lips tilt. So, it's like that? Huffing, I turn back to my meal, refusing to be lured into whatever game she's playing. Sometimes living with Fanny is like living with another demon—the difference is that the sort of battle I want to have with her has nothing to do with territorial skirmishes and all to do with wrestling in a mating hold while I rut her senseless.

With some effort I dislodge my brain from the route it's eagerly going down and thrust my corndog a little harder into the mustard cup than is warranted, rewarding myself with a lewd splatter of mustard everywhere, several drops of which land on Fanny's cheek. Although the color is wrong, the sight of it sprayed on her cheek and neck makes my cock jump with interest at the surge of lust that suddenly barrels through me. It doesn't get any better when she wipes a larger dab off with her fingertip and promptly sticks it in her mouth.

Hissing to myself, I hunker over my food and resume eating, refusing to look her way or make any more remarks or questions about the damn bag. She will see that Pashar is not a demon she can play with.

Three days later

I grit my teeth and remind myself that I'm hating every minute of this as I watch her put up the decorations that she somehow coaxed me into agreeing to. The damned bag still preys on my mind and Fanny is clever as a fox when it comes to using my distraction against me. It's as if she knew and was waiting for just that moment to attack as I stewed over the mystery bag that I still refuse to ask her again about. Despite that, I must grudgingly admit that she is a worthy component—one that I desire even more to wrestle and pin down to have writhing beneath me in a mating hold. My fantasies are turning regularly to vanquishing her in the manner of courting done by nightmare demons when they find the female they desire to nest with.

I fist my cock brutally under the table as she bends low to pick up another decoration, her pert little ass swaying in time with the music pumping through the shop. This is torture, and I know torture even if that isn't entirely in my job description.

I bite back a groan as I strangle the feral part of my anatomy that is misbehaving but immediately release myself when her head turns in my direction to flash a brilliant smile at me. I usually get off on watching humans scream in terror and yet it is Fanny's smile that is currently making me want to release in my pants. I covet them to the point of being irrational jealous over any customer she smiles at. I want to stroke myself and watch my seed spray all over her while she pants and smiles ever so sweetly at the droplets coating her tits and face. My cock gives a heavy pulse and I immediately unwind my tail just enough to rapidly shove the tip down the front of my pants and curl snuggly around my swollen shaft.

"What do you think?" she asks as she takes a few steps back from the window, her dark eyes shining with obvious happiness.

I'm tempted to tell her what I'm really thinking but I sink my teeth into my tongue, using the pain to refocus. The little vixen doesn't need any more help toying with me. Instead, I make an effort to tear my eyes from her and actually look at the display. A surprised grunt leaves me.

She selected several of my comics and set them out in a curious display. I also see why she insisted I drag the small table and old, velvet-upholstered chairs that I had stolen from a castle during a very brief jaunt in the 1600s. A business trip but one that I sufficiently rewarded myself with after delivering the commissioned nightmare personally. It was a stroke of good fortune that the nobleman whose room I was kicked into had some very nice, very luxurious things. I was quite happy to make a few choice selections. Among them were those two chairs and the small ornate table sitting between them. I also recognize the gold candelabra perched in the table and several ornately carved boxes that lay open overflowing with all manner of items. The majority of them are cheap props that she acquired in the mall; the rest are very expensive ones that she took from among my belongings.

The cheek!

What they never possessed was the fake webbing that clung to them from cotton batting that I watched her patiently stretching for part of the morning. Nor the incense ash coating everything. That is going to be a nightmare to clean out of the upholstery and I wonder which fiend in the mall I have to blame for supplying her. Despite this, it looks... good. It looks exactly like a ghostly sitting room from a bygone era, complete with two plastic skeletons slouched in the chairs. Horror comic books lay strewn on the table and resting in hands or on laps. And there are more plastic spiders and bugs than I care to count.

Pulling my cock firmly against my body with my tail, I stand and wander over to get a closer look. It's actually quite impressive. And it ties both the concept of the holiday with the theme of the shop. It may even draw more customers to enjoy my nightmares. From the corner of my eye, I can see the excitement filling her. Now would be the perfect time to lie and tell her how much I hate it and just pop that joy so I can feast upon the sorrow and suffering.

Strange how unappetizing the thought is when it comes to her. Instead of being aroused by the idea, my cock withers and my stomach lurches with distaste. Enjoy Fanny's joy—only hers. So, I grunt and nod as surly as possible.

"Looks good," I admit.

The squeal that comes from her makes me want to slap my hands over my sensitive ears, but I don't have the opportunity because suddenly I'm being overcome by a little bundle of femininity hurdling against me. Throwing her arms around me, Fanny hugs me tight.

"I just knew you would love it!"

That's not what I said, nor what I inferred, but I like her body pressed against mine too much to correct her. My tail grips hard against my cock as the beast surges to life once more the moment I breathe in her unique scent of candy and spice. The rusty purr that rumbles from me is embarrassing and I'm just glad that there are no demons nearby to witness it or hear her soft, throaty laughter in response.

CHAPTER 8

FANNY

I'm starting to hate this couch. It was a dream to sleep on for the first several nights but then that is easy when one is accustomed to sleeping in terrible conditions and always waking sore and tired in the morning. I had thought the couch was for a night or two, but it seems like the demon is planning on keeping me on it for the long term. It hadn't entirely bothered me until I caught a glimpse of Pashar's bedroom and saw exactly what sort of comfort he enjoys. If he could do all of that for himself, how hard would it be to set up something comfortable for me?

All it took was a single brief glimpse when he stepped out as I happened to be on my way to the bathroom and I've coveted it ever since. It's ridiculous that he can do all of that and not even bother to make up a reasonably comfortable guest room for me to sleep. One that doesn't make me shiver at times while I wait for my body to warm the blankets. I know that he's a demon and this is my punishment but come on. I don't need much; it hardly seems fair to deny me an actual bed when his entire bedroom is the epitome of a den of luxury. Granted, it looks like a vampire decorated, but I like it. He could keep to his home's color scheme, austere spaces, and touches of overdone elegance, and it wouldn't bother me in the least once I moved my own brightly colored little homey touches out of the living room.

But as I have nothing but a couch, his bedroom just begs me to enter, and I have a poor ability at resisting what I want. I want to explore the entire expanse of the bed and find the coziest spot on it. There is a forbidden, naughty part of me that really wants to do it while he is stretched out bare on the bed which makes me both blush furiously and grow wet.

I'm not a virgin. That was the first of my mother's warnings of my shameful future that I practically ran headlong into. But as most men I've encountered while roving were complete pricks that I wouldn't let anywhere near my pussy, my experience hasn't exactly been copious or widely varied. In fact, until just recently, I've been pretty sure I could take or leave having a sex life of any kind. Pashar may be a complete dick and a monstrous demon of nightmares, but he's one that makes me squirm with desire the moment he drops his human disguise.

Funny. It should be the hot human look that makes me want to jump him. He certainly picked an attractive model to emulate. I discovered that quite by accident when I happened to glance at a magazine and was forced to take a second look in surprise. The model's hair was short and well-groomed and his face lacked the scruff that Pashar's human look had, but all it took was for me to squint a little and I saw it. And yet that still doesn't make me all hot and bothered. He's nice to look at, but the real him has me curious and wanting to take a look and see what he hides in his pants.

I can't even begin to imagine what he looks like there but picturing his dark purple body and long wings stretched out over the black sheet, his long hair pooled behind him. And that tail. A soft pant leaves me as I imagine that long coil of his tail and the way it loops and twitches provocatively. Having all that between my legs and a bed with the thickest mattress I've ever seen to curl up on afterward is my most immediate and torturous fantasy.

Not that he looks at me that way. As much as I enjoy messing with his head regarding the Halloween stuff, I really wish I could actually capture his attention. I've been doing my best, but my best doesn't seem to be getting results. Even wiggling my ass in the air at every opportunity hasn't had the desired reaction. At this point, I'm pretty sure I could go tuck myself into his bed in my Hello Kitty pajamas and he wouldn't even notice.

I bite my lip and smile. He's never explicitly said that I couldn't sleep in his bed. He just told me to not dig through his things with my clumsy human hands. I have no intention of touching anything in the room but the bed... and maybe him if he doesn't object to a cuddle partner... so, what's the harm? Especially considering how surprisingly chilly his home is. Isn't this the world of demons? I imagined it would be hotter. He has to be cold as well if his bedroom is as cool as the rest of his home. I certainly can use a warm body to curl up to or at least share heat under the blankets with. While sleeping on the couch with the bedding I was given kept me at a tolerable temperature, the chance of being truly warm and comfortable sets me in motion.

I don't allow myself a moment to second-guess the questionable brilliance of my plan to worm my way into a more comfortable sleeping spot and hopefully, eventually, a certain demon's arms. Truthfully I wouldn't mind working my way into his twisted heart either. I've never met anyone that I felt such synchronicity with. It's like why are tied together by more than just the magic he has bound me with. I'm actually certain that we must be soul mates. I read about it in Cosmopolitan magazine and that is what I know I'm feeling. Our stars are aligned—or likely would be if he weren't a demon and in a completely different world than the one that humans experience. Even though I've never been outside of his home, I'm pretty certain that we are in another realm which is pretty fucking dope. I would give anything to be able to take a peek and see something of it. But first, I want a closer look at that bed and, if I'm lucky, the demon occupying it.

With a little quiet hum to myself, I slip off the couch and leave the living room, taking a hall to its very end where a large door bars entrance. The handle turns easily under my hand and the door opens with barely a whisper of sound. The room is completely black outside of the strange illumination from several mounted crystals that give off a faint glow of light. It's enough for me to see enough by so I don't hesitate to step into the room. It's lucky, too. I know from experience that they react only to magic, so I have no way to brighten them to make it safely around the room. If they had been too dim or darkened, I would have been out of luck.

Not that I can make out much detail, but I can see the dark imprint of the enormous bed and the bulk of the large demon stretched in the middle of it. Without hesitation, I tiptoe over, making as little noise as possible, and peer down at him. The rumbled fabric of the bedding is more of an impression than anything else, but his wide, sculpted chest is hard to miss as it moves rhythmically with every breath he draws deeply into his lungs. I lean forward, noting as I do all of the empty space between his body and the edge of the bed.

I bite back a laugh. He's not going to even notice me on the bed. There is enough room to easily fit two people on either side of him. With how firm the mattress looks, and his own large bulk considerably outweighs my much smaller body, I doubt he will even feel a hint of me crawling onto the bed beside him. I just have to stay below wing level so I'm not sleeping on it. Not a problem. It will put me at an awkward crotch level but I'm not going to be paying any attention to the beast while I'm fast asleep.

Adjusting my position lower down the side of the bed, I put my knee on the edge of the mattress and pause when the wing closest to me twitches. My eyes snap from his wing to his face but when he doesn't so much as frown or make any other move but continues to breathe evenly, I slide stealthily onto the bed and drop down low on the open mattress to the left of his hip. I'm well below the bottom edge of his velvety wing and all the strange peacock feathering at its base, while still being far outside any accidental touching distance—not without a lot of starfishing going on. Curling up on my side, I wiggle into the blankets and carefully tuck them in around me. The tiniest sigh of contentment escapes me before I can smother it.

Oh, wow that's comfortable. With the weight of the bedding draped over me, I'm forced to bite back a louder sound of pleasure.

I can't, however, hold back the startled squeal that I shout when his large body suddenly goes still for a heartbeat before his entire body moves. He is like a massive shadow engulfing me as he smoothly covers my body with his own. His hot breath stirs my hair and I swallow back my whimper. Not of fear but of desire. A flash of intense heat is rushing through me as the firm weight of his body faintly presses in against mine. It's not enough to crush me but to hold me in place beneath him. A growl vibrates between us but then he sniffs and the growl shifts, dropping down into a rattling purr. It doesn't last for more than a second before he seems to remember and it cuts off just as quickly as it started.

"What are you doing here?" he snaps, jerking me up the length of his body so that we are hip to hip rather than hip to mouth as I lay beneath him.

I give him a defiant look, put off by his attitude. It wasn't like I was trying to grope him or do anything pervy. "Don't get your tail in a twist. I'm just trying to sleep and enjoy some of this huge bed you're hogging to yourself," I hiss back, undeterred and unwilling to back down when he has demonstrated once again—and very convincingly—that he will not hurt me, not even when taken by surprise. But it does look like playing tag with the demon will have to wait until he's a little more receptive to the idea. That's fine, for now I'll be happy just to sleep comfortably. "The couch is cold and hard. It's killing my back and I'm going to end up sick if I'm not warm enough. Besides, I'm not taking up much room. So just go back to sleep."

"Impossible," he huffs. "You have no sense of self-preservation if you are crawling into a demon's bed and expecting that nothing will happen except sleep."

I go still and peer up at him, my heart galloping with excitement. "Are you going to devour me?" I whisper, sincerely hoping he will.

Though I can't see his frown, I can feel it and notice the way his glowing eyes narrow. "Of course not," he scoffs.

The sound of it grates on my ears but I smile sweetly at him since I'm sure he can see my expression just fine.

"Wonderful. Then this shouldn't be a problem. Now scoot over and quit being a blanket hog or let me take a turn on the bed while we work out better sleeping conditions for me."

It isn't exactly what I wanted but at least I'll get the bed, and that's something. I grab a hold of the blanket wrapped around him and give it a tug. To my surprise, his hand snaps down onto it and latches on so tight that I'm unable to get more than an inch or two of fabric to budge. He rumbles in warning at me, his long tail snaking along my legs as it whips around us.

"Stop!"

His snarl falls on deaf ears because I pull harder until suddenly the blanket shifts and I'm aware of the thick bar of Pashar's arousal bearing down on me. The grunt and moan that breaks from him startles both of us and we jump, causing our bodies to crash together unexpectedly, his cock pressing against me. For a moment I forget to breathe, and he seems unable to move because I can't help but to be aware of the impressive size of his sex printing its outline against my belly. His tail swishes and curls and I'm aware of the deep shadows of his wings flexing above us.

Then he's gone. Settling himself on the other side of bed, he gives his back to me, his wings twitching with annoyance.

Perhaps I pushed a little too hard but dammit I'm tired of not getting a really good night of sleep. I push up onto my side and bite my lip as I watch the random movements of his wings. "Pashar, I..."

"Sleep," he growls testily.

An unhappy frown pulls at my lips, but I fall back onto the mattress without another word. Thankfully, I am just as tired as I let on and although I'm disappointed that there was no mutually satisfying exploration that happened, I find that I am so comfortable that I slip quickly and easily into sleep as his tail lashes slowly around me.

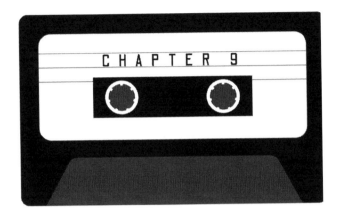

CHAPTER 9

PASHAR

I tap a claw impatiently on the countertop as I watch the human purse his lips and attempts to decide between the issues that he has brought to the counter. I want to crack his head open because I don't understand why this is happening here rather than back at the shelves where he could have returned them. He is just creating more work for Fanny, and that annoys me as much as the way he's obviously been eye-fucking her the entire time since he's entered the store. It makes me wish he had been drawn to some of the more violent nightmares on the far shelves. Unfortunately for me, the ones he chose were minimal grade nightmares that will give a rush of a chill but little else.

I scowl in disappointment at his selection as he finally slides two toward me.

"Just these, dude," he says with a laid-back smile as his eyes slip once more toward my female.

My fingers itch with the desire to grab my weaver and quickly stab out his eyes later in the comic for looking at what's mine—or better yet, feed him to Chewy—but I manage to restrain myself. Paperwork. I have to remember how much fucking paperwork it would be to murder a human on my vacation. The human standing in front of me is fortunate that demons are not only incredibly hierarchical in terms of power but have a fondness for complex systems of checks and balances to keep everything running as it should. Without that, not only would demons run willy-nilly everywhere as they pleased but this idiot would be dead before his body hit the floor.

"Six twenty-five," I growl, and the moron doesn't so much as register that I've spoken at all, his attention still firmly glued to Fanny's ass while she bounces in time with the music and mists Chewy with the water bottle.

My venomous spines threaten to burst through my skin and my illusion-cloaked corethi shifting out from under my wings. I'm still debating on whether the paperwork is worth it as eyes linger on my female a little longer, but the male wisely remembers himself long enough to hand me the money.

"Oh, hey, I totally forgot why I came in here." He chuckles to himself, brushing his hair back out of his eyes. "Do you have any Advanced Dungeons and Dragons manuals?"

"Dungeons and Dragons," I repeat, mystified, but if the human wants to be eaten my dragons—

"You know what, I think they have those at Walbrook Books on the second floor," Fanny interrupts.

I grind my teeth together as the male's face lights up.

"Oh, do you play?"

She blinks, caught off-guard by his obvious enthusiasm. I eye the byplay between them, that paperwork looking more appealing by the moment, but then she gives him an apologetic grimace and it's all I can do to keep from crowing at the disappointment crashing over the male.

"No, sorry. I just wander a lot during my lunch breaks. The books caught my attention because one had a pretty gnarly dragon on the cover. It did look kind of cool though," she rushes to add which makes him brighten a little once more to my considerable disappointment.

"Oh! You are welcome to join my group. We are a small adventuring party right now, but I heard that there was a newer manual out that I wanted to get that could add some more interesting components to our adventures. We are always looking for new players to join!"

Fanny slants me a questioning look and I know what she wants without even hearing it, and no, I say. No!

He also notes the direction of her gaze, his smile is far less enthusiastic this time. "You can both come. It will be great. Here, let me just write down where we are meeting and when. It's just right here in the mall. We rent out a party room on the second floor for a few hours once every other week to go on our quests."

Quests? This guy has to be kidding me. Unfortunately, Fanny's eyes gleam with interest as he begins going into detail while he writes of some of their latest adventures. Sitting back in my chair I snort silently to myself, hating the way that has clearly ensnared my female's attention while I fume. Chewy clearly doesn't like it either—or she is keying into my mood after all these months sharing space with me in this shop—and several tendrils sneak toward the male with obvious intended avarice.

My lips curl in a wicked smile as I watch them slide over the floor, the struggle with my hatred for paperwork being overcome by my sheer loathing for the human flirting with *my* human. Fanny's eyes flick to me and her brows furrow slightly. I tear my eyes away from the approaching vines and grin at her, but it seems that I wasn't quick enough because she quickly looks over and her mouth drops open for a full five seconds before she suddenly pushing the customer toward the door, his back of comics books clutched to his chest.

"You know, what, we will think about it. It sounds like a real blast. You should definitely grab that manual because it does sound like it will add some pretty bitchin' stuff to your game. You should probably head up to Walbrooks if you want a chance to really look around before they close," she says rapidly as she steers the human toward the door.

He doesn't even notice the plant's vine trailing after him, his infuriatingly infatuated smile fastened on Fanny the entire time as he listens to her chatter at him.

Besotted twit is going to get himself eaten. I cackle to myself as I lean forward, eager to see the moment when they strike. A quick glance behind her, Fanny picks up her pace and manages to stay ahead of them long enough until they come to a frustrated stop just short of the door. Her entire posture relaxes and she shoots a scolding look to both Chewy and me as she pats the human on the shoulder and waves after him as he trots like an obedient little mutt toward the escalator that will take him to the second floor.

I give Chewy a sympathetic look. "Foiled."

"Very funny," Fanny grumbles as she steps back into the store. Chewy's vines slide along her legs.

I watch with interest as they seem to curl in tiny little affectionate coils against her skin. I've never heard of a malcante plant bonding with anything other than its mate. Unlike non-sentient plants within the nightmare realm, malcante pair bond, despite having both female and male reproductive parts. In fact, they spend a significant portion of their early life cycle seeking out a desirable mate—which usually ends up being a pain in the ass when they do because then they start breeding and there is often an infestation that has to be dealt with if the offspring don't disperse quickly enough. If I didn't know better, I would be convinced that Chewy had chosen a mate. The tentative curls of her vines are not unlike the testing pats that the malcante give each other to demonstrate interest and then affection.

Fanny doesn't shrug them off, which makes me wonder how long this has been going on outside of my notice. Picking up the spray bottle once more, she returns to spraying Chewy's massive fronds and my eyes narrow suspiciously as more vines and fronds reach for her as if wanting to enjoy even the briefest contact.

Like hell! First thing upon closing I'm going to do what I should have done when I first realized that the malcante plant had followed me here but had been too lazy to do—I'm going to boot Chewy out of my shop and someplace very, very far from my den. The thing has been a damned nuisance, but this is the last straw! I'm sure as hell not sharing my female with a plant either!

What if she has bonded to the human?

I palm my face, digging my claws in just enough to deliver a small amount of pain beneath my scales as I hiss in frustration. If Chewy has attached herself to Fanny, it will actually cause problems to separate them. I'm pretty sure I won't be devastated if Chewy died pining away, but if she has bonded that means she has likely already injected Fanny with her venomous barbs. One hand this will extend Fanny's life way beyond a normal human which is a plus since I'm in no hurry to let my human go, but without regular venom from Chewy specifically it will do the opposite and cause Fanny to waste away within a matter of weeks.

To the fiery pits with it!

"You know, it could be fun if we go," Fanny says conversationally as she opens a box tucked behind the counter and retrieves one of the mice she bought from Twisted Whisker.

"Go where?" I suspiciously ask as I watch her toss the rodent to the plant quivering with jubilation at the sight of its meal.

If she expects me to take her around the nightmare realm, she can think again. It is not a safe place for a human to be mucking around.

Rolling her eyes, she fetches another mouse from the box. "To the game, of course. It could be fun exploring imaginary worlds. I mean—that's kind of what you do here, right?"

I scowl at the comparison. "It's not the same. Although," I grin slowly and lean back in my chair once more, "it could be entertaining," I admit. "I could spin such a nightmare that it will take their 'immersion,' to a whole new level of—"

"Never mind," she interrupts with a laugh, tossing the second rodent to Chewy's snapping pods. "Forget that I asked. I think their game is immersive enough for them."

I grin lazily, my wings flexing playfully beneath my glamour though she can't see it. "I can always just kick them into the nightmare realm and watch them scream."

Shaking her head, she picks up the spray bottle and

spritzes me like a misbehaving cat before resuming Chewy's daily misting. My uproarious laughter fills the comic book store. I've never enjoyed a vacation so much. The seed planted within my mind from Chewy's bonding to my female grows rapidly and I'm suddenly very certain that I don't want this to end. And thanks to Chewy's bizarre mating instinct, now I don't have to. I never told her when I would release her. There were no promises made—and now, it would be unethical to do so since she will need Chewy to survive. Sooner or later, I will have her in the nightmare realm with me and then I can test the waters of allowing her to venture out with me, but until then I'm determined to enjoy the reprieve... and my female.

Nightmare demons don't like others in our territories or dens. We don't even actively look for a mate. But once our mate comes along, we are possessive fuckers who are so attached to our mates that it's no wonder that we fuck enough offspring into being to compensate for the majority who never mate at all. Of course, a human can't carry a demon offspring, no matter what their movies say—Fanny recounting the plot of The Omen to me being probably one of the most ludicrous things I've ever heard—but a human never stays human long when they are mated to a demon.

Sooner or later, they change, and I'm fascinated to see what changes eventually come. Because we are going to mate. Right now, it is merely delayed while I enjoy this little courting game we now play ever since she snuggled into bed with me and pulled out my heart with her little hands.

But it won't last for much longer. My testicles are heavy and full and my cock in a constant state of arousal while the venom in my fangs leaks continuously. Soon we will rut, and the first true hit of essence will flood into her with my seed.

And it will be glorious.

CHAPTER 10

FANNY

Pashar's chest moves beneath my cheek, and I yawn widely as his wing unfurls from around me, letting in the dim light from the crystals. I don't bother moving just yet since his tail is still lashed tightly around my middle. It's kind of cute. He never admits that enjoys having me cuddled in this great big bed with him, but I can tell. Even that first night, I wasn't in bed with him for more than a few minutes before his tail wrapped around me. What started with his tail had rapidly progressed from there. Now, the moment I crawl into bed, his tail is sliding around my waist to tug me to him as his arms and wings pin me against him.

Some might find it frightening to be pinned completely against a demon, but I really enjoy it. His heat radiates through me all night and I've never felt safer than I do when his bulk is surrounding me in every conceivable way. It makes me feel loved and appreciated just for being me. In the dark bedroom at night, there is nothing else but me and him curled up close, raw in the most basic of ways as we find comfort and pleasure And Pashar holds me as if I'm the most important thing in the world to him that, even in sleep, he can bare to let go of.

It makes me wonder whether the tight leash he likes to have on me at the mall is just him getting a thrill from trying to punish me—which, if that's the case, the joke is on him—or because he likes having me tied to him. That it comforts him knowing that I can't be removed from his side.

So... yeah... it's cute.

Scooting up in his grip as much as I can, I press my lips on his large jaw, marveling at the softness beneath my lips despite its brutal appearance. A rumble escapes him and one yellow eye cracks open and slides over to peer down at me. His massive, clawed grips the back of my night shirt and I giggle when he hauls me effortlessly on his enormous chest. His width is so much greater than mine that my arms can't even close around his sides to touch the bed. His tail slides up my inner thigh and I squirm, enjoying the way his half-stiffened cock rears up and thumps my ass as a deep groan shakes him.

Pushing myself up onto my forearms braced against his torso, I smile at him and wiggle a little against his shaft so that the already wet head of his cock is rubbing against me. His eyes slit as he watches me and his big hand presses against the small of my back, holding me in place as his hips rock up against me. If not for his hand, I probably would have fallen off him with the way his body rolled beneath mine. My tongue slides over my lips with excitement.

"What are you doing, Fanny?" His deep growl vibrates through me, lighting me up like a pinball machine.

I gasp and press against his thick length, suddenly hating my cute pajamas. They don't do anything to disguise his massive erection, but it frustrates my need to feel the full intensity of his cock rubbing against my pussy. And they just get in my way. Of course, he is as naked as ever but it's not like I'm any closer to catching a peek at that monster. Somehow Pashar always gets to bed before me and the lighting cast low enough that I've never seen him though the lighting has never been such to allow me to take a good look at what he's got between his legs. Whatever it looks like, it has girth and contours for ages. I shiver as he immediately thrusts up against me, introducing me to several protrusions that run along his length that I can feel but can't see.

"I asked you a question," he grumbles, and I lift my head to give him a mischievous smile as a fresh wave of lust sends a pleasurable haze over my vision.

Those eyes. They are so bright that they penetrate me. Hell, I want him to penetrate me and not just threaten it with his unhinged stare full of arousal. I'm sure I look like a doped kitten the way I'm scraping my fingernails languidly against his chest but damn he does this to me way too easily. The flutter of excitement within my belly just gets bigger with every movement of his big body beneath mine shuttling the thick head of his cock against my entrance.

"I think it's pretty obvious," I point out with a lust-addled smirk.

A deep groan rumbles hollowly through him and his straining cock pushes harder. "Temptation. You are playing with fire. Were you never told to not play with demons, little girl?"

"I know what I want," I whisper as I stroke my tongue against the thick muscle of his chest.

His skin shivers beneath my mouth, his breath panting as he continues to lift his hips, thrusting against me, grinding against my pajamas—defiling Hello Kitty in ways that just delight me. Every stroke hits my clit, making my whimper as I cling to him.

His other hand grips my hips as he begins to rock faster and harder against me, bucking and straining between my legs as I'm brought down against him in time with his every thrust. A trembling spark lights within me and begins to burn brighter and brighter as he grunts beneath me. I wiggle in his hold, needing more but the hot brush of his tail against my back makes me grow still with anticipation. Even my breath stops as I feel it slide into my pajama bottoms. I expect him to use his tail to pull them off me, but he doesn't.

His sinuous, slick tail slides between my ass cheeks, dropping lower until it brushes my entrance and parts the lips swollen with arousal so that it can glide between them. It is a deliberately slow sensation that is confusing when his cock is battering at my clit. The tip of his tail brushes the bottom of it, curling and thrumming as his cock grinds against me. I make a choked sound in my throat at the conflicting sensations. I feel as if my breath, heart, and soul are all being stolen at the same time I cling to Pashar and gasp. That gasp turns into squeal when his tail suddenly slides just enough to reposition itself against the mouth of my pussy and press deep as his tail sinks into me.

His yellow eyes burn up at me he rocks me onto his tail and against his cock. "Come for me, little pet. Come, now," snarls as his tail presses up against the most sensitive part of my channel as his cock shuttles violently against me.

I explode into a thousand starry fragments, my pussy gripping and dragging on it with its pulsing squeeze. I can tell that Pashar likes it because he rumbles triumphantly, picking up the pace and stroking his long tongue along my neck between sucking nips of the skin there while I tremble against him like a butterfly pinned to a board. My orgasm threatens to shake my bones into dust and I'm crying out against him, my fingernails digging into his scales as I anchor myself through the storm of sensations crashing through me.

My mouth gaping, I strain against his hold, my breasts

pressing against his chest, and I arch into him, pressing myself more firmly against his dual instruments of pleasure. I gasp and moan with the tiniest of whimpers as his tail begins to plunge in and out of me in time with the savage rocking of his hips. His growls and grunts are becoming deeper, his muscles bunching beneath me as we rock together. Being rammed by both his cock and his tail, it doesn't take me long to come apart again, my orgasm burning bright as it combusts and shoots through me. This time, however, Pashar's big body stiffens beneath mine and I can feel his swollen cock jerk sharply against my pussy, making me see stars as I feel the intense heat of his cum splatter against the soaked crotch of my pajamas, baptizing Hello, Kitty with sweet, creamy musky of his cum.

Poor Kitty. The wrong kitty got all that goodness.

I drop down slack against him and his grip lightens so that his hands stroke over my back and bottom, a deep, resinous purr rattling from his chest. His tail remains firmly lodged within my pussy for several minutes, allowing me quiver and clench repeatedly on it unless the last of my pleasure finally subsides and I shiver with a soft moan as he pulls it wetly from my body.

"Good girl," he croon-growls into my hair, and I smile breathlessly against his chest.

I don't know if I'm any kind of a good anything, but I sure as hell got my treat. And I can't wait for my fill of many more come Halloween.

CHAPTER 11

PASHAR

A lthough this is my first Halloween in the mall, I can already tell that it's going to be trouble as the day draws nearer. A small group of young vampires slink nearer to my shop with their eyes lit up with mischief. I assume that they think Fanny and I are easy pickings but the moment I let out a true growl they stop warily just outside the entrance of my shop and peer at me uncertainly.

Whatever thoughts of devilry that they have considered carrying out at my expense quickly leaves their minds as they quickly drop back and hurry with preternatural speed from my shop's entrance.

"You do realize that the whole point of the Trick or Treat Street is that we won't be scaring the kids, right?" Fanny wryly points out as she pours an obscene amount of sugary treats from a bag into an enormous bowl decorated with various smiling ghouls and witches printed around the outside of it.

"I promised nothing." I make sure to add an extra surly growl to my statement. "Besides a bunch of young, rabble-rousing vampires is the last thing anyone needs cruising through here. You are more the sort of sweet that they are looking to nibble on—not what's in that bowl of yours."

"You really say the sweetest things Pashar, but don't worry I don't have eyes for any other creature of the night but you."

Her giggle fills the shop and I find my own lips tipping in a begrudging smile in response, my hard heart warming like that foul pumpkin pie she returned with the other day. Soft, warm, probably slimy—and utterly smitten with the little human female.

"Just keep it that way," I grumble. "A vampire filled with human blood from their recent snack makes an even worse mess to clean up."

Less paperwork, though, thank the demonic overlords.

She shakes her head at me, her eyes sparkling with amusement. "You do recall that we do have vampiric patrons of the mall—even a whole shop that caters to them."

"An excellent idea," I retort sarcastically. "It makes the food court lines a lot shorter when they can pick off their buffet from the humans wandering the mall before they can congest The Good Char. I hate lines," I mutter.

Fanny rolls her eyes, a soft snicker escaping her as she heads over to tend to Chewy. "I'll have you know that Damon and Max are not only way cool, but they also treat their employee Star well—as in, you know she actually gets paid."

Leaning back in my chair, my irritation with the bloodsuckers vanishes as I smirk over at her. "With as much shopping as you do with my coin, I can safely say that you are being more than adequately compensated, thief. Do not worry. I have nothing against blood suckers. They provide a good service so long as they aren't looking to nibble off what's mine."

She grins over her shoulder at me, but her face suddenly contorts with surprise and pain as she hisses and snaps the side of her hand up to her lips. "Ouch, shit!"

I stand abruptly, concern rippling through me—and apparently my illusion at the way her eyes suddenly widen at me and then dart to the door. Right. Drawing in a deep breath and expelling it, I wrestle my control back into place as I stomp over to her and tug her hand away from her mouth.

"What happened?" The growl is barely out of my mouth when I see the telltale red barb from Chewy's vine sticking deep into the side of her palm. Or what's left of it. It has already begun deteriorating and finishes the promises within a heartbeat, right before my eyes. There was no maybe about it. It was exactly as I thought. I rub my finger over the spot and glance up at her. "Does it hurt?"

A look of surprise crosses her face, but it is quickly replaced with a pleased smile as she tucks in closer to my side. "It stung a bit, but it's not the first time. Sometimes she just gets a little over excited when I'm misting her."

"Yeah... right. Chewy has not done that to anyone before," I bluntly inform her. As content as she seems to be with me, she has always erroneously believed that her life would eventually go back to normal. The time for playing games is now done with reality laying all the cards on the table. "I've had dozens of human and non-human employees and the most she's tried to do is eat them. She *likes* you," I emphasize slowly.

Fanny blinks. "Oh. Well, I like her, too. She is a pretty wicked little plant."

"No." A heavy sigh like the bellows of a demonic forge leave me. "With demons and entities for our world, it is not so casual. She is bonding with you. How many times have you been pricked by her?"

Fanny shrugs. "I don't know. Once a day since shortly after I started."

"Yeah, that would about do it," I mutter, both annoyed at how slick the malcante carried out its intentions, and absurdly pleased by it. "So, there's good news and bad news about that."

"Oh? Okay, hit me with the good news first," she replies

with a grimace as she turns her hand in mind to inspect the red wound already fading from her hand.

I grin evilly. "Your servitude can now last for centuries."

She jerks in surprise and laughs. "Okay, how exactly is that good news?"

"Well, it is for me," I grumble in an attempt to sound annoyed. "There is plenty more work I can get out of you when I've got centuries to space it out. Besides, you've gotten under my scales and skin like a hell-fly maggot chewing its way to feast on my heart and entrails," I admit in a gruff voice.

A thoughtful look crosses her face, her brows furrowing slightly. "Is that gnarly demon way of saying that you love me?"

I grunt, exasperated. "It's what I said, isn't it?"

The smile that lights her face is like the dawn that steals all dreams. It steals my breath and my heart every time and that moment especially as she flings her arms around me, nearly tipping us over since I still remain somewhat crouched beside her. My wings snap and flare wide and I nearly lose all control over my illusion as her warmth and scent surrounds me in a wonderful cloud of bliss. If this is what dreams are, then I guess I can tolerate one—because there is no better dream than Fanny.

Tail slipping up around her waist, I curl my arms and wings around her as my corethi skates gently over her as they descend from my wings. My arms tighten when she attempts to draw back, my wings rustling in warning so that she laughs and playfully swats at them. I loosen my grip just enough to peer down at her as one of my corethi slides against her cheek, leaving a smidgeon of dust in its wake. A hint of my magic, already seeping into her bit by bit with every touch.

"This is absolutely wild, and I totally love, like, so much, but I have to tell you a secret—" she grins, "I don't have a clue how I suddenly have centuries just because of Chewy stabbing me. Or what this even means for us."

"Ah. Right. Details. Chewy has bonded with you. Normally it's something malcante plants do when they mate—"

"Oh man, please don't tell me a plant thinks I'm her mate!" Fanny moans and slumps, her forehead smacking hard against my chest.

I scowl down at my beloved flesh-eating parasite of my heart, somewhat worried by her pained grimace that she might have cracked her skull on the bony plating that runs beneath my skin there. Lifting her face, I rub a finger over her brow, inspecting it carefully. Once I'm reassured that everything is intact as it should be, I sigh.

"Of course not. You don't have the right sort of equipment for her to even want to make the attempt. But she has made the unusual decision to bond with you for whatever reason. To be honest she probably sees you as her offspring that she's decided to keep within her nest," I mutter, giving the malcante a suspicious glower.

If that thing even tries to take a bite of me for touching

my female, I will pop off her heads so that she will have to suffer a restrictive diet for months while they slowly grow back again. Thankfully, Chewy not only seems content but quite pleased with herself as her fronds ruffle and her vines slink around her and us in obvious delight. Fanny giggles sat the display until I touch her chin and turn her head so that she's once again meeting my eyes.

"This bonding means that she has envenomated you. It connects your life-force to hers more quickly than I ever could," I concede. "I can't magically halt your aging the way her bonding venom does, as a demon I can only corrupt your humanity until after a great many years—decades most likely —you finally transform and shed it to be who you are meant to be."

She likes up at me, her big, wide-set eyes staring in the dark abyss of my soul. For whatever reason she finds me pleasing, I cannot complain, I can only hope that she will find the same pleasing in herself as well when the changes come.

"I won't be human anymore?"

"No," I rumble in agreement. "It is the price for being with me." I grit my teeth, hating the fact that she might try to refuse me. "Object all you want, but even if you don't mate with me and don't change, you can't escape me. You need Chewy now that you've become envenomated. You need each other, and I have to keep her here under my supervision. You can rail and scream—"

"Pashar, shut up," Fanny laughs, pressing her finger against my lips. "I love you too. And what I'm hearing h ere is that what Chewy did is ultimately a pretty awesome gift. I'm not going to be a hag when I finally change—which is kind of a relief. If I have an eternity to spend with anyone, I would much rather be hot when it happens."

"And the change doesn't scare you?" I narrow my eyes on her, not quite believing my female.

She giggles and tucks her sweet little body against mine. "Please. I get to become some badass demonic creature. That is legit wicked as fuck. Being human is overrated. I want to explore all possibilities. So long as I can remain hot," she adds, tilting her head to squint up at me. "I will stay hot, right?"

Chuckling, I kiss the tip of her adorable little nose. "You will look mostly as you do now, thanks to Chewy... just accentuated with whatever gifts the change gives you."

"Wicked," she breathes against my scales. "And how do we get this things started?"

I peer down at her, a strange ball of emotion squeezing my throat. "When we mate and I introduce my own venom into you, it will begin the process."

Her eyes slit contently, a pleased smile spreading across her face. "And can I pick when we mate?"

"I...uh... sure," I grumble, my own eyes narrowing on her as I lean in close. "What do you have in mind."

Her little pert tongue slips out from between her lips to flick my mouth and I nearly groan with the pleasure of it.

"Halloween night. The Witching hour. Let's really get magical for our first night of forever," she whispers.

Tomorrow night. I tremble with happiness as I hug her close to me. I was almost afraid that she would ask years from me just to playfully watch my squirm. It pleases me that my mate is as eager for me as I am for her. The game of torture, of master and servant are coming to and end. All of the games are done. All except one.

"Now tell me what's in that infernal bag?" I growl.

Her laughter bursts out and I have a feeling there is one last game still that she is determined to wait to play out.

CHAPTER 12

FANNY

"No. Absolutely not." Pashar growls in offense though he meekly sits before me as I adjust his costume.

"Come on, don't be like that. You promised to cooperate. You wanted to know what was in the bag, after all," I sing out in reminder as I adjust the cheesy, plastic red devil mask on his face. With his cartoon-like appearance and wide smile, it is just the thing that my demon needs.

"It is insulting to demons everywhere," he complains. "It's stupid."

"It's not stupid. You look great," I rush to assure him.

"Look at it this way, you can be a demon and not only not terrify every human in the mall but give the fake impression of being friendly and approachable to the children with minimal effort."

"I will be mocked by demons everywhere," he hisses, but I huff in amusement at that.

"Oh quit. It's a family appropriate costume that you can hide behind. What more do you want? I'm dressed up, too," I point out, gesturing with my gloved hand at the small red demon horns attached to the red headband on my head that somewhat match the paint coating my face.

"It's not the same at all," he grumbles. "You are just wearing color and soft horns. If you are going to torture me, why not provide me the same costume?"

"I suppose you didn't catch the part about looking approachable," I reply dryly. "I love you, Pashar, but your idea of looking friendly will frighten small children which is the opposite of what we are trying to do. Besides you left all the Halloween prep stuff up to me since you didn't want to deal with it—and this is what you got. So just relax. Besides, who is going to see you to tell, anyway?"

"What in Satan's twisted bowels..." a deep voice booms and I wince as I practically feel Pashar's annoyance hit the roof with Dzik's bark of laughter. "That is quite a costume, Pashar," he chokes out as Kimmy tips her head back and gives the big male a pinched look.

"I think it's cute," she says, doing her best to be helpful.

"Oh, it is," Dzik agrees, his smile growing eviler by the minute.

The exchange hits its mark and my demon glares, his glowing eyes spitting furiously at Dzik as they narrow dangerously behind the plastic smiling face.

"Shouldn't you be perched over your hell pit?" Pashar shoots back from behind the mask.

Dzik just chortles, his loud laughter carrying far enough to draw several curious gazes in passing.

"Oh, we haven't opened yet," Kimmy chirps cheerfully, her eyes shining as she peers around the shop. "Dzik's just taking me around because I wanted to see what everything looks like before we get busy. This looks great! Like the haunted mansion of some sorcerer whose demons are on the loose," she adds.

I smile in response, delighted with the compliment. I have to admit, I did a good job. In addition to the display at the front, the inside of the shop is littered with fake spiders, plastic pumpkins and grinning wicked witches along the displays and hanging from the ceiling.

"I just do not know why I have to wear anything," Pashar grumbles. "I can simply adjust my illusion if I must do this."

"Where's the fun in that?" I challenge as I pick up the floppy fabric demon tail and give his denim-clad lower body a thoughtful look.

Although it takes a very large size to accommodate his frame, I'm glad that he at least wears real clothing and merely adjusts its appearance for the sake of his illusion. Giving how monstrously huge his true form is, I'm actually gratified by the fact that he can compress himself enough so that his size beneath his illusion is more along the lines of just a really big man. It all makes my job with this much easier. Plucking up a safety pin, I circle my finger in the air with a sweet smile until he begrudgingly gets up from his chair and turns to present his backside to me, his arms crossing over his chest. Dzik ignores his warning glare and laughs harder at my demon's indignation. Even Kimmy can't quite hold her giggle in as I pin that tail right above where his actual tail is concealed within his pants.

It looks really tiny on him as it flops and dangles with his every movement, not even reaching his knees. He gives it a disgusted look, missing Kimmy's apologetic smile as she waves goodbye and practically hauls the snickering demon out with her to see more of the mall. The trickle of activity is slow, but soon customers are pouring through, many of them stopping to admire the decorations. Because it's hours yet until Trick or Treat Street is underway, for now I don't bother opening the bags of candy I have stashed behind the counters. I attend to my usual work, my fake tail swinging behind me as I walk. It must be as distracting visually as it is wearing it because more than once I catch Pashar watching it with obvious interest. It makes me wonder what it would be like to really have a tail. If I did, how would it feel to have him grab it and give it a tug?

Does he like his tail pulled? I bite my lip as I consider

curling my fingers on the base of his long, thick tail and yanking on it. Maybe I will give it a try and see.

As if sensing my thoughts, Pashar looks up from the art he's carefully creating and enchanting. His true eyes glow brighter from behind his illusion, and I feel an answering heat rise within me. We've been fooling around quite a bit, working up to the main event, and man am I ready. I've been aching to feel the length of his cock pushing into me. The lack of penetration is the only thing that has helped Pashar keep his fangs—and subsequently, venom—to himself. As tempting as it is to just go for the gold and enjoy it, I really want it to be the best end to the spookiest day of the year. Finish off the holiday in an extra special way.

How many girls can say that they spent their Halloween mating a demon?

I give Chewy a giddy smile as I feed and water her. With a fond pat to one of her vines I continue on my usual route around the shop, straightening here and there, cashing customers out when there's nothing that requires my immediate attention so that Pashar can continue to work. We make a good team in every way. Granted, there are a few tense moments when a few flirtatious comments regarding my costume make my demon straighten in his chair, emanating pure violence, but I make it a point then to hurry them along and out of the shop before Pashar explodes. Despite that, I'm enjoying myself and don't even mind the fact that I have to touch up my makeup after lunch to repair the small smears around my mouth. Or that the thick goop itches unpleasantly. It's all worth it, especially when the first stream of Trick or Treaters arrives.

Although he grumbles, Pashar doesn't object when I move his stool from behind the counter to the corner just outside the entrance. Instead, he picks up the enormous bowl of candy and lowers himself onto the stool as I dole out the treats to the kids who, with a little encouragement from their parents and more than a little cajoling from me as well at times, hesitantly make their way to him with wide eyes.

From the first dutifully rumbled "Happy Halloween" from my demon and his deep chuckle at their sudden awe-filled gasps, my already conquered heart melts a little more. Especially when he goes the extra mile for the littlest among them, I acknowledge as I watch a little girl who can't be any older than four warily approach us, her hand tucked into her brother's hand as they follow behind a stream of older kids.

Dressed all in pink like a fairy, she gives Pashar an uncertain look and appears to be on the verge of tears as a little boy dressed as a skeleton walks her up to us. I wiggle my fingers at her and give her a cheerful smile, but her gaze is fastened entirely on Pashar looming on his chair like a vulture on a perch. Although having him sit on his stool brings him a little closer to the level of the kids trick or treating, he is admittedly still huge. So much so that I'm pretty sure she doesn't even see me.

"Come on, Sally," the boy murmurs. He sighs and throws back his head with a groan when she whimpers. "Don't cry. It's Halloween, remember? People are just in costumes. And look, he's got that big bowl of candy. You want some, right? Let me show you, it's simple." Striding forward, he holds his bag. "Trick or Treat."

Pashar rumbles in approval, keeping it lower than usual so that it doesn't spook the little one too much as I fetch a small handful of candy from the bowl and toss it into the kid's sack. He turns to the little girl with a triumphant look. "See. Just like that."

As if on cue, Pashar shakes the bowl in her direction so that the little foiled wrapped pieces rustle together. Her tiny teeth sink into her bottom lip, but she nods and moves closer. Blinking rapidly, she holds up her little bag.

"Twick o Tweat," she lisps in a very little voice, her eyes like saucers in her head.

"Happy Halloween, brave little pixie," my demon murmurs, his voice pitched low in a soft purring sound as her bottom lip wobbles.

She blinks again, her lashes spiky with her unshed tears as she regards him with surprise as he continues to purr. Gradually, the corners of her lips tip and a tiny, watery giggle escapes her.

"Just like kitty," she observes.

Pashar nods solemnly. "All the best monsters are," he assures her. "And all the best do a little magic... just for special pixie princesses."

Wait, what? I give him a confused look, but he frees one of his hands from the side of the bowl and curls it low in the air between them, spinning shadows and a pearly gray mist gathering between his fingers and palm as tiny fairy lights spring up to zip around before dancing merrily around his hand. Her little mouth gapes open and she leans in closer. The lights make little bell-like sounds as they rise up to her, their soft glow illuminating her face and shimmering on her eyes.

I'm pretty sure I am gaping a little as well as I watch the interaction between them. Pashar is always so utilitarian about his skills. There is nothing visible to see outside of his art when he is working on a new comic, and his glamour settles around him instantaneously without a lot of fanfare. This is honestly the most show I've ever seen from him and the fact that he's doing it for a frightened little girl her first time Trick or Treating is the cutest thing ever. His gaze shifts, his eyes eating mine and I swear I see a hint of amusement in those glowing depths that makes me want to screw my face up and stick my tongue at him to show him that I'm definitely not impressed. It would be a lie, but I would do it. Except that it would also draw attention to what he's doing and it's obvious that it is meant to be a small thing just for her as her brother digs through his bag.

I give myself a hard mental shake, grab a big handful of candy, and drop it into her bag. The fairy lights are immediately forgotten and wink out of existence as her head drops to investigate her loot. A happy squeal leaves her, and she runs over to show her brother her score, or shop left behind as the children hurry off to their next stop. My demon stares after them for a moment until he realizes that he's still purring, and the sound cuts off like an engine.

"Not a word of this to anyone," he grumbles before levying a menacing growl towards a group of teens dressed who grin with delight in response.

"Of course," I murmur. "A demon enjoying Halloween would be just terrible."

"I'm not enjoying it," he denies, but I smirk at the blatant lie in his voice. "Experts say that sugar gives nightmares, so I'm just fueling them and prepping them for their nightmare demons."

What a bunch of bull crap. I bite back a laugh because we both know he would do nothing of the sort if he truly believed that.

"Absolutely. It can't be for any other reason. If it was, what would the other demons say?"

The look he gives me as they rush away with their candy is one that promises the best kind of retribution. A punishment I definitely mean to collect.

CHAPTER 13

PASHAR

I am glad when we are finally able to close up. Although I refuse to admit it to my mate, the festivities were surprisingly enjoyable, especially seeing the children weaving their little fantasies all around them as they raced through the mall in their various costumes. As a nightmare demon I was able to see the trails of those subtle magics and I gently tease them into the right direction so that they sleep well and explore their little adventures in the dream world fearlessly. Something else I refuse to admit if my mate catches on, but I wager she already suspects some of my softness. She keeps it to herself, but I see it in her knowing smile as we go about our routine, closing up the shop.

I pull off my mask and set it on the counter, happy to be rid of it. It takes a little more work to unpin the tail, but that soon joins it. I consider tossing the ugly thing into the garbage bin but I look down at the costume and shake my head. Humans masquerading as demons. It seems bizarre to me but then perhaps not so much as I recall more than one devilish mask during the Carnevale in Venice even in the midst of the plague. I had worn one myself, I recall, before I traveled south to Florence. I had stolen it from a vendor and worn it out of mockery as I laughed at the ridiculousness of masquerading in something so close to my true form as I frolicked among the humans. Boldly revealing the truth as I wandered among the company of many others similarly masked in the hope of going unnoticed by the rampaging evil, unaware of actual demons in their midst.

Although the time of year is wrong, staring down at the mask brings it to mind. That previous mask I had tossed into a fire, chortling with amusement but with little other thought for the mask itself. I had not thought of it for some time. Strange that the memory returns so sharply to me now when, in contrast to this Halloween, that carnival bore no true delight for me. This mask is a pale, ridiculous imitation of the artfully crafted masks I wore before and yet this time, I do not wish to throw it away. It is a novel feeling for me as I'm seldom one to keep mementos.

I believe that this one I shall keep.

Picking up my bag, I slide my work into it and follow with my supplies and tools before at last slipping the mask in with them all. Dropping the bag back onto the table, I don't bother to pick up the cloth tail that falls to the floor. Instead, I head over to the entrance and pull down the grating, my gaze straying to my mate, and her little fake tail swinging behind her, as she bends to clean up a mess. Lust hammers through me at the sight of her pert bottom rising into the air, even with that ridiculous tail attached to it, and a smirk curls my lips as I drag the grating down the rest of the way to the floor and lock it into place. With a final shake to make sure that it's secure, I abandon the entrance and slip quietly between the shelves, my gaze fastening on my female as my desire flares and fans through me, the curling with greater intensity as my cock throbs within my pants.

I'm unable to restrain my growl as I slide into place behind her. She freezes for a heartbeat and then slowly straightens as tiny bumps break out of her flesh. It is exquisite how responsive she is. My nostrils flare, dragging in the scent of her nervousness and arousal mingling together. I haven't moved even an inch closer when the lights in the mall click off one by one, plunging us into darkness, broken only by the glow of the signs. I lean forward in the darkness and slip my long tongue from my mouth so that it trails along the sensitive skin of her shoulder and up her neck. I can taste and smell her readiness and it makes my cock tightens and rises in response, pushing through my genital slit, eager to finally claim my mate.

There is a dance of subtle energies in the air, their dance winding faster and more vibrantly with the season of the hunt. I ignore it as I always do since demons do not involve themselves in the hunts of the fairy and other beings that take what is theirs in the waning months. And yet, I feel aroused with my impending claim like any male who had secured a mate by the laws of the hunt. It thrills me, winding a fiery path of pleasure deeper than ever into the core of my being. I tremble, my hands shaking slightly as they come up to settle along Fanny's shoulders. I stroke her upper arms and drop my head lower to nuzzle her neck as I deeply breathe in her scent. I could easily push my bag aside and fuck her on this counter, her pale golden breasts lifting in offering to the darkness as I bend her over it. It tempts me and I'm not usually one who ignores my temptations but not this time.

Fanny is right. We only mate once and this time should be perfect. So, I file that highly arousing image away to explore later and bend just enough to tuck my arms securely around my mate so that she is easily lifted off her feet the moment that I stand. Fanny clings to me in reaction, her small arms curling tightly around my neck as she gasps in surprise. A pleased purr rattles through me and I hug her close, my nose brushing the soft skin beneath her jaw where her scent is the richest.

"I guess it's time," she observes with a small, nervous laugh.

I don't respond with words, but my purr kicks up a notch as I adjust my grip on her just enough to scoop my bag up and loop it over my shoulder before curling my arm possessively around her again. Fanny's small body fits perfectly within my arms and against the giant bulk of my body. She is mine and I don't leave any doubt in her mind of my claim as my tongue slips out once more to bathe her neck in more of my saliva that has become pheromone rich ever since my body began priming for mating days ago. There is an extra something else in it as well and I know when she feels it because she gasps and wiggles provocatively against me as her scent blossoms with the ripest flavor of need. Her nipples scrape against my chest through her shirt.

"Oh!" That word slips from between her lips as her body shivers against mine.

That little gasped word is pure ecstasy for a demon like me. To feel it breathed upon the scales of my neck by my female, never has there been anything more erotic. I am aching as I navigate our way through the portal, the sensory burn of shifting worlds rocketing through me. Fanny twists and moans, her desire heightened by the energy-burst. I feel it too. It catches fire to the heat rushing through my blood, stirring an inferno within me as the first hot burst of precum spurts from my cock and smears against the inside of my pants, making the fabric rub irritatingly.

I drop my bag on the floor and shift my hold on my female. I need to remove the rough pants and spare the sensitive head of my dick—for all our brutal strength and deadliness, our sexual organs are more sensitive than most other species. Like other nightmare demons, mine are internal but it takes little stimulation for them to extrude and cause considerably more discomfort with my mounting arousal. As much as I need some relief from the overstimulation, I don't want to release my mate for even a moment.

An impatient, clicking growl rises from my throat, the sound an entirely new variation from my usual. It takes me only a moment to reach back far into my memories and recall what it is. Mating growl. It is both used to inflame our mates and warn rivals away. If it did anything for the latter, I haven't a clue, but its effect on Fanny is instantaneous. She jerks in my arms with a soft cry, a gush of her arousal spilling free from her as she trembles from the small climax that shoots through her. It's delicious and fans my hunger for her to even greater heights. I can't wait any longer! Clutching her tightly to my chest, I race to our room, my heart pounding with excitement in time with my heavy footfalls hitting the floor.

The layout of my den allows me to reach the room quickly and lay my mate on the bed, her bottom tucked close to the edge of the mattress. She smiles up at me and pulls off her sweater, her small, delightful tits bouncing with the movement before laying back to watch me, her dark eyes shining with excitement. Her hips promptly lift as I reach for the waistband of her pants, assisting me as I unbutton and peel them off her, taking her underwear down with them. Her sweet perfume immediately floods my nose as I bare her cunt, and another clicking growl vibrates through me in response as my cock leaps in its silent demand. I am eager to shred my human clothing from my body to climb over her and mount her, but I don't wish to scare her, or use my mate harshly and potentially harm her.

Forcing some patience into my movements, I step back and remove my clothes, allowing them to drop to the floor as I abandon the last vestiges of my human disguise and stretch to my fall height, my breath billowing into me as my body expands to its true girth once more. Fanny's eyes follow me, the lust within their depths deepening as I drop my glamour. With another clicking growl, I prowl toward the bed and her thighs part at my approach in silent invitation. Stepping between them, I lower myself to a crouch and drop my hand to her slick sex, luminous with her arousal, and press against the heat gathering there. A groan of pleasure escapes me from the feel of it, and I rub my thumb back and forth over the little nub of flesh at the top of her slit as my tongue slips from my mouth and ventures along the delicate flesh there, lapping her sweetness up. With feverish snarls of pleasure, my tongue slips along over cunt, teasing her and lapping her sweetness from the source as I press my tongue deep within her, hunting for more.

Fanny moans, her hips trembling as I thrust my tongue in and out of her as my thumb resumes teasing her little pleasure spot at the top. I delight in the kick of her hips and the soft whining pants that burst from her lungs as I tease her and worship her. I can't get enough of her flavor. I could probably feast on her for hours if the ache of my cock weren't so demanding.

She is so incredibly soft here that I can't help but marvel at it all as I explore her folds and retract my claws to dip a long, thick finger into her heat. Fanny makes a choking sound in response, her head tipping back with the intensity of the sensation rushing through her and the plush, wet heat of her squeezes against my finger. My eyes close as a shiver rushes through me and I fan my wings wide, stretching them fully from where they have been compressed and shriveled against my body all day. My corethi descend from where they are coiled at the base of my wings and lower around her like so many vines, the feathered ends trailing over her, their barbs scraping, delivering tiny, insignificant doses of my venom to my mate.

They stroke over her flushed skin, and I enjoy the way her flesh reacts to their delicate, venomous touch with every shiver and smattering of tiny bumps raising and prickling. More importantly, it is her scent that compels my hunger to greater heights. Her perfume of excitement and need fills my nose as distinctly as her cries of pleasure fill my ears. She is a sensory masterpiece: taste, sound, and touch satisfying my every need.

Almost every need. My cock is hard enough to bludgeon a hapless enemy to death but there is only one thing that will ease it and make the ache tormenting me go away. Such sweet pain. Sweet torment. Even as I desperately want relief, I relish the sensation as I bring my female quickly to another climax, her sweetness bursting into my mouth and over my tongue clenched within her cunt. I growl in satisfaction and only with great reluctance withdraw it from her body to lick her flavor coating my mouth. She watches me with glazed eyes, her pulse leaping in her throat.

She is so tiny and prey-like as I slowly climb over her. But there is no fear in her passion-filled gaze. Only a want that burns me down to my dark soul. A louder growl rumbles in my chest, hungry and possessive. Her pink lips part with a gasp and her pupils expand further in reaction. Has she been reacting that way all along? If so, it is a revelation and one that I will keep tucked close to savor and implement as I see fit.

I lower my hips to hers and a hiss of pleasure slips from beneath my teeth as my straining cock brushes her slick folds. Her pelvis leaps up in reaction, sliding in a tantalizing fashion along my length, making a thick stream of precum pump out from the tip of my prick. I want to skewer her on my dick so that she writhes, caught on its length filling her, as I plunge into her hot sheath. It is only with a surprising modicum of self-control that I didn't know I possessed that keeps me from doing exactly that.

Rocking my hips slowly, I mimic our earlier bouts of eager and adoring fornication, sliding the tip of my cock and the length of its shaft back and forth along her beckoning slit. Fanny instinctively rocks responsively into each graze, pressing the little swollen bud of her pleasure and unfurled sex opened up for me firmly against my cock in invitation.

Her sheath is so tiny, my cock like a lead pipe settled against it, but we will fit, and the mating venom beginning to course through her will see to it that it does not hurt. A quiver runs through me as instinct roars higher between us with its hungry demands.

Take. Sate. Hunger. Devour. It is a wordless pulse of instinct rushing between us, demanding the completion of the mating act that we've danced around. I can feel it beneath my scales and Fanny arches more desperately against me in her silent demand telling me that she feels it just as keenly. A pleased rumble echoes through me and I lean forward, snaking my tongue up her neck and jaw. It glances lightly against her lips before pressing deep even as I adjust my angle and press in the large head of my cock.

Her lips swallow the thick, tapered tip of my tongue even as her cunt opens and begins to swallow my cock. Her moan of pleasure vibrates through me, skating over my skin like the most pleasing of aphrodisiacs that the succubae possess. My tail curls around her thigh and my corethi cling to her as I pull out a little and press in a little deeper again. I taste the drops of venom filling my mouth from my fangs and know that she is drinking them in with every lurid suck on my tongue as she gasps around it with pleasure, her little body rising to meet my every thrust. Another growl of pleasure breaks from me as my hips jump forward, pressing the entire length of my cock home.

Fanny's squeal is muffled around my tongue but her channel attempts to strangle my cock as warm heat bursts around my length with every squeeze of her internal muscles. My cock jumps in response, eager to spill but I withdraw from the brink and pin her hips with mine so that she remains motionless beneath me and withdraw my tongue from her mouth as I work to regain control. It doesn't stop her from attempting to wriggle beneath me with frustrated whimpers. I stare down at her, watching the expressions crossing her face as she is caught within her need. So gloriously responsive.

Her little heels rise up and kick into my flanks like she's trying to urge on a hell stallion, her face screwing up in her frustration.

"Pashar, move!" she complains, and I chuckle darkly before withdrawing and giving her exactly what she needs.

Her squeal of pleasure is a delight to my ears as I plow into her, and I grunt as the head of my cock taps the deepest recess within her. I can taste the venom filling my mouth again, my gums aching with the need to strike and claim my mate, envenomating her so that she is eternally mine and mine alone. It rides me as I rock back and thrust deep again, my hips moving slowly at first and then picking up speed as our bodies come together violently with our mutual need. Fanny's little weak claws score my scales, bringing little shivers in their wake, her cries driving me on, her teeth sinking into my chest making my cock leap and my testicles shift with the rapid accumulation of my seed.

She does wicked things with those little pitiful human teeth and claws as they scrape ineffectually at me and yet stir my ardor to greater heights by ferocity with which she does it until I am slamming into her, rutting her as my hand clamps around her neck, dragging her firmly back down to the mattress and keeping her pinned beneath me as our bodies slap together with our primal need. Heat fills her gaze, and she smiles, her head tilting, exposing her neck to me. I try to distract myself with the bounce of her breasts as I rut her, slowly only to grind into her with her climaxes to milk her every orgasm to its greatest peak. The clench of her cunt around my cock is bliss, drawing my sap higher, threatening to shatter my control as I continue to ride her.

Her enthusiasm never flags as she meets me thrust for thrust. Her breath is coming in little pants now, a shin of sweat coating her skin as I feel her body prepare to climb to its pinnacle once again. It coils within her, growing as it tightens with every stroke and I am helplessly caught in it, my cock swelling and jerking with my strokes now. My lips peel back from my sharp teeth as I pump deeply into her cunt as it slowly begins to tighten around me as her muscles clench with her impending orgasm. I slam into her clenching heat, my eyes rolling back at the way her grip caresses my cock with every thrust. Her legs quiver around me and her channel spasms hard, milking my length so fiercely that my own climax barrels through me, exploding with such force that a roar tears from my throat seconds before my teeth snap onto her shoulder, savaging it as my venom flows undiluted directly into her veins.

Fanny's scream of release comes again as she rides her

orgasm anew, her body drinking in my essence with a desperation that I understand all too well. I growl triumphantly as I give her my gift as she gives herself to me.

My sweet Fanny. My mate.

Life will never be peaceful again with this female at my side. I can hardly wait to see what our future brings.

EPILOGUE

FANNY

It's safe to say that the mall has become my home and a large part of my life. In a way it has become my home just as much as my mate's den. I spend my days wandering along its halls, visiting with the friends that I've made there. I've seen so many movies at the movie theater there that I've lost count and wasted a crap-ton of Paschar's money at the arcade. Not that he minds. Money doesn't really have a meaning for him in the same way it does for humans. Demons have their own currency so human money doesn't mean dick so long as he has enough to supply us with what we need while in the human world. It's his vacation and he really treats it as such, his nightmare comics and little shop being more of a hobby project than anything else. He is happy to let me dip into the cash and take what I want even if he growls and threatens to take it out of my ass later—which always turns out to be a lot of fun, I have to admit.

It also turns out that vacations last a really long time for demons since their time runs differently than human time. And since we are mated, he is on official extended leave anyway until it's safe for us to really go home and not be isolated within the confines of his den. So I try to remember this as well. I've caught most of the good movies that have hit the cinema and shopped my heart out as years have marched past. The eighties were hard to let go of but then as the late nineties came with everyone dialing in, the world expanded further, growing and changing while I mostly stayed the same.

I mean, personal internal growth aside, and the random change of my hair styles on whim, I can't say that I look any different thanks to Chewy. Well, and not counting *the changes*. They are slow to come but I started noticing them after the first three years we were together. Small things at first, like setting fire to an entire shelf of comic books one day, and then bigger things such as when I woke up with a tail that had sprouted overnight while I slept—which does turn out to be every bit as erotic as I had imagined. Unlike Pashar's sinuous tail, mine is fluffy—like that of a fox. I blame my mate entirely for calling me his little fox so much. I swear that my body just decided to just work with what he was shoveling, but I can't complain. I love my tail, even if it's a pain in the ass to keep hidden. But more than that, I love Pashar's grumbly, surly, growly ass day by day, and he never fails to show me exactly how much I mean to him even if it is in the little things, like going with me to see my favorite movie at the theater for the third or fourth time, or bribing the cook at one of the nicer restaurants in the mall to stay open a little later for our dinner.

Surprising me on my thirty-fifth birthday with a laptop was everything! I know he hates the new booms in technology. There is no dragging him into the digital age as of yet. I can't even persuade him to put up an online storefront for selling his comics. He says it cheapens his work, but all I can see is new avenues opening up before me as I explore the world beyond what was ever possible before.

And the years keep rolling. Music changes, fashion changes. Politics. It is fascinating to watch even if I feel like I'm an observer, seeing everything from a distance. And we do leave our mall sometimes to make little trips elsewhere, but we never stay away long. We go to the beach from time to time, and we visited Disneyland, but never further out than California. I don't like to be gone long, and really neither does Pashar since he feels nervous traveling with me in the open away from the security of the mall and all the monsters who work there. There he feels safe to let me out of his sight. I like going down from the shop, through the portal to our den and sleeping in our big bed every night.

I take a bite of cold pizza, the extra cheesy slice making me hum with pleasure as I finally shut the lid on my laptop and give him a sidelong look as I slide my hand over its sleek top. This is the fifth laptop that he's bought me since the first one. Although he claims to still have no use for them, he understands how much I appreciate having access to the world at my fingertips and so sees to it that I have up to date equipment. He didn't even make any of his usual comments about nosy humans when I joined the world of social media. I think he gets the fact that I need to feel like I'm still a part of the human world in some small way even as I grow further and further apart from the last vestiges of my humanity.

I wonder if we can get internet service in the demonic world.

I make a mental note to ask him about that. Although I've loved our vacation, I know that with my transition nearing its completion that Pashar will soon look to return home. I'm excited for the new adventure stretched out in front of me but also nervous. I worry sometimes that if I lose those human parts of myself that Pashar fell in love with that he would feel differently about me.

Licking the greasy cheese and sauce from my lips, I eye my mate speculatively, my tail twitching against the back of the stool where I'm sitting behind the shop counter, the rest of the surrounding mall dark beyond our little shop. His eyes track my tail and I give it a teasing little flick, a giggle bursting from me when a lustful smile curls his lips, his glowing yellow eyes rising to meet mine.

My tail curls against my belly and I hug it to me, enjoying the teasing bristle of the soft fur. My long, pointed ears twitch, twisting with the subtle sounds of the denizens of the mall. Essentially, becoming a huyao, a fox demon, certainly hasn't been any hardship. Or perhaps I always was a fox demon and just found a way to wear a human form for a while to be born to my parents. I certainly never fit in right among my family, and there are all kinds of legends of foxes becoming humans, several of which my grandmother used to tell. I can't help but think that my parents would be horrified to see me now. They are very old and although I don't visit them since it was kinder than the truth of my decision, I got in touch with them some years ago and have kept tabs on them. Knowing that they would be unhappy with what I've become makes my chest squeeze the way that it had during my youth when I tried desperately to meet family expectations before rebelling against them.

I don't think they would recognize me now nor see any trace of the human that I was. They would be disappointed. I can live knowing that; that's nothing new. As long as Pashar loves this me as well, then I am more than pleased to have my nifty abilities. That doubt is insidious though and I find it slipping out my mouth between bites of pizza before I can stop it.

"I think my transition is almost complete," I confide quietly.

His eyes narrow slightly on me as if staring deep into some part of me that I can never see in a mirror, and nods. "A few more months at most," he agrees and takes another big bite from his slice.

Okay. No words of excitement or adoration there. No need to panic, though.

"I mean, this new me is pretty neat right? I can't imagine how it can get any better," I observe with a giggle, as I blow a tiny flame from my fingertips.

Pashar's lips curl faintly with amusement, but I'm a bit disappointed that he only grunts as he continues to eat. I mean, that's just how Pashar is. It's not like he has been demonstratively excited about my transformation, but it never bothered me before since I never felt like he was displeased with it. Our sex life certainly hasn't suffered. He is as enthusiastic as ever—and in fact gets more inventive and willing to push my boundaries as time passes. But now that my change is almost complete, the doubt has flared to life, and I don't understand why he can't see that I need a little more than that.

I wrinkle my nose at him with a huff and he looks up at me in confusion, his mouth stuffed full of the ridiculously large slice he's feeding into it.

Leaning forward, I meet his gaze and fold my arms on the counter. "Babe, I love you but seriously... you need to be just a teensy bit more reassuring than that."

His brow dips into a scowl and he quickly chews his mouthful of pizza before speaking. "Reassuring of what?"

"Of what?" I gape at him. What exactly does he think we are talking about? "Of this!" I gesture to myself in one sweeping motion. "I need to know that you love this transformed me as much as you love the human me. That you aren't going to get tired of me the way that I am now and drop kick me."

He snickers quietly but there isn't a hint of cruelty in his gaze when he looks over at me. His eyes glow with the fierce love that is so uniquely Pashar. "My love, is that what's worrying you?"

"Well, yes. This is a new adventure for me, but I need to know that you are into it as much as I am."

He chuckles loudly and reaches over, snatching me off my seat to haul me into his lap. "My little fox, it doesn't matter to me if you were a slime ghoul of the foulest swamps of the demonic world. The female I love never changes even if your form does." He presses a kiss to my mouth, his long tongue delving past my lips and deep into my mouth, past my sharp teeth, and lingers there, his tongue twining around mine as if savoring me. When he at last lets me come up for air, his grin is wolfish as he stares down at me and curls his fingers around my tail. "That said, there are many delightful advantages to this new form. Claws and fangs to tear and bite into me as I fuck you is something I will never tire of. Or this," he adds, giving my tail a short tug, sending desire licking through me.

I shiver, a ragged pant escaping me, and he chuckles, lifting me up higher into his arms as he stands. With one sweep of his arm, he flings aside the pizza box so that he can drape me over the bare counter and tugs off my jeans. My arousal spikes and I can feel the wet silky material of my panties clinging to my pussy and clit in a way that makes me moan and twitch when his hot breath fans them. He grins wickedly up at me before pressing his mouth over my panty-covered sex to nip gently with his dangerous teeth, swiftly sending me teetering close to the edge as I whimper aloud.

He responds with a growl of pleasure that sends heat tumbling deeper through me in a way that had never affected me before until our need to mate hit us. But now I reach for it greedily, basking in it that vocalized affirmation of his desire and his claws tear off my panties. But it's his large body rising to settle over mine and the way his arms close around me and hold me so tenderly and reverently to him as he whispers soft words of adoration as he kisses and licks my flesh that proves me how much he loves me exactly as I am—the now me, however it changes and remains the same.

He is mine. He is with me to explore this new adventure with me, and I just can't wait to get to the demon world and see what happens next.

For more tales of demons and their human mates, check out the Demonic Realms series!

ABOUT THE AUTHOR

S.J. Sanders is a mom of two toddlers and one adult living in Central Florida. She has a BA in History, but spends most of her free time painting, sculpting, doing odd bits of historical research, and writing. While she has more research-oriented writing under another pen name, her passion is sci-fi and paranormal romance of which she is an avid reader. After years of tinkering with the idea, and making up her own stories in her head, S.J began to seriously pursue writing as an author of Sci-fi Romance utilizing her interests in how cultures diversify and what they would look like on an extraterrestrial platform with humans interacting with them and finding love.

CREEPY PASTA

BE KIND
AND REWIND

EVANGELINE PRIEST

Chesa Rizal is a harried mall admin who finds comfort in a cheesy bowl of pasta at the end of a stressed-filled workday. Things get stranger when she gets lost in the back hallways of the mall and attracts the attention of a shadowy creature.

Rufus Halliday, once known as mindbreaker hellspawn, Vhelloss, is now the proud owner of a kitschy Italian restaurant. Hopelessly infatuated with the charming overworked admin who graces his restaurant each night, Rufus knows better than to involve himself with humans.

However, when Chesa doesn't pick up her standing dinner order, he follows her trail through limbo to find her.

Content Warning:

Even though this is a cringetastically sweet story, there will be animated mannequins; voyeurism; shadowy tentacled monsters; nightmarish hellscapes; pasta-eating; garlic knots; age gap between an elder god and a human woman in her twenties; and graphic sex between consenting sentient adults.

Featured tropes include: instalove; stalk-her-to-protect-her; size difference; tentacles; mind-linking.

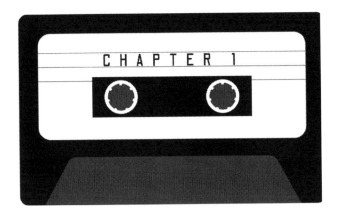

C H A P T E R 1

CHESA

S nowy static on the TV screen made Chesa Rizal's heart sink.

Not again.

Chesa fast-forwarded the VHS tape but knew it would be pointless. Yet another day's work and hours of film were destroyed. She swallowed her frustrated groan as she skimmed through the footage she had.

Interspersed among the sweeping panoramic shots of mall grounds were long stretches of warped video.

All the cute interviews that she had with most of the store

owners of Creepy Court Mall were virtually unusable. Same with most of the candid shots she thought she had captured. At least there were some salvageable moments, like the adorable dogs in the Twisted Whisker and a few clown antics from Frankie's Funhouse. It could be enough to create a B roll. She made a note for the marketing team.

So much for having a local television spot for promo done by tomorrow. She moved the deadline to Friday. If this kept up, she would never finish this project for her boss.

Speaking of whom, Jaime Barbosa's office door opened, then closed with a jangling of keys. Like clockwork, he rolled out of his office at 5:00PM precisely. The perks of being the mall's general manager.

Chesa was usually alone in the management office on a Sunday, but the management team decided to rotate working one Sunday a month for the last quarter of the year. Not that they lightened her workload any...in fact, they usually added a little more to her plate whenever they saw her. But, at least when they were here, she felt like she could get all the other mall stuff done without having to man the office.

With the videotape messed up, and the pile of props she still needed to take to storage, Chesa would need to wait until after the mall closed to finish up so she would be here for the last hour of the business day in case a customer or tenant needed anything.

At least the mall closed at 6:00PM on Sundays.

Jaime's curly hair preceded him as he poked his head into her office. He wore a bright red and pink Hawaiian shirt with light-colored khakis. A tuft of chest hair peeked up from where he left his top button undone. "Hey, hey Ches, what's the word? How's the project coming along? Do we have anything to send over to marketing this week?"

A smile strained her facial muscles. "Sure. Just a few more interviews and I'll be able to send this raw footage over to Judy and the marketing team to edit this week."

Jaime shot her with a few finger guns. "That's my girl! Don't stay too late!"

"I won't," she said to his retreating footsteps. She only half-believed herself.

It was already October, and the big new Halloween event that she was spearheading was circled in red on her desk calendar. A trick-or-treat street, something that hadn't been done before, at least to her knowledge.

And right after that, she needed to somehow turn the mall from a spooky haunted house on October 31 to a winter wonderland with a countdown to Santa Claus coming to town before opening on November 1 ... the visual merchandising team was going to love her for that.

So much to do, too little time. Yet, she was determined to make this year their most trafficked year yet. And maybe that would mean a promotion to a position where she could have at least one day off a week.

Chesa pushed aside all the impending color-coded deadlines that blared like sirens at her. "I can do this," she said to her calendar.

Her spiking adrenaline fueled her second wind as she

slashed and rearranged her priority list until she narrowed her tasks to three items:

1. Fix video
2. Take props to prop room
3. Pick up dinner at Creepy Pasta by 6:30PM.

Okay. Not bad. All she needed to do was re-record some interviews and film some more candid videos and hope the footage didn't get destroyed ... again.

Who was she kidding? Even assuming her videotape came out perfectly, she couldn't get that done in less than an hour.

The thought of the densely packed shrimp fettuccine Alfredo and fully loaded garlic knots that would be waiting for her made the frustration welling up inside of her even worse. A part of her wanted to willfully forget about the ruined tape and leave that for Monday morning's problem. But she knew herself. She wouldn't be able to sleep knowing there was a pile of work she left undone.

Her brainstorming was interrupted by a few phone calls and customer service questions. She directed one customer toward the restrooms and handed another one a map. As she refilled the mall maps in the displays, her gaze landed on the store directory.

Red Light Videos.

Maybe they could do something about her tape this week.

Chesa called the video store and chatted with Seren, a

new store clerk there. A glimmer of hope fluttered inside her when Seren turned out to be an aspiring film student who would love to help Chesa figure out her videotape issues. In fact, not only would she try to fix the tape, but she even offered to help record more footage and interviews this week.

Chesa twirled in her seat as she hung up her phone. Finally, a light at the end of a long, long tunnel! She checked her watch. Not quite 5:30PM. Plenty of time to drop off the video and store the props before the mall closed.

She chewed on her lip thoughtfully. She shouldn't leave the office unmanned, and yet the thought of actually leaving on time to enjoy a delicious dinner tugged at her. It was close enough to closing, that no one should need her.

Decision made, Chesa called mall security to let him know she would be leaving the office, but had her walkie on her in case she was needed.

"Copy that," he replied.

Buoyed by a possible solution to her problems, Chesa bounced out of the office.

CHESA DROPPED OFF HER VIDEO TAPE WITH RELIEF, AND SEREN, HER new hero, assured her they'd be able to get something together by this week. Along the way there, Chesa had handed out a few more flyers to stores on her route, unloading the rest of her pile to mall security when she passed him. The man took it with barely more than a grunt of acknowledgement.

She was ahead of even her own timetable.

One more stop, then dinner, then home.

Chesa returned to her parked dolly, which was laden with old mall props. She had parked it just outside of the door marked for Employees Only.

The endless maze of concrete hallways always gave her a touch of anxiety. Normally, she would make one of the mall security guards walk with her, so she wouldn't be alone. But, she figured since the mall was still open, she wouldn't have any issues. Besides, the guards were supposed to make their rounds in about half an hour.

Chesa followed the series of turns until she reached a T in the hallways. Turning right led to the fire exit while turning left led deeper into the mall storage locations. She turned left.

The lights flickered a bit as she dragged her load past a few more exits toward Storage Room B. She unlocked the unit, used a cinder block as a doorstop, and dragged her dolly inside. The storage room was nothing more than an unleased store space, so there was no electricity hooked up. She balanced the flashlight on the floor like a torch. It lit up the entrance adequately enough for her to tuck the dolly away. The merchandising team could spot it immediately next time they needed it.

Chesa plucked up the flashlight, checked that her keys were dangling from her arm, and that her walkie was clipped to her jacket pocket. Only when she compulsively checked again that she had all those things, did she confidently push the cinder block away and allow the storage room door to close.

With an enormous sigh of relief, and visions of creamy, cheesy pasta in her head, she backtracked her way toward the mall.

The lights flickered some more, casting a dim yellow haze into the area. She made a mental note to call Mall Maintenance to replace the bulbs with something brighter and far less flickery.

She quickened her stride as she approached the door back into the mall. Normally she would be too distracted to let her childhood fears of the dark bother her. But today...

Chesa scurried the last few steps of the hall and pushed the door open with a sigh of relief.

As she stepped through, Chesa noticed the smell. Fetid and dank, it was nothing like the citrusy-sunshine fragrances that were pumped through the HVAC system. She reached for her walkie to call Mall Maintenance. As she did, she realized something was very, very wrong.

The mall was no longer a hub of frenetic energy, with last-minute shoppers darting into shops. She wasn't even sure she was in a mall.

A maze of empty office space stretched before her. Instead of the bright lights and Top 40s hits over the speaker, everything was hazy and eerily quiet.

"Maintenance, do you copy?" Her radio was on, but the

usual squelch was gone, along with the usual chirps that would accompany the call. "Security? Anybody?"

As she played with the dials on her radio, she became conscious of a discordant tapping. It was soft at first, but it grew louder. Closer.

She peered into the increasingly darkening stretch of space that should have been the mall. Instead of the clear line of sight to the nearby anchor store, a dark plume of shadows billowed in from that end of the hall like a black tidal wave.

Chesa scrambled back into the hallway and let the door slam behind her. She twisted her key into the crash bar, locking it out. Moments later, something big crashed into the door.

CHAPTER 2

RUFUS

Rufus Halliday noticed the untouched to-go bag under the heat lamps. The promise-time of 6:30PM faded on the carbon copy receipt of Chesa Rizal's order. He had waited until the last moment to fill her garlic knots, knowing she couldn't resist tasting one before she left for home.

The owner and head chef of Creepy Pasta had been looking forward to seeing Chesa's face light up with rapture upon seeing her dinner. He lived for the unabashed pleasure that would take over her face as she popped a garlic knot into her mouth. Of sucking the buttery garlic from her fingers one by one.

Yet, it was approaching 7:00PM and there was still no sign of the charming little human who swooned so beautifully for his food.

Rufus swept his gaze over the dining room. Every table was taken and the waiting area and bar were standing room only with a forty-five minute waitlist. A stretch of his shadows confirmed everyone was happy. His staff—from his managers to his busboys—were balancing the workload like a well-oiled machine, just as he liked it.

The forgotten takeout bag was an anomaly to what should have been a smooth evening.

Rufus tapped his hostess on the shoulder. "Heather, did Ms. Rizal call? Did we make her a different order?"

Heather shook her head, her halo of curls immovable. "No, sir, I haven't seen her. I even called over to the office to remind her about her order—no answer. Maybe she changed her mind?"

Of all the humans that inhabited this realm, Chesa Rizal did not change her mind. Her unwavering, single-minded focus in all things was what fascinated him about her in the first place. Though he gave up his mantle as a mindbreaker Hellspawn for this lifetime, he still appreciated a well-ordered mind and Chesa's was a beautiful tapestry of intricate design that he could revel in for hours if she would let him.

How she so passionately immersed herself in work–or a bowl of pasta–was also infinitely refreshing.

And as she treated herself to shrimp fettuccine Alfredo with an extra side of garlic knots every Sunday, her absence was troubling.

He slipped his hand into his jacket pocket, toying with the slip of silk there. It was a hair tie, one of many in Chesa's collection. This one was a simple black style that the females of his staff called a scrunchy. He had meant to return it to her but never got around to it.

Heather had been rambling as he was obsessing over Chesa. "Maybe her closing routine is taking longer than usual. She had that big dolly she was pulling around. It's not like the other mall managers help her," Heather added on conspiratorially.

It was no secret that Chesa was the only mall admin worth a damn. "Perhaps you're right," he murmured. Chesa tended to overwork. But she always called to confirm that she still planned to pick up her order. Whenever she had called, stating she would be later than planned, he would give away what had already been prepared for her to his staff, and make a fresh one in its place.

Worry wormed its way into his gut. Dammit. He wasn't supposed to care about anyone in this realm. Especially a human. They were too fragile. Too helpless.

Too mortal.

Rufus gestured to the order. "Go ahead and donate that

food to any of the staff that wants it. If or when Ms. Rizal comes for her order, we will remake it fresh."

Heather beamed. "Got it, Boss."

Rufus glanced at the dining room once more, twirling the hair tie in his pocket around his finger. Slowly, cautiously, so as not to draw the attention of any outer lord that might be near, he unfurled his power from his human disguise. A shadowy tentacle extended from under his jacket sleeve to twine around the silk scrunchy in his hand–his connection to Chesa. As he focused on her, disjointed images of tangled limbs, confusing hallways, and menacing shadows flooded his mind's eye.

Icy dread raked down his back. Chesa was in danger. "I'll just step out for a moment, Heather. You have the floor?"

"Of course, Boss. This is nothing. Take your time."

Without a backward glance, Rufus slipped out of the back of the restaurant and into the shadows of the mall.

FADED YELLOW LIGHT AND STALE AIR GREETED RUFUS AS HE STEPPED into the liminal space that existed in rolling pockets throughout the mall. Under the shallow layers of reality that mortals see was the shadow realms. The time that was and could be.

It was like taking a polaroid, and having the images

appear minutes later. In that moment of blankness, where the photo had yet to appear and the potential for everything and nothing existed at once...that was this space.

Not quite the past, not quite the present.

The Elder races did not experience it, as their presence was so large. But spawn and other halflings were just small enough to entire these in-between spaces.

There was no real name for this realm, this hidden echo of what was left behind after the living world moved on. If so, it had been lost to time, too insignificant for the Elders to note.

Rufus liked to call this space the Aftermath. He thought the name fitting as the mortal realm seemed always to be at the tipping point of chaos.

And beyond that, the endless sprawl of the outer reaches from which he and his kindred have spawned.

It had always made him nervous to know that Chesa often walked the back hallways by herself. Her clever mind would be a tasty delicacy for any of the Elder spawn that might venture this way.

At least here, he had the power to protect her.

With an exhale, he unwrapped the human guise of Rufus Halliday.

He stretched from the confines of his human form, allowing his power to seep into him once more. Lengthening tendrils of shadows unfurled from his back as he grew to his full height. Like the density of a black hole, energy and matter flowed into him, feeding him the knowledge of the universe in a single glorious inhalation.

Gone was the mild-mannered businessman with the nondescript features and olive skin tone who wore custom-tailored Italian suits.

Here, he was Vhellos the Mindbreaker. The Hellspawn who wrestled this territory from many an eldritch creature before they knew to stay away.

Rufus reached for the tangled web of shadows that he used to mark his boundary from the outer reaches. As if they were antennae attuned to Chesa's mental frequency, he found her.

Unfortunately, she was not alone.

CHAPTER 3

CHESA

C hesa didn't know how long she ran. All the hallways
looked the same. Even when she tried to sus out a
pattern by only taking left turns, she never doubled back the
way she came.

Her initial panic simmered to a dull throb of anxiety. She
could deal with that. She had weathered many a holiday
season fueled by stress hormones alone.

Though there were no visible threats, she still couldn't
shake the feeling that she was being watched. It was the

reason she continued to run even now, albeit at a steady jog rather than the breakneck sprint from earlier.

The thought of that roiling crush of black shadows tumbling toward her like a tidal wave was enough to seize her mind in icy fear.

It was like something could reach into her nightmares and make her re-live them.

Chesa took another turn at random, hoping that she sees something other than an expanse of stale rooms filled with old cubicles or an endless stretch of cinderblock hallways. She ended up in another batch of offices.

She stopped to catch her breath. Her calves burned and sweat rolled down her back. She wore only her undershirt and trousers—her matching jacket had slipped from where she had tied it around her waist and was most likely in some forgotten stretch of hallway, along with her walkie, which was just as well since it was like lugging a brick with her.

At least she still had her key ring and flashlight. The thought of being in the dark made her shiver, and for the tenth time, she checked the flashlight for a fraction of a second to make sure it still worked.

This must be hell. She must have somehow died, and this was her new eternity.

No! She refused to die in an office. If—*when!*—she escaped from this nightmare she somehow found herself in, she would take a vacation.

She would eat whatever she wanted, sleep in until noon, and watch so many movies. The last one she had seen was back in January, when that movie, *Legend*, came out. She went to a late-night showing, indulging in a post-holiday treat because she had a glorious two days off in a row.

Boy, she had savored every moment.

Even though Chesa was supposed to be rooting for Jack, the hero, she secretly wished the Lily character had been with Lord Darkness. He was so big! And that voice—Chesa had melted every time he spoke. Lord Darkness still featured in a few fantasies of hers in those few times she was too restless to go to sleep.

A rustle of movement shifted her attention away from the cozy thought of dancing with a dark lord in the direction she had come from. Chiding herself for stopping for too long, she continued jogging once more.

She only got a few feet away when she tripped over a telephone cord that appeared as if from nowhere. Instead of falling, more cords wrapped around her until she was buoyed upward in a net of coiled cables.

The familiar chittering noise grew louder. Chesa desperately tried to pull herself free from the elastic bands of this trap, but the more she struggled, the more it coiled around her until she tired herself out.

She needed to reserve her strength.

Movement above her caught her attention. The paneled ceiling overhead was pulled open by unseen hands. Slowly, she was being pulled up into the ductwork as the black tide of shadows tumbled into view. It was still a ways off, but she didn't want to be anywhere near it.

Whatever fate waited above her, it was favorable for the black tide. She didn't want to be engulfed by whatever was in the shadows.

As the dull roar of tumbling waves filled the room, Chesa was rushed up into the ducts above her.

CHESA WOKE TO PAIN THROBBING FROM HER TEMPLE. SHE MUST HAVE hit her head when she was being pulled up from that office she had been in.

She had a hard time focusing her eyes in the dark.

The stale scent of old cloth was replaced by the dankness of stagnant air. The smell was familiar. It reminded Chesa of the storage rooms in the mall, the ones that had been converted from old store fronts.

She carefully reached for her flashlight. It slipped from her grip, tumbling to the floor. At least it was heavy duty enough not to break. It clicked on, and a dull cone of light illuminated toward a random corner with stacked boxes and industrial shelves.

The net that held her had been tacked to a hook on the wall as if she were a prop. Chesa worked through the tangles that bound her in order to get free. The cords were elastic enough that she could create a hole large enough for her to shimmy out of.

As her vision adjusted to the scant light, she noticed movement around her.

Along the far wall, mannequins swayed on their feet or were stacked on top of the other. Many were still pinioned to their stands. All of them moved against each other, a writhing mass of friction.

In the middle of the space, a couple of them were piled separately here and there, each with their legs scissored between each other. Their hips clacked together in a steady rhythm; their rigid arms encircled each other in a crazed embrace.

Chesa was enthralled by it all, and couldn't help but openly gape at the sight before her. The rise and fall of their torsos, the quickening pace of pistoning hips, the loud smacking that mimicked the sweet release of gasping pleasure—all of it made her own breath hitch as she realized her own rushing pulse. Of how liquid heat gathered between her legs, and how her muscles clenched around the emptiness there.

She wanted to touch herself, to relieve herself of the pressure that now throbbed in her most secret place. She wanted to know this manic energy that surged even inside these inanimate objects.

Embarrassed by her reaction, Chesa filed away the shock of what she was seeing to a dark corner of her mind. Later, she would analyze it, and in a furtive moment, indulge in some darker fantasies, but for now, she redoubled her efforts to getting free while her captors were distracted.

She squeezed through an opening in the net, dropping onto silent feet. Getting her bearings, she resolutely ignored the orgy happening around her.

Chesa desperately wanted to pick up the flashlight but didn't want to gain any attention. She peered into the darkness, calculating where the door would be in a room like this. Decision made, she tiptoed across the concrete floor on silent feet. Once she found the door, there would be light from the hallway.

Something wrapped around her ankle, and only a hard plastic hand held to her mouth kept her from crying out. She could make out the mannequin on the ground, its grip on her unyielding. The other mannequin, the one that silenced her —stood behind her, its arm around her torso squeezing the air out of her.

Chesa tried desperately to get out of their hold when they took her to the ground. Two more joined the first pair, and soon, she found herself wedged between four mannequins.

She searched the smooth contours of these figures for any weakness, any place she could poke, prod, kick, or gouge. Nothing. Worse, they seemed to out think her, anticipating her moves and restraining her before she could do anything about it.

What were they doing? What did they want from her?

She wished she could ask them, but it wouldn't matter. It wasn't like they could say anything.

During the struggle, Chesa realized she was fully in the

circle of light left by the flashlight. It was within reach. She just needed to free her arm.

As she thought about it, the pressure around her middle lessened just enough for her to free her arm. She reached just enough to push it and it skittered away a little.

The mannequin's hold tightened around her once more. A presence descended into this space. It was nothing that Chesa could see, but it was something she could feel, like the pressure from a coming storm front.

Fear coiled inside her, freezing her in place. She allowed the frenetic energy of the mannequin orgy to happen around her. She squeezed herself ever smaller within the midst of the tangled limbs, hoping to remain hidden from whatever lurked in the dark.

Whatever it was growled. The pitch of it was so low, she felt its vibrations more than heard it.

She couldn't track it, but one thing was clear: it stayed wholly in the shadows.

Without another thought, she reached for the flashlight and arced its light into the darkness.

There, illuminated before her, was a horror so great that she couldn't make sense of it. Her brain couldn't process the variegated limbs and eyes; couldn't perceive a color that was darker than black.

It did not like the light. Tentacles slashed out, raking through the downed mannequin forms. In the chaos, something clipped the flashlight and sent it spinning away from her. In the strobing light, she saw the exit door.

Chesa didn't dare pause. In the confusion, she ran away, dragging a clinging mannequin with her.

She burst through the door and back into the yellow and stale world of the back hallways.

She was in the light, and that was all that mattered. Anything with light. That was what she craved. She ran through the hallways once more.

Whispers were catching up to her and she could see the black tide rushing toward her.

This time when she turned down another length of hallway, she saw a familiar emergency exit door. She sprinted toward it and burst through the crash door in time for a shadowy silhouette to stand before her.

Skidding to a halt, she registered someone shouting, "Get down!" and complied.

Tentacles of smoke and mist rippled over her in a rush to knock out the thing that was pursuing her.

She fought for consciousness, but the overwhelming suggestion to *sleep now* pierced the mist of panic in her mind. Her vision narrowed to pinpoints of light as she succumbed to the feel of being wrapped in a downy blanket.

CHAPTER 4

RUFUS

Rufus poured his energies toward the night horror pursuing Chesa. Pulsating dark matter rippled toward it, binding it before it could escape his grasp.

He spared a glance at Chesa, who curled into a ball at his feet, her hands protecting the back of her neck. He plucked her from the floor with one of his tentacles, nestling her against his side.

Sleep. It was the softest command he could press upon her until he could assure himself of her safety.

Damn Aza. The foolish pain lord thought he could encroach upon Rufus's territory with no repercussion.

Even now, the black tide that had rolled through the backrooms and dared seep into his territory in limbo evaporated into gauzy mist. Rufus stretched the mantle of his power, easily deflecting the sniveling Elder spawn, pinning it with its own tentacles. "Did you not notice the web marking my territory, Aza?"

"I noticed, Vhellos. I did not care." Aza attempted to drag Rufus into the abyss of his mind, inviting him into chaotic agony.

Greater gods than he attempted to take this realm—and lost. Rufus indulged in a smile. "You will care. I will make sure of it."

"Why? Because you were once the Mindbreaker?" It sneered at him. "You are nothing. Look at how weak you are. How you protect these insignificant humans. I will crush you right after I suck the soul from that mortal you favor."

Aza would soon learn what it meant to be broken. "Whatever makes you happy, Aza." In a blink, Rufus captured Aza's gaze, forcing the pain lord to purge itself of the misery that it thrived upon. Black clods of crystallized despair spewed from its central orifices. Aza shrunk down even further until it was nothing more than a black cloud.

Rufus clawed a runic script in the air, and the being that once was Aza, the Elder spawn pain lord, was separated and bound within a shower of tokens. The golden currency rained down, with a cartoon character on one side and the words *"Where everyone is always smiling"* emblazoned on the other.

Rufus flicked the coin in the air and watched it spin before catching it again.

"See, Aza? You'll always be smiling now." Stretching forth the shadows from his back, Rufus gathered the piles of tokens together and directed them toward the Frankie's Funhouse in the mall. Trapped and bound in a place where a unique type of happiness lived, Aza would be weak and lethargic without its usual sustenance for eons to come.

It would take that long to distill enough of it from all these random coins.

Rufus lifted Chesa in his arms. She was so small cradled against his body, especially in his true form. For one infinitesimal moment, he considered where to take her.

He could return her to her office and make it so she fell asleep and what she had endured was a terrible nightmare? Rufus dismissed that idea immediately. What if there were other minor lords that have attuned to her mental frequencies as he did?

Chesa was lucky enough to survive the backrooms.

But there really was no better place for her to be than with him. There, he would be assured of her safety.

In one step, Rufus went from the backrooms to the liminal space he called home.

RUFUS PACED THE CONFINES OF HIS ABODE IN LIMBO AS CHESA SLEPT. Though the human world was now his adopted home, he needed the respite of this in-between space whenever he encountered others of his kind. The mere wisp of their presence would taint the mortal world.

Perhaps she would like some tea?

Rufus busied himself with making a platter of snacks to go with both tea and coffee.

She woke as he approached her, asleep on his couch. She immediately startled, sitting up and staring at him with those large, expressive eyes.

He could lose himself in them. Even now, her clever mind moved from panic to calm as she assessed her surroundings.

"Do not worry, Ms. Rizal. You are perfectly safe here. Do you know who I am?"

Her brow furrowed as she looked up at me. "Of course I do. Rufus Halliday, owner-operator of Creepy Pasta. I only go there almost every day to eat. Where am I?"

Rufus couldn't help but smile. This human was such a delightful surprise. Did nothing faze her? "I found you unconscious. I thought it best to take you back to my place, as it was nearby."

"Unconscious?" She closed her eyes, trying to remember what had happened to her.

She sported bruises around her neck and jawline. Dark circles marred her otherwise perfectly glowing skin. Her lips trembled, though she valiantly pressed them into a firm line to keep from crying.

Chesa was uncomfortable.

Rufus gripped the little scrunchy in his pocket. He should have taken her some place familiar. He had already smoothed over her memories, so her appearance with him was well out of the ordinary.

He hadn't wanted to, but it was for the best. After all, nice mortal humans, especially exceptional ones such as Chesa, didn't need to know about the horrors this universe offered.

With a light touch of one of his tentacles, he wiped away her confusion so she could rest if needed.

"Would you like anything to eat, Ms. Rizal? I know you like fettucine Alfredo? I could whip you up an order right away?"

Chesa looked at him expectantly. "You cook, too? And here I thought you were just the restaurant owner?"

Rufus shrugged. "I am always open to learning new things. Besides, it is always in my best interest to be nominally helpful in the kitchens in case I need to step in and cover."

A hint of a smile appeared on Chesa's lips. "I know a little bit about covering for co-workers." She chewed on her bottom lip contemplatively. Rufus found it utterly distracting. "I am happy to eat, but why are you pretending that you haven't just pulled me out of some nightmarish hellscape?"

Stunned, Rufus didn't know what to say. Instead, he probed her mind just a little and saw her recent memories bubbling up to the surface. Chesa running through the backrooms and endless hallways. Realizing that mannequins reanimate when they are left alone. Of her flight from Aza's black tide and its desire to feed from her fears.

Chesa was immune to his mind tricks. "You remember that?"

She looked at him as if he was the one to have lost his mind. "Yeah," she drawled out. "I tend to remember those moments when I have to run for my life. Do you do this so often that the events blur together? By the way, who or what is Vhellos?"

Rufus gave up trying to lie to her. "That would be me. My old name."

"Your old name," she said dully. "I'm assuming it's not from a random country that you emigrated from."

"No."

"And where did you come from?"

Rufus gazed at her once more. How much did she remember? Did she see him in his true form? No, that couldn't be. She would run in fear rather than be bright eyed with curiosity.

Chesa threw up her hands. "Look, I don't know what kind of Superman-Clark Kent thing you think you're doing, but you cannot possibly think that I don't know that you were the one that saved me from the large meatball blobby thing with all those eyes and teeth."

He blinked. "Blobby thing?"

"Yes! That dark blob that floated around like a meatball with a million eyes and teeth. There was a big black tidal wave filled with monsters at its back? And then you held it back with your magic jazz hands?"

Rufus looked down at his hands. "Jazz hands?"

Chesa bounced where she sat. "Yeah, because you were like big and tall and had all the tentacles rippling around you? Dude, I know it happened. You can't lie to me, so don't even try."

Rufus didn't think he was trying. "I'm not trying anything. I'm just...surprised. Most humans would babble incoherently right now if they remembered the horrors you've seen."

"I'm not like most humans—" she countered.

"Clearly."

"—but honestly, 'babbling incoherently' is a bit much. Shocked, perhaps, but it's not *that* brain melt-y."

Not that brain melt-y? "I will have you know, Ms. Rizal. I was known as the Mindbreaker in my previous life."

Chesa put her hands up in mock surrender. "Okay, okay, I'm getting it now. You had thought I'd forgotten about it all, and hoped I'd believe I had an awful nightmare, is that it?"

Rufus no longer knew who was trying to comfort whom. His delightful little human had more resilience and nerve than he had given her credit for—and he had already given her the utmost credit. "It seems there is no reason to speak. As you seem to know all, Ms. Rizal."

"Chesa, please. And, no, I don't know all, but I know what I lived through." She tossed the blanket away from her and stood. "You said something about dinner? I'm starving!"

He shook his head with a chuckle. "Your dinner awaits."

THEY PASSED THE TIME IN IDLE CONVERSATION. THERE WAS ONLY one minor mishap when Chesa accidentally opened the door to limbo rather than the powder room. She noted the few asteroids floating in space, before closing the door and opening the correct one.

What a revelation she was. In her presence, Rufus felt at ease. He could listen to her for hours. She spoke fast and was excited over the littlest things.

And the best part was that she remembered him. Not just what he needed her to remember, but all the random little insignificant things as well. He said as much to her. "Few people remember me, as I am doomed as not to be remembered."

Chesa ripped apart a garlic knot with a manic glee. "How in the world do you manage a restaurant if people keep forgetting you?"

"It isn't a sudden thing. It's more like a gradual fade. And when I need people to remember me, I do."

After a moment of thoughtful chewing and comfortable silence, Chesa asked, "So what now? Are you going to kill me?"

He choked on his limoncello. "After I went through all that trouble to find you and cook for you?"

Chesa laughed with her entire body. "Man, you should see your face." She wiped the tears from her eyes as Rufus contemplated finding a mirror. "How long have I been gone? I feel like I've been asleep for hours based on how rested I feel. I don't remember the last time I slept for over four hours."

Pride swelled in Rufus's heart. "You've only been here a few hours. But if you ask me, I feel you need a full day's worth of rest. You work too much. We all think it."

Chesa froze mid-forkful of pasta. "All? Who's all?"

Rufus ticked off the answers on his fingers one by one. "My waitstaff for one. I'm pretty sure everyone who works in the food court. Anyone who's met you..."

She hushed him. "Regardless, I still need to get back. The updates need to be done, and the marketing team needs to know changes ASAP. They're waiting for my reports—" As she spoke, her hands gestured faster and faster.

Rufus captured one of her elegant hands and nested it between both of his. "I don't think you quite get me. This place—limbo—is out of space and time. Just as the backrooms were a liminal space outside time where you were lost in for hours. You can spend hours here—days, even—and only a minute would have passed." He looked at her meaningfully. "If you truly wish to go back to your home, I will arrange it. But if you wish to stay here, eat, rest, you may do so. You will inconvenience no one else, least of all me. Which will it be?"

Chesa didn't hesitate. "I want more Alfredo and garlic knots, please."

CHAPTER 5

CHESA

One night stretched into three. After the carb loading, Chesa slept for most of the next day. And the next. She only woke for food and showers.

Rufus had supplied all she needed, including her own suite of rooms, clothes, and skincare products. All of which were of better quality than her current collection.

"I told you. You needed sleep."

Chesa sipped her coffee. Even his coffee was better than hers. "I'm going to be so spoiled after this."

"You are welcome here any time you need to rest. Seriously."

She laughed half-heartedly. Man, she wouldn't want to leave. "I don't think I'm strong enough to withstand that kind of temptation."

"You don't have to be strong."

Chesa felt the mood shift, and she didn't want to follow where it would lead. Instead, she asked the second biggest question in her head. "You know what's funny? Filipino food is nothing like this cheesy pasta, and yet your food always tastes like home." She shoveled a brick of lasagna onto her plate, pulling a pinch of cheese and placing it into her mouth.

Rufus ducked his shoulders. "That might be my fault. Whenever I cook, especially for you, I wanted you to feel the comfort of home."

She fell for him then. Sure, he was ridiculously handsome with his cheekbones and dark features and a deep voice that spoke to her so gently. And, yeah, he was also this enormous dark lord that embodied her most secret fantasies.

But when he said stuff like that? Screw rules and what was the proper way to do things?

Rufus had to have felt the same. Infinite lifetimes played out in his eyes. His tentacle wrapped around her chair leg and pulled her closer to him. He dragged her onto his lap. She had all the time in the world to stop him, to pull away. She didn't do any of that.

Chesa tilted her head back as he descended, pressing his

lips against hers. She dug her fingers into his lion's mane of hair.

It was a chaste kiss. At first.

Tentative. Exploratory.

But one sweep of her tongue against the firm line of his lips flipped the switch on his control. He had her on the table. Long, elegant fingers skimming her body. The scraps of her clothes disappeared.

She gasped as he placed sucking kisses down her neck and chest. Rolled one nipple between his fingertips. Tasted the other one. Murmured appreciative words against her skin.

His fingertips softly glided up her body, finally resting at the crease of her hip before he gently cupped her femininity. The warmth of his hand on her wet heat caused her to shiver with pleasure as he murmured sweet, unintelligible words against her skin.

He teased her senses, exploring every inch of her most intimate parts with his fingers, his tongue. She became completely absorbed in the sensations that coursed through her, allowing herself to forget everything but the pleasure he was giving her.

She came in a glorious surrender, her back arching as she screamed. Rufus did not let up, filling her with his fingers, pushing her to go again. Chesa could not deny the onslaught of sensation that trembled over her.

In the aftermath, she admitted out loud that she needed

to go back, and he said, "I know. I will take you when you go. Just tell me when."

She bit her lip. "We don't have to leave right now."

A slow smile spread across his face. "What do you want to do instead, little Chesa?"

CHAPTER 6

Rufus

He thought Chesa was beautiful when she swooned over his food; she was even more so when she wrapped that delectable mouth around his cock. He buried his fingers in her hair, careful not to hurt her, but she didn't need to do this.

"Chesa, I—" His words died on a groan as she swallowed his length, taking nearly all of him in. She wrapped both of her hands around his base while she bobbed her head up and down.

Where had she learned this? She didn't have a partner of note in the year he has known her.

He brushed the surface of her mind carefully. He wouldn't pry, but superficial thoughts were fair play. It would be like hearing someone speak to themselves aloud.

He didn't have to push at all. The tapestry of her mindscape rippled before him, desire and curiosity as vibrant threads woven throughout.

Chesa Rizal was a virgin. And she wanted this. Wanted *him*.

He should have known. After all, she was an eager over achiever in all things. With her ordered mind and meticulous focus, her virgin mouth was his undoing.

He should take things slow, but he was too far gone. He gasped when she took him in deeper, touching the back of her throat.

Her tongue moved in circles over the head and she moaned when he pushed in deeper, her hands gripping him tighter in encouragement.

Rufus felt his climax close as she swirled her tongue around him, coaxing ripples of pleasure in him. He reached down and wrapped one hand around her neck, fingers brushing lightly against her skin.

He watched her, mesmerized, as she wrapped her lips around him and sucked lightly.

He bit his lip and tried to hold back, wanting to make sure that Chesa felt every bit of the pleasure he was feeling. But despite his best efforts, his body surged forward, pushing him over the edge.

Rufus groaned as his orgasm rocked through him and she kept up her nimble ministrations until the last of his spent pleasure left his body.

Chesa pulled away and smiled up at him. He caressed her cheek, feeling so much admiration for her willingness to please him. She blushed as he pulled her up to tuck against his body.

He liked the feel of her there, in the hollow of his neck. He curled his fingers over her cheek, tilting her face up so he could press a tender kiss onto her forehead. The tip of her nose. Her pillow soft lips.

He wanted more.

Rufus pushed her back until she was laid out before him. She moaned when he settled his weight on her, wrapping her legs around his waist for more friction.

He would give her all she desired and more.

He pulled back, trailing slick kisses along her neck and collarbone. His hands explored her curves, her breasts, her inner thighs, and the heat between them. He trailed his fingers lightly around her clit, teasing it with gentle circles.

Her breath came in quick pants and her eyes fluttered shut as the pleasure rose. She locked her legs around him and he pressed against her, finding that special spot.

Rufus used the shadow tentacles from his body to invade her, sending out an army of tendrils to explore her body. He wanted to be inside her, just like she had been living inside of him for months. He wrapped the tentacles around her legs and arms, binding her gently and caressing her skin. They skimmed over her body, exploring every inch of her, every crevice.

The pleasure inside him surged higher and higher, and he felt his control slipping. He gritted his teeth and pushed forward, sinking in deeper and deeper and sending her over the edge with him.

Finally, he pulled out, panting heavily. He held Chesa close, cocooning her in his embrace and cradling her head against his chest.

The room was heavy with satisfied silence, both of them overwhelmed by the exquisite pleasure they had experienced. He held her like that for a few moments longer before pressing a sweet kiss onto her forehead.

"We need to do that again." Her voice was thick as she finally succumbed to sleep.

He smiled, tucking her in and settling himself beside her.

Yes. Soon. He would make sure of it.

CHAPTER 7

CHESA

It was wild to wake up and walk into the office early on Monday morning after spending a full week with Rufus. Recuperation and rest were exactly what she needed to get that pep in her step.

Well, that and orgasms. So. Many. Orgasms.

Chesa finished her work and promptly clocked out at 5:00PM, ignoring the not-so-vague hints that Jaime dropped for her to pick up some extra work—otherwise known as his slack. She didn't even acknowledge his words, only waving a quick goodbye before she dashed out of the office.

Rufus had invited her to a proper date, and she didn't want to be late.

He was there to greet her in the foyer. She was barely in his arms when he pulled her in for a kiss. "Ready for dinner?"

"Where are we going?" she asked.

He smiled that devastating smile that sent her heart into convulsions. "We are already here, my love."

Chesa wanted to ask what he meant when her gaze rested on the structure behind him. The Eiffel Tower soared into the sky.

She was in Paris. She couldn't believe it. One moment, they were at the mall. The next, they were in Paris.

He had taken her to Paris!

Rufus lifted her hand and brushed his lips over her knuckles. "This is only the beginning."

They had dinner and dessert, after which he whisked her away for a private dance on the Eiffel Tower. Then, riotous lovemaking back at his place.

The next day, Chesa picked up the tape from Seren at the video store. She paid her $200 from the mall's petty cash, and Seren was super excited about it.

Rufus confessed he had been the reason Chesa's videos kept messing up. He made it up to her by taking her out for a pizza picnic in Rome, and then licking her to multiple backbreaking orgasms as she cried out to the stars.

He sank himself inside of her in that slow way that made her eyes flutter shut.

"Tsk, tsk, my sweet Chesa. Look at me. I need all of you."

She met his gaze and lost herself in the galaxy of stars she saw there. She let him dive deep inside her mind as he took her body...her very soul.

Rufus ground his hips against hers, eliciting a deep groan from her. "After this, where to next?"

He was determined to take her to all the places she longed to go. But right now, she was exactly where she wanted to be. Chesa reveled in the way he looked at her. How he pressed himself even closer against her. "Anywhere with you."

Sign up for my newsletter for bonus scenes, extended scenes, and other exclusive content:
https://evangelinepriest.com/newsletter/
For more monster romances, check out *A Cherry on Top* at https://books2read.com/monstrousappetites1. Set in the underworld of Obsidian City, it is a slice of life novella that is part of the *Monstrous Appetites* series.
Taming the Viscount Viper features the same naga family mentioned in Monstrous Appetites. It is available as part of The Monsters Ball on Amazon.
For more stories in the Obsidian Rift universe, *Claiming Her Orc* is available for pre-order. Links are available at https://evangelinepriest.com/links.

ABOUT THE AUTHOR

Evangeline Priest writes love at first bite paranormal romance featuring growly alpha heroes and women strong enough to tame them. She writes "monsters in space" science fiction romance as Eva Priest. Try out The Legion universe, starting with *Hunted:*
https://evangelinepriest.com/book/hunted-the-legion-savage-lands-sector-1/

She is usually within reach of coffee, chocolate, or a bowl of noodles.

Join her VIP community on Patreon where she shares NSFW art, excerpts, cover reveals, and featured stories each month.

For more news on releases, you can sign up for Evangeline Priest's newsletter. Enter this link into your favorite web browser:
(https://evangelinepriest.com/newsletter).

patreon.com/evapriestwrites

tiktok.com/@evapriestwrites

instagram.com/evangelinepriest

facebook.com/evapriestwrites

x.com/evapriestwrites

ALSO BY EVANGELINE PRIEST

AFTERWORD

Thank you for reading!

Creepy Court Anthology

If you enjoyed the anthology, please consider leaving a review
on Amazon.

Made in the USA
Middletown, DE
29 October 2023

41472068R00336